LORNBUR

A Vaeldor Adventure
written by

Ronald G. Bellar

Brighton, MI 48114

LORNIBUR

To my father and father-in-law,
Ronald and Stanley.
May they rest in peace.

Dear Reader,

Lornibur is a stand-alone adventure. However, it is also Book 5 of the Vaeldor Series, a telling of stories from the world of Vaeldor as time marches on. For your convenience, a detailed Glossary of Names and pronunciations is provided at the back of Lornibur.

Some entries may act as small spoilers.

Vaeldor Series (in reading order)
    Alas! The One that Evil Brings
    Might and Strength of Evil Bone
    Eyes Open in Shadowy Hall
    The House of Elgarroth

Visit Ronald G. Bellar's website at:
    http://ronaldgbellar.com
Or his Facebook page at
    https://www.facebook.com/vaeldorhouse

CONTENTS

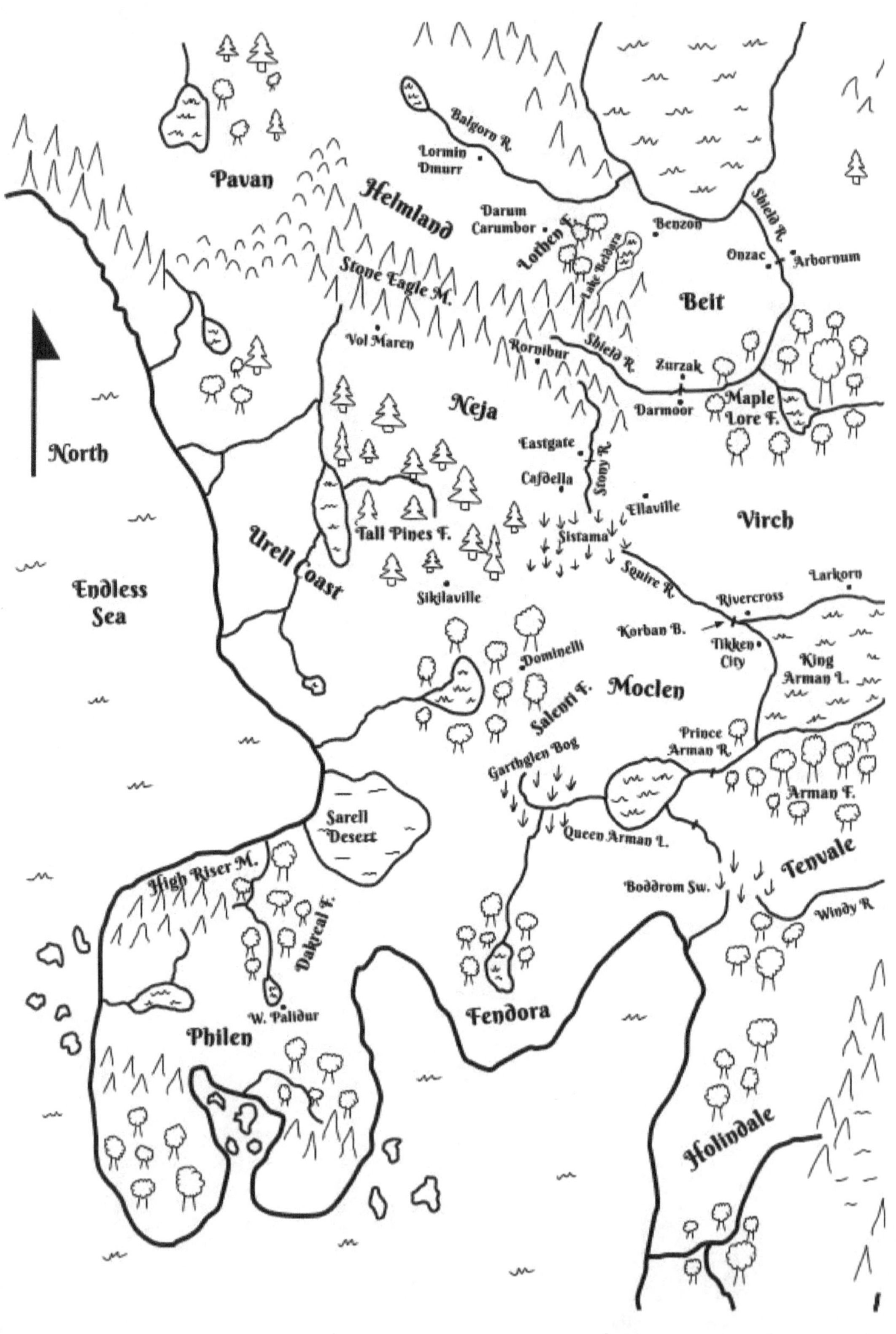

North
Pavan
Helmland
Balgorn R.
Lormin
Dmurr
Darum
Carumbor
Lothen
Benzoll
Shield R.
Onzac
Arbornum
Beit
Stone Eagle M.
Vol Maren
Kornibur
Shield R.
Zurzak
Darmoor
Maple Lore F.
Neja
Eastgate
Cafdella
Stony R.
Ellaville
Virch
Sistama
Tall Pines F.
Urell Coast
Squire R.
Larkorn
Rivercross
Endless Sea
Sikilaville
Dominelli
Korban B.
Tikken City
King Arman L.
Salemi F.
Moclen
Prince Arman R.
Arman F.
Garthglen Bog
Queen Arman L.
Tenvale
Sarell Desert
Boddrom Sw.
High Riser M.
Windy R.
Dakreal F.
W. Palidur
Philen
Fendora
Holindale

Andria
Wornduir
Coranthiar M.
Ekland
Bouldertown
Harbnum
Echo Valley Rapids
Selt
Lake Charal
Vermallon F.
Nira
Batorn Gulf
Steadshire
Maple R.
House of Elgarroth
Pelfagarr
Orlenfel F.
Tribenor
Benasti F.
Batorn R.
Orlenfel R.
Sendorum
Great East R.
Candermane Tunnel
Varlimor M.
Morimont R.
Kalmaar
Tedonis
New Palidur
Morimont
Lake Garaard
Serpent's Range
Sardina
Starlight L.
Southwood
Darmhorng
Burmagaard
Barraday
Charadova
Ironside Keep
Border Hills
Denvale
Fire Hills
Belsai R.
Marcove
Ludal M.
Mud Lake
Moon Lake
Kembald
Menfrial F.
Endless Sea
W. Twin R.
Krimbror R.
Lambrak
Borlean M.
E. Twin R.
Stronghold
Desert of Fire
Trethel R.
Dright Sw.
Nomedd
Tarn Arüm Jungle

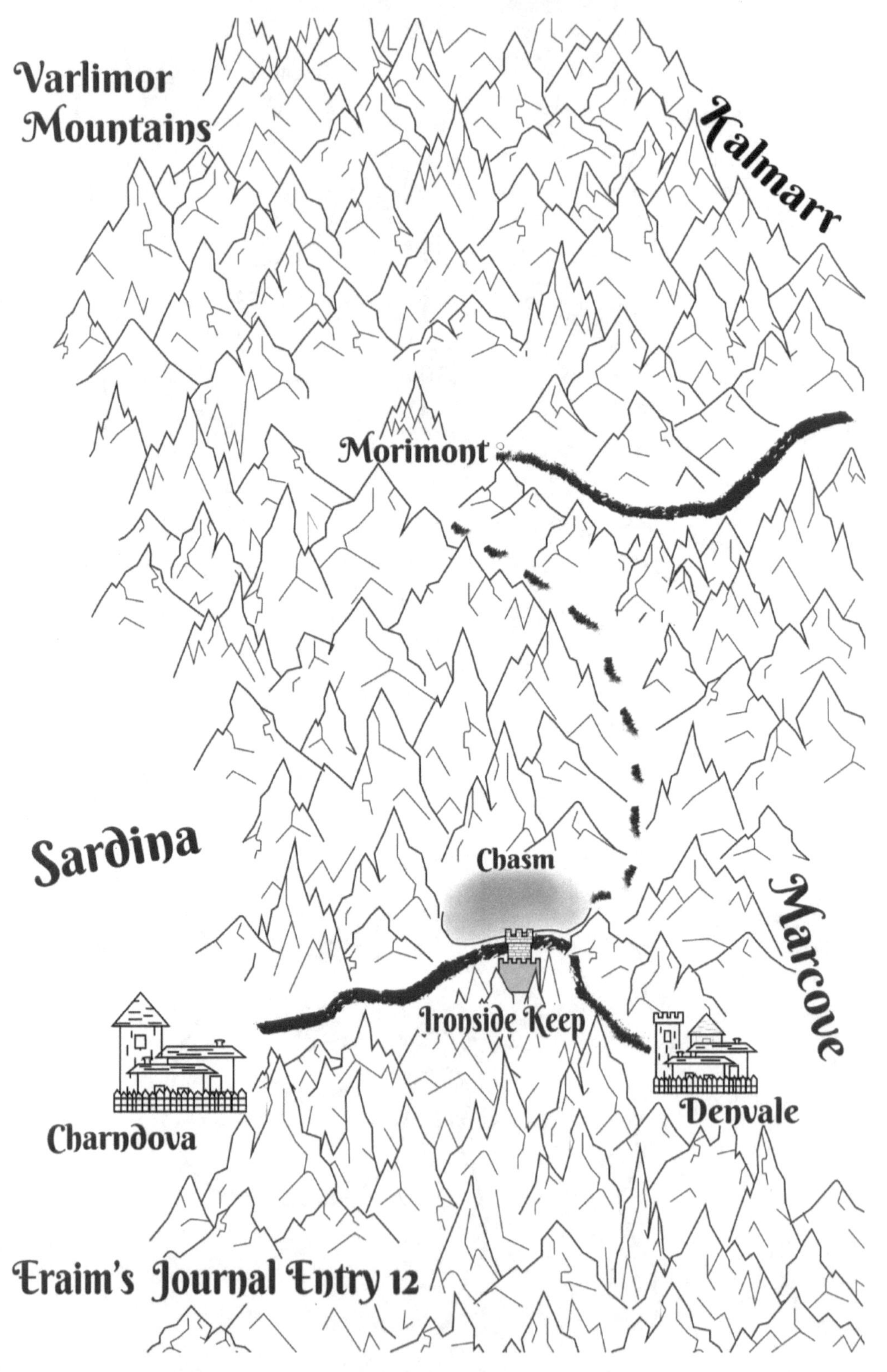

Varlimor
Mountains
Kalmarr
Morimont
Sardina
Chasm
Marcove
Ironside Keep
Charndova
Denvale
Eraim's Journal Entry 12

Prologue

Final Days

Balmorak watched his scout enter the chamber where he and his warriors awaited news. By Dowar's expression, it wasn't good.

"The blasted creatures are everywhere!" said Dowar. He barred the door he had just slammed shut and spun to face the weary soldiers, his long beard momentarily caught in the doorjamb. His whiskers were longer than any other dwarf's in the room — his family prided themselves on how quickly theirs grew. "We're too divided, and there's not enough of us left. We can't win."

"*Brakkeet!*" Balmorak spat. How had things gotten so bad? "We've already collapsed half the mines. What use is victory if there's nothing left?"

"We must close off the forge," Hardor insisted.

"Our own are down there!" Brunux barked in response.

The two had argued that point for days.

"They're not warriors!" Hardor's face reddened, making the gash across his extra-large nose moisten with blood. "There's probably no one left." He turned to Balmorak. "The forge has got to be the source. Anyone still down there is lost to us."

Both Hardor and Brunux had valid points. Even as the enemy fell, more of the hellish monsters appeared. And the sudden influx of giant lizards didn't help matters.

"Are the upper quadrants evacuated?" Balmorak asked Dowar.

The warrior nodded once. "As are the northern and western quadrants. We've lost contact with the eastern and lower quadrants."

"What say you, Balmorak?" asked Hardor.

As much as Balmorak hated to admit it, Hardor was correct. They needed to bury Lornibur, and the evil with it. He looked down at his battleaxe, Clanghorr. For nearly a hundred years, he had held the title of King's Champion, now serving his second king. He concentrated, his mind melding with the weapon as he searched for its mate, Torrac. Nothing. There had been nothing for over a month. Whatever happened to Torrac and its wielder, Mattasun, it couldn't be good. Without them, Hardor's point made even more sense.

"Collapse it all." Balmorak nearly choked on the words. He viewed the dwarves around him, meeting Hardor's gaze last. "You will make sure it is done."

Hardor frowned. "Me? What about you?"

"Clanghorr and I have unfinished business." Balmorak focused on nothing. "I know a way into the royal chambers. A secret passage." He eyed his followers again. "Velgaad will pay for his treachery."

Everyone nodded, their expressions grim. No one would argue the decision.

"You'll not make it alone," said Brunux. "I'm with you."

"And me," added Dowar.

Balmorak raised his calloused hand before anyone else could speak. "I accept your service," he said to the volunteers. "But it ends there. The rest of you must make sure nothing escapes this place. We will find our own way out, Meldar willing."

More nods answered, though slower and less convincing.

Balmorak turned to Brunux and Dowar. "Follow me."

Chapter 1

The Small Room

Greyor sat in his small room, reading a scroll by candlelight. Most dwarves used their small rooms for writing letters, keeping an inventory of goods, and planning parties or events. For Greyor, his small room was where he prepared for his return to Lornibur, a task over three decades in the making.

Lornibur… The birthplace of the dwarfish race, thought to have been destroyed for centuries. In its day, all dwarves called it home. Now, Greyor's people were divided into four major clans: Varlimor, Stone Eagle, High Riser, and Serpent's Range, each with its own king. Then there were smaller communities scattered about—rumors claimed dwarves inhabited the Coranthiar and Ladal Mountains. Folks considered each clan its own race of dwarf, but they were meant to be one people under Meldar, a status that ended during the rule of Velgaad over a thousand years ago. The evil king brought doom upon the ancient underground city, killing half of its citizens, according to history. Velgaad met his own demise as well, but the vermin returned during the Necromancer War as a Death Lord, an undead minion of the necromancer Trannum. Greyor had had the pleasure of destroying Velgaad's new form after traversing Lornibur's mines, and once the war ended, he swore to return and reclaim the city for all of dwarf-kind.

While venturing through the extensive tunnels during the war, Greyor had completely lost his way and was lucky to have emerged alive. That wouldn't happen this time. This time, he planned to discover everything there was to learn before even thinking about reentering. On the right side of his desk were a stack of books and scrolls he removed from the royal library, all relating to Lornibur's history. To the left were additional scrolls and books covering topics such as mining, farming, and architecture—subjects to conceal his true interests. The task needed to remain secret for now. Besides being a dangerous place full of pitfalls and giant lizards, the mines were home to strange humanoids that helped Greyor to survive. His cousin Millord had been with him, and wanted to exterminate the mine dwellers for trespassing, but the creatures were not evil. They were hunters and gatherers and wished only to endure. Greyor suspected most of Morimont's citizens would feel the same as Millord had, and he couldn't allow the innocent humanoids to come to harm.

Thus far, Greyor had been patient. At no time did he feel pressured into acting too soon. He was only one hundred forty-four years of age—at least another eighty would pass before he was considered old by dwarfish standards. But recently, strange occurrences had encouraged him to speed up his plans.

First, there was Clanghorr. The legendary axe was over three feet long, with a bronze handle wrapped in leather and ending in a spike, and along its silver blades were runes no one seemed able to understand. Occasionally the runes glowed, as if with the brightness of a forge. The fabled weapon of the dwarves had been in the possession of Greyor's cousin Poluran before the Necromancer War; Greyor had no clue how Poluran came to own it. After Poluran's demise at the hands of a Death Lord, the battleaxe passed to Millord. Though Greyor had been cousin to both, Millord was the obvious choice as the next recipient, for Poluran and Millord had been counted among the Stone Eagle clan while Greyor was of the Varlimor clan. If there existed a reason some of Greyor's kin had left Varlimor after the fall of Lornibur while others remained, it was lost. And although relationships between citizens of separate mountains were considered severed after the abandonment of the ancient home, for Greyor and his cousins, blood was blood.

During the journey through Lornibur, Millord was killed by a monstrous two-headed lizard or snake—Greyor was unsure exactly what the creature was. The mine dwellers called it Maak Maak. Millord gave Clanghorr to Greyor before vanishing down one of the reptile's throats, and the weapon had been with him ever since. Already held in high standing among Morimont's warriors, Clanghorr elevated Greyor's status all the more, and he led missions to eradicate goblins attempting to bring harm to Morimont's citizens. As well, he deterred ogres from venturing into Varlimor from Benasti Forest, and fought off a rampaging giant.

As time passed, Greyor sensed something buried deep within Clanghorr. It was as if it had a soul; as if capable of more than simply carving into his enemies. And throughout the most recent war to defeat Trannum and Uustaag once and for all, that feeling intensified. During the Battle of the Broken Land, Greyor swore he heard whispers, though he couldn't understand them. He was sure Clanghorr had been trying to communicate with him. Somehow, the weapon had awakened, and a strange yearning drove him to return to Lornibur to learn more.

The other occurrence urging Greyor to speed up his expedition into the lost city happened a couple of hours ago. He had arrived home to find a small box on his dining table. No one other than himself had a key, so how did it get there? Upon opening the package, Greyor found scrolls and sheets of parchment within. Dust covered much of the contents, and the discoloration told him the pages were very old and needed extra care. He was further shocked to learn the subject of every piece related either to Lornibur or to the months following the collapse of the city.

Though the gift filled Greyor with excitement, he remained wary of where the box had come from. The only living members of the company that survived Lornibur other than himself were Selanna and Eraim, but they were elves, and probably not too interested in dwarfish history. Even if one of his companions had mentioned the journey beneath Varlimor to another, he doubted any would have divulged the location of its entrance. Access to the mines lay within a hidden escape tunnel between Ironside Keep and the Fire Hills, and none of his friends would have willingly betrayed the lord of the stronghold governing the mountain pass between Marcove and Sardina. No. Greyor's concern was that someone had discovered what he was up to, even though he had told no one of his plans—no one, except for Eraim and Lorylla, a couple of elves he absolutely trusted to keep his secret. If it were King Kolermane who had found out, or any of the dwarfish lords, the undertaking would likely become a royal affair. Kolermane was old, and might wish to take credit for the resurrection of Lornibur before passing on. If that were the case, the mysterious box could have come from one of the Lords' Houses, and Greyor would surely receive an invitation to visit the royal quadrant before long.

Greyor shook the thought. Regardless of how the box had arrived, there was nothing to be done but try to learn something he didn't already know. He had hoped the package included a map, but it wasn't so; just various stories and notes written by several hands, all of them in the Dwarfish language. The current scroll before him was intriguing. As with most of the parchments, stains, tears, and holes marred the page, and Greyor couldn't decipher every word.

> ...Brunux was not so lucky. The King of Treachery's flail wrapped him aside the head and he perished. The task of scattering the pieces of Lornibur's destructor then fell upon Balmorak and myself ...

It was then illegible for most of the page.
On another parchment, Greyor read:

> ...and I fear Balmorak places the blame fully upon his own shoulders. I do not expect he will overcome ...

And on yet another page:

> ...Balmorak refuses to remain. He is shamed, and does

> not wish to bring disgrace to his lineage. He will not
> tell me where he plans to serve out his self-banishment,
> and he forbids my companionship and plans to leave
> his family behind. What then will become of
> Clanghorr? I fear to...

The rest was smudged.

On another page, written in a different hand, was mention of the last Ellibrus Lords to serve before Lornibur's fall.

> The Houses are split. A new king cannot be chosen.
> Ellibrus Zambror plans to lead his House to the
> northwest in search of a new beginning. Ellibrus
> Juskarn is at odds with Zambror and intends to head
> southwest. Because Velgaad was of Brisomer's House,
> no one wishes to associate with Ellibrus Brisomer and
> his following, and they have gone east. Ellibrus
> Bormungdaher refuses to forsake Lornibur and will
> remain...

Greyor pondered the last name. Bormungdaher. The first king of Morimont, best known to non-dwarves for his contributions to the construction of Palidur and Palidur Bridge. But he was so much more. King Bormungdaher was the only dwarf king to reestablish the four Lords' Houses after Lornibur's fall, while the other clans became more human-like, with monarchs taking complete control. Had they not realized Velgaad's goal had been to do the same? To do away with the Houses? At least, that's what the scrolls seemed to indicate.

Each House comprised thirteen lords. Eight of those lords were Broxen Lords, chosen by their constituents, and they worked with nobles and commoners alike. The next four members were the Harkan Lords. Originally of the Broxen Lords, they were selected by their peers to ascend, and associated mainly with the Broxen Lords and nobles. Then there was the Ellibrus Lord, or High Lord, who ascended from the Harkans. The entire House took on the Ellibrus Lord's name, and he worked as a counselor to the king. Unlike human realms, the throne did not fall upon one of the king's descendants when he retired or passed on, but upon one of the Ellibrus members—that was why non-dwarves often referred to them as princes. It was a system Greyor believed in, and was the way Varlimor continued to run things. Why humans allowed children to assume rulership, regardless of their qualifications, he would never understand.

Perhaps the most intriguing name from the box was Balmorak. From the information available, Greyor determined the dwarf to be the King's Champion, a practice long forgotten. Unlike the hierarchy of dwarfish rule, the King's Champion was not an elected station, but an inherited right. If there was a reason for the position's abandonment, it was lost. The parchments and scrolls provided no answer.

Ding-a-ling. Ding-a-ling.

Greyor sighed at the small bell attached to the ceiling above his head. A thin rope ran from the bell and through a hole in the wall on its way to the front door. He wasn't expecting visitors. After concealing the mysterious box beneath his desk, he exited.

Outside his small room, Greyor followed a short hallway. A door on the right led to his bedroom, and one on the left was open, revealing the guestroom, unused for decades. Greyor had no time for entertaining. In the room ahead were three overstuffed chairs and a fireplace. Just about every room possessed a fireplace, but none of them burned at the moment. Through an archway on the left side of the chamber were the dining room and a kitchen beyond, and to the right was the foyer. He turned right.

Upon opening the front door, anxiety invaded Greyor's chest to see Lord Stromburn. Stromburn was a Broxen Lord of the House of Basallor; the House Greyor belonged to. Greyor hadn't spoken to the Broxen Lords since they tasked him with making sure goblins vacated a nearby grotto nearly a year ago.

"Evening, Lord Stromburn," Greyor greeted his visitor.

"Good evening, Greyor." Stromburn gazed past Greyor as if to see if he interrupted anything. The dwarf was at least fifty years Greyor's senior, but the deep creases crossing his forehead and extending from the corners of his eyes suggested several more years. "I trust you and Clanghorr are well?"

Greyor snorted. "We're fine." He glanced beyond Stromburn. The lord was alone. "Is there a task demanding my attention?" He doubted that to be the case. If it were so, a messenger would have summoned him to the manor of the Broxen Lords. What could have brought one of them directly to his home at this hour?

"No nightmares?" Stromburn raised his brow. "Others who returned from the War of the North claim nightmares haunt their dreams."

"It's been seventeen years since that war ended," Greyor said.

"Still," Stromburn shrugged, "others can't seem to shake them."

Greyor knew it to be true. The creatures Uustaag had unleashed into battle… thousands of minotaurs, trolls, and Dun Soldiers. Worse still were the Death Lords, krahluks, zreekans, and four-armed flying demons. Somehow, the nightmares plaguing the other dwarves had skipped Greyor's bedchamber.

"All the same, good to see you're doing well." Stromburn smiled. "And of course, we are in your debt, as you know. The heroics described by our returning soldiers—"

"Is there a purpose to your visit?" Greyor didn't wish to sound crass, but if the lords were aware of his research, Stromburn should just come out with it.

"I apologize." Stromburn bowed. "It is never our intention to inconvenience Morimont's most treasured hero." There were no hints of sarcasm or patronization woven into the statement. "I am actually here on an official visit. Lord Basallor requires your attendance."

Greyor held his breath. The Ellibrus? If the summons was regarding Lornibur, he should first be taken before the Broxen Lords, who would determine if his plans were worthy of the Harkan

Lords' time. The four of them would then decide if Greyor should meet with Lord Basallor. From there, Basallor might hold a discussion with the other Ellibrus Lords to see if the issue demanded Greyor's presence before the king. Not knowing the reason for the appointment stirred a deep annoyance inside. "What is the meaning of this invitation?"

"I'm afraid that is for Lord Basallor to share." Stromburn smiled again, as if to put Greyor at ease. "I'm sure it is all well and good. But he expects you tonight."

Greyor sighed. "I shall report within the hour."

Stromburn nodded. "Very good."

Chapter 2

Morimont

Greyor's home lay in the upper-south quadrant within Morimont. Most homes were in the upper quadrants. Each section was perfectly carved into the mountain interior, as were the homes themselves. Dwarves could go years without setting foot outside Morimont if they so chose, and many of them did. The more venturesome citizens consisted of merchants, craftsmen, diplomats, soldiers, shepherds, and adventurous souls such as Greyor. For the mountain-bound, Morimont contained nearly everything they needed for survival, and the rest they procured from those daring enough to obtain it from outsiders.

The ceiling towered overhead, allowing room for the various staircases ascending to higher tiers of personal residences, each one set farther back than the last. Greyor lived on the ground floor, and the standard five feet of stone separated his home from those of his neighbors'. The expansive ceiling wasn't necessarily for the stacked housing; when creating a world inside a mountain, space was required. Brightening the great above were suspended braziers of brass, each larger than any of Greyor's fireplaces and illuminating veins of gold and silver running in random patterns, like glittering outlines of clouds. Smaller braziers dotted the stone floor to highlight the walkways.

Greyor exited the quadrant, following a wide northward tunnel. The veins continued high overhead, with copper added in, and pillars carved to resemble hammers held up the ceiling at thirty-yard intervals. After two hundred feet, he descended a wide staircase spiraling around a ten-foot-thick column to reach the Grand Center.

It was the section housing merchants and craftsmen, as well as all the shops. Corridors ran like streets between buildings ranging from ten feet high to nearly touching the forty-foot ceiling. The majority of the taller structures housed multiple businesses, while a number of them stored most of the city's goods. Beyond the buildings to the northeast, hidden from Greyor's view, were the arched stone doors separating Morimont from the outside world. Each stood twenty feet high, and one winch existed to open them while another pulled them shut. But Morimont citizens used normal-sized doors not far from the grandiose entrance, as the monstrous doors opened only for ceremonies, or when Morimont's army marched.

From the Grand Center, Greyor could go north, south, east, or west to the quadrants bearing the Broxen Lords of the four Houses, but he continued downward along the stairs to the next level, where the Harkan and Ellibrus Lords resided. As he reached the lower-middle quadrant, the odor of moist dirt and mushrooms tantalized his nostrils. Unlike other quadrants, the area was not cavernous. It was separated into large rooms to house flora and fauna, such as mushrooms and cave lizards, and several ponds supported various breeds of fish.

Greyor detected a distant roar. The forges below were in use — music to his ears. At one time he yearned to be a weaponsmith, but all members of his family were warriors, and he settled for tinkering in the forges once the smithies were done for the day.

He traveled a few corridors until entering the lower-southern quadrant. The space opened up, and more housing greeted him. The residences were larger and spread out, as most of the noble families lived in the lower quadrants, and deposits of natural gemstones along the high ceiling and walls sparkled in the light of several braziers, creating a myriad of flickering lights. Between the structures was the tunnel Greyor sought, and he followed it to the manor of Lord Basallor.

Beveled edges and images of hammers, axes, picks, and shields in bas-relief adorned the three stories of the lord's dwelling. Staircases approached entrances on the second and third levels, while two doors existed on the ground floor. Just like the other homes, there were no windows.

A dwarf Greyor did not recognize stood outside the lower door on the left. "Master Greyor?" the soldier asked, glancing at Clanghorr hanging at Greyor's side. Admiration shone in the dwarf's eyes.

Greyor gave a slight nod.

"You are expected." The guard opened the door.

Greyor took a deep breath and released it as he entered. The foyer of Lord Basallor's home was much larger than his, and a fireplace contained a small flame to warm the room. Until that moment, Greyor hadn't realized how cold the undermountain had been. A pair of archways provided access to hallways. From past visits, Greyor knew the arch on the right led to a library and a pair of guest rooms. Lord Basallor's office lay through the arch ahead.

A servant rose from a chair to acknowledge Greyor's arrival. It was a young dwarf, perhaps forty years of age. Probably a nephew to Lord Basallor. "Right this way, if you would," the dwarf said, and they entered the corridor straight ahead.

Greyor followed the servant along a tall passage, past a grand archway to a formal dining chamber able to seat twenty, and to an eight-foot door of oak bearing carvings of stalactites and stalagmites, as if it were an entrance to a cavernous room. The servant opened the door, revealing Lord Basallor's den.

Sitting behind a desk of darkened bruskiin, a wood-like material harvested from giant mushrooms, was the Ellibrus Lord. The desk supported a lit candle, three stacked books, an uncut lump of blue quartz, and a few loose sheets of parchment, and the den smelled of pipe smoke, though no pipe was visible. To the right, a tapped keg lay on its side. Basallor eyed a sheet of parchment through a monocle; it was common knowledge his eyesight had diminished over the past decade.

"Ah, Greyor!" Basallor set down the page and leaned back.

Patches of gray seasoned his red beard, and the top of his head was perfectly smooth while his whiskers continued over his ears to connect around the back. "Come. Come in." He motioned toward a pair of vacant chairs before the desk.

Greyor took a seat in the chair on his right. "I'm intrigued by the hour of this invitation."

"Most unusual," the lord nodded. "I agree. And I apologize. But disturbing news has reached my ears, and the topic cannot wait another day."

Greyor tensed, his heart racing.

Basallor leaned back. "The mines have been especially giving lately," he said, changing the subject in a vain attempt to lighten the mood. "Have you seen the silver lodes of late?"

Greyor shrugged. When you lived underground, polite conversation didn't include talking about the weather. He wished the Ellibrus would get to the point.

"Can I pour you an ale?" Basallor stood and walked to the keg.

Well… there was always time for ale. Greyor nodded.

The lord filled a couple of mugs and returned, placing one in front of Greyor and sitting with the other. He took a deep drink, and Greyor did the same. The brew was refreshing.

Basallor wiped foam from his thick mustache. "Seems no one's seen you much lately. You haven't been ill, I trust?"

"Nah." Greyor lowered his mug to his knee. His father taught him long ago that a mug never left the hand until empty. "Been resting my bones. Have a lot on my mind."

"To be expected." The lord shook his head. "No dwarf can claim to have experienced all you have, young or old. The monsters you've fought, places you've been… I cannot imagine having faced Death Lords." He shuddered.

Death Lords… The undead bodies of horrible kings. Not only did Clanghorr destroy Velgaad in the Necromancer War, but the axe assisted in the destruction of Radaam in the Battle of the Broken Land. Beyond that, Greyor and his majestic weapon slew many hairless black gorillas and tentacled spell-casting creatures—krahluks and zreekans from the world of Thard'Dun, an evil deity bent on decimating all of Vaeldor. The memories nearly caused Greyor's blood to boil, but a wave of calm intervened as Clanghorr's whispers returned; words uttered in a strange language seeming familiar, but quiet enough to be incomprehensible.

"Clanghorr is a fine weapon, to say the least," Basallor said.

Greyor noticed his free hand now resting atop his battleaxe, between the blades. He attempted again to focus on the whispering, but it faded.

"It is the very reason I have summoned you," added the Ellibrus Lord.

Greyor raised his chin. Why would his summoning concern Clanghorr?

Basallor took another deep drink, emptying his mug. "You see, the Stone Eagle clan believes it belongs to them."

"What?" Outrage led Greyor to use a stronger tone than he had intended. "They know Millord bestowed it upon me. They have known this for over thirty-five years." He almost spilled his ale, and drained the mug so he could set it down. "Why is this brought about now?"

Basallor nodded. "I agree completely. But it seems King Blorin of Rornibur has passed, and his son sees things differently. There were no dwarves present to witness Millord's dying wish."

Greyor frowned. "Lrindon wants it for himself!" he growled.

A sour expression captured the lord's face. "And he is sending an entourage to stake his claim."

Greyor had met Prince Lrindon several times when visiting Poluran and Millord in the past, and a few times since his cousins' deaths. The prince-turned-king wasn't necessarily a greedy dwarf. Something had changed Lrindon's mind.

"What does King Kolermane say?" Greyor asked.

Basallor sighed. "The king is old. We know this. He is wary of starting a feud with Rornibur, especially in his final years."

"But he wouldn't be the one starting it," Greyor protested.

"The House of Basallor supports you," the Ellibrus leaned forward, "and we always will." He sighed again and then smiled. "I assure you that no decision has been reached. I have conferred with my peers, and we are split as to our counsel for the king. I'll not reveal those who oppose me, but I will say that their concerns are nothing more than a need to keep our bond with our kin strong. One even suggested you move to Rornibur as a representative of Morimont, and thereby retain Clanghorr."

A horrible idea. Clanghorr's home was with Greyor in Morimont.

"When does this entourage arrive?"

Basallor sat back. "End of summer."

Spring was nearly spent. Greyor had a bit more than three months to figure it out.

"I suggest you think hard on this," the lord added. "I do not wish to lose our greatest warrior. But I cannot bear to think of Clanghorr in another's hand. I will continue to fight for you."

"Thank you, Lord Ellibrus," Greyor said, barely above a whisper. "Will that be all?"

Basallor nodded. "That is all… for now. Sleep well."

Greyor walked absently from the room and along the hallway to the foyer, where the servant opened the door. He exited, and the soldier outside uttered something he didn't hear. His focus was on Clanghorr; on Lornibur. He couldn't free the ancestral home without his axe. The mission could wait no longer.

Upon arriving at his house, he returned to his small room. But instead of continuing his research, he pulled a blank parchment from the drawer of the desk. He then grabbed a quill and dipped it into a vial of black ink and began to write.

> Dear Lorylla,
> I hope you are well.

His hand moved from line to line, writing the first of four letters.

CHAPTER 3

ANOTHER JOB

Baylun squatted behind a large boulder and peered around the side. The hobgoblins walked about their encampment, unconcerned with the world. There were ten of them, and they posted no guards. With multiple squads of six hobgoblins roaming the forest to the north, the main party surely could fathom no one making it this far south. Baylun looked at Kiryanna and nodded.

The marteese warrior grinned to one side. She was as beautiful as when they first met during the War of the North, and had not aged a day over the seventeen years since they married. Though most folks mistook Kiryanna for a full-blooded elf, her friends knew better. Her human half could be savage at times, but this didn't bother Baylun. He loved her fire! She wore her golden breastplate, perfectly molded about her modest curves, and strapped at her side was her golden sword. A matching headband held back her curly red hair, which spiraled to just below her shoulders, and her green eyes were alight with excitement. Kiryanna enjoyed the hunt!

Baylun smirked in return, but the stretching of his lips reminded him of the single tooth protruding from his lower jaw. The flaw earned him the nickname Fang when he was younger, and it was a constant reminder of the hobgoblin blood mingling with the human blood in his veins. He was a krukari, and there was nothing he could do to change that. His smile faltered.

Kiryanna frowned as her left eyebrow rose. A familiar reaction. Though Baylun's appearance displeased most onlookers, Kiryanna found him handsome inside and out, and reminded him of this every day. When he first encountered her in Neja, she was the bodyguard of Brem, a devoted priest of Frayorna, Mother of Nature. A marteese himself, Brem made an occupation of preaching to half-breeds, insisting they have a place in the world. Upon Brem's death at the hands of Uustaag, the Ancient Enemy of the North, Kiryanna did her best to keep the priest's mission alive, and Baylun had been subject to all of her lessons. He didn't mind. He still couldn't believe someone so beautiful could love and marry a krukari such as himself and bear three wonderful children. And although their sons' krukari heritage was noticeable only if one looked for it, their daughter's hobgoblin blood was buried deep enough as to be nonexistent. Of the three, she came the closest to matching their mother's good looks, and every year she closed the gap further.

Baylun thought about his children, as he often did when away from home for so long—it had been three weeks. At seven years old, Teliya was the youngest. Though she had Baylun's brown eyes, her hair burned with the same fire as her mother's, and her complexion was fair. She was perpetually happy and saw the beauty in everything; rarely did Teliya cry. Baylun's sons were protective of their sister, but there was no need, for all of West Palidur adored her.

Daymyn was born three years before Teliya, and was as competitive as his mother. Kiryanna had hesitated to name their second born after Baylun's late cousin, a warrior that had strayed from the path of goodness, but Baylun still wondered if he might have prevented Daymyn's ill-fated decisions had he not been so focused on himself at the time. He and Daymyn were trapped behind enemy lines for months before the War of the North, forced to blend in with the evil forces of Darum Carumbor to survive. The pressure had been too much for Daymyn, and bent the warrior's will toward darkness. Although everyone held Baylun blameless in the matter, it was a feeling he couldn't shake. In the end, Kiryanna accepted what she referred to as Baylun's need for atonement, and agreed to the name.

Nidor was the eldest, nearly fourteen years in age, and named after a barbarian paladin of Silcor, the fire deity. The original Nidor, a dark-skin of Holindale, had been the noblest soul Baylun had ever met, and was instrumental in ending the threat of annihilation Uustaag and the evil deity Thard'Dun imposed on all of Vaeldor. The paladin had been best friend to Baylun's father, Gruelenor, and the greatest "uncle" a child could have hoped for. Though Baylun's son failed to echo Nidor's purity of spirit—an unachievable goal—the lad was good-willed, strong, balanced, and excelled with the sword faster than even Baylun's older brother, Romik, had done as a young teen.

Presently, Baylun noticed Kiryanna's lips twisting to the side. He then realized he was clasping the small fire opal around his neck. A symbol of Silcor, he always clutched it when thinking about his children—or the late paladin Nidor. Kiryanna knew this.

"Will we rid Philen of these despicable creatures today?" she posed.

Baylun took a deep breath and returned his focus to the camp. The largest tent surely contained the Philanders the hobgoblins had snatched in the middle of the night over three weeks ago. He tightened his grip on Torrac, the mysterious axe his brother had given him on his eighteenth birthday, before the War of the North began. Forged out of bronze, it was a magnificent weapon with a spike at the bottom of the handle and runes etched along its blades. The battleaxe was heavy, but well-balanced, and never in need of sharpening. Without it, Baylun would never have survived the journey through the evil citadel of Lormin Dmurr during the Battle of the Broken Land.

Turning to Kiryanna, he held up five fingers and pointed left to reveal the number of hobgoblins in that direction—Kiryanna loved using hand signals. He then showed three fingers and pointed right. After flashing two fingers, he made a fist to represent the hobgoblins that had entered tents.

She nodded her comprehension and held her fist to her chest before motioning to the right.

Normally, Baylun and Kiryanna wouldn't be alone on a mission such as this. But the rest of their squadron busied themselves with distracting the roaming patrols to allow Baylun a chance to locate the enemy camp. His father taught him to track when he was Daymyn's age, and he had followed the hobgoblins' trail to this very spot. The thought of gathering his soldiers before the assault crossed his mind, but he didn't know what shape the captives were in, nor how much longer they would remain alive. He needed to act.

He nodded to his wife and stood, towering over her petite figure. She unsheathed her golden blade, her grin returning. Baylun stooped to give her a kiss before rounding the boulder and sprinting toward the five hobgoblins.

The enemy noticed Baylun immediately and pulled their swords while shouting. To Baylun's right, Kiryanna closed on the other guards much more swiftly. Two of the hobgoblins met Baylun. They were large, but paled compared to him, and his powerful swing sliced one and cleaved the other.

Of the other three hobgoblins, one balked at Baylun's presence while the other two attacked. Baylun parried aside a sword with his haft and jumped back from a hammer. He countered, chopping the head from the second attacker before planting the spike of his handle into the face of the other.

The fifth hobgoblin charged, its eyes still wide and fear evident in its half-hearted slash. Baylun knocked its weapon to the ground and punched the worm in the jaw — his gauntlet left gashes across his foe's cheek, and the sound of snapping bone reached his ears. The hobgoblin collapsed, screaming with its hands over its face.

In Baylun's peripheral vision, two hobgoblins exited a tent and raced for the larger one — towards the prisoners. He stepped at them and threw his battleaxe. The runes along the edge lit up, and it didn't matter that he took no time to aim; the blades twirled faster, and the weapon hastened toward its target. It was a handy trick he learned during his time in Helmland, when he heaved Torrac at an undead dragon beyond even the range of a crossbow. Just as the axe had destroyed the skull of the skeletal beast, it split the lead hobgoblin in half.

The final kidnapper hesitated at the sight of its comrade's fate while Baylun charged. He was prepared to tear the hobgoblin apart with his bare hands if he had to, but Kiryanna arrived first, and pierced the bandit's heart with her golden blade.

Baylun glanced over his shoulder. The hobgoblin he had punched was gone.

"They're here!" announced Kiryanna, standing just outside the flap of the large tent. "And they do not look so good."

Baylun nodded. After retrieving his weapon, he pulled his herb pouch and hastened to join his wife.

❋❋❋

The trip to West Palidur lasted two weeks. Easily an eight-day journey, the condition of the captives slowed things considerably. The healing herbs Baylun had applied, small plants called silver eye, were working, but they treated only injuries, and not the lack of food and water nor the mental trauma that made the prisoners weak. Baylun's soldiers arrived shortly after he administered the herbs, and offered shoulders to lean on; and once they reunited with their horses, plenty of food and water were provided. But the four men and two women still needed time, and received it while Baylun carried an easy pace into the north. Thank goodness summer had only just begun — the Philen heat was yet to reach its full force. The journey might have been much worse otherwise. By the time they reached West Palidur, color returned to the captives' cheeks, and they appeared closer to how they had when last seen by loved ones.

The city guard recognized Baylun and his men, and the tall doors of the southern gate swung open. Baylun then left his lieutenant to escort the rescued prisoners to their homes and report to Duke Magneer's castle. Uncle Magneer would surely rather hear of the mission's success from Baylun himself, but he desperately missed his children.

Kiryanna did not oppose the decision.

Baylun lived in the northern reaches of West Palidur, where the houses were not so crowded and grass was plentiful. His particular residence was two stories, with a barn and a large backyard, and was given to him as a gift for his services to Philen and the part he played in defeating Uustaag — one of several perks he received after the war. The citizens regarded him as a hero, and rarely did he pay when visiting taverns. This filled him with guilt, as if he were stealing, for the War of the North depended upon many brave souls, least of all himself. But over the past eight years, notions of guilt withdrew enough to allow the occasional enjoyment of a night on the town with his wife.

Baylun's father sat on the front porch with Teliya. Like Baylun, Gruelenor preferred to remain at home most days, away from the eyes of the city. Baylun inherited his strong resemblance to hobgoblins from his father, as well as Gruelenor's resentment of that fact, but Gruelenor was a bit more extreme, only leaving home to visit Baylun or Duke Magneer. Presently, Baylun's father and Teliya played a game where they attempted to make the ugliest face — a pastime Gruelenor detested, but saying no to Teliya was impossible. Upon seeing Baylun's approach, Gruelenor ended the competition by pulling down his lower lip to bare his large bottom fangs while sticking out his tongue and crossing his eyes. Teliya jumped for joy and bowed in surrender to the King of Ugly Faces.

Gruelenor diverted his attention to Baylun. "Go well?" His voice was even more gravelly with his advancing age, and deep wrinkles cut into the leather-like skin of his large forehead all the way to his receding hairline. Perhaps the only benefit of having krukari blood was his jet-black hair, as hobgoblins and krukari never grayed.

Baylun nodded.

"Father!" Teliya rushed from the covered porch and into Baylun's arms — thank goodness Kiryanna insisted they clean their armor before returning home.

Kiryanna stood to the side with a grin. She never minded their daughter's attachment to Baylun. On the contrary, she encouraged it. Baylun pretended Teliya's embrace was crushing his bones — her arms didn't come close to reaching around his ribcage — and the small girl convulsed with giggles.

"All those taken have been returned," Kiryanna said to Gruelenor. "A flawless mission."

Gruelenor grinned to one side.

"Did you tell them?" shouted Lorin from the house thirty yards to the left, where Baylun's parents lived. His mother was as lovely as ever, defying the gray hair giving away her years.

Baylun frowned. "Tell us what?"

Gruelenor shrugged. "A message arrived. The herald was from Ironside, but the letter is from Morimont. The soldier said it was of utmost importance."

Baylun's frown deepened. He received letters from his brother, the Lord of Ironside Keep, several times a year. But Morimont? He knew no one from the dwarfish city. "What does it say?" he asked.

Gruelenor shrugged again. "It's sealed."

Perhaps it was a past acquaintance of Kiryanna's. Baylun looked at his wife. She shook her head. She didn't know either.

"It's on the dining table." Gruelenor nodded toward Baylun's house.

"Thanks," Baylun said as he walked up the porch steps, his daughter clinging to his leg and giggling harder with every step.

Kiryanna tickled Teliya until the child released her grip, freeing Baylun to open the door. Mother and daughter then began a gleeful conversation about everything that transpired over the past month.

Baylun entered the family room. A plush divan faced the hearth, and four comfortable chairs surrounded a game table. His family played games at least once a week, including card games like Save the Maiden and King's Conquest, and some nights they held tournaments of chess. Kiryanna often made games up, and though a bit silly, the kids enjoyed them. Baylun secretly did as well. On the mantle was a large piece of citrine gifted to Baylun from the dwarves of the High Riser Mountains, chiseled to resemble fire. The crystal was extremely valuable and a symbol of Baylun's family's dedication to the fire deity, Silcor. Though many were aware of its splendor, thieves wouldn't dare enter Baylun's home—rumors of Torrac's powers were greatly exaggerated, and he said nothing to correct them.

On the far wall, a pair of doors flanked an archway leading to the backyard. The left door led to the study, and the right door to a workroom. On the left side of the room, a stairway rose to the house's second story. The dining room lay beyond an archway to the right.

Baylun entered the dining room, where a sweaty Nidor studied a sheet of parchment. Nidor was quick to read and write and already stood well over five feet in height. From a scratch on the young man's left forearm and a bruise on the right hand, the lad had surely been sparring with Daymyn in the backyard. Both of Baylun's sons aspired to become warriors and worked hard to achieve that goal. The only benefit of Baylun's captivity in Darum Carumbor had been the weeks he spent training soldiers in combat, and he utilized those skills to instruct his boys. When he was away on missions with Kiryanna, Gruelenor took over those duties, as well as teaching them archery and how to track.

Nidor looked up. The leather-like skin most krukari inherited from their hobgoblin ancestry wasn't noticeable in any of Baylun's children, but he could not help but see it. Of course, their slightly pointed ears helped to detract from any half-hobgoblin characteristics, a contribution from Kiryanna's marteese blood. Too bad Kiryanna couldn't prevent Baylun from passing his flattened nose to the boys. Theirs were not nearly as large or as wide as Baylun's, but he had hoped they'd avoid all the traits that plagued his childhood. Kiryanna claimed their noses to be perfect.

"You're leaving again?" Nidor's tone made the question more of a statement. His voice was deepening, and not a trace of the gravelly quality Baylun and Gruelenor shared was evident, much to Baylun's delight. Draped around Nidor's neck was a fire opal shard, the very one Gruelenor salvaged from Lormin Dmurr after the Battle of the Broken Land. It was the only surviving piece of the original Nidor's existence, before the paladin closed the opening to Thard'Dun's world. Gruelenor had given it to Baylun's eldest as a gift when Nidor turned eight.

"I've not seen the letter," Baylun pointed out.

"You're always going somewhere," muttered Nidor, dropping the parchment onto the table.

The growing population of hobgoblins to the south had kept Baylun and Kiryanna especially busy lately. But what could he do? Leaving the wandering marauders to pillage was out of the question.

Nidor eyed Baylun. "I want to earn my place among Duke Magneer's Honor Guard. Not be *given* the position because he's my granduncle or because you're their captain. How am I supposed to do that if we don't finish my training?" His shoulders slumped. "Gulson is already scheduled to perform before the Honor Panel."

Baylun sighed. Gulson; son of Lord Mundwes, one of the wealthiest nobles in West Palidur and a good friend of Uncle Magneer's. That Gulson was six months younger than Nidor didn't help matters. "Granduncle Magneer prefers his candidates to be sixteen years old," Baylun said, attempting to ease his son's angst. "Even with an invitation, it doesn't mean he will be accepted. So be patient." Noting the lack of respite, he added, "Besides, you're twice the warrior as Gulson, and you know it."

Nidor held a wry smile. "I suppose. I best him every time we spar. But I'm still not scheduled to perform."

Baylun's attention moved to the parchment. He wanted to know what was written.

"It's an invitation to Ironside," said Nidor.

Baylun's spirits rose. He hadn't seen Romik for almost a year. His brother's visits to Philen dwindled after the birth of Ameilistari, Baylun's niece. She was a year younger than Nidor. But Gruelenor claimed the message was from Morimont. Baylun stepped around the table and lifted the letter.

"Who's Greyor?" asked Nidor.

Sure enough, the end of the parchment bore Greyor's name.

Baylun was familiar with the dwarf's reputation as one of the greatest heroes in the Battle of the Broken Land. He had never spoken with Greyor, but caught glimpses of the dwarf, and his father and wife once traveled with the warrior and talked about the fancy battleaxe named Clanghorr. "Its bronze spike reminds me of Torrac," his father had said, and Kiryanna agreed. The same dwarfish smith had likely forged both weapons.

"Greyor?" Kiryanna asked, standing in the entryway. "The dwarf?"

Baylun nodded while he read the message.

Dear Baylun,

I hope you are well.

Though we have not officially met, I'm sure you know of me, as I do of you. Your accomplishments in Lormin Dmurr are widespread, and they are the reason I send this note. I need warriors such as yourself for a most urgent task. Unfortunately, the dangers are unknown, and I cannot guarantee your survival. If you accept this request, please meet me at Ironside Keep on the next new moon from the arrival of this message. I should also mention that the reward will be well worth it.

Yours Truly,

Greyor of Morimont

CHAPTER 4

FAMILY REUNION

Baylun said goodbye to his parents. Gruelenor and Lorin stood on their porch, waving while the wagon pulled away from the house. Baylun preferred riding his horse, but with the whole family going, the wagon was the only option.

After Baylun had finished reading the letter, Kiryanna seized the parchment to have a look. A smile crept across her cheeks, and she turned to Baylun.

"This is perfect!" she said. "We've not had a vacation in ages. And I *know* you miss your brother."

"Why can't *we* go?" asked Nidor.

Kiryanna furrowed her brow. "Of course you're going. I'm sure you miss Uncle Romik and Ameilistari. And your brother and sister have never been to Ironside."

Baylun cleared his throat to gain his wife's attention. "Did you read the *whole* letter?"

She raised an eyebrow. "Yes, I did. And do not think for a moment that I'm staying behind."

"But the danger…" Baylun protested.

Kiryanna almost laughed. "My dearest, nothing will *ever* compare to what we have faced. Now let Mother and Father know we will be gone for… I'd say until early autumn. I'll send word to Duke Magneer."

Baylun took a deep breath and pushed it out. There was no arguing with the woman. He loved and hated that about her.

"And we'll need to take the wagon," added Kiryanna as she glided from the dining room.

And they were taking the wagon…

Nidor smiled.

Nearly a week had passed, and they rode slowly north through Fendora while the southern heat continued rising with each passing day. Daymyn complained it was his turn to drive the horses. From inside the wagon, Teliya reminded Baylun that he promised to take her to Tikken City someday, and that it wasn't fair her brothers had been there already. Kiryanna hummed a tune while pulling salted meat from a sack for lunch, and Nidor renewed an earlier protest that he didn't intend to eat the tough meat throughout the entire trip. Kiryanna informed their eldest that if he wished to be a true warrior, he needed to get used to traveling rations. The whole affair was almost enough to drive Baylun mad. Instead, he grinned. It was also what gave him purpose.

"It's not your turn yet, Daymyn," Baylun said. "Nidor has a few miles to go." He turned to the opening into the wagon to speak to Teliya. "We can't spend time in Tikken City on the way there, princess. Maybe on the way back, if you all behave." He looked at Nidor. "I hate that meat too."

Yes, this was the life.

The grueling heat relented as they passed into Moclen, and the temperature stabilized. A couple of days later, Baylun's family stayed in Tikken City, much to Teliya's delight. But they arrived at night and departed in the morning, much to her chagrin. They spent the following night in Rivercross, and then additional nights in several villages throughout Virch and Sendorum.

As they turned south at last, they stopped in Tedonis, a city holding a special place in the hearts of many. Originally a war camp before the Necromancer War, it flourished after the affair, becoming the attraction it was today. It was a settlement where holy soldiers, priests, and paladins of New Palidur mingled with normal folks, sharing meals, drinks, and laughter. It was where those among the living had made their stand against the undead, and the war to free Vaeldor from the great evil of the not-too-distant past began.

Baylun recalled a story his father told him about a group of friends arriving at the encampment to receive orders from the legendary paladin Merssa. That group included the likes of Gruelenor, Nidor, Uncle Magneer, and Romik's father, Ballrik. They accepted a mission that took them into Nira, where they met their future wives. Unfortunately, the mission also led to Ballrik's courageous death at the hands of demons. Ballrik's wife, Lorin, had been pregnant with Romik at the time, and father and son never met before the warrior's ill fate; and although Romik never admitted it, Baylun knew a hole existed in his brother's heart for the man. But not everything that followed the event was regrettable, for it led to the union of Gruelenor and Lorin, and consequently the birth of Baylun. In essence, the war camp, now a city, was where it all began for Baylun's family.

The following morning, Baylun slowed the wagon as they passed the grand statue of Merssa before Palidur Bridge. Morimont dwarves carved the twenty-foot-tall monument a few years after the War of the North ended, commissioned by Vayla, Grand Paladin of New Palidur and granddaughter of the late paladin hero. Beyond the bridge stood the Holy City, its white buildings standing tall and flags dancing in the breeze.

"Though the statue makes her appear giant," Kiryanna told their children while gazing upon the monument, "Merssa Goldmace was no taller than myself. But her courage and strength rivaled even Vecnor the Destroyer."

The kids seemed genuinely impressed. Baylun chuckled at the nickname his wife had given to Vecnor, fitting as it was. The temptation to correct her crept up his throat, to tell their children the legendary warrior had been called Black Death and Rogue Knight, but she was enjoying herself, and he didn't wish to spoil the fun.

They moved on.

Though Palidur Bridge was wide, Daymyn demanded they straddle the middle and proceed slowly, as if they might go over the edge and plunge into the Great East River far below. Luckily, no other wagons opposed them. After exiting the opposite side, Teliya expressed a desire to enter New Palidur and see how it compared to West Palidur. Baylun had only ever visited the Holy City once, after receiving an invitation to Vayla's wedding. Although rumors held the Grand Paladin to be related to Baylun's late cousin, Daymyn, Baylun had no intention of attending until Kiryanna informed him he was going. In the end, he had a grand time. It was good to see the faces of those he had battled alongside in the War of the North laughing and having fun. Kiryanna had also insisted Baylun dance with her, and although he was sure he appeared a total clod, her smile brought him joy.

"I'm sorry, princess," Baylun said to his daughter. "There's no time to go in." To try and placate her curiosity, he added, "A paladin named Rholmar was duke in Philen before your granduncle, when the city was called Crynora. He was originally from Palidur, and renamed Crynora West Palidur so he wouldn't get homesick."

Teliya stuck out her lower lip in disappointment.

Baylun compromised by following the road nearest to the city, so his daughter could view the taller buildings from outside its walls. It added a half hour to the overall trip. Kiryanna enhanced the experience by describing everything she remembered from their visit years ago. Teliya sighed, not completely satisfied, but her frown diminished.

There was then little else to distract Baylun's family while trekking south, and several days later they reached Charndova, nearly four weeks after leaving West Palidur. It was almost lunchtime, and though the new moon was yet a couple of evenings away, Baylun dreaded the thought of entering the large city outside the mountain pass. It meant another day of strangers giving his family strange looks. He opted to press on.

The kids were silent as they entered the pass. Towering walls of rock moved in on either side, casting shadows, and the horses labored to tow the wagon along the climbing road. Baylun had made the trip many times in the past, but never with a wagon, and he pushed the mounts as fear of not making it before evening crept in.

The breeze rose and fell, carrying cool mountain air and inspiring all but Baylun to don cloaks while the road twisted left and right, moving them in and out of patchy sunlight. As the way straightened, Baylun steered the wagon to the northern side of the pass to remain in the sun's warmth. The wall to the left then ended, revealing a thousand-foot drop to the north, and rising winds danced with all loose clothing while the path arced northward. As Daymyn's face drained of color, Baylun hugged the cliff wall to ease his son's anxiety. But the poor boy remained ashen for miles, and Baylun found it hard to move his right arm with Daymyn wrapped around it.

The pass then turned eastward, and the embrace eased at last when Baylun steered the wagon away from the chasm and up the snaking climb toward Ironside Keep. He might have pointed out the approaching towers carved into the living rock earlier, had his arms not been busy controlling the reins and giving Daymyn security. It was nearing dinnertime when the stronghold's gate came into view.

The keep was a prime example of the splendor of dwarfish architecture. It sat at the apex of a long curve, positioned to repel an army of thousands with a muster of only two hundred soldiers. The windows along the base of the structure suggested two stories, with most of the openings on the second floor, but Baylun knew a couple more levels existed below ground. Towers rose high above, riddled with additional windows and arrow slits at varying heights, and atop the largest tower in the center waved the flag of Ironside: a red banner sporting a shield split by a downward pointing broadsword, with mountains to its right and a pick to its left. The pick represented a deep friendship with the dwarves of Morimont, a bond stretching centuries.

Originally constructed as a guardian of the mountain pass, the fortress once deterred hostile forces of the east from entering Sardina. But years of peace led its lords to convert a portion of its interior to an inn. The stronghold passed from father to son since its creation, until Romik's granduncle Arkor took possession after the Necromancer War due to the death of Romik's father, Ballrik. It was Baylun's understanding that Ballrik had never presided over the keep.

Baylun expelled a relieved breath when the elderly gatekeeper, Morsum, stepped from the entryway, calling for servants to gather their gear and take care of the wagon and horses. It was time for a good meal and a solid night's rest.

Teliya ran to Morsum and gave the soldier a grand hug. Even in the man's advancing years, he insisted on performing his duties—Romik was uncertain of Morsum's age. Still, Romik declared Morsum the best guard a lord could ever hope for. After Ameilistari's birth, the gatekeeper doubled as nursemaid, a position Romik claimed Morsum was most excited to undertake. And Baylun had to admit the guardsman had a way with children. Romik had brought Morsum to Philen twice on past visits, and Teliya adored the man.

"I've learned a few new faces," Morsum said to Teliya as she took his hand and they stepped beneath the raised portcullis and into the keep. "I believe you'll need to crown me the King of Ugly Faces before your visit ends."

Baylun and the others followed.

Within the entry hall stood Romik, smiling from ear to ear. The long sleeve of his silk shirt concealed his wooden left arm, with only the hook at the end showing.

"Not a chance you can beat Grandfather," Teliya said to Morsum, her eyes scanning the chamber. "But first you must show me *every* room in this place."

"Of course, Lady Teliya." Morsum bowed low before leading her away. "We'll begin with the privy."

"Eww!"

Romik chuckled and turned back to Baylun, his grin remaining. "Good to see you, brother. The Philen air has been kind." He embraced Baylun with his good arm. "You look the same as ever."

Baylun returned the hug, watching his daughter disappear down a dungeon-like corridor. Romik followed Baylun's gaze and laughed.

"You needn't worry. She'll be fine."

Baylun relaxed, knowing his brother's words to be true. Morsum would allow nothing bad to happen to the children. The old man adored them.

"It's great to see you, Romik." Kiryanna hugged the Lord of the Keep.

"Hello Uncle," Nidor and Daymyn said, almost in unison.

Romik smirked. "Well, if it isn't my favorite nephews."

"I'm more favorite," declared Daymyn with a devilish grin.

"That remains to be seen." Romik frowned. "Let's see who can distract Ameilistari from her studies the fastest." He looked at Nidor. "She's in her room."

Nidor bolted through an iron door and up a long staircase, and Daymyn chased after, shouting, "Not fair! I don't know where her room is!"

"Is it safe to interrupt her?" asked Baylun. His brother discovered early on Ameilistari's aptitude for the magical arts, and she was advanced for her age. At least, that's what Selanna had said. The elfish mage was the most powerful wizard Baylun had ever met, and was the main force behind Uustaag's defeat in the War of the North. Selanna insisted on training Ameilistari in the beginning, when the girl was eight years old, so the young mage wouldn't hurt herself—or anyone else. The thought of Nidor and Daymyn making an incantation go awry put Baylun's nerves on edge.

Romik waved off the concern. "She's only reading."

Baylun nodded, hoping his brother wasn't just humoring him.

"Do you know why we're here?" asked Kiryanna.

"No," Romik replied. "All I received was a letter from Greyor of Morimont to make room for you and a few others, and a coffer of gold to cover all expenses." He narrowed his gaze at Kiryanna. "Well, for *Baylun* and a few others."

She lifted her brow.

Romik laughed, raising his good hand as if to defend himself. "I'm just saying what the note told me. I didn't think for a second you'd be left behind."

"Who are the others?" Baylun asked.

Romik wrinkled his forehead in thought. "There's Eraim… and Lorylla. Remember the gray elf that traveled with Grand Paladin Vayla?"

Baylun recalled the elf. Lorylla hailed from Orlenfel Forest, and was tall enough to look him eye to eye with her strange white irises on black eyes. And though her features were slender, she possessed an inner strength obvious to anyone paying attention.

"Any of them here yet?" posed Kiryanna.

"You're the first," Romik answered. "And I'm glad. Gives us time to catch up."

Romik led them deeper into the keep and to the tavern. To the right was a throne-like chair atop a dais, and several tables littered the floor between the stage and the bar at the opposite end. The room was half-full, with patrons enjoying meals, drinks, and conversations. Most of them lifted their glasses to Romik.

"Tell us a story, Lord Romik," hollered one man.

"Tell the one about the bone dragon," shouted another.

Romik raised his hand. "All in good time. Have you met my brother, Baylun, and his lovely wife, Kiryanna?"

Some patrons gazed nervously at Baylun while a few smiled at Kiryanna. Most showed confusion—whether with Romik's relationship to Baylun or Baylun's union with Kiryanna was anyone's guess. They were reactions Baylun was accustomed to.

"To Baylun and Kiryanna's health!" yelled the first man who had spoken, and he chugged from his tankard.

A spattering of "Hear! Hear!" shouts followed, and more drinks were consumed.

Romik led the way to a table in the corner, providing a bit of privacy, and they sat down. A barmaid arrived immediately. She was attractive, with long blonde hair and hazel eyes, and her cheeks reddened when she spoke to Romik.

"What shall I bring you, milord?" she asked.

Romik looked at Baylun and Kiryanna before turning to the servant. "Three bowls of stew and beers."

"Very good." She curtsied and walked away.

"You tell stories now?" posed Baylun. "I've never seen you on that chair."

The large seat had existed since Romik's grandfather, Vikur, placed it there to regale customers with adventurous stories. Granduncle Arkor never used the chair while running the keep, but kept it on display out of respect for his late brother. Romik followed his granduncle's example, or so Baylun had thought. The decision to bring the tradition back to life must have occurred within the past year.

Romik shrugged, his smile faltering. "These days, stories are all I have." He glanced at his false arm. "The dwarves did a fine job with this, and Granduncle Arkor was the best teacher on how to use it." He sighed. "But I feel pity from everyone who looks at me."

"It's your imagination," Kiryanna said with a wave of her hand. "It's *you* who pities you. And it will remain so until *you* do something about it."

Baylun could always count on his wife to be brutally honest.

The barmaid returned with the drinks.

"Thank you, Naydrel." Romik smiled.

She bowed and headed toward the kitchen.

"Naydrel seems smitten with you," Kiryanna said.

Romik held a wry smile. "Several people blush before lords. Besides, she's a dozen years younger than I."

Kiryanna frowned. "I am much older than Baylun." She turned to Baylun. "Age holds little meaning after a certain point."

Baylun preferred not to think about their ages. Yes, Kiryanna was over eighty years old, while he was thirty-five, but the difference wasn't what bothered him. It was that she was half-elf and would live another hundred-fifty years or so, while he would grow old and wither long before that. It was a worry that constantly ate at the back of his mind.

Morsum entered the tavern with Teliya and Daymyn.

"Ameilistari must have ignored Daymyn," muttered Romik. "I'll have to have a word with that daughter of mine."

"Oh, I remember being her age," Kiryanna said with a smirk. "It's completely natural."

Baylun chuckled. "Nidor probably wants Ameilistari to help him woo your captain's daughter." He lowered his brow. "What's her name?"

Romik grinned. "Sybin." He glanced from a young man sweeping the floor to another cleaning a window. "And I have never had so many strapping lads begging for jobs since she began to blossom. According to Morsum, the keep had only taken experienced soldiers in the past. Now, I have a dozen trainees hoping to earn permanent positions." He gazed at Baylun. "I'm afraid your son has more competition than he knows. And she sees *them* every day." He shrugged. "As for Sybin, she aspires to follow in her father's footsteps, and wishes to become the first woman captain of Ironside. It keeps her quite busy."

Nidor and Ameilistari entered the room. Baylun's brother spoke of Sybin's beauty, but did Romik realize his own daughter's heart-melting smile? The young men working in the tavern certainly did. Though only thirteen, Ameilistari was approaching womanhood as if she were sixteen. Her curly dark hair gathered behind her, secured by a green ribbon to expose more of her light brown skin, and as she laughed at whatever comment Nidor made, her voice was angelic. Baylun felt sorry for Romik. Teliya had Kiryanna to help her become a woman. Romik's wife, Azoumee, passed away a few years after Ameilistari's birth, and Romik was alone. Hopefully, Azoumee had done enough to prepare her husband for the task.

Azoumee had been a lovely person, and a descendant of Holindale. The dark-skinned barbarians had sent thousands of Dales to battle Trannum's forces in Marcove during the Necromancer War, her parents among them, and many remained after the affair to begin life anew. Having grown up on a farm, Azoumee was knowledgeable about living off the land, and she started the first garden throughout Ironside Keep's existence. Romik ordered loads of dirt to be transported to the top of the central tower to make this possible, and an immense bed was constructed to hold it. To this day, Romik maintained the garden in her honor, and outside of the winter months, it helped to keep his pantries full. Azoumee had been attractive in her own right, but Ameilistari would surely exceed the woman's comeliness.

Nidor and Ameilistari sat on either side of a table and whispered to each other. Ameilistari then noticed Baylun watching, and cupped a hand around her mouth, as if Baylun might read her lips.

Kiryanna followed Baylun's gaze. "What are those two up to?" she asked no one.

Ameilistari pointed her finger and spoke a word to light the candle on her table. The young men working in the tavern applauded, and she blushed.

"Nice work, Ameilistari!" hollered one.

"Psst." Romik gained his daughter's attention. "Not here."

She rolled her eyes and cupped her hand again to speak to Nidor.

"Does Selanna still teach her?" asked Baylun.

"No," Romik replied. "She was around for the first couple of years. Now Ameilistari learns from a marteese named Rauzel. The woman seems to know what she's doing, and Ameilistari likes her enough." He looked at his daughter and shook his head. "I just wonder how she plans to run the keep with all of her time spent on wizardry."

"She's a capable young lady," stated Kiryanna. "She can handle anything you put before her."

Romik released a nervous chuckle. "I hope you're right." He turned to Baylun and changed the subject. "Have you seen Desser?"

Baylun grinned. "He and Barrelda visited three months ago."

"Did he bring his kids?"

Baylun puffed out his cheeks as he exhaled. "Yes. And they

are…" He shook his head, holding in a laugh.

"Spirited young warriors," Kiryanna finished for him.

Baylun nodded. "Uncle Magneer strongly suggested we keep them busy *outside* the castle after the first night." He chuckled. "Desser just grinned while they climbed everything in sight!"

"What about Barrelda?" Romik asked.

Kiryanna laughed. "She joined her kids' little competition. While wearing a gown!"

Romik smiled, as if imagining the spectacle. "Sorry I missed that."

Naydrel delivered three bowls of stew.

"Thank you, dear," Romik said.

Her smile grew wide. "It is my pleasure."

"When does the dwarf arrive?" Baylun asked as the barmaid walked away.

Romik stirred his food. "Tomorrow." He furrowed his brow. "I know not why he wishes to meet here." Looking at Baylun, he added, "And his advance payment is much more than necessary."

"He's paying for your discretion," Kiryanna said without hesitation.

Baylun looked at Morsum eating dinner with his younger children. Whatever Greyor had in store, he hoped it wouldn't keep him from his family for too long.

Chapter 5

A Crowded Meeting

Greyor scaled the secret stairs, zigzagging from the chasm floor to the mountain pass outside Ironside Keep. It was a thousand-foot climb known only to the dwarves of Morimont and the lords of Ironside. Upon reaching the top, he approached the rock wall before him and listened. Through tiny holes in the stone, he heard nothing; no voices, no horses. He eased a loose brick from the wall to the right of the secret door, creating a small window to spy on the road. Nothing. After replacing the stone, he pushed a mechanism to open the hidden door and quickly exited before shutting it. Typically, dwarves used the stairs only during the dark hours so they remained unseen entering or exiting, but time was pressing. The Stone Eagle entourage to discuss Clanghorr's proper home was to arrive at Morimont by the end of the month.

Greyor headed west on the barren pass. Ironside Keep wasn't much farther, and he soon ascended steps that mirrored the snaking path leading to its entrance. Not long ago, perhaps a couple of decades, the stairs presented the only access to the keep's gate. Romik had changed that, adding a narrow road to make the stronghold more inviting to guests. Greyor disagreed with the alteration. It created another route for invaders to reach Ironside. But that was the way of humans: shortsighted and optimistic.

The late sun still shone, so the portcullis was up when Greyor arrived. He stepped into the entry chamber under the scrutiny of three sentries.

"You Greyor?" asked a guard.

Greyor nodded.

"Everything is set," the soldier said. "I'll lead you to your room and inform Lord Romik you've arrived."

"Very good." Greyor gazed past the man at the archway leading to the tavern. "But first I require an ale."

The gatekeeper smiled. "Please follow me."

Though Greyor had visited the keep's tavern many times in the past, he appreciated the respect Ironside soldiers always extended toward his kin, and didn't object to the escort.

Upon entering the tavern, he spied Lorylla. The slender gray elf was alone, and all other patrons were gathered at tables farthest from where she sat. It was a typical reaction to gray elves, even after the Necromancer War and the War of the North. It wasn't the gray skin so much, nor the elf maiden's height or deep voice. Folks were distrustful of the white irises on black eyes. But Greyor couldn't speak too ill of the keep's guests; the eyes surprised him the first time he met Lorylla and her father, Xorlunder. Some people just needed more time to adjust.

Lorylla smiled at Greyor's approach. It was a warming smile he hadn't seen in almost four years, and he breathed a pleasant sigh. Of all elves, Lorylla was the one he tolerated best. It wasn't her grace or beauty that Greyor found pleasing, as did many humans that came to know her, but her understanding of dwarfish ways. She didn't make jests like Selanna and Eraim, or shun non-elves like the wizard Wezlok had. She was a serious sort, like a Vermallon elf. But unlike that warrior clan, she did not shy away from delving underground to learn of Vaeldor's buried secrets. She was the perfect companion for the journey ahead.

"Ah! My little friend," Lorylla said in her sonorous voice.

Greyor had gotten used to the greeting. Had anyone else addressed him so, he might have reached for Clanghorr. As he sat across from the elf, a young human approached with a mug in her hand.

"I was informed that ale is your drink." The lass placed the cup on the table.

"You best have another on the way." Greyor winked. "This one's only to wet my lips."

"As you wish." The barmaid bowed slightly and walked away.

Lorylla eyed Greyor. "They would not take my coins for payment." She ran her index finger around the rim of her wineglass. "You paid even for the drinks? Am I to believe you are truly ready?"

Greyor nodded. Other than Eraim, Lorylla was the only person he entrusted with his plan to return to Lornibur, though he had only done so a decade ago. As Lorylla rarely left Orlenfel Forest, there was no one of consequence she might tell, and he wanted to be sure she would join the venture. Eraim discovered his plans five years ago. The small elf became suspicious when Greyor pestered her with questions about their past journey through the mines — Eraim had an exceptional memory! She pried into the reason for his interrogation, and as he realized he'd need her help, he divulged his intentions.

Greyor lifted the mug and began chugging. Once every ounce had passed down his throat, chased by every last bubble of foam, he slammed the cup onto the table, earning a glance from the other patrons. He wiped his lips with his arm, and the barmaid dropped off a second mug.

"I've gathered all the information I could find," he said to his companion once the young lady was gone. "Truth be told, I don't think I'll *ever* be ready." He stared at the ale in his hand. "But I have put it off long enough."

"Very good." Lorylla smirked. "*Qes perishanta.*"

Greyor chuckled, recognizing the elfish phrase, for she had spoken it several times before. My quiver is yours.

"You invited Eraim?" Her question sounded more like a statement.

"Of course," replied Greyor. "She was the only one who seemed able to navigate the maze. And she knows I'm going."

"From what I know of her and things I have heard," Lorylla said, "I am surprised she agreed."

Greyor nodded. "She's much tougher than she pretends to be. I just hope the four of us are enough."

He drained the mug.

The barmaid returned—empty handed!

"Master Greyor," she said. "Lord Romik has sent word that the meeting room is ready, and everyone is present."

"Very good, lass." He reached into his pouch and pulled out two silver coins. After placing them in her hand, he stood. "And I know the way."

They rose, Lorylla standing more than head and shoulders above Greyor, and he led the way from the tavern. They followed the corridor back to the entry chamber, where soldiers passed the time with a game of cards. To the left, an open iron door revealed stairs to the upper levels.

Without a word, a gatekeeper interrupted the game and rushed to the stairwell. "Please follow me," the soldier said, and he went through.

The steps rose steeply, and Greyor and his companion followed the guard up three stories, passing through additional iron doors— all of them open—and entering a long hall traveling left and right. Their escort proceeded to a closed door across the hall and knocked. After a muffled invitation to enter, the guard opened the door and stepped aside.

Greyor walked in and looked about the meeting room. It was a decent-sized space with a long table, three smaller tables, a few shelves laden with books, a fireplace, and stairs leading to a balcony hosting a couple more tables and additional bookshelves. The dying light of the sun shone through a skylight, a fire flickered within the hearth, and candles burned upon the long table, where more guests than Greyor expected stared back at him.

Romik was at the head of the table, and Baylun sat to the lord's right while Eraim was to the left. Next to Baylun was Kiryanna, the krukari's wife. Though Greyor knew firsthand about her abilities from a past adventure, he had not invited her—he didn't wish to make their children orphans should things go poorly. Seated by

Eraim was an elf, one hailing from Salenti Forest, judging by his height. While Eraim possessed a hidden strength, her companion had more muscles than any elf Greyor had met from any clan. Eraim's bow leaned against the wall behind them, alone. Where was her friend's bow? Greyor wasn't sure he trusted a bowless elf.

He sighed.

"Welcome all," he said hesitantly. "But other than Lord Romik, this meeting is only for those I invited."

Kiryanna's brow started rising.

"So, if the rest of you... would... just..." He stopped talking. Kiryanna's eyebrows had reached their maximum height, and the muscular elf winked at him.

Winked?

Kiryanna stood. "If you wish to have the likes of Baylun and Torrac at your service, I will be going as well. We do everything together." She retook her seat.

With the mention of the name given to Baylun's weapon, Clanghorr's whispers began, louder than before. Greyor heard them clearly. They were indeed gibberish.

"This is Tewlon," Eraim said of her companion. "He does not speak, and understands only Elfish, so your secret is safe with him. And he is very capable with the sword. I believe him to be necessary for the road ahead."

Lorylla took a seat next to Tewlon. She and Eraim exchanged nods, and Lorylla did the same with Baylun and Kiryanna.

Greyor sighed again, taking the chair opposite Romik. "It seems I have no choice," he said. "So we'll get started." He looked at Romik, in case the meeting's host wished to say anything.

The Lord of the Keep bowed his head. "This is your meeting. You may proceed."

"Has anyone *not* heard of Lornibur?" Greyor posed.

The occupants of the room eyed one another. Romik then spoke.

"Only stories from my cousin Desser. But they were tales passed on to him by Uncle Magneer. Desser's grandmother, I believe, accompanied you and Eraim into those mines."

"That is correct," stated Eraim. "Arrikan was significant in our survival there."

"I was told about a two-headed snake by Brem," said Kiryanna. "I could never tell if he made it up to make the tales more interesting." She frowned momentarily. "Oh! And there was a demon of ice."

"Marfesna," said Eraim, her expression touched by malice.

Greyor bobbed his head. "All correct. But it is much more than that. Lornibur is a grand city. The birthplace of my race, before we separated into the clans of today. A place of splendor. The last king of Lornibur was a vile worm named Velgaad, and he was its downfall. Lornibur was thought to have been collapsed, and Velgaad and his evil buried with it, but we learned that rumor to be false. Me, Eraim, and your grandmothers or cousins or whatever they were have been there. And I aim to reclaim it in the name of all dwarves."

"So why not recruit dwarves?" posed Kiryanna.

"The mine dwellers," replied Eraim.

"The what?" asked Romik.

"A people living in the mines," Greyor explained. His mind went back to the skinny folk who shied away from light and spoke a strange language. When he had lost his weapon, a group of the creatures returned it to him, and led him and Millord when they got separated from their friends to find Maak Maak. The dwellers fought valiantly behind Greyor and Millord against the enemy they long feared, and most of them died for their efforts. Four survivors continued to accompany Greyor and his companions after Maak Maak's defeat, and all but one perished at the hands of Marfesna.

"Millord wished to dispose of them," Eraim said to those at the table.

Greyor raised a hand. "Yes, my cousin was hasty in his desire to clear everything not a dwarf from the mines. And that is why I have invited *most* of you." He scanned the room to see if anyone had caught his sarcasm. Apparently not. "While my kin would likely share in Millord's original view of the folks living there, he learned before his demise that the mine dwellers were not evil. They are just… different. And I do not wish to bring them harm."

Eraim gave a firm nod.

"I invited Eraim for obvious reasons," Greyor continued. "She has been there, and without a map, she's least likely to get lost." He looked at Lorylla. "Lorylla is an exceptional warrior with a good head on her shoulders." He turned to Baylun. "And your reputation precedes you, Baylun. From everything I've been told, I am certain you can empathize with a people misunderstood."

"That is a trait we both share," said Kiryanna. It was obvious the marteese did the talking for them both.

"But also, there is this." Greyor pulled his weapon from his waist. "This is Clanghorr."

Baylun eyed the battleaxe with interest.

"And from what I understand," Greyor gazed at the krukari, "it would seem you possess a similar weapon."

Baylun nodded. "I left it in my room," the krukari's voice was gravelly, "but it is very similar to yours."

"Was Clanghorr made by a large dwarfish smith?" asked Romik.

Greyor frowned at the Lord of the Keep.

"I bought Torrac from a dwarf out of Morimont," Romik explained. "He said it was the greatest weapon he had ever forged."

"Indeed," muttered Greyor. No mortal hands could have forged Clanghorr! "That remains to be seen."

"What exactly is our aim?" Kiryanna asked. "Once we're inside Lornibur?"

"Right. Right." Greyor turned his mind back to the mission. "When we explored the mines during the Necromancer War, we traveled a specific route, more or less, to enter Nomedd unseen. We did not discover any rooms of consequence. No living quarters, no Lords' Houses, no forge. I aim to find such places. As with all cities, the forge will be at the heart of Lornibur, and if I can breathe life into her, I feel the rest of the city will awaken."

"What are the dangers?" posed Kiryanna.

"Exceptionally large lizards that blend with their surroundings," replied Eraim. She narrowed her eyes at Greyor. "Not ordinary *cavern* lizards." She returned her attention to Kiryanna. "The two-headed… I hesitate to call it a snake, for it had claws… was a monster the mine people called Maak Maak. It was giant and powerful."

"And although we wounded it," added Greyor, "we didn't kill it. It may have died from its injuries, but that remains to be seen."

"Could there be more than one?" asked Kiryanna.

Greyor shared a glance with Eraim. He hadn't thought of that. But something that large would be a predator, and predators did not share hunting grounds. "That is unlikely," he said.

"Hmm." Kiryanna pursed her lips. "What are its weaknesses?"

Greyor snorted a chuckle. "Clanghorr!"

"And Selanna's spell of fire," added Eraim.

Kiryanna nodded. "What if there is no forge? What if we wander aimlessly for weeks with nothing to show for it?"

"You will be compensated, regardless of the outcome," replied Greyor. "I am prepared to pay each of you one thousand gold coins."

The room was silent. The amount was surely more than any but Romik possessed—it was nearly all the wealth to Greyor's name. Still, the Lord of the Keep appeared shocked.

A muffled voice sounded from the balcony, and all eyes turned upward.

"Who's up there?" demanded Romik.

A pair of youthful faces peeked over the railing. A girl, obviously of Dale descent, and a boy. Though subtle, Greyor detected krukari features in the lad's face.

"Just us, Father," replied the girl.

"Come down," ordered the Lord of the Keep. "Now!"

The couple descended the stairs, their expressions of shame more likely at having been caught than at having spied on the meeting.

"You will tell no one of what you have heard." Romik eyed them both. "And we will speak more on this later." He aimed the last part at the lass.

"Yes, sir," the youths responded in unison.

"Now be gone with you," Romik said.

The two left.

Kiryanna looked at Greyor. "I apologize on behalf of Nidor."

The name was a surprise. Greyor had traveled with Nidor the paladin, and suddenly recalled the Dale as having been good friends with Baylun's father, Gruelenor. "It's quite all right," he assured the marteese. "I suppose it won't matter much after today."

Kiryanna made a few hand gestures to her husband. Baylun hesitated before making return gestures.

"We accept your terms," she said to Greyor. "When do we depart?"

"Tomorrow," Greyor answered. "I'd go now if I thought any of you were up to it."

Kiryanna frowned. Perhaps she had wanted more time.

"Why did you hold your meeting here?" asked Romik. "And why am I present?"

"Well…" Greyor rubbed his nose. "You see, you have the key. The entrance to Lornibur lies in Ironside's secret passage. You know the one I speak of. I need you to give us access." At Romik's lowering brow, Greyor added, "You needn't worry about us speaking of your tunnel. Eraim and I have been there already, Baylun is your brother, and Lorylla —"

"I have not the faintest interest in the tunnel's existence," Lorylla said in a calm demeanor. "And neither would any of my kin."

Greyor smiled. "There you have it."

Romik slowly grinned. "Very good."

The meeting adjourned, and Greyor headed to his room, hoping to gain some rest. But his nerves were alive, and the dawn couldn't come soon enough.

Chapter 6
The Journey Begins

Baylun strapped on his belt while Kiryanna checked her gear. The hour was early; he doubted the sun had risen. He was uneasy about leaving his children with Morsum for… however long it took. The soldier was ancient. Morsum might have been fine playing nursemaid for Ameilistari five years ago, but Baylun's children could be a handful. Beyond that, he still worried about Kiryanna joining the quest. In truth, he didn't see the danger in fighting large lizards. It couldn't differ greatly from exterminating alligators, a task he had performed in Philen when the population of the reptiles grew to an extraordinary amount. But Greyor planned to enter the mines with no maps to guide them. They might get lost and never find their way out. Kiryanna belonged with their children, but there was no convincing the woman.

A small hand on Baylun's shoulder stole his attention.

"Everything will work out," Kiryanna said softly. "You'll see."

As usual, she knew what he was thinking.

"An escort awaits outside the door to take us to the crypt," she added.

He turned to meet her gaze; her emerald eyes sparkled. "We must see the kids before we go," he said.

Kiryanna smiled. "Of course."

She could still melt his heart with her smile. He reflected on the first one she bestowed upon him years ago in an evil land when they faced much greater dangers. Perhaps fighting hobgoblins, goblins, and bandits in Philen had become too predictable. Or maybe he had lost his nerve. The thought of his children losing their parents had never crossed his mind during missions before, so why did it bother him now?

Kiryanna rose onto her toes, and Baylun leaned over to kiss her. Everything was right again.

The kids were awake when Baylun and Kiryanna arrived. Nidor was fully dressed, including his leather armor and weapon belt.

"What are you up to?" Baylun asked.

Nidor shrugged. "Ameilistari said Sybin is training this morning. Thought maybe she might need a sparring partner."

Baylun chuckled. "Take it easy on her."

Kiryanna raised an eyebrow. "From what I hear, you had better be on your guard."

Nidor held a sarcastic grin. "Ha ha."

Teliya raced into Baylun's arms. "Don't be too long." After a squeeze, she added, "But stay gone at least a week. Morsum says King Cavalor will be in Denvale, and that he can take us to meet him."

Baylun frowned. Cavalor was a fine and courageous man—he had battled beside the Marcove king in Lormin Dmurr during the Battle of the Broken Land. But Denvale was a less-than-tidy place, and home to many sketchy characters. Of course, outside New Palidur, every city had areas to avoid at night. In West Palidur, it was the southwestern region. But in Denvale, it seemed half the city fit into that category.

"Relax, Father," said Daymyn. "Ironside soldiers are going with us."

Baylun sighed. "Stay away from the edge." He hugged Nidor and then Daymyn. "No peeking into the chasm."

Kiryanna finished hugging Teliya. "They'll be fine." She eyed Baylun. "You forget too often they have elfish blood as well. They are very nimble, with grace and balance you will never comprehend."

Baylun held a wry smile.

Kiryanna turned toward the door. "Now let's go before they leave without us."

The escort led them down the stairs of the central tower. After passing archways showing a kitchen, a dining room, and the lower library, Baylun heard Kiryanna whisper something he didn't quite catch.

"What?" he whispered back.

She frowned. "I said nothing."

Baylun glanced about, confused. There was no one else around. He then noticed the whispers hadn't stopped, and they didn't come from his wife nor the soldier leading them. He shook his head, but couldn't disperse them.

An opening appeared below. The inner wall then ended, and they followed steps arcing around the circular storage room at the bottom of the tower. Organized about the chamber were crates, barrels, and sacks, and on the wall opposite the final step was a painting of the keep's original lord, Grellmor, which also served as the door to the crypt. The warrior appeared as a giant, with one foot atop a mountain and his sword almost piercing the sun, and several locks adorned the portrait's side. Baylun was told that ghouls had marred the fresco before the Necromancer War, but one could no longer tell.

Gathered in the room were Greyor, Lorylla, Eraim, Tewlon, Captain Marlajin, the captain's daughter, Sybin, and Baylun's brother. Romik wore a chain shirt, and the Sword of Ironside hung from his waist—odd attire for seeing the company off. His wooden arm was no longer covered by a long sleeve, leaving the hinges and straps at the "elbow" joint visible—unlike Granduncle Arkor, Romik had lost most of his arm. Along the outer edge of the "forearm" was a metal strip, and small hooks accompanied the larger one at the end, like twisted fingers.

Romik stood to the side of Grellmor's image, giving orders to his captain. Sybin paid close attention, as if being issued the instructions herself—evidently she would be late for her battle practice. She appeared confident, and her budding figure, sleek raven hair, and piercing gray eyes made Nidor's infatuation with her understandable. Once the orders were complete, the captain handed Romik a burning torch and gave a nod—Sybin mirrored the gesture. The pair then climbed the steps to exit the room.

Romik sent a smug grin Baylun's way.

Greyor turned to Baylun with a frown. "Would you talk some sense into your brother?"

The strange whispers grew in volume, but only slightly. Was Baylun going mad? He ignored them and asked, "What's wrong?"

"Romik says he's joining us," Eraim said.

Baylun eyed his brother.

Romik winked.

"Romik…" was all Baylun managed.

The Lord of the Keep stepped away from the painting and led Baylun by the elbow to the stairs. "I'm going," he stated in a hushed voice. "There's nothing you can say to—"

"Please." Baylun glanced at his wife. "It's bad enough I cannot talk Kiryanna into staying." He stared hard into Romik's eyes. "We have children to think of."

"As your loving wife put it," said Romik, "nothing will change until *I* do something about it."

"She was just…" Baylun fell silent, unsure of how to finish the sentence.

"She's right." Romik's gaze was stern. "Granduncle Arkor was a great hero, even with one arm. If I turn out to be half the warrior he was, it'll be quite an accomplishment."

"What if you…?"

"Die?" Romik raised his brow. "We all die at some point. It's what we do before that time that lives on. You have Torrac, and stories about your heroics travel from Urell Coast to Kalmaar." He grinned. "Come now, Fang."

Baylun hadn't heard that nickname in years. It almost made him laugh. But this was no laughing matter. "You're Lord of Ironside," he reminded his brother.

Romik held a satisfied expression. "Yes, I am." He spoke louder and faced the room. "And as lord, I possess the only key into the crypt." He turned to Greyor as he pulled a small chain from his pouch, from which a key dangled. "And if you want access, you'll accept my terms. I shall receive no gold. My reward is the adventure."

The dwarf's frown deepened, and his eyes sought Baylun.

Baylun shrugged.

"Brakkeet!" Greyor shook his head. "So be it. Now open the blasted door!"

Romik's victorious smirk was unwavering as he approached the mural of Grellmor. He then had everyone turn their backs—including Baylun—while he opened the door. As the Lord of the Keep protected the secret of the entryway, Greyor handed each member a backpack and two waterskins.

"These have food and water," the dwarf said. "Enough for several weeks."

"You may turn around," announced Romik.

In place of the image was an opening. Beyond, a second circular chamber awaited. A score of niches penetrated the wall at various heights, each nearly seven feet long and one foot high—large enough to house a corpse. Three were boarded shut; the rest were empty. The first sealed niche bore the inscription: VIKUR. Below it, another read: ARKOR. The final inscription, beside the first, read: BALLRIK. Baylun knew the latter to be vacant. Romik's father was lost after leaping through a demonic gate to save thousands of lives. And although Ballrik had never been Lord of the Keep, Romik honored his father in such a way.

A matching mural of Grellmor marked the opposite side of the room, and between the niches to the right, several faded paintings of past Lords of the Keep lined the wall, including Romik's grandfather, Vikur. Newer paintings occupied the spaces to the left, the first depicting Arkor the One-Armed Warrior, the second resembling Ballrik as described by Arkor, and the final portrait was of Romik. Romik had chosen to be painted with both of his arms and holding the Sword of Ironside in two hands—the same weapon clutched by all but Arkor. Blank spaces existed for future lords between Romik's image and Grellmor. Perhaps Ameilistari's likeness would occupy one.

Again, Romik insisted everyone turn away. Upon the sound of grinding stone, they looked back to see a secret panel opening. Beyond was a tunnel, rough in its construction.

Romik gazed into the dark corridor. "Though I have opened this door before, I have never passed beyond it."

"Still can't believe my kin carved that passage," grumbled Greyor, eyeing the uneven walls and shaking his head. "Disgraceful."

As Romik stepped through the opening with the torch, Baylun realized another issue with his brother joining the party. The Lord of the Keep was the only one who couldn't see in the dark. Though Baylun preferred light, the risk of darkness was ever present where they headed. He would need to stay close.

The company moved on, and the grinding of the closing door faded behind them. The tunnel bore them straight for long stretches, at times descending crude steps—Greyor again shook his head at the craftsmanship—or twisting left and right. Occasionally, stairways spiraled around solid pillars. The air was stale and moist, and puddles spotted the floor, but nothing hindered the group's progress.

The day was long, and Greyor called for a halt upon reaching a chamber containing a well, firepit, and several flattened piles of old straw beds, unused for quite some time.

"We should stop here," said the dwarf. "I'm sure you folks need your rest." He walked to a tunnel exiting the room on the opposite side and peered into the darkness. "I believe the breach is another day's travel."

"Some of us are just as capable as you," Kiryanna stated, showing her annoyance with the dwarf's insinuations that they were of weaker races. "Still," she added, "stopping for rest is the *smart* thing to do. For all of us."

Greyor looked at Eraim, who smiled with a "told-you-so" expression. A grin spread the dwarf's mustache, and he chuckled at some unknown jest.

Tewlon pulled a few narrow logs from one of his packs and placed them in the firepit. Baylun thought it odd to have been carrying wood all this time—that left little room for necessary equipment. The strong elf then withdrew a blanket and laid it on the floor, and Eraim sat atop it.

"This straw is positively disgusting," remarked Eraim. "Probably infested with bugs." She looked at her elf companion. "You had best share my blanket."

Tewlon smirked and settled next to her.

Greyor brought flame to the logs before claiming an area on the cold floor. Romik extracted a blanket of his own, as did Lorylla.

Baylun had no blankets. He and Kiryanna usually slept on the grass in Philen, as the weather was always pleasant. He sat on one of the straw piles, placing Torrac beside him. It was like sitting on stone. Kiryanna sneered at the discolored chaff, and with a sigh, she joined him.

Greyor rose and relocated to a spot between Lorylla and Baylun, and the faint whispering in Baylun's head strengthened. It seemed to say, "anger… anger… anger…"

He ignored it.

"So that's Torrac," said Greyor, gazing at the battleaxe. "It has runes along the edges."

Baylun nodded as he lifted the weapon onto his lap. "One blade says *honor*, and the other says *courage*. I don't know which is which."

Greyor eyed him. "Who told you that?"

"Romik." Baylun glanced at his brother, who focused on the fire. "That's what the dwarf smith told him."

"Is that so?" Greyor pulled Clanghorr. "Because those are akin to the writings on my axe." He presented the weapon.

The letters appeared similar. A few runes were identical.

"When I heard stories of your weapon," Greyor said, "I knew I must meet you one day." He glanced at Torrac. "Do your runes ever light up?"

Baylun slowly nodded. "Do yours?"

Greyor bobbed his head. "Is it easy to throw?"

Again, Baylun nodded.

"Other than the lengths of the handles," Greyor said, "the only difference I see is that my blades are of silver while yours are bronze."

The likeness *was* uncanny.

Suddenly, Baylun realized the whispers didn't say anger. They repeated Clanghorr over and over. Why did the spirit invading his mind speak the name of the other weapon? Baylun looked at Greyor. The dwarf stared at the axes as if perplexed.

Greyor turned to Baylun. "Perhaps this journey will provide some answers."

Baylun thought of mentioning the whispers, but decided against it. If he were going mad, it would end the mission for him and Kiryanna. He couldn't do that to his wife; this was where she wanted to be at the moment. He would keep it to himself. If it got any worse, he'd tell her.

Greyor seemed satisfied with the conversation, at least for the time being, and pulled rations from his pack. Everyone did the same, using the food the dwarf had provided, which comprised salted meat, flatbread, nuts, and cheese.

Romik brought his own rations, and tossed a handful of colorful, shriveled, waxy shapes into his mouth—pieces of dried fruit. His late wife had shown him the process for preparing the fruits so they lasted for months, and he had developed a taste for them. With the garden atop Ironside Keep's central tower holding an apple tree, a pear tree, grapevines, and berry bushes of several varieties, he possessed a nearly endless supply.

After everyone finished eating, they turned in for the night.

❋ ❋ ❋

Greyor was first to guard. The fire had died down, and the chamber and tunnels were dark. Though he couldn't see much in the way of details, he saw well enough, and nothing approached.

While pacing from one exit to the other, he gazed often at Baylun's axe. Romik claimed the weapon to have been forged by a dwarf out of Morimont, but that was impossible. It was ancient, of that Greyor was certain.

He peered down the tunnel leading toward the Fire Hills. "Torrac," he said softly to himself, and glanced in the weapon's direction as he realized the whispers in his head repeated the name. The axes knew each other. Brothers? Cousins? He pondered the runes. If the weapons were connected, why did Torrac's runes glow in Baylun's hand? The warrior was a krukari. Then again, Clanghorr's writings had never come to life while Millord possessed it. Had Poluran ever seen them light up? Greyor returned his attention to the passage. He needed to learn more about the axes. He wasn't sure why, but he was positive Lornibur held the answers.

There were no sounds to alarm Greyor through the night. At one point he detected the squealing of distant rats, and he chased a few away from the food packs. As his shift ended, he woke Eraim and settled in for some sleep.

❁ ❁ ❁

Baylun awoke at Tewlon's touch. Apparently, the elf had guarded the final leg of the night.

Kiryanna slept with her head on Baylun's right arm, and the tingling of the limb was almost painful. She opened her eyes when he pulled it free, allowing blood to rush to his fingertips. His back was a bit stiff as he climbed to his feet—sleeping under the stars was much preferred. As Baylun stretched, he realized the whispers had stopped, and he released a relieved breath.

Tewlon finished rousing the others, and once everyone was ready, they lit three torches and continued.

The tunnel was unchanged from the previous day as they trudged along. They paused briefly for lunch within the confines of the corridor, and as the monotonous trek felt it would never end, Greyor

57

halted. A hole existed in the wall ahead. It was high enough for the dwarf to walk through without ducking.

"Lornibur," Greyor said in awe.

❊ ❊ ❊

Greyor eyed the breach. Decades ago, it had been much smaller, and Millord became wedged while trying to squeeze through. The sorceress Selanna turned the constricting rock into mud to widen the entrance and free the warrior.

Clumps of dirt marked either side of the wall, and a boot print sat undisturbed on the other side. Greyor placed his right foot into the impression. Though he wore different boots back then, it was a perfect fit.

He stepped through and lifted his torch. The tunnel was exactly as he remembered. The ceiling rose fifteen feet overhead, just as finely chiseled as the walls and floor. It was expert craftsmanship. Along the corridor, exquisite arches stood every twenty feet to the left and right, each topped with images of hammers and anvils in bas-relief. To the left, the fading trail of a muddy boot approached a larger arch with runes etched around its arc.

Greyor moved closer to inspect the writings. The lines, curves, dots, and dashes… They seemed familiar. He compared them to the runes on Clanghorr. The style of the symbols appeared to match.

"We go this way," he said.

"It is the same way we went last time," commented Eraim. "We have to be sure of where we step."

Greyor nodded, looking at the others. "Maak Maak dug many tunnels, some of them hidden. We don't want to fall into one."

"The one that separated us last time was just beneath the floor," Eraim added, "and the flagstones crumbled when we trod upon them."

"Yes," Greyor said. "Watch your step, and follow the person in front of you." He exhaled hard through his nose, eyeing Eraim.

"Perhaps you should lead."

Eraim glanced at Tewlon and back to Greyor. "I… suppose."

"Everyone else, two by two," Greyor instructed. "Me and Lorylla go next. Then Baylun and Kiryanna, and Romik and Tewlon. Stay ten feet from those before you." That should keep them from wandering where they ought not to.

Eraim puffed out her cheeks and moved to the lead. Thus far, she had appeared relaxed and confident, but nervousness now crept into her eyes. She pulled Mithkahr, a weapon known to emit a reddish tint when evil was near. The blade remained dull, and Eraim seemed to breathe easier.

The tunnel continued with arches throughout its course, and smaller corridors branched to the left and right with rails running along their centers. Etched upon some walls were more images in bas-relief, these showing dwarves engaged in various activities. The first set depicted miners swinging pickaxes. The next portrayed miners harvesting ore. A third wall revealed dwarves wielding battleaxes, warhammers, swords, and spears, as if entering battle. A few dwarves held crossbows.

"This is the tunnel we took last time." Eraim's soft voice echoed as she stood before a corridor branching right. A rail followed it from a hallway on the left, and the wider passage continued forward.

Greyor furrowed his brow in thought. They could follow the same route to the mine dwellers and lizards, or find an alternative path to unknown dangers. Probably better to face the former. He nodded to Eraim to go right.

They proceeded, walking on either side of the rail. Though the magnificent arches were absent within the narrower corridor and the ceiling dropped to ten feet, the hallway was no less impressive with its perfect angles and smooth surfaces. The company then entered the first of several vaulted chambers Greyor knew to lie ahead. The ceiling rose into darkness, and along the walls, veins of gold and silver reflected off the torchlight. A beautiful sight to behold!

"Mees! Mees!" Eraim called, her eyes darting about the room.

At first, Greyor saw nothing. Then a movement to his right revealed an enormous lizard slithering across the floor while attempting to blend with the gray stone. The last time Greyor passed through these halls, he didn't encounter the reptiles for a week. The creatures had evidently expanded their domain.

He charged with a torch in one hand and Clanghorr in the other. The lizard must have realized its failure to remain unseen, and it shifted from gray to dark green as it lunged. Greyor brought his axe across, easily separating its head from its body, and the monster collapsed.

A lizard on Greyor's flank hissed, but Baylun cut its message short when Torrac cleaved it in half. Another reptile leaped from the wall, and one of Lorylla's arrows pierced its skull—Greyor sidestepped its corpse. On the other side of the room, Eraim held her bow and released an arrow to slay a lizard, and Kiryanna and Tewlon claimed a kill each.

Silence captured the chamber, but only for a moment. A crash stole everyone's attention as the archway they entered through collapsed. A large hole now replaced the floor in the nearby corner, and from the opening came a strained voice.

"Help!"

Tewlon was first to arrive at the pit, moving slowly so as not to increase its size—it encompassed an area roughly ten feet in diameter. The rest of the company kept their distance. As the elf peered into the hole, his shoulders slumped and he shook his head. He reached down and pulled up Ameilistari. And then Nidor.

Chapter 7

A Plan Gone Awry

Ameilistari sat at her desk, an open tome before her. It was the last of the required reading assigned by her mentor, Rauzel; an extremely boring book about trees. What did Ameilistari need to know about trees? If not for the few flourishing atop the central tower, she would barely recognize one.

Of course, that wasn't true. Ameilistari had been to Marcove many times to visit her late mother's family, where trees were abundant. Still, she missed the days when Selanna instructed her. The elf was a legendary mage rumored to have defeated both Trannum and Uustaag! When pressed by Ameilistari, however, Selanna answered no questions on the subject. But Selanna was fun and knew everything about magic. Rauzel was knowledgeable, but lacked the elf's personality. Plus, Selanna often brought Eraim to the keep, and Eraim was an absolute treat!

Beyond enjoying the elves' company, it was nice putting faces to the stories Ameilistari's father had told her of his adventures of the past. Romik spoke fondly of Selanna and Eraim, as well as several others. Unfortunately, after Selanna began mentoring Ameilistari, her father's attitude toward the elf changed. That was when Rauzel took over. Boring, dull Rauzel.

Ameilistari looked out her tower window at the orange sky and sighed. It was nearing dinnertime. If she were to poke her head through the window, she could spy the gate far below. But that would only make her more anxious. Her father received word that Uncle Baylun and Aunt Kiryanna were on their way, and the message had arrived weeks ago. Where were they?

Ameilistari loved her uncle and aunt. Baylun was scary at first, but he turned out to be a real pushover, and his mere presence made her feel safe. And Kiryanna… the best aunt ever! Daymyn and Teliya were comical to watch, and Ameilistari looked forward to seeing the two, but she most eagerly awaited Nidor's arrival. Nidor was a bit older than her, but they always had fun together. Of course, he would inquire about Sybin: *What's Sybin been up to? What's Sybin been reading lately? Did Sybin talk about me?* In reality, Sybin thought Nidor an interesting person. Of course, the captain's daughter found several of the young men around the keep interesting. The boys found Sybin interesting in return, but over the past couple of years, they began paying attention to Ameilistari as well. And with Ameilistari's skin tone darker than everyone else's within the keep, she intrigued the onlookers all the more — Ironside needed more girls.

The problem was that Ameilistari didn't have time for romance. Her studies kept her busy, and she couldn't afford distractions. That was another benefit of having Nidor around: he tended to keep the boys at bay. Not that anyone feared Nidor — he looked nothing like his father — but his presence created the appearance of companionship. Ameilistari wondered if they knew she and Nidor were cousins.

Although she anxiously awaited her relatives' arrival, Ameilistari's impatience on this occasion wasn't solely driven by the excitement of seeing them. Her father had received a letter from a dwarf named Greyor, and she managed to read most of what was written. The dwarf planned to meet with Uncle Baylun, Eraim, and some other person about a quest. And a quest was just the thing Ameilistari needed to advance her skills. Practicing magic on stone walls was getting tiresome; she needed to test her skills in the real world. She had a plan, and it required Nidor's help to make it work.

Her door burst open, and Nidor ran in, out of breath. He was taller than when she last saw him, and a light fuzz covered his upper lip and formed slight sideburns. He smiled. A few seconds later, Daymyn crashed into Nidor's back. The boys shared the same wide nose, dark hair, and slightly pointed ears, appearing much like the brothers they were.

"I won!" Daymyn declared, pushing his way past his brother. He then looked at Ameilistari and whistled.

"She's our cousin," said Nidor.

"Yeah, but…" Daymyn didn't look away. "She looks way different than last time."

"Excuse Daymyn." Nidor shook his head. "He's just noticed girls back home."

Ameilistari smirked. It was no different than how the keep trainees acted. She dropped her smile and narrowed her eyes at Nidor. "What took you so long?"

Nidor glanced at Daymyn. "Kids…"

Daymyn moved closer to Ameilistari. "Show me some magic!"

She held a measuring gaze. "On one condition."

"What?"

"Nidor and I have things to discuss," she said. "So if I show you a bit of magic, you must leave us for at least an hour."

Daymyn scrunched his face in thought. "Only if you tell Uncle Romik I distracted you from your studies."

"Deal!" She looked about, trying to decide on what spell to cast. Gazing at her younger cousin, she asked, "How would you like to touch the ceiling?"

Daymyn's eyes widened. "You're going to make me taller?"

She laughed. "Not quite."

Standing up, Ameilistari moved her fingers about, as if independent thought controlled each. She then mouthed her incantation, shifting the magical forces around the room to swarm beneath Daymyn's feet—though invisible to non-casters, Ameilistari saw them plainly. She lifted her hands, and her cousin rose atop the energy until reaching the ceiling.

"Amazing!" Daymyn put both palms upon the stone above his head. He then eyed the floor. "But I think you can put me down now."

Ameilistari lowered him until his feet settled on the floor. Even Nidor appeared impressed.

"Now go back the way you came," she told Daymyn, "and I'm sure you'll find your family."

"Yeah, yeah," he said with a sly grin. "I can see you two are up to something. But a deal is a deal."

Ameilistari waited until the door shut before sitting again.

"So…" Nidor looked around the room and out the tower window. "Has Sybin mentioned me since I left?"

Ameilistari rolled her eyes. "Later. First, what do you know about this meeting with the dwarf?"

"Why?"

She grinned. "Because we're going to join their little adventure."

Nidor lowered his brow. "The note mentioned danger. They'll never permit it."

She bunched her long curly hair behind her head and tied it with a slender green ribbon. "They cannot prevent what they don't know."

✿ ✿ ✿

Ameilistari frowned. Nidor had shared with her the entire contents of Uncle Baylun's letter, which was nothing she didn't already know. She had hoped it contained more information. They needed to learn more.

They headed downstairs toward the common area, where the keep was set up as an inn. When Ameilistari wasn't studying, practicing magic, or training to one day run Ironside, she could normally be found there—it was more interesting than conversing with soldiers or doing chores. Upon reaching the entry chamber at the bottom of the long stairwell, the guards on duty looked her way.

"Your father is in the tavern," said a soldier.

"Very good." She tilted her head in appreciation of the report. At the current time of day, she could have guessed that fact.

She and Nidor made their way along the corridor to the tavern.

Seated at a table were Father, Uncle Baylun, and Aunt Kiryanna, and Naydrel the barmaid was blushing like a fool again while serving them. At another table, Daymyn sat with Morsum and Teliya. Ameilistari couldn't help smiling while the old gatekeeper made the young girl laugh. Not long ago, that was *her* playing with the elderly man. He was dear, almost like a grandfather.

Patrons occupied most of the tables, but there were a few to choose from, and she led the way to one.

"We should be able to hear them from here," she told Nidor.

He looked doubtful, measuring the distance between their tables with his eyes and gazing at the score of customers holding conversations. "My hearing isn't *that* good."

Ameilistari laughed before batting her long eyelashes. "You forget with whom you sit."

She noticed Uncle Baylun looking their way, and cupped a hand to one side of her mouth, so he wouldn't see her lips moving. After uttering the proper phrase, it sounded as if Aunt Kiryanna were speaking from under the table.

"What are those two up to?"

Nidor's jaw dropped.

Ameilistari pointed her finger at the unlit candle between her and Nidor, and the wick came to life. The boys working in the room applauded.

"Nice work, Ameilistari!" said one.

"Psst," hissed her father. Only he could quiet the tavern with such a noise.

Ameilistari looked his way.

"Not here."

She rolled her eyes and cupped her hand again to speak to Nidor as the patrons resumed their discussions. "Father doesn't like my doing magic. Like it's going to hurt me or something." She shook her head. "He just doesn't understand it."

"Does Selanna still teach her?" Baylun's muffled voice said from beneath the table.

"No," her father answered. "She was around for the first couple of years. Now Ameilistari learns from a marteese named Rauzel."

Ameilistari rolled her eyes.

"The woman seems to know what she's doing," Romik continued, "and Ameilistari likes her enough."

Ameilistari shrugged at Nidor. She didn't dislike Rauzel, but the marteese would never be Selanna.

"I just wonder how she plans to run the keep with all of her time spent on wizardry," her father added.

"She's a capable young lady," said Kiryanna. "She can handle anything you put before her."

Father chuckled. "I hope you're right." He turned to Baylun. "Have you seen Desser?"

Ameilistari wiped the table, as if removing crumbs, and the voices stopped. She sighed. "The thing is, I don't know if I *want* to run the keep. Sometimes I think I do, and others..." She eyed Nidor. "Maybe you can do it."

Nidor shrugged. "It's a long way from Philen."

"But it's closer to Sybin." Ameilistari smirked.

He blushed.

Getting back to business, Ameilistari glanced at their parents. "We'll learn nothing here." She took a deep breath and blew it out. "We will have to sneak into their meeting."

Nidor checked to make sure no one was listening. "How?"

Her grin returned. "I know when and where they're having it. We'll just have to arrive before it starts."

❖ ❖ ❖

Ameilistari spent the rest of the evening with Nidor, walking the castle grounds. Nidor spoke of life in Philen, and his issues with a young warrior named Gulson receiving an invitation to something he referred to as an Honor Panel. It was a topic Nidor was obviously passionate about.

"Give it no further thought," said Ameilistari. "I saw you sparring last year, and if you are any better today than you were then, who cares if Gulson has an invitation? He probably had his father use his position to get it. He's obviously jealous of you."

Nidor couldn't fully contain a smirk.

"And if he's still a bother once you're running West Palidur," she added, "just summon your inner-Nidor."

"I'd rather have an inner-Vecnor," Nidor mumbled.

She lifted her brow. Lessons about Paladin Nidor were taught every month, and the respect in the eyes of Ameilistari's Dale relatives never escaped her notice when the topic arose. Many stories seemed made up, telling of impossible feats, but she was positive her kin believed each and every one. Even Selanna spoke highly of the Silcor paladin. "You know, Paladin Nidor is sacred among my people," she told her cousin.

"As he is in my house," Nidor said. "I apologize." He stood tall. "All praises to Almighty Silcor, and to Nidor, Angel of Salvation."

Ameilistari smiled. Though he exaggerated the gesture, his eyes revealed genuine respect. "Much better."

That was another good thing about Nidor's family. While Ameilistari's father worshiped several deities, with an emphasis on Cafior, God of the Land, her mother had been a devout follower of the fire deity, a trait shared by Nidor's family. And not only did Uncle Baylun and Aunt Kiryanna name their firstborn after the greatest Dale ever to live, the two had also bathed in Paladin Nidor's flaming spirit in Lormin Dmurr, the evil citadel of Uustaag, after the paladin's spirit closed the door to Thard'Dun's world. When it came to the gods, Ameilistari's father encouraged her to follow her heart, and even though few soldiers understood it, she kept the Word of Silcor alive within the keep. Still, she left room for Cafior in her life, as well as Vou, God of Magic. Selanna insisted on the latter in order to open herself to the forces of magic surrounding them.

The next day, Ameilistari dragged Nidor along while she accompanied Captain Marlajin during his monthly check on the towers. They scaled each tower to speak with soldiers, make sure all doors were sound, and check on the stronghold's overall integrity. Very boring. Nidor shot her a look of annoyance, but after Sybin joined them halfway through, forgiveness was swift.

While the captain dutifully went about his business, it was obvious Nidor's presence affected Sybin. Normally wearing the face of a hardened soldier, the girl appeared more her age during the tour, sometimes glancing at Nidor, sometimes smiling, and other times giggling silently when Nidor made gestures Ameilistari couldn't see. A throat clearing from Marlajin always brought the antics to an end. A couple of times, Ameilistari distracted the captain with questions about the workings of certain pieces of equipment, or plans of action for situations she invented, allowing the two to share a few words. But Marlajin was no fool and put a stop to the inquiries.

After the chore, Sybin joined Ameilistari and Nidor for lunch in the tavern. Sybin was older than Ameilistari, and her figure nearly fully formed, and before the meal she released her raven hair from its usual ponytail, allowing it to hug her high cheekbones and drape over her shoulders. Times like this, Ameilistari couldn't compete with the girl's beauty. She wished Sybin relaxed more often, as it took the focus off of herself. Hopefully, Nidor didn't notice the glares aimed his way by the young men in the room, now that he sat with the both of them.

"Do pointed ears feel differently?" Sybin asked while they ate, her gray eyes narrowing on Nidor.

"I don't know what other ears feel like," Nidor replied. "Do you want to compare?" He turned his head so she could reach.

Sybin giggled while running her fingers over the top of Nidor's ear. It wasn't so pointed as Kiryanna's, but definitely more so than a human's.

"Will you live long, like a marteese?" Sybin asked. "Or does your krukari blood spoil that?"

In most places, Nidor might be confused for a marteese. But those living in Ironside Keep knew his father and were cognizant of his krukari heritage. And though Captain Marlajin hid it well, the man had no love for half-hobgoblins. Ameilistari knew this to be true, regardless of her father's ignorance on the matter. And so did Morsum. Was the same prejudice seeping into Sybin? As Ameilistari's temper got the better of her, she flicked her finger, overturning Sybin's drink without touching it.

Sybin stood up with a squeal as the liquid splashed onto her lap. "No!" She brushed the excess moisture from her breeches before it could reach her fine boots.

Guilt struck Ameilistari. She didn't know for a fact that Sybin felt as Marlajin about krukari. Perhaps the captain's daughter meant nothing by the comment. And though Sybin emulated the man most times, it was no excuse for what Ameilistari did. One did not act in such a way when sitting with friends.

"Should I dry you?" she offered.

Sybin turned angry eyes on Ameilistari, obviously aware of how the drink had spilled. "No, thank you." She looked at Nidor. "Perhaps I'll see you later."

She stormed out of the tavern.

"Why did you do that?" Nidor asked, visibly upset.

"Do what?" Ameilistari gave her best innocent expression.

"Come on, Stari."

He used her father's nickname for her. She hated it.

"She needs to learn manners," Ameilistari said plainly. "And you need to stand up for yourself."

Nidor sighed. "It doesn't bother me, being part-krukari. Most people don't even know." He eyed Ameilistari. "And I thought you two were friends."

"We are." Ameilistari twirled her finger to dry the table. "But we argue now and again. And as soon as she realizes I'm right, she usually apologizes."

Nidor chuckled, lightening the mood.

"We'd better get going," Ameilistari said. The meeting wasn't far off.

They exited the tavern and passed hastily through the entry guardroom, where soldiers waved as Ameilistari headed for the long staircase leading to the towers. She couldn't count the times her father informed her that the stairwell existed to constrict would-be invaders and make assaulting the towers practically impossible. Throughout the keep's history, only once had the upper levels been breached. But that was by the undead before the Necromancer War, so it didn't count.

She and Nidor passed by additional iron doors meant to further hamper invading forces—she had only ever seen them closed when Captain Marlajin performed his monthly checks. Beyond the stairwell exit, the Great Hall connected to all towers. Additional doors led to meeting rooms and barracks, as well as a kitchen and dining chamber for soldiers. Ameilistari's room was in the central tower, as were her father's and Morsum's.

Lieutenant Bleer walked by with a nod and an unofficial one-finger salute. He was an expert crossbowman and generally manned the east tower's turret overlooking the mountain pass toward Denvale. Ameilistari waited until he was out of sight before heading to the room her father had set for tonight's meeting.

"Do you have the key?" asked Nidor.

Ameilistari rolled her eyes. "Key…" She wiggled her fingers just so, and the lock disengaged. After opening the door, she stepped aside. "After you."

Nidor smirked and entered. "Can you open any lock?" he asked after Ameilistari shut the door behind her.

"Most of them," she replied. "The more intricate the lock, the harder it is. And magical locks are another matter." She used a reverse spell to relock the mechanism.

They stood in one of three libraries the keep possessed. This was the one with the fewest books, as most soldiers seemed uninterested in reading. A table with a dozen chairs sat in the middle with three smaller tables farther on, closer to the bookshelves. The fireplace burned with a flame started an hour ago, as the room tended to get drafty and Father wished for his guests to be comfortable. To the left, a staircase ascended to a balcony, where a few more bookshelves and a couple of tables were kept, and sunlight shone through a skylight within an angled portion of the ceiling. Ameilistari led the way up the stairs.

"We simply keep quiet," she said, "and we'll learn everything we need to know."

"They won't come up here?" posed Nidor.

Ameilistari gave him a level gaze. "There's more dust up here than any other place in the keep. We're safe."

Nidor nodded, putting on a brave face. But his eyes remained nervous.

Ameilistari chuckled. "You'll see."

They sat against the far wall from the railing overlooking the room below—one would need to walk up the steps to spot them. To pass the next hour, they conversed quietly. Nidor again brought up the Honor Panel, explaining how a warrior had to perform before elite soldiers to earn their way into the Honor Guard of the Duke. Ameilistari wondered why he fretted. The Duke of West Palidur was his granduncle. Surely he had just as good a chance as anyone of joining the Honor Guard. Probably better. To change the subject, she talked about her training to run the keep—her cousin wouldn't understand the workings of magic. Nidor, of course, asked more questions about Sybin.

"What you need to realize about Sybin," Ameilistari said, "is that she's very focused on replacing her dad when the time comes. So if your aim is to woo her, it is a nearly impossible task. She wishes to be a great fighter." She stared Nidor in the eyes. "Just keep that in mind when you next speak to her. That is where her interest lies. And… be careful. Don't show her too much affection if she doesn't reciprocate."

The door below opened.

"You may wait in here," said a guard, and the door shut shortly after.

Soft footfalls suggested two people had entered. Very small or very light people—or both. A female voice then spoke in Elfish. Ameilistari was learning the language, but the words were uttered too quickly for her to keep up. She was sure it was Eraim. A male responded in the same tongue.

The door opened again.

"Ah!" said Ameilistari's father. "Eraim. Always a pleasure to see you."

"It has been much too long," Eraim acknowledged in her tiny voice.

"And who is your friend?" Father asked.

"This is Tewlon," Eraim replied. "He is a skilled warrior, but he does not speak."

Ameilistari and Nidor shared confused looks. Probably just a Salenti jest. Father had mentioned that elves of that forest tended to enjoy pranks, and Ameilistari witnessed some of their shenanigans firsthand when Selanna was her mentor. Once, Selanna soured the drinks of every customer in the tavern to impress upon Ameilistari the possibilities of magic. Father wasn't amused.

The door opened again.

"Baylun!" Eraim said. Then, in a less excited tone, she added, "Kiryanna, you're late!" A giggle followed, but Eraim's was the only one.

Ameilistari mouthed the words, *I love your mother*, to Nidor.

Eraim introduced Tewlon to Uncle Baylun and Aunt Kiryanna. Small talk among the guests ensued, none of it important. Baylun then asked Romik if he had gained any proficiency with the crossbow attachment for his false arm.

"I don't use it anymore," Father said. "I can't seem to get the hang of it. Nowhere near the talent Granduncle Arkor possessed."

Ameilistari vigorously shook her head in agreement with her father's words, mouthing, *he's horrible*.

"Granduncle was only missing his arm from the elbow on," Father explained. "Not the whole thing. So I've gone another way.

From things I heard about the Death Lord Radaam's sword, I thought, why not see if I can do something similar? The dwarves fashioned an attachment with additional hooks. Perhaps I'll get to try it out soon."

A knock sounded, and Romik called out.

"Enter."

The door opened, and heavy footfalls stepped into the library. After a moment of silence, a deep voice spoke.

"Welcome all."

It had to be Greyor.

Introductions occurred, and Ameilistari grinned when Aunt Kiryanna gave the dwarf no choice but to accept her into the quest. She wished she could join that way instead of sneaking. Eraim again made a jest about Tewlon being unable to speak, and Ameilistari still didn't understand the prank. The sliding of chairs followed as everyone sat, and the meeting began.

Greyor spoke of Lornibur, and the others chimed in, speaking of mines and monsters and even a demon. The dwarf declared Lornibur to be the birthplace of his kin, and he aimed to take it back. They then spoke about mine dwellers, and that Greyor didn't wish to bring the creatures harm.

Next, Greyor explained his reasons for choosing his company. Apparently, Eraim had been to the mines before—where hadn't the elf been? Uncle Baylun and someone named Lorylla possessed unique skills, earning them their invitations.

The dwarf also discussed Clanghorr and Torrac. Ameilistari knew the former from her studies, while the latter she had seen personally. Uncle Baylun had even allowed her to hold Torrac, but it was far too heavy. Regardless, it was a magnificent weapon. Her father then spoke about Baylun's axe, claiming a dwarfish smith had crafted it. Greyor seemed to harbor doubts about the statement.

The meeting returned to the subject of the mines. Apparently, large lizards that were not cavern lizards infested the tunnels, whatever that meant. The two-headed snake's name was Maak

Maak, and it might not be a snake. Maybe it was dead, maybe not. And there probably wasn't another one. According to Eraim, Selanna blasted the monster with fire. Ameilistari grinned. She wished she could have seen that!

Greyor revealed a reward of one thousand gold coins to each person in the room, and the voices silenced. What anyone could do with so much gold was beyond Ameilistari. Of course, she already had everything she needed; her father made sure of it. The amount thoroughly impressed Nidor.

"Silcor's Flame!" he whispered. Too late, he cupped his hand over his mouth.

"Who's up there?" said Romik.

Ameilistari recognized the tone. There was no hiding and no trying to talk their way out of it. She crawled forward to peer over the balcony, and Nidor followed.

The room's occupants came into view. The well-muscled elf was surely Tewlon, there was no mistaking Greyor, and the final visitor must be Lorylla. The elf was obviously tall, her skin was gray, and silver hair draped down her long neck to below her slender shoulders. She was beautiful. Even more exotic were the elf's captivating eyes — white irises upon black. Fascinating!

"Just us, Father," Ameilistari answered.

And she and Nidor were promptly invited to leave.

"That was your stupid mistake," she said once they were out of the chamber. Seeing Nidor's hurt expression, she grinned so that he realized she spoke in jest, and he relaxed. But it *was* his fault.

They returned down the long stairwell and to the tavern for a late dinner. The room was less than half full.

"Did you see the gray elf?" asked Nidor after they sat.

"You mean Lorylla?" Ameilistari posed. "She was —" She noticed the gleam in Nidor's eyes. "You realize she's probably three hundred years old, right?"

Nidor shrugged. "I know. It's just… Father talked about the eyes of gray elves, but… And she was so…"

"All right." Ameilistari rolled her eyes. "Any more of that, and I'll have to have a word with Sybin."

Nidor chuckled. "So what's next?"

"Next, we follow them."

He frowned. "They'll see us."

"No one will see us." Ameilistari grinned. "And no one will hear us."

She glanced across the room to where Morsum was eating dinner with Teliya and Daymyn. She missed those days. Of course, Morsum would be more than happy to dine with her on any night, but she needed to leave behind her childish fun if she wished to be taken seriously as a mage. Sometimes the notion made her lonely.

She looked back at Nidor. "Just be ready in the early morning. If anyone asks, you're sparring with Sybin. They'll believe that. Meet me in my room before sunrise."

Nidor agreed.

❊ ❊ ❊

The next morning, Ameilistari gathered everything she might need. She packed some light provisions, her waterskin, and put on the emerald ring her father gave her last year. She loved how it sparkled against her skin. On second thought, she put it back, not wanting to risk losing it. After tying her curls back and out of the way, she peeked out the door. The hallway and stairs spiraling upward to the right and downward to the left were vacant. She shut the door and sat on her bed.

Moments later, a soft knock fell upon the door. It opened, and Nidor stepped inside. He wore leather armor, with a sword and two hatchets strapped to his waist. He looked like a proper warrior.

"Where have you been?" Ameilistari asked. "We need to get moving."

"My parents came to say goodbye."

She sighed as she opened the door. "Well, we must hurry."

They rushed down the steps of the central tower. Surely the group would gather in the meeting room before they left. At least, Ameilistari hoped that was the case. Upon nearing the Great Hall, however, she spotted Nidor's parents and stopped, causing her cousin to bump into her. Luckily, the collision made little noise, and their presence remained undetected. A soldier escorted Uncle Baylun and Aunt Kiryanna deeper into the tower. Strange. The only things below were a storage room and the family crypt.

"Hold my hand," Ameilistari whispered with urgency.

Nidor frowned.

"Just hold it!" she ordered. "The spell won't hide you if we're not in contact."

Nidor grabbed her hand.

Ameilistari focused on the surrounding energies. The incantation was powerful, so she gathered all magical forces within reach—the nearby torch extinguished. She then spoke her arcane words, and the air grew thick, as if it were water. It was a taxing spell, one Selanna claimed would grow less fatiguing with repetition, so she had practiced often, usually within her room. To make sure it worked properly, she spent time in the tavern eavesdropping on random conversations, and the speakers had no idea she listened—most folks coming to Ironside led such boring lives. Now, she considered herself an expert.

She nodded at Nidor.

"Nothing's changed," he whispered.

She almost laughed, and replied without fear of being overheard. "Not for us. And as long as we're holding hands, no one can see or hear us."

"That's truly impressive," admitted Nidor.

"Yes, I know." She pulled him down the steps. "But you can tell me how impressive I am later. There's no time to spare."

They followed Nidor's parents into the dungeon, and the two reported to the storage room outside the family crypt where the group awaited. Ameilistari's father stood next to the mural of

Grellmor, the original Lord of Ironside—Greyor planned to use the secret tunnel! But how did the dwarf know of its existence? Ameilistari learned of the passage a few years ago, to be used in the case of an emergency, as well as where to find the key. To her knowledge, no soldier within the keep had that information except for Captain Marlajin. Her father then revealed his intention of joining the quest.

Ameilistari's jaw dropped. He mentioned nothing to her about going with the dwarf. Were she not hiding at the moment, she might have been cross with him. He didn't even say goodbye!

While Uncle Baylun attempted to change her father's mind, Ameilistari pulled Nidor around the room to stand next to the painting; the door to the crypt. Several locks adorned the panel, but they were a ruse. Her father would insert his key into a natural-looking crack to find a cleverly hidden mechanism and open it. She and her cousin would have to time it perfectly.

"Be ready to move when I tell you," Ameilistari said.

Nidor nodded his assent.

The dwarf agreed to Father joining the party, and he returned to the mural of Grellmor, directing everyone to turn their heads. Once they did as instructed, he inserted the key and gave it two turns.

As soon as the door slid halfway open, Ameilistari commanded, "Go," and pulled Nidor through. "Over here!" She dragged him to the other side of the family crypt, where a second hidden door existed. The one leading to the tunnel. She scooted sideways into a niche near the floor—a resting place for the dead. It was creepy, but necessary, as the chamber was smaller and someone would surely bump into them. "Squeeze in," she said, maintaining hold of Nidor's hand.

He did his best, but the space was meant for a single body, and he jutted out a bit. Hopefully no one meandered too close.

Luck was on their side, and they remained undiscovered while her father opened the second door. Ameilistari prayed that luck continued.

"Out! Out! Out!" she said, urging Nidor from the niche as the last member of the group stepped through the doorway.

They climbed to their feet, but the secret panel was nearly shut. Not even she could squeeze through. Nidor released her hand and jammed one of his hatchets into the opening, preventing the door from closing all the way. His face then contorted in the sliver of light spilling through the crack as he attempted to force it open.

Ameilistari worked a spell, pooling magical forces within the seam—she had to hurry. She put forth her hands with palms out and felt the door wanting to complete its task. Sweat beaded on her forehead as she struggled against the pressure, using strength both physical and arcane, and she moved her hands apart, as if they were inside the crack. The panel slowly opened, allowing a bit more torchlight and making a slight grinding of stone on stone. She stopped so that the noise would cease. The gap was only a foot wide.

"Go," she said with a strained voice.

Nidor complied. It was a tight squeeze, but he made it through. Had he been his father, he would never have fit.

Ameilistari moved one step, then two, and jumped through the opening and into the tunnel. The door closed, and everything went dark as the torchlight disappeared in the distance.

"Where are you?" Ameilistari whispered.

A strong hand grasped hers.

"I'm right here," Nidor said quietly. "We're okay. I can see well enough."

Of course! Her cousin's krukari and marteese blood afforded him the ability to see in the dark. Ameilistari had focused so much on her magic, she forgot about that. She breathed easier.

"Give me a moment to recast my spell," she whispered. She repeated her incantation, summoning the bubble to hide her and Nidor. Upon completion, she said in her normal voice, "Lead the way. We must catch up."

Her cousin's firm grip pulled her forward, dragging her left and right and down several steps—she appreciated him warning her and slowing for each stairwell. A light then appeared in the distance, and her stride grew more confident.

Though maintaining the spell added to her fatigue, she pushed herself until the faces of those they pursued became clearer. Nidor then slowed, and she was grateful to catch her breath. How was it he wasn't panting? It didn't matter. They had caught up.

They followed the tunnel for more than a day. To maintain her strength, Ameilistari allowed her spell to expire once the group halted to sleep, and she and Nidor alternated staying awake so as not to be left behind. The hallway was extremely uncomfortable, but there was nothing to be done, and without the silencing bubble, they took extra care not to make any noise.

When the company stopped to eat lunch the next afternoon, Ameilistari and Nidor did the same while maintaining their handhold. It wasn't easy, and it disappointed Ameilistari to learn Nidor had brought no food of his own. Now, hers would deplete twice as quickly.

"Well, that's your second dumb mistake," she teased him.

Hours later, the group stepped through a hole in the wall. Ameilistari and Nidor followed, discovering what must be Lornibur. The passage was magnificent, and she recognized similar styles of rounded and angled wall transitions to those within Ironside Keep.

The company moved on, even though it was obviously late — none of them seemed ready to rest. Upon entering the first chamber, an immense room with a ceiling shrouded in darkness, giant lizards attacked. The creatures had hidden themselves by blending with the surrounding stone, but they did not fool Eraim, and the elf readied her companions. While the group fought, an eight-foot lizard lunged from above the archway where Ameilistari and Nidor held hands — somehow the monster had sensed their presence.

Ameilistari yanked Nidor's arm as she darted to the right, and the reptile landed and scrambled after them. She continued to the near corner while Nidor attempted to pull his sword, but the floor cracked and gave way. Ameilistari was suddenly weightless as she and Nidor fell toward the darkness below, and in that moment, her concentration on the hiding spell failed. The descent stopped abruptly when Nidor squeezed her hand hard enough to cause pain. He had caught hold of something, and the lizard disappeared below her dangling feet.

"Help!" Nidor managed through clenched teeth, strengthening his grip on Ameilistari. She hadn't realized how strong her cousin had grown, and she winced as the pressure on her hand doubled.

The room quieted, and Tewlon's face appeared above. The elf shook his head and his shoulders slumped as he lowered onto the floor to offer his hand.

Nidor strained to lift Ameilistari, and Tewlon pulled her out. While the elf rescued Nidor from the hole, she gazed at several sets of eyes exhibiting anger or shock, and a few held disappointment. To her left, the entrance had collapsed.

"That was your stupid mistake," muttered Nidor once he stood next to her.

Chapter 8

No Way but Onward

Greyor stood back while chaos unfolded. The voices of Romik, Baylun, and Kiryanna echoed about the vaulted ceiling as they questioned their children. He eyed the collapse at the entrance, tracing cracks to the new hole in the floor. The two events were connected. How did Maak Maak construct such effective traps?

He walked to the pit, following a path he was sure wouldn't cause the opening to widen. There was no doubt the hole was intentional. A thin layer of flagstones was all that had covered it, ready to break. The lizards surely communicated to have avoided triggering it themselves. Greyor kneeled and removed his gauntlet to feel the rough wall below. It wasn't that old.

A slender hand with long gray fingers settled on his shoulder. "What do you see?" asked Lorylla.

Greyor sighed. "Maak Maak lives." He faced the room, where the family squabble continued. "Enough!"

All eyes turned to Greyor. Eraim and Tewlon stood apart from the others, watching the far exit during the melee of excuses and exclamations. Good. Some of them had some sense.

"We must go back," stated Romik.

"That's not going to happen," said Greyor.

"Our children must be returned to the keep at once!" the Lord of Ironside demanded.

"We aren't children," mumbled Ameilistari, receiving a glare from her father.

Greyor let out a controlled exhale. "You notice the entrance has collapsed?" He eyed the rubble. "There's no digging through. We haven't the tools." He looked at Romik. "And I'm only one dwarf."

"We have strength," said Baylun, glancing at Tewlon. "Surely it will take some time, but—"

"And cause a total cave-in?" posed Greyor. He lifted Clanghorr towards the debris. "That pile climbs high. Much higher than the ceiling. It isn't done falling. It's waiting for ignorance to test its resolve."

Baylun furrowed his brow, gazing at the rubble as if trying to see what Greyor explained. The others mimicked his action. But Baylun wasn't a dwarf, and neither were they. All they saw were rocks and dirt.

"There's a bigger issue at hand." Greyor pointed at the hole. "This was intentional. A trap. It seems our last venture through these halls has encouraged its keeper to protect against future intrusions. Maak Maak isn't dead."

"All the more reason to get the children to safety," said Romik.

Baylun nodded in agreement. Kiryanna narrowed her eyes, as if considering Greyor's words.

"I mean no offense," Greyor said to Romik, "but you're not lord down here. The kids aren't the only ones in danger while that beast roams the mines."

Romik held a level gaze. "At the first opportunity, my daughter and I shall leave."

"There is only one other exit I am aware of," Eraim said. "To the far south, near Nomedd."

Romik released a frustrated sigh.

"What's done is done," stated Kiryanna. "Nidor and Ameilistari have evaded our detections and followed us on this venture. They're to blame. We're to blame. Who cares?" She looked at her son. "Nidor, keep your sword ready and remain at Ameilistari's side." She turned to her niece before the lass could object. "Every mage needs a warrior to keep them safe." Glancing at Eraim, she added, "Eraim was there to protect Selanna."

Eraim nodded.

Romik shook his head, but didn't contradict the marteese's words. Baylun sighed.

"What do we do next?" asked Lorylla.

Greyor glanced at the hole. "There will be more traps like this." He turned to Eraim. "Probably too many for you to detect before someone else is caught in one. And if it's like the last time, this monster will attempt to separate its food." He returned his gaze to the pit. "I say we hunt the beast."

Gasps and muttered words of shock and disagreement followed.

Eraim silenced the room. "Greyor is correct. We do not want to get separated. That plays to Maak Maak's favor. We are stronger together." Her shoulders slumped as she looked at the hole. "As much as I detest the thought, we must find Maak Maak before it finds us."

Greyor nodded. Whether Eraim's fear was genuine or she enjoyed playing the part, she always spoke the truth when it mattered. Her friend, Tewlon, didn't appear so confident. Perhaps he wasn't as good with the sword as Eraim believed. If he were, he would have fought in the Battle of the Broken Land.

"How do we hunt this thing?" Kiryanna asked Greyor.

He looked at the marteese. "We go down." Scanning the company, he added, "How many ropes do we have?"

❀❀❀

Baylun hadn't felt so much stress since being trapped in Darum Carumbor before the War of the North. Nidor and Ameilistari had a lot to answer for. It was bad enough Kiryanna had joined the quest, and now she seemed accepting of the situation. Was she more interested in hunting the giant snake-lizard than getting the kids to safety? Of course not. Baylun pushed the thought from his mind. Kiryanna simply recognized there to be no other options. And she had always had more confidence in Nidor's abilities than did Baylun. She often accused him of taking it too easy on their son in combat training; that the lad was ready for more. Maybe she was right. During the long journey to Ironside Keep, Baylun overheard Kiryanna telling Nidor she would have a word with Granduncle Magneer when they returned to West Palidur, to clear up the whole invitation bias. And she would probably do just that. Baylun often noticed his uncle cringing whenever Kiryanna spoke.

Presently, Kiryanna stood next to Greyor at the edge of the pit, tying knots into Romik's rope at five-foot intervals. Her expression was the same as when performing missions in Philen: focused and prepared for anything.

Baylun looked at his son. Nidor held the sword Baylun had purchased last year, an exceptional weapon forged by West Palidur's finest weaponsmith, and hanging about the lad's neck was the Nidor-shard. Baylun prayed the paladin's spirit watched over his son.

❁ ❁ ❁

Greyor measured the darkness below. Times like this made him miss having Arrikan around. The mountain ranger had journeyed with him through the mines during the Necromancer War, and was more skilled at climbing than anyone he had known. But being human, she passed decades ago. Greyor regretted having lost touch with her family afterward. Her son and grandson were skilled rangers as well, but Magneer was Duke of Philen and Desser lived a barbarian life in Pavan, which Greyor still didn't understand. *You were raised a barbarian; you didn't become one.* Romik and Baylun were cousins of Desser, but lacked his mountain expertise. Without Arrikan, Greyor would have to lead the way.

He began with his own rope, a knotted length of forty feet, and spiked it to the floor a few feet from the opening. Positive it would bear his weight, he moved to the edge of the pit and handed his torch to Tewlon. The darkness wouldn't hinder him unless lizards were lying in wait, as the cold-blooded monsters weren't so easily detected against the stone. Hopefully, that wasn't the case.

"Just a moment," said Eraim, and she produced a bauble from her pack. It was three inches in diameter and appeared to be made of brass. "Selanna gave me this."

The sphere took on a glow, beginning with the strength of a candle and expanding to illuminate twice the area of a torch. Better still, it lifted from her palm and hovered into the hole to light up the shaft. Why didn't the elf reveal this little trinket earlier?

Greyor entered the pit. The rough wall provided plenty of footholds, and he easily worked his way downward. After ten feet, the rope above him moved as Tewlon lowered into the tunnel. Tewlon? Greyor shook his head. If danger awaited at the bottom, Eraim, Baylun, or Lorylla would have been preferable.

He reached the end of the rope, where a loop was tied, and placed his foot into it for support. Greyor then pulled Romik's rope from his shoulder and spiked it to the wall. He resumed his downward trek, and fifteen feet lower the hole split into three directions—the point at which Maak Maak had hoped to separate its prey for easier kills. Greyor listened. Nothing. He sniffed. A slight odor suggested decay, but he couldn't determine where it came from. Tewlon was then right above him and peered down. Farther up, the others followed.

"Can't tell where the smell comes from," Greyor whispered.

Tewlon closed his eyes for a moment. After reopening them, he pointed at the tunnel veering left.

Perhaps the warrior was good for something. Elves heard things better than most; maybe their noses worked better as well.

Greyor swung the line into the passage Tewlon indicated and continued until Romik's rope ended in another loop. The shaft below curved away, becoming almost level, but the floor was eight feet down—a long fall for a dwarf. The angle of the wall slanting toward it wasn't too steep, however, and Greyor released his hold and slid the rest of the way, praying to Meldar there was not a drop-off after the bend.

There wasn't.

He breathed a sigh of relief and moved forward as he detected the sound of Tewlon sliding to join him. But then Eraim's light arrived, and Greyor halted. The tunnel plunged after a few paces. He barely noticed Tewlon slamming into his backside, though the elf's grunt was unmistakable—the warrior failed to move him in the slightest.

Greyor crept ahead to have a look, and the stench of rotting carcasses intensified as he peered downward. Several bodies covered the floor of a chamber twenty feet below. He heard nothing moving, and spiked Baylun's rope to the wall and dropped the slack. There was plenty of length to reach the floor.

Greyor descended, careful not to step on the body of a mine dweller upon reaching the bottom. Dozens more existed in various states of decay, all of them displaying areas of missing flesh with obvious bite marks. None of the wounds were large enough to have come from the jaws of Maak Maak.

Tewlon arrived, and Greyor walked farther in to provide space. Eraim dropped next, followed by her glowing bauble, and her little nose wrinkled in disgust as she tiptoed away from the bodies, careful to avoid the carnage. The hovering light then expanded, revealing the room in its entirety. Three archways offered exits to one side, each twenty feet apart, and long claw marks marred the walls and floor in several places. A large tunnel not crafted by dwarves bore into a wall adjacent to the arches.

Greyor pulled Clanghorr and headed toward the Maak Maak passage. Eraim joined him with Mithkahr in hand.

"Any thoughts?" he asked.

Eraim twisted her lips to the side. "You might owe me more than a thousand gold."

Greyor smirked while containing his chuckle. "We succeed, and I'll build you a castle."

She smiled. "No thanks. My house is perfect."

He glanced back to see Lorylla touch down, having detached the rope and jumped the distance. The gray elf coiled the length of hemp and stepped past the others to hand it to Greyor. He stuffed it into his pack—one should never be without rope when traversing mountains, inside or out.

Everyone appeared ready. Nidor stood near Ameilistari toward the rear, and Romik was behind them. The young mage was the only one not holding a weapon.

"Let us find this monster," said Greyor, and he nodded at Eraim to proceed.

The elf followed the tunnel, and Greyor trailed a step behind. The passage was roughly ten feet in diameter, but due to the rounded walls the group walked in single file. At times it slanted upward or downward, but mostly it remained level. After fifty yards, it entered another chamber, this one longer than it was wide. Corridors exited to the immediate left and right, and crumbled statues lined the walls ahead, eight to either side, with only their bases and parts of their legs intact. At the end of the hall was a dark archway topped by a diamond shape in bas-relief.

As Greyor stepped forward, the statues were suddenly whole. The dust and debris vanished, and torches in sconces illuminated the long hall. Eraim was gone. The company was gone. He was alone. From the right corridor marched three dwarves in armor. In the middle dwarf's hand was... Clanghorr? The warriors looked through Greyor as if he weren't there.

"You're sure Velgaad met with him again?" asked the dwarf holding the replica of Greyor's weapon.

The dwarf on the right answered. "Without a doubt. And the krukari asked about Torrac."

The dwarves stopped short of Greyor.

"Excuse me," he said.

They paid him no heed.

"I believe the worm is setting things in motion," the middle dwarf said. "We can sit idle no longer."

The dwarf on the left glanced along the hall before speaking in a hushed tone. "Balmorak. Do you know what you're saying?"

Balmorak... One of the names from the documents in the box

delivered to Greyor's home. The King's Champion. But how was Balmorak here? And where was Greyor's company?

The torches fluttered and failed, and Eraim's light filled the hall as the dwarves vanished and Greyor's companions reappeared. The statues returned to their state of ruin.

"I am not sure which way we should proceed," Eraim said. "But I would wager the archway leads to a place of import."

"Throne room," Greyor uttered without thinking. He frowned, unsure if he had guessed, or if he knew it to be true.

Eraim nodded and proceeded until Greyor grabbed her arm. Though her limbs appeared dainty, he felt nothing but muscle.

"Did you see anything peculiar just now?" he whispered.

She lowered her brow and shook her head. "Only crumbled statues. Did *you* see something?"

Tewlon was then next to her, and the strong elf gestured before pointing at Clanghorr. Eraim eyed the weapon as if considering, then returned her gaze to Greyor.

"Did the runes on Clanghorr take on a slight glow a moment ago?" she asked.

Greyor sighed. If they did, he hadn't noticed. Evidently Tewlon had. Unknowing how to respond, he said, "Possibly."

Kiryanna joined them, her eyes revealing impatience. Perhaps apprehension. "Where are we going?"

"Forward," Eraim replied, still staring at Greyor.

They proceeded, walking between the ruined statues. During Greyor's vision, the sculptures had distinct faces, but they were unknown to him. Why had Maak Maak destroyed the visages? What did a reptile care? Maybe it had been the mine dwellers. He would probably never know the answer.

"Wait," said Romik as they neared the archway. "It's late. Perhaps we should find a place to rest. I would hate to face this Maak Maak without our full strength."

Greyor stared blankly ahead. He had to bear in mind that he wasn't traveling with dwarves. Humans, elves, half-elves, and krukari—and whatever Nidor was—needed sleep. He glanced beyond the arch. It opened into a grand chamber. Though eager to see more, he relented.

"We'll go back and turn left," he said, again speaking without thought. If there were usable rooms in that direction, he'd soon find out.

They doubled back, and Greyor led the way into the left branch and up a short flight of stairs. The passage turned right and left a bit farther, the right corridor stretching into darkness while small archways lined one side of the hallway to the left. Greyor headed for the archways.

The first opening gave way to what must have been a lounge—he had certainly discovered the living quarters of Lornibur. Greyor moved to the next arch. Beyond was a hallway with a door on either side and another at the end, all made of bruskiin. It was surprising they were still intact, despite the rusted metal reinforcing them. He stepped to the first one on the left and tried it. It was stuck. Perhaps swollen. Using his shoulder, he forced it open.

The room beyond was an apartment appearing to have been undisturbed for some time, and dust covered everything. Four stone chairs faced a wall holding a hearth and a shelf of ancient books. A few books appeared to contain parchment, while the others were worn-out leather casings, and mildew covered all of them. In the corner rested a keg, a stain below ending any dream of a potable liquid within. At the rear of the chamber was a dark archway.

Greyor coughed, stirring up a whirl of dust, and covered his mouth with his arm as he approached the arch.

"I do not think this is such a good place to rest," commented Eraim with a sneer.

Beyond the archway was a bedroom containing a single bed, a nightstand, and a desk, all made of stone.

A breeze tugged at Greyor's beard, and he turned to see a rush of air swirling about while Ameilistari spun her hands. He lifted his arm over his nose, but the miniature whirlwind pulled all dust into it and vanished. A handy talent. She'd make a fine maid one day.

"Thank you," Eraim said to Ameilistari.

The lass smiled. "Just a minor trick." She noticed her father's glare, and her smile retreated.

The lord's hesitation to accept his daughter's wizardry was understandable; Greyor wouldn't want any of his offspring playing with magic. But it wasn't a typical trait among dwarves, so he doubted it would ever be a concern. Still, there was nothing wrong with her cleaning the room.

"This should do," Greyor said. "Let's settle in."

Baylun forced the door closed.

"Rest on this?" asked Eraim, frowning while she sat on a stone chair.

"There were once cushions," Greyor told her. "I'm sure young Ameilistari swept away any proof of their existence."

Everyone spread out through the small chamber and sat against the walls. Some laid down blankets, but that mattered little on the hard floor. Greyor was perfectly comfortable.

❊ ❊ ❊

Ameilistari's frustrations grew. Her father's contempt for her magic was baffling. He had lived a life both horrific and heroic from the stories she had heard, and more than once magic saved him. Of course, it had threatened him as well. But showing disdain for a simple cleaning spell made no sense. It was for everyone's benefit. Except maybe Greyor. The dwarf might prefer dusty, dirty conditions. He lived underground, after all.

Nidor appeared uneasy and remained standing while most of the others found places to sit against the walls. Uncle Baylun claimed one of the dwarf-sized chairs, and it was comical how his knees bent above his waist. Somehow, he didn't seem uncomfortable.

Ameilistari turned to her cousin. "It'll be fine," she whispered. "You'll see."

Nidor sighed. "Did you believe our little deception could lead to this?" he whispered back. "Hunting a giant monster lizard?"

"Look around us," she said. "We are surrounded by heroes. The best Vaeldor has to offer." She smiled to ease his apprehension. "We'll see things that stories are made of. And this time, our names will be mentioned when those stories are told."

Nidor shook his head. "You're braver than I."

She lifted her chin. "Of course I am."

They sat on the floor, and Ameilistari followed Nidor's gaze to Lorylla. The tall elf rested in the corner near the hearth, opposite the bookshelves, her eyes shut.

"What captivates you about the gray elf?" Ameilistari asked.

Lorylla's eyes opened and shifted their way. For a moment, the elf's gaze froze Nidor—those penetrating eyes! He broke free and faced Ameilistari.

"I don't know," he said, quieter than before. "Mother and Father spoke often about the grays. Grandfather called them the greatest clan of warriors he had ever seen. He said one named Xorlunder was the wisest among them, but the elf died in the Battle of the Dead Fields."

As Lorylla stood and walked their way, Ameilistari wondered if she had heard their conversation. The elf sat next to Nidor and revealed a rare smile. She was truly beautiful.

"Is there something you wish to know about gray elves?" she posed softly, her voice deep yet feminine.

Nidor's mouth opened, but he said nothing.

"Did you know Xorlunder?" Ameilistari asked to fill the awkward silence.

Lorylla's smile broadened. "He was my father." She looked at Nidor. "And yes, he died in the Battle of the Dead Fields at the hands of the Death Lord Gruzim."

She *had* heard them talking! Nidor evidently realized this as well, and his eyes widened.

Ameilistari furrowed her brow. "Why are you here? I didn't think elves enjoyed being underground."

"Eraim and Tewlon are here," Lorylla pointed out.

"True." Ameilistari glanced at the smaller elves. "But Eraim has been everywhere. I notice her name in nearly every story about the wars of the past century."

Lorylla chuckled. "She is quite unique." She considered Ameilistari. "A dear friend asked me for help, and here I am."

"Do gray elves not detest the underground?" posed Ameilistari.

"Though I prefer the forest, my folk are not so anxious about delving deeper. We do not fear Vaeldor swallowing us up."

"How old are you?" Ameilistari asked.

"Not quite halfway through life."

"Are you married?"

"Yes."

"Any kids?"

"Yes."

Ameilistari looked at Nidor. He stared at the elf like a gaping idiot with nothing to add.

"I think that is enough for tonight." Lorylla stood. "Try to get some rest. Heroes always find time to rest, so they stay strong." She walked back to her corner.

Ameilistari punched Nidor's arm, breaking him from his trance.

Chapter 9

An Old Enemy

Greyor guarded for most of the night, sharing that duty with a rotating partner. First he watched with Eraim, then with Tewlon. He rested during the next couple of hours and resumed the final watch with Baylun.

Baylun sat awkwardly on a chair by the dark fireplace. The air was cool, but not cold enough to require a fire. Greyor paced the floor, pondering the vision of Balmorak and the other dwarves. Was Clanghorr using images to speak to him?

"Does the name Balmorak mean anything to you?" Baylun asked quietly.

Greyor held his breath. Eyeing his sleeping companions, he approached the krukari and spoke in a hushed voice. "You heard them?"

"The voices?" Baylun asked.

"By the statues?"

Baylun nodded.

Greyor sat in the neighboring chair, his heart racing. "Did you see the dwarves?"

"Dwarves?"

Greyor nodded, excitement driving him to lean toward the krukari.

Baylun shook his head. "Just one dwarf. The other was human. He called the dwarf Balmorak, and the dwarf called him Mattasun."

"Mattasun…" Greyor repeated, and an explosion of names invaded his mind. Within the storm, a few stood out: Mattasun, Gruelenor, and Baylun. Gruelenor? Baylun's father? He glanced at

Baylun, then searched the fireplace. The dust-free, crumbling bricks provided no answers.

"What's it all mean?" asked Baylun.

Greyor narrowed his eyes. "I don't know." He looked at Torrac, the axe lying on Baylun's lap. "But we were meant to come here. Rather, the weapons *needed* to come here. This is where they began." He eyed Baylun. "This is where they will tell us their secrets, and how they are connected. Surely you feel that."

"I've heard whispers," admitted Baylun. "They say Clanghorr."

Baylun's attention fell to Greyor's battleaxe. Greyor had felt the same pull the last time he uttered Torrac. A thought then occurred.

"What if we touch them together?" he whispered.

Baylun shrugged. He lifted Torrac and extended it between the chairs. Greyor did the same with Clanghorr, and the blades connected.

Nothing happened.

"That was pointless," muttered Greyor, pulling back his weapon.

Baylun appeared disappointed as well. "Should we mention something to the others?" he asked.

Greyor scanned the company. "I don't see what help they'd be." He looked at Kiryanna sleeping in a seated position with the golden sword on her lap. Was it painted gold? A sword made of actual gold would be too heavy and likely bend or break from use. No doubt a combination of materials went into its making, as well as her breastplate's. "Does your wife know?" he asked.

Baylun sighed. "I don't want to worry her. Wasn't sure if I was going mad."

Greyor bobbed his head. "Probably best to keep it that way for now." He stared at Baylun. "But tell me everything from here on. We're in this together."

Baylun nodded.

They spoke no more, and Greyor returned to pacing.

What would Greyor's friends say if they saw him now, working with a krukari? He shook his head. He didn't care. Lornibur and

Clanghorr were all that mattered. And besides, Baylun came from excellent stock. Greyor had traveled with Gruelenor into Trannum's crypt of undead apprentices before the War of the North, and the krukari proved honorable and brave. Add to that paladin Nidor's trust of the half-hobgoblin… that was good enough for Greyor. He still wondered why the voices mentioned Gruelenor's name, but it was best not to mention that yet. Baylun seemed to be dealing with enough at the moment.

They woke the others half an hour later. After a brief meal of salted meat, Greyor forced open the door and they returned to the hall of broken statues.

Greyor moved slowly to the far archway, hoping Clanghorr would speak to him. The weapon remained silent. Darkness cloaked the chamber beyond until Eraim's light entered, expanding its reach to reveal a throne at the opposite end, as well as illuminating the vaulted ceiling. Striations of gold, silver, and copper rose from the floor and up the walls, converging on a diamond set at the apex of the dome, and the gem created dancing lights while Eraim's bauble moved farther into the room. The jewel was surely more valuable than all the riches in Ironside's treasury.

Additional ruined statues lined the walls to the left and right with exits between them, and a deteriorated carpet of indeterminable color made a path across the center of the floor and up two steps of a dais that held the throne. Constructed of granite, the chair appeared untouched by age, and jewels sparkled red, blue, and green from its high back. Something small rested atop its seat that Greyor couldn't make out. Behind the throne on either side, large archways led into darkness, and from them issued steam. Mithkahr took on a red tint.

Greyor raised a hand to halt the company. He nodded at Eraim, and she sheathed her elfish blade and pulled her bow. Tewlon stood next to her with sword drawn while Lorylla nocked an arrow. To the rear of the group, Romik corralled Ameilistari and Nidor near the entrance, and Baylun and Kiryanna stepped forward with Torrac and the golden sword at the ready.

"I'll flush it out," Greyor whispered, and he proceeded, gripping Clanghorr until his fingers ached.

Sweat beaded on his forehead as he neared the left arch. The heat was moist, and steady breathing from two distinct sources was obvious. Eraim's light remained behind, and Greyor halted just outside the opening to allow his vision to adjust. An enormous creature seemed to be sleeping. Unlike the lizards they battled yesterday, this monster's blood ran hot, making it easy to detect, and as Greyor's sight penetrated the darkness further, he saw two necks stretching from the massive body to a pair of large reptilian heads. Powerful claws descended from strong shoulders, and the back end of the beast tapered to a tail with no rear legs. Maak Maak was at least fifty feet long.

The neck on the left side bore terrible scars; Clanghorr had painted that picture. Upon the right head was a discolored left eyelid, and Greyor had a flashback of the behemoth's massive jaws devouring Millord. Taking a calming breath, he suppressed his rising anger and the urge to attack—that's what Millord would have done. But he wasn't Millord. The mission was about more than revenge, and this battle was for the entire company.

"Get up, Maak Maak! You vile worm!" Greyor bellowed.

The creature stirred. Its heads lifted and all but one eye opened— the discolored eyelid remained shut.

Greyor retreated, running to the throne.

Three loud calls echoed from the room behind the granite chair, like the blasting of a horn. A massive head then peered through the left archway, and the one-eyed head did the same through the opposite arch.

Lorylla and Eraim released their bowstrings toward the right opening, but a gushing stream of scalding water issued from the reptilian mouth, engulfing the projectiles. Tewlon grabbed Eraim with surprising speed as the blast continued across the chamber, pulling her to the floor near the middle of the room. Lorylla leaped above the stream, and Romik and the young ones ran safely from its path as it struck the far wall.

The other giant head made a motion to mirror the attack of the first, but only steam billowed forth, floating harmlessly to the ceiling after ten feet. Perhaps Clanghorr's damage from years ago had done more than just leave scars.

Greyor charged the one-eyed head, eager to avenge Millord, but it withdrew before he arrived. Both heads then emerged from the left archway as lizards ranging from five to eight feet long issued from the smaller arches—Maak Maak had called for reinforcements!

One-Eye turned Greyor's way, lunging as Maak Maak's claws pulled it farther into the room. He used the throne as a shield, and its crocodile-like teeth clamped shut short of the chair.

As the monster reared, Greyor charged. The head rose above his reach, and he continued toward the body now halfway into the chamber. Its claw reached for him, but an arrow struck it, delivering a small explosion—Lorylla had empowered the missile with the ancient magic of her race. The blackened appendage retreated, and Greyor sliced through the scales of Maak Maak's side, releasing greenish blood and gaining the attention of both heads.

"You'll not make a meal of me!" He issued another gash.

Maak Maak scrambled forward, trampling Greyor and burying him beneath its massive body.

❀ ❀ ❀

Baylun tightened his grip on Torrac as the giant reptile peered through the enormous openings. They were the biggest heads he had ever seen—much larger than a bone dragon's. As the head to the right breathed scalding water across the chamber, his thoughts went to Nidor, Romik, and Ameilistari. Thankfully, the three evaded the attack. Dozens of lizards then stormed into the room from the archways to the sides, and Greyor charged as Maak Maak moved both heads to the left arch.

Baylun hesitated. The dwarf couldn't possibly fight the monster alone, but the children and Romik would soon have more than they could handle.

"Kill that thing!" Kiryanna yelled at Baylun, sprinting toward Nidor.

Perhaps having her on this mission was a blessing.

Baylun ran at the giant beast. Behind him, the clamor of combat and minor explosions resounded. Greyor inflicted a second deep gash upon the monstrous lizard while an arrow struck the head on the left, and the creature pounced on the dwarf with all of its weight.

"Maak Maak!" yelled Baylun, gaining one head's attention.

He heaved Torrac, aiming for the head with one eye—it had lowered to search for the dwarf. The upright head hissed, as if warning its other half, and the targeted neck moved quickly from the axe's path. The runes then lit up, and Torrac spun faster as it veered toward its target, cutting deep and showering the throne in green blood. As the head wavered, a ball of fire streaked over Baylun and exploded upon the monster. Billowing flames forced him to drop to the floor, and searing heat washed across his back.

As the fire dissipated, Baylun suppressed his pain and looked to see Maak Maak had collapsed. Lorylla arrived at the corpse and struggled to lift a section of its body to reveal Greyor, and the dwarf scrambled from beneath the unmoving monster—his bones must be truly thick!

Around the room, the attacking lizards were down to a few, and Tewlon decapitated one while Kiryanna skewered another. Eraim pierced the final reptile between the eyes with a long-shafted arrow.

The battle ended.

"Uncle Baylun!" Ameilistari cried, running toward him with wide eyes. Tears were forming.

The burning sensation across his backside had not eased. Regardless, he pushed himself to stand.

"Ameilistari!" scolded Romik as he chased after his daughter. "You have to be more careful! You might have killed your uncle!"

"I'm so sorry." Ameilistari hugged Baylun, intensifying the pain.

"Oh!" She released him as he winced. "Sorry about that too."

Kiryanna arrived with a concerned expression. "Are you all right? Can you continue?"

Baylun bent forward, then side to side. Though uncomfortable, the burns didn't match the frozen torment he endured when faced with Radaam in Darum Carumbor nearly two decades ago—the very air surrounding the Death Lord had been unbearable. Nor did it come close to the crushing agony of Uustaag's hammer in Lormin Dmurr. He nodded to his wife.

Nidor approached with lizard blood dripping from his blade.

"Clean your weapon," Baylun told his son.

❊ ❊ ❊

Maak Maak was more horrifying than anything Ameilistari had pictured from heroic tales of the past. She froze when the heads emerged from the alcoves, unable to think straight, and one of them released a burst of smoking water.

"Move!" her father ordered, pushing her and Nidor clear of the attack.

Dozens of lizards then arrived from the side archways. Though much smaller than Maak Maak, any one of them could kill her with a single bite.

"Nidor!" yelled Father. "Take the left."

Nidor didn't hesitate, and he reported to Ameilistari's left flank while her father moved to her right. Luckily, no lizards entered through the opening behind them.

Her father employed his false arm to fend off a lizard while slashing another with his sword. Though wounded, the recipient of his attack lunged, and her father swung the hooks serving as a hand to impale the creature's head. With a jerk, he pulled the monster in close and buried his blade to the hilt.

Ameilistari calmed her scrambling thoughts enough to cast a hasty spell at the second lizard before it pounced. It was the only incantation she could bring to mind under the circumstances, and a spark of light flashed from her palm. Though not a lethal attack, it temporarily blinded the creature and caused it to reel. Her father skewered it with his sword.

Turning, Ameilistari saw Nidor had defeated the only lizard to threaten him. He eyed the reptiles racing about, remaining like a sentinel between her and the melee, just as his mother had instructed.

A roar stole Ameilistari's attention. Maak Maak stood in the left archway, making the room seem smaller. As the giant reptile crushed Greyor, Eraim's words from the meeting back at the keep came to Ameilistari, of Selanna defeating Maak Maak with fire. She pooled energy before her, forming a ball of flame, and pulled her hands apart to enlarge the spell—the monster wouldn't go down easy. She thrust her arms forward, launching the fire across the chamber.

Ameilistari hadn't noticed Uncle Baylun. He was dangerously close to Maak Maak when her spell struck, and there was nothing she could do as the flames washed over him. The fire dissolved, having completed its mission—Maak Maak had collapsed—and Uncle Baylun lay face down, his armor blackened. Her heart leaped into her throat and she couldn't breathe. She had killed him.

Baylun moved—he wasn't dead! Oxygen rushed into her lungs as she ran to him. None of the stories ever mentioned heroes almost killing other heroes through carelessness. She would need to be more mindful in the future. But first, she needed to make sure Uncle Baylun was okay.

❁ ❁ ❁

The full weight of Maak Maak pressed down upon Greyor, but his metal shell kept the beast from crushing his bones. Intense heat then surrounded him—had it breathed its steam again?

The creature suddenly became heavier, and it stopped moving. Greyor wriggled to escape, but without success. The body then lifted slightly to reveal Lorylla. She did her best to provide an exit, and

Greyor squirmed toward her until free of the reptile.

Maak Maak lay motionless, its corpse badly burned before blackened walls, and slain lizards littered the room. Baylun pushed himself from the floor, the krukari's backside charred as well. Everyone else appeared to be all right. Lying near Greyor was Torrac.

"Are you okay?" Lorylla asked Greyor.

He nodded.

A family squabble ensued, with Romik scolding his daughter while Kiryanna made sure Baylun was fit to continue. What other choice was there for the krukari?

Greyor lifted Torrac.

Lorylla vanished. Maak Maak disappeared. The company and the lizards, all gone. Several torches illuminated the chamber, but other than perfectly chiseled statues of unfamiliar dwarves, it was empty. The throne was empty. A dwarf then entered from a side hallway. It was Balmorak, and Clanghorr was at his side.

A man entered through another archway. He wasn't very tall, but he was no dwarf. He stood just over five feet in height and was clean shaven, and strapped to his back was Torrac. The man was surely human.

"Mattasun," Balmorak said. "I'm glad you received my summons."

Mattasun chuckled. "Clanghorr practically shouted in my head."

"I believe Clanghorr senses the urgency," Balmorak remarked.

The smile dropped from Mattasun's face. "What is it, old friend?"

"King Velgaad." Balmorak shook his head. "He's been dealing with the dragon priests."

Mattasun glanced about the chamber. "Is it safe to discuss this here?"

Balmorak held a wry smile. "Probably the safest place at the moment. Velgaad's down in the forge, playing host to a couple of the clerics right now."

"The forge?"

Balmorak shrugged. "He says the fires of Demoligius will strengthen our steel beyond that of anything known to dwarf, elf, or human."

"To what end?"

"It's a ruse," replied Balmorak. "Velgaad desires power, both within and beyond Lornibur. He wishes to rule all races."

Mattasun was silent while digesting the information. "What's your plan?"

"Don't have one. Not yet."

"Then why summon me?"

Balmorak drew in a slow breath. "It is my belief Velgaad has put a price on your head. When he finally makes his move, he does not wish for Clanghorr and Torrac to unite against him."

"I don't fear assassins," Mattasun stated. "Torrac can sense them before they strike."

"Not assassins," Balmorak warned. "He looks for strength. One who can defeat you and claim Torrac as his own."

"Torrac would never consent."

Balmorak nodded. "Just... watch yourself."

Suddenly, Lorylla was staring into Greyor's eyes. Balmorak and Mattasun were gone, and the only illumination came from Eraim's bauble, still floating in the center of the room

"Are you sure you are all right?" the gray elf asked. "You seem far away."

"I'm fine." Greyor patted her arm. "Thank you, friend."

He glanced at Baylun. The krukari looked his way as well. Greyor walked over and returned Torrac to its master.

"Come look at this!" called Eraim.

The elf stood near the throne, gazing at the seat. Greyor joined the others to see what had caught her eye.

Maak Maak's blood splattered most of the chair, and a broken egg lay on the seat. It would have been well over a foot in length before whatever rested inside claimed its freedom, and pooled in the bottom half of the shell was a smoking, blood-red substance.

Apparently, the properties of the eggshell made it impervious to the liquid, but it was not so for the throne. Some of the fluid had escaped, resulting in several holes in the granite to various depths. A couple passed completely through the chair and into the floor a few inches deep.

"What *was* this?" asked Eraim.

Nobody answered.

"Let's return to the room we rested in," said Greyor. "I need to think."

CHAPTER 10

RUNES

Greyor forced the apartment door shut. Baylun had entered the bedroom with his wife to remove his armor and assess his burns while everyone else settled in the front room. Romik sat on a chair, rubbing his temple with his eyes closed, and Tewlon was on another with Eraim perched on the arm, the former cleaning his blade and the latter inspecting her arrows. Ameilistari waited at the bedroom entrance, appearing anxious. Nidor must have stepped into the other room with his parents.

"These silver eyes are insufficient!" Kiryanna's voice held frustration. She then appeared in the archway. "Anyone have more useful herbs?"

"Stone crawlers," replied Greyor, reaching into his pouch and extracting a few mushrooms from the stock he had brought. They were special and grew only within caverns in the mountains.

Kiryanna eyed the gray toadstools with black spots. Her brow lowered. "How do you prepare them?"

"With a bit of salt." Greyor winked.

Her frown deepened. "Will salt not burn the open wounds?"

"It makes them taste better."

"You do not eat them!" Eraim dropped from the chair and approached. "Not if you want their full potency." She opened a pouch and pulled out some weeds. "But in Baylun's case, Vermallon dusk will be more effective." She handed a few of the herbs to Kiryanna.

Kiryanna's brow rose. "Do you have fifty more?"

Eraim half-smiled. "Place them over the burns and gently rub them in circles. It may cause a little pain, but he will be better for it."

Greyor shrugged and popped the mushrooms into his mouth—his arms and legs still ached from being pinned beneath Maak Maak. One mushroom would have done the trick, but he didn't feel like returning the others to the pouch. He then took a swig from his smaller flask—the one containing ale.

Kiryanna returned to the bedroom, placing a hand on Ameilistari's shoulder as she passed by. Moisture filled the young mage's eyes.

"Do not fret," Eraim said to Romik's daughter. "Baylun is as tough as anyone." Her eyebrows drew together. "But why did you summon a ball of fire?"

Ameilistari sighed. "Before, you mentioned Selanna had defeated Maak Maak with fire. And I saw it crush Greyor. I was only trying to help."

Greyor appreciated the sentiment. But he was nowhere near defeat at the time. A dwarf would have known that.

Eraim gave the lass a firm look. "What Selanna would tell you is that you must consider your surroundings before casting such a spell. When she summoned fire, Maak Maak was in a lake, and she struck its head." Eraim frowned, then added, "And she would also tell you to limit the source of power to reduce its effect."

Ameilistari nodded.

Eraim bit her lip. "And… I guess… she would also be very impressed with how much you have grown."

Eraim sure had a lot to say on Selanna's behalf.

Tewlon shook his head. What part did he disagree with?

Nidor emerged from the bedroom. He placed his hand on Ameilistari's shoulder and gave a nod. The young sorceress let out a relieved exhale.

Kiryanna exited the room next. "Well, that Maak Maak was certainly impressive."

"I thought it would be more dangerous," commented Nidor.

"It was not at full strength," said Eraim. "It was obviously hampered by the wounds we inflicted years ago, and it did not manage to separate us."

"And it had just awakened from slumber," added Greyor as he headed into the bedroom.

❋ ❋ ❋

Ameilistari exhaled with great relief as she slid down the wall into a seated position. Baylun was all right. Kiryanna's amiable tone reinforced the notion.

Nidor sat next to her with a grin. "When did you learn to cast fireballs?" he whispered, appearing genuinely impressed.

Ameilistari shrugged. "It's really no different from the spell I used to light the candle. Just on a much larger scale." She looked Nidor in the eyes. "I honestly didn't know I could generate one so powerful."

"I don't think I'll ever tease *you* again," Nidor kidded.

She smirked.

"Except to say that was another dumb mistake on your part." He glanced at the ceiling, as if calculating. "I believe we're even."

Though she didn't enjoy having her near-failure thrown back at her, she was glad Nidor could joke about the situation. Uncle Baylun must truly be all right. She would be more careful in the future.

"Did you see Lorylla in the battle?" Nidor asked softly.

Ameilistari held a wry smile. "I was trying to stay alive."

"She jumped twenty feet into the air." He shook his head, enjoying the memory. "Her sword was smoking, and she must have slain seven lizards without breaking a sweat."

"She's married," Ameilistari reminded her cousin. "And probably two hundred years older than you."

"It's just…" Nidor sighed. "Grandfather says hers is the most ancient race in all of Vaeldor. And the things she can do… Can you imagine having such skills?"

Ameilistari gave him a sidelong glare. "Don't make me hit you with a fireball."

❀ ❀ ❀

Greyor entered the bedroom to find Baylun sitting on the bed. The krukari was buckling his leather vest.

"You good now?" asked Greyor.

"I was fine before," Baylun said in his rumbling voice. "A few burns won't slow me down."

Greyor chuckled and peered over his shoulder. No one had followed him. "I saw Mattasun."

Baylun lowered his brow. "Walking through Lornibur?"

Greyor shook his head. "What exactly did you see before?"

Baylun scrunched his face in thought. "He walked through hallways identical to the ones we've seen. Dwarves stopped whatever they were doing as he passed, but said nothing. He entered the throne room, and Balmorak was there."

"To warn him?"

Baylun nodded.

"Anything after that?"

"No." Baylun slid his chain shirt slowly over his head and around his torso. "What do you think Mattasun meant about being summoned?"

Greyor furrowed his brow. "Not sure. Somehow, Clanghorr spoke to Mattasun." He looked at Baylun. "I wish Selanna were here. I sent her an invitation, but Eraim claimed she was too busy. She'd probably figure all of this out." He sighed. "Let me know when you're ready to move on."

Baylun lifted Torrac from the side of the bed. "I'm ready now."

Greyor grinned.

Though Kiryanna insisted they allow Baylun time to rest, the krukari waved off her concerns, and the company exited the apartment. Baylun showed minor discomfort, but made no complaints while they walked back to the throne room—Greyor appreciated the warrior's strength more and more every second. Minutes later, they arrived.

Nothing had disturbed the reptile corpses, and Greyor led the way to the granite chair. The eggshell remained undisturbed as well. Unsure of what to do with a broken shell, Greyor left the investigation to Eraim and passed beneath the right arch to the room where Maak Maak had slept.

The chamber was a staging area, where the king's royal servants would make final preparations before proceeding to the throne room. The ceiling was twenty feet above, and Maak Maak filled the other archway, its tail stretched along the wall between the two rooms. A pair of washbasins were permanent fixtures of stone, one protruding from either side wall and their bowls completely dry, and flanking the basins were benches, also attached to the walls. Remnants of what must have been a carpet were strewn about, and the air was warm and moist. A hallway exited the far end of the room, likely approaching the royal chambers.

The group entered with Eraim's light.

"Whatever hatched from that egg," Eraim said to Greyor, "it could not have been very long ago."

"A baby Maak Maak?" posed Romik.

Eraim shook her head. "Time will tell." She gazed along the ceiling and about the room. "Who knows how long before we encounter it?"

"If it didn't hatch long ago, it can't be very big." Greyor shrugged. "How dangerous can it be?"

Eraim held a wry smile. "You never know in a place such as this."

There was nothing to be done but move on, so Greyor walked across the room and into the adjoining passage. The group followed. The corridor was eight feet wide and twelve feet high, and faded murals along its length were impossible to discern.

Another vision struck, lasting a fraction of a second. Balmorak swung Clanghorr, cleaving a human wearing red robes with orange and black trim in the very hallway where Greyor stood. It was almost as if he had swung the axe himself. He glanced at Baylun, who shrugged. The krukari didn't see it.

Twenty paces farther, another brief vision occurred. A human in robes of black with red trim, his eyes glowing red, stood in the hallway. A Demoligius priest! Greyor looked at Baylun again. Again, the krukari shrugged.

"Is something wrong?" asked Eraim.

Greyor shook his head and moved on.

The corridor turned left and right. To the right were five doors, two on either side and one at the end. The passage to the left was no different, except the doors were taller and decorated with square panels.

Greyor followed the latter and approached the first door on the left. It was another bruskiin door, reinforced with rusted iron bands and blackened about the edges. As he reached for its latch, he saw Balmorak doing the same, and fire erupted from the other side. The dwarf lifted Clanghorr, and as the runes on the axe lit up, the flames washed around the warrior and brought him no harm. Balmorak forced the door shut, cutting off the fiery burst.

"Don't open this one," Greyor said, lowering his hand and moving to the door across the hallway. Better safe than sorry.

No vision came, and the door opened easily into a bedroom that appeared to have hosted a scuffle. Greyor went to the bed and searched while Eraim checked a stone chest of drawers. The drawers were of bruskiin, but unlike the door, they were in ill repair. The bed was also bruskiin, and too long for a dwarf.

Greyor found nothing, and he looked back. Eraim lifted an item from a drawer. It was a tiny black talon, and something dark and shriveled was in its clutches. She spoke in Elfish to Tewlon, a language Greyor understood very little of, but two words were clear: Demoligius priest.

"What is it holding?" he asked in the Common speech.

"What used to be a tiny heart," the elf replied. Ire suddenly consumed her. "I will not say from what."

"Velgaad must have been dealing with Seltans." Greyor's tone grew heated, finally able to admit something he knew to be true. All

Demoligius priests hailed from Selt. "I wish I could kill him again! His Death Lord form wasn't satisfying enough."

Lorylla eyed the object, her grimace holding as much contempt as did Eraim's. Maybe more.

"Let's move on." Greyor pointed his axe at the nasty trinket. "Right after I destroy that thing."

Eraim nodded and placed the talon on the floor.

With a single swing, Clanghorr shattered the unholy relic, but upon contact, the briefest flash of fangs gnashed at Greyor's mind. The runes on his battleaxe were aglow, and the light quickly faded. Clanghorr had protected him from something undesirable.

"What is it?" asked Eraim.

Everyone stared, including Baylun. By the krukari's expression, he hadn't seen the fangs.

Greyor shook his head. "Just remnants of evil. But it's gone."

They exited and moved to the next door on the left. Beyond was another room in disarray, this one appearing to have been a lounge. Stone furnishings lay cracked or broken, the hearth had collapsed, and several shards of crystal littered the floor atop ancient stains.

Greyor went to the door at the end of the hall and opened the latch. A spacious bedroom that had surely been luxurious at one time lay in ruin. Furniture existed, some made of stone, but most was constructed of oak and utterly destroyed. Why would a dwarf want wooden furniture?

Greyor entered, and Balmorak interrupted his thoughts again. The warrior and two others fought a team of dwarves in royal uniforms. One of Balmorak's enemies wore an ornate suit of plate armor with intricate etchings and spikes upon the shoulders, and swung a flail with a pair of spiked iron balls—the same weapon Velgaad the Death Lord had wielded during the Necromancer War. The evil king struck one of Balmorak's companions across the side of the head, felling the dwarf.

"Brunux!" called Balmorak, rage obvious in his voice.

A passage came to Greyor from the letters in the box back at home… *Brunux was not so lucky. The King of Treachery's flail wrapped him aside the head and he perished…* The other dwarf accompanying Balmorak must be the author.

Balmorak closed on Velgaad, slaying three guards in the process. The king was hopelessly outmatched, and Clanghorr cleaved the worm in half. Balmorak didn't stop there. The dwarf severed each of the king's limbs—both legs in a single swing.

"Greyor?" asked Eraim.

He turned to the elf. The vision faded.

"Why do you keep staring at nothing?" she posed.

Greyor didn't know what to say. Not yet. No one but Baylun would understand.

"This is curious," said Lorylla.

The gray elf kneeled by a fireplace. She pulled her knife and worked the blade between two bricks, pulling one loose and revealing a small cavity. With a delicate touch, she reached into the dark hole and removed a scroll. The rolled parchment was yellowed with age.

"Be careful!" cautioned Eraim with wide eyes. "That is ancient."

Lorylla issued a level gaze at the shorter elf. She returned her attention to the scroll and moved to the nearby stone desk. Taking a seat on a chair too low for her, she hovered over the parchment as she placed it on the desktop.

Greyor stood on one side of the gray elf and Eraim on the other. It seemed like time crawled while Lorylla unrolled the page little by little. A drawing of a flame occupied the top left corner, and below it were the numbers 10, 2, and 3 written in Dwarfish, each followed by an unfamiliar rune. Next, a sketch of an oval with lines extending from either side appeared. Parts of the parchment then cracked, and Greyor's gasp halted Lorylla.

"Dare we go any further?" he posed.

She turned to him. "My little friend, leaving the rest unknown is as useless as destroying it in the process."

Ameilistari stepped next to the desk to peer over Eraim's shoulder. "I might be able to help."

Lorylla looked from the young mage and back to Greyor with a questioning gaze.

He sighed. Selanna had taught the lass, and he counted the elfish sorceress higher than even Elgarroth. The old wizard from Vermallon never did much beyond advising, while Selanna was in the thick of everything throughout the wars against Trannum and Uustaag. Greyor nodded to Ameilistari to proceed.

❋ ❋ ❋

Ameilistari stared at the aged parchment while Lorylla rose from the chair. Once the gray elf was out of the way, she took a seat. It was like sitting on a boulder. With all the beautiful creations made by dwarfish hands, it amazed her they were so bad at making furniture.

She eyed the scroll. It had attempted to reroll itself after Lorylla released it, but a couple of breaks in the hardened paper prevented it from moving very far. Years ago, Selanna showed her how to handle aging books without causing damage. A scroll was a little different, but she was positive the spell would work.

Sweat beaded on Ameilistari's forehead as she whispered an incantation. With a deep breath, she blew lightly onto the parchment, and steam issued from her lips, relaxing the page. The paper then darkened slightly, and she ceased blowing—going too far would make it illegible. She gently unrolled it farther, and below the oval were additional runes.

The scroll crumbled into pieces, most of them becoming dust.

Ameilistari gasped. She had failed.

❋ ❋ ❋

Greyor placed his hand on the young mage's shoulder. "Don't worry, lass. It was bound to happen." He doubted anyone else would have gotten as far. Looking at Eraim, he asked, "Did you see it?"

She nodded slowly with a perplexed expression. "May I see

113

Clanghorr?"

Greyor chuckled. "I'm afraid Clanghorr is too heavy for you."

"I do not wish to use it," Eraim said. "Just to look at the runes."

To this, Greyor had no objection. He extended the axe for her inspection.

Eraim sucked in her lips, her eyes moving over the runes along the blades. She looked at Baylun. "Can I see Torrac?"

The krukari held out his axe, and she scanned it as well.

Eraim turned to Greyor. "The writings on your weapons use the same letters."

Greyor nodded. It was an observation he had already discovered.

"Selanna believes the runes to be ancient," Eraim said. "Perhaps they are to dwarves what arcane runes are to mages. Except of course they hold no magic."

Greyor frowned. What in Meldar's Forge was she saying?

"And some of the axes' characters were on the scroll as well," Eraim added. "Excuse me."

She pushed her way onto the stone chair, making Ameilistari stand. Pulling a sheet of blank parchment from one of her pouches, Eraim set it on the desk and withdrew a sturdy vial and a quill. After opening the vial, she dipped the quill into its black ink and sketched everything the old page had revealed before deteriorating. At least, it appeared to have every line, rune, and marking the original scroll possessed. Very impressive.

She turned back to Baylun. "Torrac says *courage* and *honor*, correct?"

Baylun nodded hesitantly. "But I don't know which says which."

"That does not matter." Eraim twisted her lips to the side. "With that knowledge, I might be able to find commonalities and decipher at least some of the runes." She looked at the krukari. "Please show me your blades again."

Baylun complied, and Eraim scrawled perfect replicas of Torrac's runes onto the parchment. She turned to Greyor.

"And now Clanghorr."

He again extended his weapon, and she added its runes. It seemed more of a task for Selanna, but as the little elf made additional markings on the page, Greyor supposed there was no harm in giving her a moment.

He walked about the room. Tewlon, Lorylla, and Ameilistari watched Eraim work while Romik and Baylun held a quiet conversation. Kiryanna and Nidor sat on the edge of the broken bed.

"By the way," the marteese said to her son, "your swordsmanship against the lizards was excellent."

Nidor shrugged. "I didn't do much."

"Nonetheless, I saw you." Her tone was firm. "You were brave and handled yourself very well. And you followed orders and remained at Ameilistari's side." Her eyes narrowed on Nidor. "Make sure you continue to do so. She is *your* charge."

A glint of light captured Greyor's attention. The illumination from Eraim's bauble reflected from the hole where Lorylla had found the scroll. He moved closer to spy something metallic inside. Reaching in, he pulled out a silver key no longer than his palm. Greyor looked back to see Baylun and Romik watching with curious eyes, and he approached the two.

"This was behind the scroll." He held out the key.

"There must be a thousand locks in this place," remarked Romik. "Who's to say what it opens?"

"I see nothing in this room requiring a key," Baylun said.

Greyor glanced around and nodded. He looked again at the key. A small marking was near the base: a flame, just like on the parchment Ameilistari destroyed. Perhaps Eraim would figure out its purpose once she completed her work. With nothing more to do until that time arrived, Greyor pulled salted meat from his pack and took a bite.

Chapter 11

Secret Passage

I believe I have something."

Eraim's announcement captured Greyor's attention. He pushed past Baylun and Romik and squeezed by Ameilistari, ignoring their grunts and protests as he rushed to see what the elf had discovered. The parchment before her displayed the markings she had recreated, plus the runes she copied from the battleaxes and several new writings, none of it legible.

"What you *have* looks just as confusing as before," Greyor complained.

Eraim frowned as if hurt by his words. "Nonsense. I used old dwarfish runes, as well as old elfish runes, arcane runes, and the dwarfish alphabet." She grinned. "From there, we believe we determined which of Torrac's blades says *honor*, allowing us to know which is *courage*. That said, I used the characters similar between the two battleaxes, and it is our belief that Clanghorr says *bravery* and *justice*." Her smile stretched from ear to ear.

"*We* determined?" asked Lorylla. "*Our* belief?"

"*I*," Eraim corrected herself. "And *my* belief."

Greyor gazed at Clanghorr's silver blades, mouthing the words… *bravery, justice*. Of course!

"And using those runes," Eraim added, "*I* believe the numbers on the scroll were directions for opening something. Something located near fire. Ten paces to the right, two feet above the floor, and turn three times." She wrinkled her little nose. "But turn what?"

"A key?" Romik asked, looking at Greyor.

Greyor pulled the silver key. "I found this where the scroll was."

Eraim considered the item. "Maybe." She held out her hand until Greyor gave her the key. After scrutinizing it, she placed it into her pouch.

"What was written below the diagram?" asked Lorylla.

Eraim frowned. "I could not fully decipher that one. But it appears to be a name."

"Balmorak?" posed Greyor.

"No," replied the small elf.

"Mattasun? Brunux?"

Eraim looked at Greyor. "No. But where are you getting these names from?"

He glanced at Baylun before answering. "Just dwarves of old." The temptation to tell her about the visions entered Greyor's mind—she seemed as smart as a wizard at the moment. But Lornibur had more to show him first. And to gain that knowledge, the company needed to move on from this room.

A grating sounded toward the rear of the chamber. Greyor turned to see a portion of the back wall sliding to reveal a dark corridor.

"What...?" asked Romik.

"I believe it was Nidor's doing," said Kiryanna, rising from the bed. She eyed the nearby bedpost, now in a bent position. "This moved when he grabbed it to stand." She looked at the hallway. "And that's when the door revealed itself."

Eagerness drove Greyor to hasten to the opening. The tunnel was narrow and short, with imperfect walls, floor, and ceiling. The shoddy craftsmanship reminded him of the secret passage beneath Ironside Keep—a poor representation of dwarfish work!

He entered, followed by Eraim, Kiryanna, and Lorylla, the gray elf hunched over to fit. Beyond Lorylla, he couldn't see the order of the others. The corridor bore straight, and then slanted downward at a gentle angle, probably unnoticed by most of the company. It continued another twenty yards before turning left. Around the bend, the tunnel sloped upward at a noticeable rate. Possibly an escape tunnel. If so, it would provide a way out for Ameilistari and Nidor.

The next turn took them left again, and a bit farther, large holes breached the walls to either side while the passageway continued onward. The openings were roughly ten feet in diameter—Maak Maak's work.

"I don't know about this," Greyor mumbled as he halted twenty paces away.

"There might be a way out ahead," said Eraim.

"I realize that." Greyor scratched his chin, eyeing the corridor beyond the Maak Maak tunnel. It continued to climb. "But I don't like the looks of it."

He detected whispering as Lorylla spoke to those behind her. Mutterings of a conversation ensued, and Lorylla turned back to Greyor.

"Romik begs you to proceed," the tall elf said. "He says he and the young ones will continue, without the rest of us if necessary."

Greyor shook his head. There was no telling what awaited them. Even if it were a route of escape, dangers might lay ahead. He sighed. "We'll all go."

He continued to the breach. The rounded tunnel was larger than the corridor, its floor four feet below the original passage—quite a step for a dwarf! Worse still, the tunnels plunged steeply to the left and right, as if Maak Maak's only intention had been to hinder anyone trying to escape, if that was truly the corridor's purpose. As a result, the lower floor was a hill, ready to send them tumbling to unknown depths.

Greyor puffed out his cheeks with a forceful exhale. "Balance could be tricky. I'll secure a rope to the other side." He looked at the elves and marteese behind him. "Wait here."

Kiryanna nodded. Eraim furrowed her brow in obvious disagreement. Lorylla's expression remained calm.

Greyor spiked one end of Baylun's rope to the floor. The other end he tossed onto the "hill" Maak Maak left behind. He then put Clanghorr away and emptied his lungs to make himself lighter.

The slant wasn't too steep, and Greyor lowered himself, sliding to the low point of the rounded floor. The pits of blackness to the left and right stole his breath, and he wrapped the rope around his gauntlet to aid his balance. Continuing to slide his boots, he inched forward, kicking rocks into the abyss on either side. Upon reaching the rising wall, Greyor briefly wondered why he hadn't sent Eraim first—the escape tunnel was six feet overhead. But he was a dwarf. He was born in the mountains and had lived in them for over a hundred years. With a deep breath, he put the rope in his mouth to free his hands.

The arcing wall was rough, with several places to brace his boots, and jutting pieces of rock provided decent handholds. But as Greyor made it halfway up, he stopped. The ledge was still two feet above, and the wall ceased offering an easy climb. And the rope tasted horrible.

"Slide down," said Eraim from below. She had followed, and Kiryanna was with her.

Blasted elves and half-elves! They knew nothing about traveling underground. Greyor worked his way back, joining them atop the crowded hill.

Eraim gracefully stepped around Greyor—he didn't even have to move. She then scaled the curved wall with little effort, and turned back with a smirk.

Greyor snorted. It was obviously due to her light weight. Kiryanna would have suffered just as he had with the gear the marteese wore.

Kiryanna moved past, hugging Greyor so she wouldn't fall, and she found holds that had eluded him as she joined the elf.

Greyor sighed.

Eraim motioned for him to throw her the rope. After doing so, Kiryanna drove a spike into the floor to secure it to the ledge. Greyor cringed with every fall of the hammer—he hadn't tested the strength of the stone. The marteese might place the spike too close to the Maak Maak addition.

Once Kiryanna finished the task, Greyor scaled to join the maidens. He turned back to see Lorylla crossing the low floor without a misstep—why not just leap across? As she passed the middle of the trench, Baylun descended while Romik watched from above. Beyond the one-armed lord, Tewlon remained with the young ones.

Crack!

A fissure appeared, traveling from Kiryanna's spike and into the reptile's tunnel. Lorylla had just grabbed the ledge where Greyor stood, ready to hoist herself up.

"Stop!" Greyor warned the others.

The crack grew, passing below Baylun and up to the spike on the other side. Lorylla hesitated while Baylun turned to go back, and Romik lowered his hook for his brother to grab. A rumbling followed, and Lorylla leaped away as the Maak Maak tunnel collapsed. The floor beneath Greyor gave way, and he plummeted.

Chapter 12

Armored Chamber

Please! Wake up!"

Greyor opened his eyes. Two Eraims stared down at him, shaking his shoulders while the room spun.

"Thank Silcor," said Kiryanna from somewhere out of view.

"You put the spike too close," Greyor muttered.

Eraim frowned. "What?"

"The spike." He squeezed his eyes shut to push away the gathering moisture. When he reopened them, the spinning slowed to a stop. "You put it too close to the broken tunnel."

Eraim looked away. "He is all right."

"Of course I'm all right."

Pain stabbed at Greyor's forehead as he sat up. Eraim's light had joined them in their descent, and it illuminated a small chamber with crumbled furniture and scattered rubble. Above, a gaping hole bore into the ceiling, and another descended to the left in the room's back corner. Two archways provided exits, and Kiryanna held her golden blade while peering through one. The rest of the company was missing.

"Not again," Greyor mumbled. "Blast that Maak Maak!" His eyes widened and he reached to his side… Clanghorr was there. He expelled a relieved breath.

"I believe we fell a hundred feet," said Eraim, extending a hand.

Greyor accepted her assistance, and she exhibited surprising strength as she helped him to stand. His head pounded, and he grabbed a stone crawler from his pouch and tossed it into his mouth.

"Did you know that if you…" Eraim made a grinding motion with one hand over the other, as if stirring an invisible bowl.

Greyor stared at her while chewing.

She stopped the motion. "Never mind."

"If we fell that far," Greyor said, "we're two levels below the throne room." He looked around. "Of course, there's no telling how far left or right we are."

"I cannot be absolutely positive," Eraim turned to the archway where Kiryanna stood, "but I believe we need to go that way."

Kiryanna gave Eraim a nod of approval. "If anyone can get us out of here, it's you."

Eraim seemed surprised to receive the compliment.

"Are you ready?" the marteese asked Greyor.

He frowned. "I'm standing, aren't I?" She must not know many dwarves.

Eraim's light moved to the arch she had indicated. "I will lead, if you wish," she said to Greyor.

He nodded, and they exited the room with Kiryanna bringing up the rear.

The corridor was eight feet wide and three times Greyor's height, and he sensed the floor to be gradually descending. Unlike the other passageways, the ceiling was rounded, and an archway provided support thirty feet ahead. Though smaller than the arches above, it was no less impressive, and replacing the image in bas-relief was a single topaz. The gemstone wasn't as large as those displayed thus far, but still worth a hundred gold in human cities.

Beyond the archway was a four-way intersection. The corridor continued, extending beyond an identical arch ahead, and it was the same to the left, except the archway held a peridot. To the right, doors lined either side of the hallway, each twenty feet from the previous one. Eraim turned right.

Kiryanna guarded the middle of the tunnel while Eraim checked the doors on one side and Greyor opened those on the other. Each led to a bedroom, and from the sizes of them, they had belonged to important dwarves; possibly priests. They were empty, as if the occupants had left in a hurry, except for one.

The fourth door on the right revealed yet another bedroom in disarray. The bed, desk, wardrobe, table, and two chairs were all crafted from stone, and the mattress, cushions, and a tapestry were long deteriorated. A dwarf skeleton sat near the corner of the bed toward the wall, and old blood darkened the floor beneath it, now brown and faded.

Greyor grunted to gain Eraim's attention, and they entered together for a better look while Kiryanna remained in the hallway. Eraim followed Greyor to the skeleton, her eyes drawn to the far leg of the bed.

"He didn't make it out with the others," said Greyor, inspecting the bones without touching them. "I wonder if he was a Velgaad faithful?"

Eraim opened a hidden compartment within the bed leg against the wall. From it she pulled a key. "He must have been trying to get this when he met his end," she said.

Greyor moved the skeleton aside to gain a better look, in case Eraim had missed anything, and an object fell free from the bones. A golden key lay on the floor, much larger than the key Eraim held.

"Another one…" Greyor shook his head. "We'll have a hundred keys and no locks before we're done."

Eraim gave a wry smile. "I do not think it will be as bad as that." She bit her lip. "That is an odd-looking key."

Greyor scooped it up. At the end were four prongs, each with its own unique design. He gazed back at the skeleton. "I wonder why nobody found this."

"If I had to venture a guess," Eraim eyed the skull, "I'd say he swallowed it."

Impressive, considering the key's size. Perhaps the dwarf died choking on it.

Eraim looked from the bones to the key she held. "The former occupant was trying to get this for a reason."

"Eraim!" said Kiryanna from outside the door. "Your light,

please!"

Eraim turned to the hallway, and the bauble hastened to the marteese. Kiryanna glanced left and right, her eyes widening, and the light followed as she stepped into the room and slammed the door shut, putting her back against it.

"Lizards!"

Strange. Kiryanna had never struck Greyor as one easily rattled. She had faced Uustaag, for Meldar's sake!

"At least fifty of them," the marteese added, "coming from both directions."

Admittedly, that would be a challenge. But Greyor was confident they would claim victory. He had Clanghorr, and Eraim was with them.

"I dislike that look." Eraim stared at Greyor. "Fighting that many by ourselves is not wise."

"I agree," said Kiryanna. "I can handle half a dozen, and Clanghorr and Mithkahr might get a dozen each. But after that, we will take injuries. Perhaps get separated."

Not a bad assessment. But she was wrong about Clanghorr. Two dozen could easily be achieved.

There was a thump on the door, followed by another, and another. Soon, it was as if someone were beating a drum, and the bruskiin door shuddered. Kiryanna dragged a stone chair to barricade the entrance.

Greyor sighed. Why not fight? They had healing herbs if any of them took injuries.

Eraim inspected the nearby wall, sliding her hand along its surface. "Ha!" she said, and fit the key into a tiny hole. As she turned it, the wall on her right opened up to a tunnel. "Inside! Quickly!"

Kiryanna rushed through the opening before Greyor could lead the way—curse the marteese and her speed! As he entered behind the half-elf, the bauble flew past. Greyor then detected the sliding of stone as the door closed behind Eraim. She still held the key.

The hallway was five feet wide and six feet high, so it presented none of them with any difficulties. It veered left and right, with occasional staircases taking them deeper, and after two hundred yards, they reached a dead end. A small keyhole was obvious in the wall to the side, and Eraim inserted the same key and gave it a turn. A secret door opened ahead.

They entered a hall running left and right. It was thirty feet to the opposite wall, and to the left, it traveled a bit farther before splitting into smaller corridors to its sides. Not far to the right, impressive doors barred the way. They appeared to be made of gold, each standing fifteen feet high and nearly as wide, with beveled edges and a score of depressions that must have once held valuable gems at various heights. On the left door was carved a pair of crossed pickaxes, with pick heads on either end of their shafts. The other door depicted a battleaxe, its haft ending in a spike.

Greyor gasped, his boots seemingly stuck to the floor while Kiryanna approached the doors. Eraim glanced back down the secret corridor once more before the panel slid shut.

"Greyor," said Kiryanna. "Come look at this."

He forced his legs into action. Was it the grandeur of the doors that held him in wonder? The etching of the battleaxe? He looked at what had caught the marteese's eye. Three feet from the floor on either side of the seam between the doors were two keyholes, and a narrow track in the shape of a circle connected all four. Scratches marred the area around the holes, as if someone had failed in several attempts to pick the exquisite lock. Higher up, additional scratches were evident, as if powerful claws had tried to gain access. But why would Maak Maak try to break through and not just tunnel around? As Greyor narrowed his eyes, he realized the scratches were smaller than Maak Maak's claws. Something else had caused them.

The floor shook. It wasn't a quake from below; it seemed to come from the wall opposite the doors.

"Use the key!" Eraim said with urgency.

Greyor inserted the four-pronged key. It didn't turn.

"You have it in wrong," Kiryanna insisted.

He pulled the key and rotated it once to the right before attempting again.

Nothing.

"Try again!" Eraim yelled, her wide eyes glancing back as another tremor shook the far wall, where a crack appeared from floor to ceiling.

Greyor removed the key and started to spin it once again to the right. But a thought occurred: that's what it *wanted* him to do. He rotated it twice to the left and inserted it. The key turned! And as it did so, the doors swung inward on their own, leaving the key in Greyor's hand.

A domed room lay beyond, fifty feet in diameter and just as high in the middle. The floor was silver and the walls bronze, and at twenty-foot intervals around its circumference, lamps issuing blue flames hung to within eight feet of the floor, strangely providing normal lighting.

"Urnumil…" Greyor said in awe as he stepped forward.

As soon as they entered, the doors began swinging shut, but Greyor paid them no heed. There was then a crash, and before the doors touched, a blast of heat raced across his back, making him turn at last. The golden doors were perfectly smooth on this side. A powerful blow struck them, but they held with barely a rattle.

Eraim shook her head, her mouth hanging open. "Dragon!"

Another thud struggled to move the doors. Then silence.

Greyor turned to Eraim. "There aren't any dragons."

"It sure looked like a dragon," said Kiryanna, gripping her golden sword in both hands while eyeing the doors.

"Probably Maak Maak's baby," Greyor suggested. "How many heads?"

"I saw only one," Eraim replied. "I do not believe it was Maak Maak's offspring." Mithkahr held a red glow, but it faded while she spoke. She inhaled deeply and blew it out.

Greyor turned back to the room. "Whatever it was, it's gone."

Kiryanna moved next to him, her sword now lowered. But her

eyes remained fixed on the golden doors.

"All right!" Eraim said to no one, as if having a quiet argument with an invisible person. She faced Greyor. "What did you say when we entered?"

Greyor frowned. He scanned the room, spying the blue flames burning atop glass globes within iron frames, and it came to him. "Urnumil. The oil in the lamps." He moved closer to one, though it was too high to be reached. "I read about it in…" He shook his head. He wasn't ready to share information about the mysterious box in his house. "It doesn't matter. It's an ancient oil that burns blue, but never does the flame consume it." He shrugged. "I guess it's been burning since the days my kin roamed these halls."

Eraim cocked her head to the side and peered at the fire. "Interesting."

Greyor glanced about the chamber as he stepped farther in. Though the floor appeared to be made of silver, he was positive it was something stronger. Probably the same with the bronze walls. That was surely the reason the room remained undisturbed by Maak Maak.

Several dwarves suddenly occupied the far end of the chamber, and Greyor approached. Four dwarves were to either side of a kneeling dwarf, and a tenth dwarf stood before the latter with a raised hand.

"Do you swear to defend Lornibur and its inhabitants with your last breath?" the dwarf with the raised hand asked.

"I so swear," the kneeling dwarf responded.

It felt to Greyor as if he had spoken the words himself.

"By the will of Meldar and the power of Clanghorr," said the dwarf who spoke first, "you shall serve as King's Champion, Hero of Lornibur, for no less than two hundred years, lest death claim you."

The kneeling dwarf was Balmorak. The warrior held Clanghorr's spike against the floor, and the battleaxe's runes were aglow.

"Being firstborn of Dornux, and by the resolution of Clanghorr, this bond is yours by right," the first dwarf continued, "and shall pass to your firstborn afterward, lest death claims them or Clanghorr finds them unworthy." The dwarf stepped aside to reveal a silver pedestal standing three feet high and supporting a thick tablet of granite. "Now place your name among the others."

Balmorak stood and approached the pedestal. Raising Clanghorr, he placed the spike onto the stone, and there was a flash of light. He lowered the weapon to his side.

The dwarves disappeared. Greyor was before the pedestal, and Eraim was speaking to him.

"It is rude to ignore us and walk away!"

"Sorry." Greyor shook his head to clear it.

Eraim said something more, but his attention fell to the tablet. Over fifty names he didn't recognize were etched onto it. The final two were Dornux and Balmorak.

"You are doing it again!" Eraim said with emphasis. "A monster has us trapped in here..."

He heard no more while he stared at the last two names. Lifting Clanghorr, he moved the spike to the spot below Balmorak's, and there was a flash of light. In that moment, several dwarfish faces sped through Greyor's mind, none of them remaining long enough for a clear picture except for the final one: Balmorak.

The room was gone. Eraim and Kiryanna were gone. Greyor stood two hundred yards from a mountain, where hundreds of dwarves burrowed into rising cliffs with pickaxes and shovels while others hauled away stone and dirt in wheelbarrows. Rough openings existed, and the sound of additional digging was evident from within each. Greyor took in the surrounding mountains. They were familiar. It was home.

"Balmorak," said a voice behind Greyor.

He turned to see a pair of dwarves making their way across the rugged terrain. The lead figure was Balmorak.

"You can't leave!" the trailing dwarf insisted. "Not now. Not with the entire clan in disarray. We need you. We need Clanghorr. We need our Champion!"

"I am Champion no longer," mumbled Balmorak. "My duty was to Lornibur, and the city is no more."

"But…"

Balmorak sighed. "It is for the best. I failed. And I will not have that failure brand my family forever. You shall tell them you escaped alone. That I didn't make it out."

"What about Clanghorr?" the other dwarf asked.

Balmorak shook his head. "The spirit of Clanghorr no longer answers to me. It has been silenced."

The other dwarf wrinkled his forehead. "But your son, Revain. What about his birthright?"

"No." Balmorak's face was stone. "For my family to have a normal life, Clanghorr and I must vanish. They'll never believe me dead if you return with the weapon."

"I'll go with you!"

Balmorak shook his head. "Sorry, but you cannot. You are the only one who can convince them I perished. You have been a good friend, Dowar. Please do this for me. For my family."

Dowar! Assuredly the author of several of the pages in Greyor's small room; the warrior who fought against Velgaad and the king's soldiers with Balmorak and Brunux

"Where will you go?" Dowar asked.

Balmorak looked at the evening sky. "I don't know. I have never been this far from Lornibur." He turned west. "But I'll find a path."

The mountains shifted. Greyor stood on a familiar road. He was in the Stone Eagle Mountains, and Balmorak followed the wide path toward Rornibur, the city less than half the size as Greyor knew it. The ex-Champion was nearly unrecognizable. Balmorak's beard was trimmed to almost nothing, falling only inches below the chin, and graying made him seem over two-hundred years in age. But somehow, Greyor realized Balmorak to be only a couple of decades removed from his conversation with Dowar in Varlimor. He couldn't be more than a hundred eighty years old. Maybe younger.

The scene changed. Balmorak sat alone in a personal dwelling, staring at Clanghorr by the light of the hearth.

"You've not spoken in years, my friend," he said, his eyes watering. "Perhaps you'll never speak again."

He entered the bedroom. In the corner was a closet, and he opened it to reveal a suit of armor, a few hanging cloaks, and a stone chest affixed to the floor. Balmorak unlocked the trunk and lifted the lid. A bundle of clothing bearing insignias of a star formed by intersecting pickaxes filled the space. He removed the clothing and wedged a metal bar into the seam of the trunk's bottom. With some effort, he lifted the slab to uncover a recess—it had been excavated recently. Balmorak placed Clanghorr upon the dirt and allowed the slab to fall back into place. After putting new sets of clothing into the chest, ones lacking the star, he closed the lid and locked it.

Balmorak carried the Lornibur garments to the hearth and tossed them into the fire, one piece at a time.

Another scene flashed before Greyor's eyes, showing Balmorak walking about Rornibur, his identity either unknown or forgotten by its citizens. Time sped up as he grew older, married, and bore a single child before passing from old age. That child then aged, married, and bore other children. And so on. Just as in Morimont, the housing passed from family member to family member, and Greyor saw a familiar face at last: a young Poluran snooping through the closet. Poluran discovered the false bottom and pulled Clanghorr from its grave.

The vision shifted yet again, and Greyor was in a different city. From the excavations, he knew it to be the earlier version of Morimont. Dowar was explaining Balmorak's death to a female dwarf and her three sons. They wept.

The scene sped up, as it had in Rornibur, and Greyor watched the eldest son age, marry, procreate, and pass on. It happened repeatedly until Greyor's grandfather appeared, then his father, and finally himself. A whisper echoed.

The lineage of Clanghorr is restored...

Had Clanghorr spoken the words?

"Greyor!" shouted Eraim.

He looked at the elf. Kiryanna stood next to her within the domed room of Lornibur, and the two seemed worried.

"What is going on with you?" Kiryanna demanded. "You have been staring at nothing, and not for the first time."

Greyor eyed the stone tablet before him. Beneath Balmorak's name was his own.

Eraim followed his gaze, and she ran her fingers over the newest etching. "What does this mean?"

"I…" Greyor hesitated, unsure. "I think Clanghorr has awakened." He looked at Eraim. "I might be the Champion of Lornibur."

CHAPTER 13
TRAIL OF REPTILES

Ameilistari gaped at the corridor before her. Or rather, the lack of a corridor. It had collapsed, taking her companions with it. Except for Nidor and Tewlon. After Tewlon pulled her and her cousin back from the falling debris, she summoned a magical light to reveal the damage, and she and Nidor stood dumbfounded. Her father, Aunt Kiryanna, Uncle Baylun, Eraim, Lorylla, Greyor… all gone. Tears welled up in her eyes.

Tewlon was the only one without an expression of disbelief. The elf's brow furrowed as he stared at nothing and nodded to no one. He then beckoned Ameilistari and Nidor to follow, and started down the hallway, back the way they had come.

"No!" Ameilistari yelled.

She cringed, peering at the cave-in. Her outburst caused no additional collapse. Had she been outside Ironside Keep in the wintertime, her shout might have had a profoundly different effect. She found it great fun to make loud noises and watch snow tumble down the high slopes. Soldiers were never appreciative when the rare mishap buried one of the stronghold's turrets, especially after the hours necessary to clear the area with shovels. Ameilistari was pretty sure snow would never have touched the keep were it not for her games.

"We can't leave them," Nidor said. "We have to dig."

Her cousin understood. Perhaps Tewlon and Eraim weren't great friends after all, if the elf was willing to abandon her.

Tewlon shook his head and pointed down the hallway in the direction he wished to go.

"Look." Ameilistari planted her feet firmly on the stone floor. "We know you can speak. I know not why you and Eraim think it funny to fool the others in such a way, but we heard you talking before everyone arrived at the meeting in Ironside."

Tewlon sighed. After a moment of thought, he spoke several words in his own language. His voice was in contrast to his physique, like a boy during puberty, not yet a man.

"I understand *some* Elfish," Ameilistari said. "But reading it is much easier than speaking it. I'm not quite there."

"I know a bit." Nidor looked from Tewlon to Ameilistari. "Father has been teaching me." He turned back to Tewlon. "He said something about no hope, and finding the mines."

Tewlon shook his head, obviously disappointed with the translation.

"Wait a moment." Ameilistari narrowed her eyes at the elf. "If you understand what we're saying, then you surely speak Common."

Again, Tewlon paused. After another sigh, he spoke in the Common tongue. "There's no hope in digging. If you wish to find the others, we must return to the mines. Maak Maak made its traps to drop prey into lower chambers. The monster didn't desire to crush its food beneath tons of rock, so there's a good chance they're alive."

Elation invaded as Tewlon's words gave Ameilistari hope. But suspicion crept in, and she regarded the elf.

"You don't speak like an elf."

Nidor turned to her with a questioning expression.

"Elves are more proper when using the Common language," she explained. "He talks like a human."

"Is there really time for this?" asked Nidor. "If he's right, we must get moving."

Ameilistari pursed her lips. "Of course. You're right." She looked at Tewlon. "What do you suggest?"

"Follow me," the elf said.

Tewlon led them back toward the royal bedroom, and Ameilistari's light followed. Upon reaching the secret panel, the elf gazed at the dead end as his shoulders slumped. The bedpost had opened it from the other side; surely there was a mechanism nearby.

"Well?" Ameilistari stared at the elf. "Do the elf thing. I'm sure there's a way to open the door."

Tewlon sighed. "I have never been good at such things."

"No?" Ameilistari raised an eyebrow. "No good at finding that which is hidden? You carry no bow? Are you sure you're an elf?"

"Ameilistari," Nidor said. "Can't you open it?"

She released a calming breath. Was expecting Tewlon to be more elf-like unfair? In truth, she had only known maybe a dozen elves in her lifetime, and although they seemed to share certain traits and skills, perhaps they were more different from one another than she believed. Tewlon was wrought in muscle, after all, and she had never heard of that attribute in his kind. In the end, he was trying to help, and he appeared to have some knowledge of the situation. That was surely why Eraim had brought him along.

Ameilistari eyed the stone wall before them, where she knew the door to exist. "Do either of you remember which way the door slid?"

"To the right," Nidor immediately replied. "No! Left."

Ameilistari sighed. "Which is it?"

"It was to the right from the other side," answered Nidor. "So it'll be left from this side."

She nodded and focused, reaching with her mind to the surrounding energies—there was surprisingly more than she expected. Drawing the magic to her, Ameilistari put her hands together with palms out and thrust an invisible force into the seam along the corner, like a pry bar. Little by little, waves of magic penetrated the crack. She then struggled to move her hands apart, and the wall slowly began to slide—it was like trying to move boulders.

Tewlon didn't wait for her to complete the spell. As soon as there was room, he placed his fingers into the opening and pushed. Together, they opened the door the rest of the way.

"Go!" Tewlon said through clenched teeth.

Nidor hurried into the bedchamber. Ameilistari maintained her spell, not wanting to risk the elf being crushed, and walked at a slow pace while his face turned two shades of red. Once through, Tewlon followed, and she released the energy. The door slammed shut. She was sure Tewlon held an air of annoyance toward her while he panted.

Nidor immediately went to the bedroom door.

"Wait!" Ameilistari halted her cousin. "We need a plan."

"A plan?" Nidor frowned. "How do we make a plan when we don't know where they are?"

"We must be ready in case lizards come," she explained.

Nidor needed to take such things into consideration if he wished to rise through the ranks of the Philen military. Or perhaps, accept a position at Ironside Keep.

"Your fire seemed to do the trick with Maak Maak," Nidor pointed out. "Just do that again."

Ameilistari felt her chin lift with the reminder of the power she unleashed.

"It was injured," Tewlon said between breaths.

"What?" Ameilistari turned to the elf.

"I'm just saying, it was injured by Clanghorr and Torrac. Do not be overly confident. And don't forget to account for the whereabouts of your companions."

Ameilistari huffed. Of course he pointed out that part. But Uncle Baylun escaped with no permanent damage, and she learned a valuable lesson. Perhaps Tewlon knew nothing of strategy. She had been training to lead others for over a year now.

"That's why we need a plan," she said. "If an overwhelming number of lizards approach, that would be a good time to stay clear."

Tewlon appeared to struggle with a response. "Do you not have magic other than devastating fire?"

"Of course," she retorted. "I have lots of spells. What kind of question is that?"

He shook his head. "What about something to slow them? Maybe something with… tiny forks of lightning?"

The elf's words triggered a memory. Selanna had taught her a stunning spell, like miniature bolts of lightning launched from her fingertips. Ameilistari could immobilize ten lizards at once without worry of bringing harm to her companions. Still, she wasn't about to be told how to use magic by an elf that didn't even use a bow.

"I shall think of something," she said.

Tewlon actually rolled his eyes. Ameilistari was unaccustomed to being treated in such a way. It was annoying.

"Okay," said Nidor. "If there's too many," he looked at Ameilistari, "you do… whatever you're going to do. If you wish to use fire, or anything else that might cause us harm, tell us to clear out."

That was better. Tewlon could learn a lot from Nidor on how to address a mage.

Nidor turned to the elf. "And you and I will do the rest."

Tewlon held a wry smile. "I'll go first," he said, and walked past Nidor.

The elf cracked open the bedroom door and peeked into the hallway. After a moment, he opened it farther and exited, waving for Ameilistari and Nidor to follow.

No one spoke while they progressed. Upon reaching the chamber where Maak Maak had been sleeping, Ameilistari found it hard to breathe as the situation fully struck her. Lornibur was a massive network of tunnels and rooms—they'd have to consider themselves lucky to find the others. She pushed away the fear with a slow exhale. A leader needed a clear head to perform properly.

They stepped through the arch on the left and into the throne room. The broken egg still adorned the granite chair, like some kind of nest, and the corpses of Maak Maak and its cohorts littered the floor. The smaller archways remained dark.

Tewlon crept along the wall and peered through the first arch. Apparently unsatisfied, he moved to the next one, and the next one.

"What are you looking for?" Ameilistari whispered.

"A way downward," the elf whispered back.

That made sense.

"Should we spread out?" Nidor asked quietly. "I see pretty well in the dark."

Tewlon shook his head without looking back, and he passed another archway. Upon reaching the next opening, he stopped.

"Several lizards entered through this one," he said, and he started to step through.

"Wait!" Ameilistari halted the elf. "Should we not avoid that tunnel?"

Tewlon sighed. "According to Eraim, the lizards were on a lower level the last time she was here." He gazed into the adjoining corridor. "I'm hoping this leads closer to their lair."

"You *want* to go closer?" asked Nidor.

"I don't plan on walking *into* their lair." Tewlon turned to face them both. "Like I said, the traps are designed to drop prey into areas where Maak Maak and its friends can feed. So we have a better chance of finding your parents if we follow the lizards."

Okay, Tewlon wasn't wrong. But he should have put it that way in the first place. He needed to improve his communication skills.

They moved along the corridor for twenty yards before a branch revealed a descending stairwell. Tewlon followed the steps fifteen feet to a landing, which connected to another flight of steps descending to the left. As yet another set of stairs became evident, a piece of the ceiling dropped onto Tewlon. But it wasn't part of the ceiling. It was a five-foot lizard that had matched the color of the stone too well.

Tewlon obviously didn't detect the creature until it was upon him, and he raised his arm at the last second. The reptile bit his forearm, and the elf slammed its body into the wall. Nidor moved to assist, but Tewlon thrust his sword through the lizard's neck, and it fell to the floor, wriggling. As Nidor's weapon readied to strike, Tewlon's blade flashed back across, decapitating the monster.

"Blasted creatures!" the elf hissed, holding his wounded arm close. He then scanned the walls and ceiling ahead.

"I know Eraim said they could blend with their surroundings." Nidor stared at the corpse. "But that was…"

"Yes." Tewlon appeared agitated. "We'll have to move slower and pay better attention."

Ameilistari could have told him that. "How is your arm?"

"It hurts." His reply held a touch of sarcasm. "I don't suppose either of you knows how to apply healing herbs?"

Ameilistari didn't. She looked at her cousin.

"Father has shown me." Nidor pulled an herb from one of his pouches.

Tewlon frowned at the plant. "Silver eye? Do you know how to work with Vermallon dusk?"

Nidor shook his head. "We have nothing like that in Philen. Can you teach me?"

Tewlon sighed. "I've never been very good with herbs."

"You can't properly apply healing herbs either?" asked Ameilistari. She thought all elves held at least a little knowledge of such things. It was clear why he traveled with Eraim—she could do anything.

Tewlon gave her a level gaze, offering no response.

"Silver eye is fairly abundant in Philen," Nidor said, "and easy to use."

He tore the small leaves into smaller portions, and put them in his mouth a moment before mashing them in his palm.

Disgusting! Even Tewlon seemed leery about the process. Still, the elf presented his arm after removing it from his leather sleeve. The bite marks didn't look too big, but they pressed deep into the muscular forearm, and blood flowed.

"Can you clean the wound?" Nidor asked Ameilistari.

A repulsive task! But if she wished to be an adventurer, it was something she needed to get used to.

Ameilistari pulled a cloth from her pack, one of four she brought in anticipation of drying sweat from her brow, and blotted the wound. Nidor then packed the saliva-herbs over the holes before taking the cloth and wrapping it around the elf's forearm. She would have thought a clean bandage was called for, but Tewlon didn't object.

Upon completion of the task, Tewlon returned to the lead, and they continued downward at a much slower pace while eyeing their surroundings.

Ameilistari estimated they descended eighty feet when the stairway ended. Before them was a twenty-foot-wide passageway moving from left to right, and the grand archways with hammers and anvils in bas-relief returned, as did the rail running along the corridor's middle. Tewlon headed left, and they traveled a short distance when he stopped, his ear cocked to the side.

"More lizards," he said, looking back the way they had come.

Ameilistari turned, and Nidor stood before her with his sword ready. Tewlon joined her cousin. At first, there was nothing. But then the patter of several feet reached Ameilistari's ears. Moments later, a group of lizards approached, not bothering to blend like the one on the stairs. Perhaps their coloring couldn't keep up with their hastened advance.

Ameilistari pulled in magical energy, focusing on the reptiles. After a couple of arcane words, she threw forward her hands, fingers wide, and tiny bolts of lightning flew past her companions. Upon striking the lizards, the bolts raced around their bodies, and ten of the creatures spasmed where they stood, unable to move any farther.

Three reptiles continued on their path, and Nidor struck one while Tewlon decapitated another. The third lizard lunged at Tewlon while Nidor evaded the teeth of the one he faced. The elf steered aside the reptile with a kick and followed with a deep gash across its chest. Nidor danced back from another attack before adding a second wound to the six-foot monster before him. As the creature reeled, he thrust his blade, and the lizard ceased to move.

The other lizards continued to convulse down the corridor, unable to overcome the energy coursing around them.

"It won't last much longer," Ameilistari warned her companions.

"Let's go!" Tewlon said, and he ran past the stunned reptiles.

Ameilistari and Nidor matched the elf's pace, and soon several hallways branched to either side, all of them ten feet wide and none of them bearing a rail. Tewlon bolted into the third one on the right. They then passed three archways, and Tewlon turned into a fourth, entering a chamber with a pair of stone tables. Ancient mining tools lay scattered among a couple of tall piles of rocks and debris.

"Help me with a table," he said to Nidor.

The two moved to one side of a table and pushed. Veins bulged from their necks as the heavy piece of furniture slid across the flagstones, and they didn't relent until reaching the archway. They then lifted their end, standing the table up to prevent entry. Although Tewlon was obviously strong, Ameilistari was reminded of how much Nidor had grown since the last time she saw him. She briefly wondered if he would get as large as Uncle Baylun.

Nidor and Tewlon panted while they leaned against the barricade and slid into sitting positions, almost in unison.

"We'll rest here a while," Tewlon said between breaths.

Ameilistari nodded. "I agree." She should have said it first. It was the leader's place to make those decisions, and she was trained to do so. "And we should have something to eat," she added, in case Tewlon thought the same thing.

"The others had all the food," the elf said with a wry smile.

Ameilistari smirked. "I have my rations."

She pulled her pack and removed enough flatbread for her warriors to have two slices each. She kept one for herself. That left six more in her pouch, as well as a few handfuls of dried fruit. Hopefully, she and her companions found the others before the food was gone. With no better accommodations available, she sat next to Nidor and nibbled on her bread.

Chapter 14

Remains

Baylun grabbed hold of Romik's hook as the ground shook beneath him, but he was too heavy for his brother to lift. The floor then crumbled, and he fell.

The last Baylun saw of his son was Tewlon pulling Nidor and Ameilistari from the crashing debris. He didn't see whether the children escaped unscathed, however, as something rammed into his side. It was Lorylla, and her momentum knocked Baylun into the drop-off on the left. His grip on Romik's hook pulled his brother along.

The Maak Maak tunnel fell a short distance before Baylun struck stone. The pit then angled, and he slid uncontrollably another thirty feet when it changed directions and became steeper. A hand then grabbed his armor, and Romik's hook jerked away. As Baylun's vision adjusted to the darkness, he saw his brother grasping his collar and using the hooks to dig into the shaft in an attempt to slow their descent. Higher up, Lorylla glided down the wall on her boots while pulling on Romik's wooden arm, and scores of stones pursued, large and small.

The tunnel shifted again, plummeting straight down, and as a stone floor approached at an alarming rate, Baylun jerked to a halt within a room. Romik's lower body hovered above him, halfway in and halfway out of the tunnel—the hooks must have snagged something. As rocks rained down, Baylun turned away to protect his face.

Romik's grip failed, and the floor rushed to meet Baylun. Reflexes from years of experience allowed him to roll into a landing without losing hold of Torrac, but he didn't escape harm, and the unforgiving flagstones and showering rocks bruised his body. A thud sounded behind him, and his brother released a grunt, having fallen as well.

After the assault of stones subsided, Baylun looked back. Romik lay not far away, facing the hole in the ceiling but unmoving. Lorylla stood nearby, her exposed skin showing various scratches and her gray leather marred along the arms and legs, no doubt from scraping the walls of the descending tunnel. She appeared to have escaped any serious injuries, and her bow was intact and ready with an arrow nocked.

Baylun checked on Romik. A crack lined the middle of the "forearm" section of his wooden arm, but the steel running along the side had apparently kept the appendage from snapping. Romik's scalp bled, and scratches marked his face. He was otherwise intact.

Reaching into his pouch, Baylun withdrew two silver eye herbs and began tearing the leaves into small pieces. After mixing them with a bit of saliva, he applied them to the head wound—a gash only an inch long, but producing a lot of blood. He then grabbed a strip of cloth and pressed it tightly over the cut.

"Baylun," Lorylla whispered.

He looked up, noticing the room for the first time. It was impossible to determine its original intent, for decades—possibly centuries—of rubble covered the floor, some atop and some below skeletal remains. Another Maak Maak tunnel exited to the right, and to the left, Lorylla aimed her bow at no less than a dozen creatures before an archway. Their skinny bodies were no taller than Greyor, and they wore filthy rags. Some sniffed the air while a few crept closer, holding long, narrow pieces of metal as if they were spears.

There was no time for fighting; Baylun's brother needed care. Lifting Torrac, Baylun stood tall and released a battle roar. The little creatures retreated through the arch, a few of them dropping their weapons in the process, and the shuffling of feet quickly faded. The room silenced.

"Those must be the mine dwellers Greyor referred to," said Lorylla.

A reasonable conclusion.

"We must try not to harm them," the elf added.

"So long as they don't interfere with me mending my brother," grumbled Baylun, stooping to apply pressure to the wound.

"You take care of your brother," she said. "I will keep watch." She approached the arch.

Baylun pulled another strip of cloth from his pouch and tied it around Romik's head to hold the bandage in place. Unfortunately, he couldn't see if his brother was pale, not even with his superior vision in darkness, so he grabbed a torch from his pack and worked his flint and steel, sparking it to life. Romik had color. All the same, Baylun placed his brother's head on his lap to allow for a more comfortable rest.

He glanced at Lorylla. The gray elf remained silent, focused on her task. "Why did you push me into the drop-off?" he asked.

She glanced his way and returned her attention to the exit. "A very large boulder was about to crush you."

"Oh." He turned back to Romik. "Thank you."

After what felt like half an hour, the thought of the mine dwellers returning with larger numbers entered Baylun's mind. They needed to get moving. With a sigh, he stirred his brother.

Romik's eyes opened, and he slowly sat up. "What happened?" He raised his hand to his bandage. "My head hurts."

"We fell," Baylun replied.

"Using your hooks to slow your descent was wise," commented Lorylla as she joined them. "Otherwise, the fall might have proven much worse for the both of you."

Baylun glanced at the elf. Though her tone made her sound arrogant, her expression suggested she only stated facts. He turned to his brother. "Thanks for that."

Romik nodded, wincing as he did so.

"Take whatever time you need," Baylun told his brother.

Romik's eyes opened wide, and he searched the room. "Stari?"

"We got separated," Baylun said. "But I saw Tewlon pull her and Nidor away from the collapsing ceiling. I'm sure they're safe."

Romik pushed himself to his feet. "I'm ready now." As Baylun stood, he added, "I'll not rest while her fate lies with an elf that can't talk." With a sigh, he asked, "What about Kiryanna?"

"She was with Greyor and Eraim," said Lorylla. "The last I saw."

Romik gave Baylun a nod. "Then she's in the best of hands, wouldn't you say?"

Baylun realized his brother meant for them to concentrate on finding the children. Were Kiryanna not a skilled warrior, the decision might have torn him in two, and her being with Eraim and Greyor made her situation even less dire. Baylun nodded.

"Good." Romik turned to Lorylla. "Any idea in what direction we fell?"

"The shafts dropped us approximately one hundred feet," she replied without thought. "And the angle carried us at least a hundred feet in the direction we were trying to proceed before the collapse."

"So..." Romik scrunched his brow, "farther away from our children?"

"That is correct," the elf answered.

Romik looked at Baylun. "That's a start. We'll need to head upward at every opportunity."

Romik's expression seemed to imply Baylun would lead the way. But he had no idea which direction they should go. If only there were tracks to follow. He headed through the archway, and Romik and Lorylla followed.

The adjoining hallway was thirty feet wide and moved from left to right. Grand pillars in the middle held up the high ceiling at twenty-yard intervals, and a single rail ran the length of the passage to either side. Baylun's torchlight sparkled off gemstones near the top of each column, sapphires on those to the right and rubies to the left. The gems were clearly valuable. Were the situation not so grim, he might have taken a moment to marvel at the splendor of it all.

Baylun turned right. Though he didn't know if it was the correct way, Kiryanna had always been partial to sapphires. Hopefully the path of blue stones brought some luck. Romik trailed after Baylun, and Lorylla guarded the rear with her bow ready.

A couple of archways lined the walls to either side, but glances told Baylun they opened into dead-end rooms. He continued, and the arches fell behind, replaced by smooth walls. There was then a lone arch on the left with a tunnel extending into darkness. Baylun considered turning, but with his lack of knowledge of the place, it was best to proceed.

Sixty yards later, smaller archways appeared on either side. Bas-relief carvings atop the openings didn't depict hammers and anvils, but mine carts, picks, or other various shapes, including wavy lines above one and a mushroom over another. Before one of the support pillars, a small area of discoloration stained the floor—old blood. A couple more blemishes marred the flagstones farther on, larger than the first, and one showed streaks, as if someone had dragged a corpse along the corridor. The trail lightened as it continued, fading altogether after twenty paces. Farther still, the skeleton of a lizard lay atop a fourth dried pool. Were all the stains from dead lizards?

"We should split and check the archways," suggested Romik. "So we miss nothing."

"Don't enter any rooms," Baylun said, handing Romik the torch. "Not by yourself."

"Hey." Romik winked. "*I'm* the big brother."

Baylun couldn't resist a chuckle.

Lorylla's expression was unchanged.

Romik moved to the left side of the pillars, placing the torch within the hooks of his false arm. Lorylla remained in the middle of the corridor with an arrow ready.

The first archway Baylun reached displayed an image of a pick. A branch of the rail system entered the large chamber beyond, where piles of rubble littered the floor. Broken tools and mine carts in various states of ruin lay about, some partially buried by debris.

"Nothing," he said loudly enough for Romik to hear.

"I believe this is a… mushroom garden," Romik called back. "Biggest mushrooms I've ever seen."

"Dwarves call them bruskiin," Lorylla said. "They use them like we use wood."

Romik glanced at the elf. "Huh." And he moved on.

The next arch for Baylun displayed a mine cart, and a rail entered it as well. Inside were ancient carts, but no exits or stairs.

"Nothing," he said to Romik.

Baylun reached the lizard skeleton and stooped to inspect the bones. Tool marks marred the ribs and spine. The skull was untouched.

"It was picked clean," he said as Lorylla stopped to observe.

"Eraim once said the mine dwellers wear lizard skins as armor," she mentioned as Romik joined them.

Baylun nodded. "Makes sense." He turned to his companions. "But their skills are lacking."

"So are the Bomahni when they skin and treat leather," Romik said, referring to the Pavish barbarian tribe where their cousin Desser lived. "But they're savages."

Baylun no longer thought of Desser's tribe as savages. But of course, he saw their cousin more often than his brother did. Were the mine dwellers similar to barbarians of the outside world? At the moment, it didn't matter. Baylun needed to find Nidor, and they still lacked a way to ascend.

"Let's move on," suggested Romik, as if reading Baylun's mind.

He nodded, and they continued.

A pair of wavy lines topped the next arch. As Baylun peered inside, he heard rushing water, but the room was too deep to see the far end. "I'm not sure," he said hesitantly.

Lorylla was then behind him, gazing over his shoulder—he'd never get used to the elf's height. She narrowed her eyes.

"Wait here," she said.

Baylun opened his mouth to object, but she pushed past him and sprinted into the darkness. Eraim would never run into an unknown room! A moment later, Lorylla returned.

"Just a river, lots of destroyed buckets, and stone basins filled with old stale water."

"Nothing!" Baylun called to his brother.

He moved to the next archway, his frustrations growing—where were the blasted stairs? The symbol above the entryway was a square, and within the room beyond were several long tables of stone, as well as the remains of more lizards that had been picked clean. Also scattered were what appeared to be armored skeletons of dwarves.

"Romik," Baylun said in a quieter tone. He wasn't sure why, but he didn't wish to speak too loudly, as if someone might overhear him. "Bring the torch."

Romik and Lorylla arrived, and Baylun took the torch from his brother and entered. It was a dining chamber. Rows of tables filled the space, with benches to seat at least fifty, and a dark archway was in the opposite wall. The armor on the skeletons appeared ancient, as did several shields scattered about, and a few stray helmets contained skulls.

The tables disappeared. Baylun was suddenly back in the throne room, and Balmorak stood in the center, speaking to Mattasun. It was the very scene Baylun saw before, where the dwarf warned of King Velgaad's desire to bring the man harm, but this vision took over where the last one left off, and Mattasun exited the chamber. Baylun knew not why, but he was compelled to follow.

Mattasun traversed the tunnels with confidence, turning left, right, and descending a staircase without the slightest hesitation. He was familiar with his surroundings. He then walked along a wide corridor with blue and red gems atop central pillars, just like the one Baylun currently roamed. Mattasun followed the rubies.

After passing several archways, a crash sounded behind Mattasun, like a cave-in, and he spun. The corridor was empty. But then a dozen dwarves approached with malice in their eyes. They held axes, hammers, spears, and swords. Mattasun turned back to see a dozen more dwarves ahead, as well as a large krukari dressed in black plate armor. If not for the armor, Baylun was sure the warrior would have exhibited as much muscle as Vecnor. A pair of fangs protruded from the krukari's lower jaw while he glared, and strapped to his back was the handle of what was surely a massive sword.

"Surrender Torrac, and you shall live," said the krukari in a rumbling voice.

Mattasun pulled his axe with a wide swing, causing several dwarves to flinch. "How can you side with this *creature*?" he demanded of the dwarves. "I am Mattasun, dwarf-friend and bearer of Torrac. By birthright and oath, I am a servant of Lornibur!"

"Never liked a human walking our halls," one dwarf hissed.

Mattasun pointed his weapon at the krukari. "Enough to take up with this half-hobgoblin? The warlord of Helmland?"

Baylun gasped. The krukari was much younger, and his eyes were brown, but it was Uustaag. The Ancient Enemy of the North wasn't nearly as tall as when Baylun faced him in Lormin Dmurr, but it was him.

"Take the weapon!" barked Uustaag.

The dwarves charged.

Mattasun ducked through the nearest archway and into a dining chamber—the one Baylun and his companions had entered. Unlike the room Baylun discovered, torches illuminated the tables and benches, the furniture appearing as if its construction was recent. As Mattasun reached the center of the room, he turned, throwing his battleaxe at the entrance. The runes glowed white as the weapon spun, picking up speed and slicing through the first three dwarves in pursuit. The stout warriors fell while their comrades sped past them. Mattasun then held out his hand, and Torrac returned! He threw it again, dropping two more dwarves, and the battleaxe again flew to him, landing perfectly within his grasp as the enemy arrived.

Dancing back, Mattasun dodged a hammer and lifted Torrac to

parry a sword. He then caught a spear with his gauntlet and pulled the attacker close enough to impale the warrior's head with Torrac's spike.

The dwarf released the spear and fell to his knees, holding a hand over the wound as it gushed blood.

Mattasun swung Torrac in a wide arc, causing the dwarves to retreat a couple of steps, and twirled the weapon overhead as he pressed. His opponents froze, and he butchered two before they overcame their fear and countered.

A sword glanced off Mattasun's chain shirt, and a hammer struck his hand. He grimaced while swinging Torrac at one of the attackers, and the axe passed through the dwarf's armor and flesh with ease, killing the warrior instantly. As three more dwarves advanced, Mattasun thrust Torrac's spike into the eye socket of the warrior before him, penetrating deep into the dwarf's skull.

Yanking the haft free, Mattasun threw the weapon, cutting through the nearest dwarf. As the other two arrived, Torrac tore through one of them as it returned to Mattasun's hand. The other dwarf thrust a sword, piercing Mattasun's stomach, but the wound wasn't deep. He ended the dwarf with a vicious downswing.

"Enough!" commanded Uustaag, stepping through the entryway and pulling the sword from his back. It was similar to the weapon the warlord wielded in Lormin Dmurr, though not quite as broad and it lacked the violet mist rising from the blade. "I'll finish this myself."

Uustaag stepped forward, towering over Mattasun, and executed a feeble lunge likely meant to draw him in. But Mattasun steered the weapon away and stood his ground. Good for him. Uustaag then brought the sword down with terrifying force, and Mattasun swung Torrac to knock the blow aside—the wide blade sparked upon the floor.

Mattasun countered with Torrac's spike, bypassing the krukari's defenses and impaling the warrior's massive thigh. Uustaag growled, narrowly missing Mattasun's head with a punch and striking his shoulder instead. The blow unbalanced Mattasun, and he dove away as the warlord performed an overhead chop.

Mattasun rolled to his feet, but Uustaag moved quicker than expected and issued another strike. Again, Mattasun knocked the sword aside, employing all of his strength to accomplish the feat. His foe followed with a powerful kick, and he tumbled across the floor.

As the sword rose, Mattasun threw Torrac from his prone position. Uustaag steered the spinning weapon from its path, and it nicked the evil warrior's shoulder, shaving off a piece of the black plate armor and releasing a spray of blood. Uustaag roared in pain, reminiscent of the krukari's final moments in Lormin Dmurr. As Torrac returned, Mattasun scooted to a bench to regain his feet, but Uustaag thrust the wide blade, piercing his chest. Mattasun slumped and ceased to move.

A memory raced across Baylun's mind from Lormin Dmurr, when he faced Uustaag before the battle atop the citadel. The Ancient Enemy claimed to have killed Torrac's owner. Now he knew those words to be true.

"Torrac is mine!" Uustaag declared, grabbing hold of the weapon's haft. He then cried out as smoke issued from his black gauntlet, and it seemed he could not release the weapon. With a violent jerk, he pulled his hand free, and the gauntlet briefly glowed red. Uustaag turned to the dwarves with ire in his eyes. "What's the meaning of this?"

The dwarves cringed. One then spoke with hesitation.

"Sorry. You see, it's got a soul. It won't work for just anyone."

"I'm not anyone." Uustaag walked slowly toward the speaker. "I am Uustaag, and all will fear my name."

"But it was bonded to Mattasun," the dwarf said. "Until he served his hundred years or died." He looked at Mattasun's corpse. "That bond now passes to his firstborn, unless Torrac finds them unworthy."

Uustaag sneered. "Why was I not informed of this earlier?"

"Um…" The dwarf glanced at his comrades, but received no help. "I know not, my lord. Perhaps King Velgaad believes killing

Clanghorr's owner while Torrac remains unclaimed will end the cycle. Maybe open the weapons to new bloodlines within the shrine."

"Perhaps?" Uustaag towered over the dwarf. "Maybe?" He scowled. "Your king is a *fool*!"

The dwarf quivered.

"But *maybe* he is correct." Uustaag peered over his shoulder at Torrac. "And you shall find out." He pointed his sword at the dwarves, his glare as menacing as when his eyes were two different colors in Lormin Dmurr, one red and one violet. "You will remain here until that weapon is freed of its master. Then you will bring it to me."

Uustaag swung his blade before the dwarf speaker could react, gashing the breastplate and spraying himself in blood. The stout warrior fell. The krukari then swiped his metal finger through the blood and tasted it.

"If you fail me," he said to the others, "your deaths will not be so swift."

The dwarves slowly backed away.

"Do you understand?"

"Yes, my lord!" they responded in unison.

Uustaag strode out of the room and disappeared.

The dwarves stared at each other, none of them brave enough to speak. Several minutes later, there was a crash, like an avalanche.

"He's cut off the only exit left," said a dwarf.

"How do you know?" asked another.

The first dwarf held a level gaze.

The second dwarf's shoulders slumped. "Of course he did."

Time sped up. The dwarves were often absent from the dining room, but returned daily to observe Torrac. Sometimes they proceeded through the rear archway and came back with food, using a table far from the bodies they apparently had no interest in removing. After several days, perhaps weeks, they didn't pass beyond the food-providing arch anymore, and returned only to stare at the battleaxe or eat mushrooms they brought with them.

The rate of time increased, and the dwarves came and went. After what seemed years had passed, the vision slowed, and six of the dwarves sat at a table, their beards much longer than when they first arrived, their stomachs shrunken, and their eyes exhibiting defeat. Still, no one dared to touch Torrac.

"We can't go on like this," said a dwarf. "I'm going mad."

"Like the others," mumbled another dwarf.

"How many have we lost?" asked a third.

"Too many," said the first dwarf.

"How many have you killed?" a fourth dwarf hissed at the first.

"We all agreed!" he snapped. "They went mad. They were a danger to us all." He glared at the others. "And I killed only those unwilling to end their own lives."

"Torrac will never submit," mumbled the second dwarf.

"What if Velgaad failed to kill Balmorak?" posed the fifth dwarf. "We'll never be free of this place."

"You want to touch it?" asked the first dwarf.

The fifth dwarf shook his head. "I still feel the energy coming off it." He scowled at the weapon. "It's will remains strong."

"I'm leaving," the second dwarf said quietly, yet everyone ceased speaking and stared at him. "We have the tools." He glanced around the table. "Die here or live on the run from that blasted krukari. What's the difference?"

The first dwarf sighed. "Fair point." He surveyed the others. "Gather picks, ropes, and spikes."

"What if Uustaag is watching?" The third dwarf grabbed the first dwarf's arm. "What then?"

"We'll have to be quick about it!" The first dwarf pulled his arm away. "Now let's get to work."

The sconces went dark. Baylun's torch was the only light, and he stood amid the tables before a headless skeleton. Mattasun's skeleton. He looked back. Romik and Lorylla watched him with troubled eyes. Before he could speak, a rush of names darted through his head: *Mattasun; deceased*, followed by many others, each unfamiliar and described as *unfound*. The final three names registered clearly: *Clarna; unfound. Gruelenor; unfound. Baylun… Speak your oath onto Torrac. Do you name yourself dwarf-friend? Do you swear to answer Clanghorr's call for no less than one-hundred years, lest death claim you?*

Baylun looked down. Torrac's runes were pulsating with a bright light, as if awaiting his answer. So many questions raced through his mind… he could discern none of them. He focused on the grand weapon he held. Torrac had been with him for years now. Without it, he would have perished in Lormin Dmurr, and many times since. The words then escaped his lips.

"I so swear."

The runes went dark.

"What's going on?" demanded Romik.

Lorylla's brow lowered.

"Torrac…" Baylun didn't know what to say. He gazed at the corpse below him. "This was Torrac's previous owner."

"How do you know this?" asked Romik.

Baylun shook his head. "I just know."

"Your weapon speaks to you?" posed Lorylla.

Baylun looked at the gray elf. "Sometimes. Usually whispers I cannot understand."

Romik frowned. "This can't be the previous owner. I bought the weapon from its creator."

Baylun held a wry smile. "Unless you bought it from a ghost… I doubt that was its creator."

"You look pale," Lorylla said to Baylun.

Indeed, Baylun felt drained of energy, and sweat covered him from head to toe. It was as if he had just run a mile, except he wasn't breathing hard. Had the visions fatigued him? Or was it the oath? He let out a slow, shaky breath.

"Perhaps we should find a place to rest," suggested the elf. "For a moment only."

Romik eyed Baylun with concern and nodded. "But only for a moment. Stari and Nidor have to be our priority."

"There's a chamber with piles of debris to hide us," said Baylun. "Across the hall."

Romik gave a firm nod, and they exited the dining room.

CHAPTER 15

SOMETHING'S BURNING

Greyor looked again at the granite tablet to make sure he wasn't mistaken. His name was still there.

"How did you carve your name?" asked Eraim. "I saw only a flash of light when you touched the spike to the stone."

Greyor scanned the chamber. "This is a ceremony hall." He followed the bronze dome to the diamond inset at the apex, then gazed at the silver floor. "The metals making up this room… they're the same substances that make up Clanghorr." He looked at the axe. "This place is the source of Clanghorr's power."

"What does it mean that you are the Champion of Lornibur?" asked Kiryanna. "And how does that help us find the others?"

Bond is reformed, Clanghorr whispered.

Greyor was suddenly aware of Torrac. The weapon was above him and to the right. He looked at Kiryanna. "I believe I can track Torrac. I feel its presence."

"The weapons *are* connected!" Eraim declared, as if to herself.

Greyor gave the small elf a questioning gaze.

"Sorry," she said. "Just something I had mentioned to Selanna."

"You sense Baylun is alive?" Kiryanna asked Greyor.

"Not exactly," he replied. "But I sense Torrac is moving."

The marteese gave a nod. "Good. I am sure it is Baylun who carries it. That means he still lives. So we will focus on finding Nidor and Ameilistari."

"Tewlon is with them… I believe," said Eraim.

"How do you know this?" posed Kiryanna. "What do you mean, you believe?"

Eraim looked unsure of how to answer. "I saw Tewlon with them before… He pulled them from the cave-in."

"You saw this?" Kiryanna narrowed her eyes. "Or you *believe* this?"

The marteese sounded more like she had when Greyor traveled with her into Trannum's crypt decades ago.

"I saw it." Eraim was firm in her answer.

"Good." Kiryanna seemed to relax slightly. "All the same, I do not know this Tewlon, nor what he's capable of."

"He is an excellent warrior," proclaimed the small elf. "If anyone can keep them safe, it is Tewlon."

"I can think of several others I'd trust before him," Kiryanna muttered to herself, with no attempt to keep from being overheard.

"They did not fall." Eraim ignored the marteese's comment. "So they will be in the area around the throne room. We need to work our way upward."

Kiryanna frowned. "Why didn't you mention this in the first place? We could have sought a way up already."

Eraim bit her lip. "I… do not know." She sighed. "Perhaps I struck my head during the fall."

Greyor saw nothing to suggest the elf had suffered a head wound. Though her hair was a little mussed up, there were no signs of blood or welts.

Kiryanna shook her head, mumbling, "How is it you ever accomplish anything?"

Eraim didn't appear upset with the marteese's words, but ashamed. Still, Greyor had to give her the benefit of the doubt. The little elf had come through too many times to distrust her now.

"In any case," he said, "we have been moving farther downward ever since we fell. We'll need to go back to where we started if we wish to ascend."

Kiryanna glared at Eraim for a couple of seconds before giving Greyor a nod.

They headed toward the golden doors, and Greyor hesitated as a thought struck him. Although he had no knowledge of Lornibur's layout, dwarves had built it, and for the most part Morimont seemed to be fashioned in a similar manner. So if this level bore an entire room dedicated to Clanghorr, it made sense that he and his companions were near the forge. The legendary forge.

"Is Clanghorr speaking again?" asked Eraim.

"Nah." Greyor focused on the doors. "Just thinking." He looked at the maidens' awaiting expressions. "I'm pretty sure the forge is close by."

Kiryanna's brow slowly rose.

"So … we could…" Greyor cleared his throat. "We'll find our way back just as soon as we gather the rest of our company."

Kiryanna's eyebrows returned to their natural state. "And I would appreciate updates on Baylun, if you don't mind."

"Of course," Greyor said. He glanced once more around the room to take it in. "Well… Let's get to it."

He used the key, and the immense golden doors slowly swung inward. Scorching marred the hall outside, but the doors were untarnished, and the far wall was collapsed, exposing an expansive cavern.

While Eraim walked to the secret door, Greyor kept watch on the crumbled wall as the golden doors closed behind him. The enormous room beyond was dark, but he spied what appeared to be several buildings. Could it be one of the lower quadrants, like in Morimont? He desperately wished to investigate further, but the panel beside Eraim slid open, and she withdrew the key from the tiny hole next to it. His curiosity would have to wait.

Greyor took the lead, climbing half a dozen flights of steps as the tunnel led them back. Upon reaching the passage's end, Eraim stepped forward with the key.

"Wait!" Kiryanna halted the elf. "What about the lizards? There were far too many to fight."

Eraim held up a hand for silence and listened. "I hear nothing."

She opened the door.

The chamber wasn't quite how they had left it. The lizards had chewed through the door and ravaged the skeleton, but none were present. Eraim entered, and Greyor and Kiryanna followed, the marteese moving swiftly to peer into the corridor.

"All is clear," she said.

They slid the chair aside, and Greyor opened what remained of the door. They then returned to the intersection and turned left. Greyor passed beneath the archway, noticing the incline of the tunnel felt more pronounced than its decline had seemed, but a few paces later, the floor was the least of his concerns. The hallway vibrated. Something large was ahead, shaking the foundations as it rushed toward them.

"Get back!" he yelled, turning to usher the maidens down the slope.

The air grew hot, and Greyor glanced over his shoulder to see fire billowing along the passage. Eraim reached the intersection and darted left, followed by Kiryanna. As Greyor made the turn, the flames washed over his back, hotter than any forge. He collapsed, and the fire continued rushing by, its radiant heat making every nerve in his body cry out.

Eraim and Kiryanna grabbed Greyor's arms and pulled him farther from the intersection. The rush of fire finally ceased after what seemed like half a minute.

"Are you all right?" Eraim asked quietly.

"Guess we're not going that way," Greyor said, his voice strained.

"Are you all right?" she repeated, a bit more forcefully.

He swallowed a lump forming in his throat. His backside throbbed with pain. Looking at Kiryanna, he asked, "How did you care for Baylun's back?"

The marteese turned to Eraim, who pulled herbs from her pouch. They were identical to those she had given to Kiryanna after Baylun was burned.

"Are we safe to treat him here?" asked the half-elf.

Eraim pursed her lips. "We will have to be." She looked at

Kiryanna. "If it was the dragon, it is too large to pursue us here. But keep watch, all the same."

The marteese nodded and diverted her attention to the intersection.

Greyor grimaced while Eraim helped him out of his armor. There was no need to remove his undershirt—it fell off as soon as they unstrapped the breastplate.

Eraim gasped.

"That bad?" Greyor asked. It felt as if he were up against a bonfire.

"I would like to say I have seen worse." She sighed. "The treatment will hurt."

Though Greyor's tolerance for pain was high, he wasn't sure how much more he could take before it showed. And he needed to be strong for the maidens in his care.

He slowed his breathing and closed his eyes, seeking a single point in his mind. It was a trick taught to him by Lorylla following the War of the North. They had become dear friends and alternated visiting each other, and during one of the gray elf's trips to Varlimor, she assisted Greyor in defeating a two-headed giant that had been terrorizing the road between Morimont and Kalmaar. The monster held a boulder three times Greyor's size, and when he sliced through the brute's massive thigh, the rock dropped onto his leg, surely smashing every bone. The pain had been so intense that he could not stand Lorylla touching him, and a tear even escaped his eye—he believed it was the left eye. Such humiliation! Lorylla calmed Greyor and led him to seek the spot in his mind, a tiny sphere of peace. Her voice was soothing, guiding him until he located it—he never would have thought a gray elf could teach a dwarf their magic! It was a blessing then, and he reached for the spot now, praying to Meldar he found it. And there it was, hovering in the dark recesses of his deepest thoughts. He focused on it until all pain faded.

Lying on his stomach, he said, "I'm ready."

Eraim went to work, and Greyor kept his eyes shut. Her delicate hands moved over his back, and though pain was unavoidable, his mind remained lost in the tranquility of the spot.

CHAPTER 16

HIDING OUT

Ameilistari stared at the darkness. It wasn't fair that Nidor and Tewlon could see and she couldn't. Selanna or Rauzel should have taught her a spell for that! It was Tewlon's idea to extinguish her light, and his reasoning was sound: it might bring unwanted attention. She cursed herself for not having thought of it first. Her father would have been disappointed—more so than he already was.

Over an hour had passed, and the mines exhibited only distant noises. She heard what sounded like a collapsing ceiling, the grating of stone on stone, and something large sliding along the floor. Tewlon claimed the sounds were too far away to cause alarm. As another half hour came and went, Ameilistari suggested they get back to finding their companions, but Tewlon insisted they stay put a little longer, providing no reason why. Ameilistari gave him the benefit of the doubt. But she could stand the silence no longer, and whispered a question.

"Tewlon. Why do you pretend not to speak?"

A chuckle from the elf was the reply.

"I don't understand the jest," Ameilistari added.

"I guess it's more a habit than a prank." Tewlon's voice was just above a whisper. "My old master preferred me not to speak."

"What about your new master?" posed Ameilistari.

"She's the same, more or less."

It was a she!

"Is she an elf?" Ameilistari pressed.

There was a hesitation. "Yes."

She nodded to herself. He was probably talking about Eraim.

"Are you from Dakreal? Or Salenti?" asked Nidor.

Another pause before Tewlon responded. "I live in Vermallon."

That wasn't an answer. And although Ameilistari had never met a Vermallon elf, everyone knew they were taller than Tewlon.

"Do you know many gray elves?" Nidor posed.

Ameilistari rolled her eyes—hopefully Nidor noticed. "Lorylla's married, you imbecile!" She spoke louder than she had intended.

"I'm not talking about Lorylla," Nidor's tone remained quiet, "but gray elves in general. Are they all beautiful like her?"

"Most elves are beautiful on the outside," commented Tewlon.

A strange comment for an elf to make.

"What about the things Father says they are capable of?" asked Nidor.

No immediate response. Tewlon was probably smiling at Nidor's ignorance. Or his obsession.

"They are something special," the elf said at last. "I have known several in my day, and Lorylla comes from a long line of noble elves."

"How old are you?" asked Nidor.

"You wouldn't believe me if I told you."

Another non-answer. The entire conversation was boring.

"Why are we sitting here?" Ameilistari posed. It was time to get back to the matter at hand.

After a pause, Tewlon replied. "The others are surely searching for us. It might have been a mistake to leave the throne room."

"But you…" Ameilistari shook her head. They had traveled here following the elf's advice!

"Like I said," Tewlon stated, "I may have erred in judgement. I'm used to taking care of myself, and not waiting for help to come. I should have thought more about the two of you."

"We can take care of ourselves," Ameilistari insisted. "My father wasn't much older than us when he fought his first battle." At least, that's what he had claimed.

"You shouldn't speak so loud," Nidor said.

Ameilistari took a calming breath. Nidor was right. She released the air slowly. "I'm just saying, the longer we sit here, the more likely something will find us."

There were sounds of shuffling feet, and they weren't so distant. Ameilistari froze. Next came sniffing, and she detected movement beside her—Nidor and Tewlon. But it was pitch black, and she saw nothing. Her companions were probably motioning to each other.

"What are you two doing?" she demanded.

The sniffing and shuffling stopped. But Ameilistari's whisper couldn't have traveled far; another reason must have halted whatever approached. Her companions rose to their feet, and she did the same.

"Summon your light," Tewlon said.

Ameilistari did so, and a score of short humanoids lifted their hands to shield their eyes against the dull glow as it rose overhead. They stood twenty feet away, beside one of the tall piles of rubble. But where had they come from? The table still blocked the only entrance.

"Mine dwellers," Tewlon said.

Nidor began unsheathing his sword, but the elf halted him with a hand on his forearm.

"They are not the enemy," Tewlon cautioned, "unless they give us no other choice."

The small folk stood no higher than Greyor, but were much thinner. Dirty hair hung below most of their shoulders while some were bald, and several bore patchy beards. They wore reptilian skins like armor, and rusty helmets covered a few of their heads, leaving their eyes and mouths visible. They all raised thin metal spears as if readying to attack.

A spell of fire came to Ameilistari's lips, but she realized the mine dwellers weren't advancing. They backed away from the light as if it hurt their eyes. She lowered the glow until the creatures became mere shadows, and they seemed to relax.

Tewlon stepped forward, his sword sheathed and a friendly hand raised. "Hello."

Three mine dwellers threw their spears.

With great agility, Tewlon dodged the missiles, and he pulled his blade as more dwellers lifted their weapons. Ameilistari brightened her light, causing the creatures to cower and back away—a couple blindly tossed their spears and struck nothing. She willed the light to fly at them, and they scrambled around the debris pile. The sound of their clamoring feet then ended abruptly, as if they had all stopped running at once.

Tewlon rounded the heap of rock and twisted railing and halted. He sheathed his sword. "They're gone." He looked about the room. "But where? Where did they even come from?"

"Obviously, there's a hidden door," said Ameilistari.

"Should we look for it?" asked Nidor.

Tewlon returned. "No. We should make for the throne room."

Ameilistari lowered the intensity of the light to that of a torch and pulled it back to hover above them. She then released her displeasure with the elf's idea in a single exhale. "I don't see why? We are just as capable of finding them as they are of finding us."

"I seriously doubt that," said Nidor.

Great. Nidor was siding with Tewlon. This was supposed to be her cousin's chance to prove himself to his parents.

"Wait." Tewlon stared at the floor, as if listening. He looked at Ameilistari. "You're right. We should delve deeper."

Did all elves have difficulties making decisions? No wonder humans ruled most of Vaeldor. At least Tewlon came to his senses before they traveled all the way back.

The elf gazed at the floor again, his brow furrowed. "Impossible," he whispered.

"What?" Ameilistari gained his attention. "What do you hear?"

Tewlon hesitated. "Nothing," he said at last.

He was acting very peculiar. It then struck Ameilistari: he was communicating with someone. But who? And how?

"Are you speaking with Eraim?" she asked.

He frowned. "Of course not. I just... tend to think out loud sometimes."

She narrowed her eyes. "And what are you thinking now?"

Tewlon sighed. "We should return to the throne room and seek another route downward."

She raised her brow. "And what's unacceptable with the route we're on?"

"I sense a strong presence below us." He issued an intense stare. "One even your parents would not willingly confront."

"I see." Ameilistari studied the elf. Although he was acting strangely, he hadn't steered them wrong. She nodded. "So be it."

Tewlon moved the table aside with Nidor's help, and they exited the chamber and slowly headed back the way they had come. Tewlon led and Nidor brought up the rear, and all three of them kept a wary eye on the walls and ceiling for lizards. None were detected. Tewlon made no wrong turns, and they encountered no resistance as they reached the throne room. Upon entering, however, the shuffling of feet echoed from the hallway behind them.

"They're coming!" said Nidor.

Tewlon looked across the hall at the opposite archways. "This way!" he said, racing toward the middle arch.

Keeping up with Tewlon was impossible, and Nidor obviously slowed so as not to pass Ameilistari. Behind them, the shuffling became running feet, and she peeked over her shoulder to spy more than a score of the mine creatures. But the dwellers halted, appearing hesitant to step into the throne room, and their nervous eyes scanned the chamber until resting upon the corpse of Maak Maak.

Ameilistari returned her focus to the way ahead. Tewlon waited at the archway with a frown, and as she and Nidor arrived, the elf continued.

The corridor was fifteen feet wide, and scattered arches lined the walls while larger ones provided support to the ceiling twenty feet overhead. The echo of their own hastened steps surrounded them, and soon shadows swallowed the entry to the throne room.

"They do not pursue," Nidor said.

Ameilistari stopped to listen, holding her breath to suppress her panting. Nidor stopped as well. Indeed, the creatures never entered the hallway. She resumed panting.

"Keep moving," ordered Tewlon. The elf was thirty feet ahead.

Ameilistari wasn't used to all this running. Her father made soldiers race up and down the towers during training, but she never joined in—mages didn't need to run when spells could see them through any situation. If only she had a spell to ease her fatigue.

"They're gone," Nidor said. "Perhaps we should catch our breath."

Neither Nidor nor Tewlon were panting. Her cousin was speaking about her!

"They're likely taking another path," Tewlon said. "Now move."

Ameilistari sighed. If Nidor could do it, she could too.

They resumed the hard pace.

She gave up trying to measure the distance they ran, and it crossed her mind that Tewlon might be torturing her on purpose. The elf only shot glances along smaller corridors as they sped by, and barely slowed upon reaching intersections before choosing their path. He then showed mercy, reducing the speed to a jog, and not long after, the jog deteriorated to a brisk walk. They encountered no lizards in all that time, and the mine dwellers never resurfaced.

Dark archways again dotted the corridor, and Ameilistari thanked the gods when Tewlon halted to peer through each. At least a dozen existed, but the elf sought no counsel from her when picking which direction to proceed. Probably a good decision. She was completely lost. Still, from the choices made thus far, it seemed like Tewlon attempted to head back toward the throne room whenever possible. The only thing Ameilistari was absolutely sure of was that they remained in Lornibur—the craftsmanship was unwavering. It must have taken decades, if not centuries, to hollow out all the stone. The maze was endless.

Finally, they encountered something other than archways and corridors. Within the next intersection, a staircase spiraled about a pillar, rising from beneath the floor and passing through the ceiling. A way down at last. Ameilistari breathed a sigh of relief.

"Wait," said Nidor as Tewlon neared the steps. "Shouldn't we rest a moment?" He glanced at Ameilistari.

Tewlon squinted back down the hallway. He then closed his eyes for a few seconds and opened them with a nod. "For a moment."

She didn't need special treatment. Sure, she was tired, hungry, and her feet throbbed, but her companions *had* to share in some of those ailments. Right?

"If you two are that exhausted," Ameilistari said, "I'll do some scouting while you regain your strength."

Nidor's expression seemed to doubt her. Tewlon smirked.

"I suppose we can go a bit farther," said the elf. And he descended.

Nidor continued staring as Ameilistari lifted her chin and followed.

The steps were narrow, and as the stairwell dropped beneath the floor, a stone tube surrounded them—Ameilistari's throat tightened as the air seemed to thin. After what must have been thirty feet, the surrounding walls ended, and she breathed easier. They had entered a corridor similar to the one they left behind, and the stairs spiraled another fifteen feet to the floor.

Tewlon froze five steps from the bottom. Ameilistari saw nothing.

"What is it?" she asked.

"Lizards," the elf warned. "Many."

She looked again and still saw nothing. Either the creatures were outside the light, or…

A movement to the right caught her eye, and she spotted a well-camouflaged reptile on the wall. It was five feet in length, and its color barely betrayed its presence. She then noticed several others shifting about. The wall was teeming with the things.

"This way!" Tewlon said as he jumped from the steps and away from the monsters.

Ameilistari hastened to the third step before joining the elf, and

Nidor leaped from seven steps up. He grunted upon landing atop a pile of rocks, and though he followed, he did so with a limp and fell behind.

The lizard-wall wriggled as the creatures turned dark green and scrambled onto the floor or ran to the ceiling. Ameilistari recited her stunning spell, and the closest ten reptiles spasmed and ceased their forward progression. Though not even half of the lizard's muster, it was enough for Nidor to gain ground, and she and her cousin caught up with Tewlon—the elf waited with an impatient glare.

They continued to an intersection. The tunnel passing from left to right was wider, with pillars along its center to support the ceiling twenty feet overhead. Ameilistari repeated her spell as Tewlon turned right, halting another ten reptiles.

Archways lined the walls, but the elf didn't hesitate to inspect any of them. They then encountered a door reinforced with steel bands, and he stopped to work the latch. It was either locked or stuck.

Tewlon gazed at the scrambling lizards, and Ameilistari cast her spell again. She then recited her unlocking incantation before trying the latch. It opened. She rushed through with her limping cousin, and Tewlon pulled the door shut as he entered.

"Can you relock it?" the elf asked.

Ameilistari spoke the reverse spell. A *click* sounded, confirming the latch's cooperation, followed by scratching noises on the other side.

"That should hold for a while," said Tewlon.

Ameilistari gazed about the chamber. It contained stone benches and a well, but no other exits. Perhaps a room for miners needing a break from a hard day's work. She followed Nidor, who hobbled to a bench, and sat beside him.

"Nice jump," she said quietly. "I believe you've reclaimed your crown as King of Dumb Mistakes."

Chapter 17

Clay'Gor

Lornibur remained quiet while Baylun and his companions sat behind mine carts he and Romik had arranged to conceal their presence. He doused the torch once all was set, but not before lighting a candle. Though complete darkness would have worked better to hide them, he didn't wish for Romik to sit there, blind and worried. Lorylla closed her eyes as soon as they settled in, but Baylun doubted she slept.

He stared at Torrac, still puzzled by the visions. Thoughts of Kiryanna and Nidor then came to mind, pushing away all concerns for the battleaxe. As fascinating as the weapon was, it paled when compared to his worry for his family. Romik's expression reflected that anxiety.

"They'll be okay," Baylun said quietly, so as not to disturb Lorylla or alert anything to their presence. Still, his deep voice rumbled, and the gray elf opened an eye as if to hush him.

"I wish I knew that to be true," Romik whispered. He released a sigh. "Kiryanna is an abled warrior," he looked at Baylun, "we both know that. And she's with Eraim and Greyor. Who could ask for better companions? But our kids are with an elf I've never met."

"I've heard Tewlon's name before," admitted Baylun. "Father said he performed chores for the wizard Elgarroth, like chopping wood and serving food."

Romik gave Baylun a sidelong stare. "That hardly improves the situation."

Baylun agreed. He wasn't sure why he had brought it up. It came from one of his father's many trivial stories about the Necromancer

War, when Gruelenor's company stayed at the House of Elgarroth to evade Benasti hobgoblins and Soldiers of Blood. "It was decades ago," he said. "He's had plenty of time to become a warrior since then. And Eraim doesn't travel with just anyone."

Romik gave a wry smile. "I suppose."

After a moment of silence, Baylun asked, "Why are you unhappy with Ameilistari's talents?" Hopefully, the question detracted from the dangers their children faced.

Romik frowned. "What?"

"Her magical talents?" Baylun said. "She seems pretty confident and capable."

Romik pursed his lips. "Selanna ruined everything." He turned to Baylun. "The day she arrived at the keep was the beginning of the whole blasted mess. Stari's life has veered from the plan ever since."

Lorylla again lifted an eyelid, as if to bring down their voices.

"*Her* plan?" posed Baylun. "Or yours?"

Romik's shoulders slumped. "You've seen the lives wizards lead. They do not run keeps. They're constantly in harm's way, trying to influence battles better decided by the blade. They live lonely lives in isolation, or move to Tenvale with its strange laws and forget about everything but their craft." After a pause, he added, "And they live longer than normal humans." He sighed. "She'll live twice as long as she should, and likely marry no one."

Though Baylun had heard of Elgarroth in stories, the only wizard he actually knew was Selanna, regardless of the thousands of spell casters residing in Tenvale, a realm ruled by mages and possessing odd customs. Selanna might not dwell in the Wizard Kingdom, but as Romik pointed out, she never married and now lived in Vermallon Forest by herself or with Elgarroth or Eraim. At least, that was the way Baylun understood it. He could not recall a single story involving a mage who had settled down to start a family. But that couldn't be true for all wizards. Could it? Eraim wasn't a mage, and to Baylun's knowledge she never married either. She and the warrior Vecnor seemed to be close for a time, but Vecnor disappeared after the War of the North. Of course, the tall warrior was human, and few elves mingled with non-elves due to the discrepancy with their lifespans. Baylun bore that weight around his neck every day. Although Kiryanna would live only half the years of a full-blooded elf, it was still more than three times that of a krukari.

Baylun drew a deep breath. He needed to refocus on Romik—his own issues had to wait. But he could think of no words to ease his brother's apprehension. "She's young," he said. "She might surprise you."

Romik shook his head. "I see her drifting more and more into a life of magic. It has her taking careless risks, such as sneaking onto this quest. And now she's pulled Nidor into her schemes."

Baylun wouldn't put the latter solely on Ameilistari's shoulders. Nidor's passion to become a warrior had surely made agreeing to join her an easy decision. Baylun narrowed his eyes at his brother. "Ameilistari has a good head on her. She's the smartest young woman I have ever met, and she seems to enjoy her life at Ironside. Give her a chance."

"Have you talked to her about it?" asked Lorylla. The gray elf's eyes remained shut.

Baylun and Romik stared, as if to see if she was truly awake. She opened her eyes and gazed at them both.

"In Orlenfel," she said, "we encourage, but we do not steer our youths into fulfilling our expectations. The spirit is meant to be free, and only the gods can guide it. Not to follow one's heart is to live a life of depressing failure." She eyed Romik. "How old is Ameilistari?"

"Thirteen. Soon to be fourteen."

"That is the *Age of Trelibrum* in Orlenfel," she said. "The beginning of the passage from childhood to adulthood, when they are to wander the forest in search of their heart's desire. They craft their own bows, hunt, prepare food, read books, and meditate. And although a priest accompanies them, it is only to offer advice and help them discover their passion."

"I appreciate your words," Romik said. "But elves and humans live very different lives."

"I have children of my own," Lorylla said, "and the eldest walks her path already. It is not one I would have selected for her, but it was hers to choose. In truth, it is a path no gray elf has *ever* chosen. And as she sees it through, I will see very little of her in the centuries to come."

When Lorylla put it that way, Baylun felt very small. A krukari or human parent might suffer such separation for three to five decades, but centuries? No wonder elves never seemed in a hurry to complete mundane tasks.

"How old is your daughter?" asked Romik.

"Two years ahead of yours."

They certainly didn't take their time raising their young. Baylun would have thought elves remained children until their thirties or forties.

"I'm sorry to hear that," Romik offered.

"Nonsense." Lorylla smiled. "I wish for her to live the best life she can find. Other than a couple of ugly wars, I have done so myself."

Romik almost smiled as the elf's words sank in. Almost.

Baylun wondered if it was time to rethink Nidor's situation in West Palidur. Perhaps he should speak with Uncle Magneer about Nidor performing before the Honor Panel.

"You ready?" Romik asked him.

Baylun nodded. His energy had returned several minutes prior. "Let's go."

They lit another torch and abandoned their hiding place, continuing along the tunnel in the direction of the sapphires. Baylun thought about the gemstones. Mattasun had followed the rubies, so the sapphires must lead back to the throne room. By contrast, the rubies surely led to an exit. But the dwarves mentioned they were trapped in this corridor. Hopefully, that wasn't still the case.

"I so swear," Lorylla said quietly while they walked.

"What?" asked Romik.

She turned to the Lord of the Keep. "Baylun whispered those words to Torrac in the dining chamber."

Baylun didn't think anyone had heard him. He didn't even realize he had spoken aloud. He sighed. "Torrac asked if I swore to be a friend of the dwarves, and to answer Clanghorr's call for no less than one hundred years. Lest death claim me."

"A hundred years?" Romik appeared confused.

"A strong magic emanates from your weapon," Lorylla said. "The same magic I sense within Clanghorr. They are linked." She studied Baylun. "You would best pay attention when Torrac is speaking to you."

Baylun's mind drifted, trying to recall everything his battleaxe had shown him. But none of it made much sense. Serve for a hundred years? Rarely did krukari live beyond eighty, and he was nearly halfway there. Even if he were to break that threshold, his fighting skills would be unworthy of Torrac after another two decades. Probably sooner. Then there was the dwarf that said Torrac passed to the firstborn once the oath was fulfilled. Did that mean Baylun was descended from Mattasun? Every krukari had a human somewhere in their lineage. Baylun's darkest secret lay in the fact that the Death Lord Gruzim had been his grandfather, knowledge only he and his father shared, but Mattasun's line couldn't have possibly spawned the ex-Lord of Benasti. As Baylun thought back, he recalled the name Torrac mentioned before his father hadn't been Gruzim, but Clarna. She must be Baylun's grandmother. He committed the name to memory. Although it was surely too late for Gruelenor to meet her, who wouldn't want to finally learn the name of their mother?

"Baylun!"

Romik's shout stirred him from his pondering, just as an eight-foot lizard leaped from the wall. Its teeth would surely have ripped out Baylun's throat had Lorylla's arrow not pierced its skull. The lifeless monster crashed into him, almost knocking him to the floor.

Around them, a score of lizards scrambled about the walls and ceiling, and farther along the hallway were a dozen more. They closely resembled the stone, their movements betraying their positions as they maneuvered to attack. Lorylla released two more arrows, dropping a pair of reptiles, and Romik flashed his sword, slaying one while another bit into his false arm.

Baylun readied Torrac as a couple of lizards lunged. With a single swing, he severed one's head and cut halfway through the other—the second reptile squirmed a few seconds before becoming still. Another lizard dropped from the ceiling, and Baylun brought his battleaxe overhead, slicing it in two.

The creatures then surrounded them, and a commotion sounded down the corridor where the reptile reinforcements were gathered. Baylun couldn't tell what had happened—the immediate threat required his focus.

He cut another lizard down before something landed on his back—it was all he could do not to fall. A sharp pain in his side followed as fangs sank in. He thrust his spike, impaling the beast, and the pressure of the jaws abated as the monster disengaged.

Next to Baylun, Romik fought with surprising skill for a warrior with one arm. The Lord of Ironside swung his sword with precision and clubbed an attacker with his wooden appendage—glowing cinders flew from the torch locked within the hooks. Behind Baylun, Lorylla had abandoned her bow, and her blade glowed red while she stood above two lizards with smoking wounds. She leaped onto the wall, seeming to defy gravity as she skewered a lizard perched there, and jumped back to the floor to stomp another before thrusting her sword downward.

Baylun continued hacking into the monsters, killing four more, and he learned why the second group of lizards had never arrived: the creatures battled mine dwellers. Six of the short humanoids fought while two lay unmoving, and the reptiles were down to half of their original number.

As Lorylla slew the final lizard around them, Baylun charged down the hallway. Another mine dweller fell, its head nearly removed, and a couple of lizards collapsed with multiple spear wounds. A reptile on the ceiling readied to pounce on an unsuspecting mine dweller, and Baylun heaved Torrac. The runes came alive with a bright glow, and it rotated faster as the creature sprung, easily slicing through the lizard's body and dropping its halves to either side of its intended victim.

Baylun suddenly recalled Torrac returning to Mattasun, and he reached out while the weapon continued along the darkened hallway. "Come back!" he said through his teeth.

To his amazement, Torrac turned back, flying as fast as it had raced to its target. Baylun's eyes grew wide—how could he catch it with the blades spinning so quickly? Mattasun hadn't hesitated, and Baylun pushed away the fear. As Torrac arrived, the handle struck his palm and his fingers closed about the haft.

The mine dwellers won the battle, and the four survivors gazed at Baylun. All but one clutched thin metal spears dripping with blood. In the final one's hand was a crude hammer, obviously made by an amateur weaponsmith. Baylun thought of roaring as he had earlier, but it seemed cruel after the dwellers lost half of their companions. He stared, unsure of what to do, and Romik moved beside him with the torch.

The mine dweller wielding the hammer slowly approached, shielding its eyes from the light. Baylun grabbed his brother's sword arm as Romik stepped forward—the creature had not lifted its weapon. It came to within fifteen feet and stopped.

"Clay'Gor?" it said, to Baylun's surprise.

Romik frowned. "Clay'Gor?"

The mine dweller pointed at Torrac. "Clay'Gor!"

Baylun shook his head. The dweller was trying to communicate, but what was it saying?

"Not Clanghorr," said Lorylla, arriving at Baylun's other side. "Torrac."

Clanghorr! Of course that was what it meant. But if the mine dweller knew that name, then it must be one of the brave soldiers that followed Greyor and Millord when the dwarves traversed the mines during the Necromancer War.

"Greyor? Millord?" Baylun asked. "Do you know them?"

"Gray'Or!" The mine dweller smiled, still holding a hand above its eyes. "Gray'Or Clay'Gor!"

It hastened to join its friends.

Still unsure of what to do, Baylun waited. The creatures held a conversation of nonsensical words and grunts. The mine dweller who spoke then turned back and motioned for Baylun and his companions to follow.

"Do we dare?" posed Romik.

"I think so," said Baylun. "I don't believe they mean us any harm." He looked from Lorylla to his brother. "That might be one of the dwellers that helped Greyor years ago."

"I say we go with them," said Lorylla. "It is preferable to wandering. Perhaps they will help us find our friends."

Baylun looked at Romik. His brother sighed and then nodded in agreement.

Chapter 18

On the Trail

"Wake up."

Greyor opened his eyes. He lay on his stomach, and Eraim was squatting with a hand on his shoulder. His back was much improved.

"Can you get up?" she asked.

"I think so." His voice was a touch hoarse, and he cleared his throat. "I think so." That was better.

He rose to his hands and knees and noticed he was no longer in the hallway. A stone table and two benches were the small chamber's only furnishings, and a well delved into the floor. His breastplate, vambraces, and gauntlets lay nearby. Next to the only door stood Kiryanna, her sword in hand.

"You are not easy to drag." Eraim sounded tired.

She helped Greyor to stand, and the lack of pain in his back was surprising—the herbs were amazing!

"How long have we been here?" he asked.

"An hour," replied Kiryanna. She approached with fatigue plaguing her eyes. But there was also concern. Perhaps their last encounter had damaged her hopes of finding her family unharmed.

Greyor stretched his hands overhead. There was stiffness, but it wouldn't hinder him. A breeze brushed the nape of his neck, and he reached back to discover most of his hair was missing—all that remained was that which had been protected by his helmet.

"I am afraid the creature burned most of your hair back there," said Eraim.

"Well…" he shrugged. "Better that than my beard!" He winked.

But his attempt to lighten the mood went unnoticed. "How far did you drag me?"

"Not too far," Eraim replied. "Maybe fifty yards."

Greyor nodded. "Now we just need to figure a way to get past that fire-spitting monster."

"Indeed," muttered Kiryanna.

"That *monster* is enormous," said Eraim. "It does not rely on stealth. We should be able to hear it coming, as long as we stay alert and move without too much haste."

Kiryanna pursed her lips.

Greyor understood the marteese's apprehension; he had lost his cousin in these mines. He would do what he could to reunite Kiryanna with her family. The forge would have to wait. "Let's get moving," he said.

As he lifted his breastplate, his back informed him it hadn't completely mended just yet. The damaged skin stretched with every movement, reminding him of the searing heat he had suffered. But there was no time for discomfort, and with Eraim's help, he donned his armor.

"Can you tell me if Baylun is well?" Kiryanna asked once Greyor was ready, anxiety haunting her eyes.

"Torrac…" Greyor whispered.

He felt a pull from within, a yearning to walk through the back of the chamber. He proceeded to the finely chiseled stone and placed a hand on the wall. It was solid.

"What are you doing?" asked Eraim.

Greyor pushed against the wall. Nothing happened.

"There are no hidden doors," the elf said. "I checked while you rested."

Greyor shook his head. It made no sense. "Clanghorr… It wants me to go this way."

"But… there is no door," Eraim repeated. "That would be impossible unless you plan to dig a new tunnel."

"Why would your weapon send you through a wall?" asked

Kiryanna.

"When I say Torrac," he explained, "I am drawn to go this way."

Eraim wrinkled her nose. "It does not wish for you to go *through* the wall, but in that direction. We must find another path."

"Can you tell how far away Torrac is?" asked the marteese.

Greyor gazed at Clanghorr. "How far away is Torrac?"

Again, the force pulled him toward the wall. It would not answer the question. He looked at Kiryanna and shook his head.

"That leaves us with a decision." Eraim turned to Kiryanna. "Do we continue searching for Nidor? Or see if Clanghorr can lead us to Torrac? We are much stronger with Baylun among us."

Kiryanna paled. Having no kids, Greyor could only speculate about the turmoil the marteese endured. Her cheeks flushed as she glared at Eraim.

"Do you swear Tewlon can keep the children out of harm's way?" There was an edge in Kiryanna's tone.

The blood drained from Eraim's face. She was like a scared child faced with a demanding parent and unsure of how to answer. She swallowed, and determination returned. "I cannot offer absolutes, but I trust Tewlon with my life more than any other being, even against that dragon."

Kiryanna stared for a few seconds before taking a deep breath and expelling it through her nostrils. "Very well." She turned to Greyor. "Let's find my husband."

Greyor nodded. He'd hate to be Eraim if anything bad happened to Nidor. And from the way Eraim chewed on her lip, she surely felt that pressure already. But Tewlon? Eraim had traveled with many heroes in her lifetime, including himself and Vecnor. Strange how the muscular elf carried such clout.

Greyor went to the door and listened. Nothing. He removed his gauntlet and touched it. The bruskiin was cool. He opened it.

A corridor passed left and right, ten feet wide with a rail running along its center. The faint odor of charred wood drifted from the right, but any heat produced by the dragon's fire was long spent.

"We came from the right," said Eraim.

That much was obvious. Greyor turned left.

"Why did you bring Tewlon?" he asked Eraim while they walked. The silence of the mines was unnerving.

"Well…" she replied. "He is an excellent warrior."

"Sure, sure." Greyor bobbed his head while scanning the way ahead. "But why Tewlon? Why not Vecnor?"

"Why would you think I had that option?"

"Please!" Kiryanna spoke louder than either of them. "A fool could see that something existed between the two of you. So why not bring the slayer of Uustaag?"

"Is Vecnor even alive?" asked Greyor.

"I am sure he is," Eraim said tersely. "But he is not my personal soldier to command."

The affair must have soured after the War of the North. Sympathy for Eraim tugged at Greyor's heart. She deserved the best. Of course, Vecnor was human, and she would outlive him by a few centuries at least. Greyor wondered if the large man's skills were even as sharp as they had been two decades ago.

Archways soon lined the walls to either side, and glances told Greyor that most of them led to deeper places for excavation of stone and ore. He couldn't avoid the thought that somewhere below were the metals used to craft Clanghorr and Torrac, as well as line the room where he made his oath. How many weapons could the materials making up the dome and floor create?

They reached a six-way intersection. The rail continued straight only. Greyor searched his mind for Torrac, and the unseen force turned him to the left. But there were two corridors passing in that direction. He looked at the maidens; they watched with trusting eyes, full of hope. He couldn't take that hope away. He took the first corridor.

They traveled a long stretch with no doors or openings. An archway at the end then gave way to a larger hallway moving left and right. The new passage was thirty feet wide, and magnificent pillars supported the high ceiling every twenty yards, each of those to the right bearing a sapphire set near the top while those to the left held rubies—each stone was surely worth no less than three hundred gold coins. The oldest tunnels in Morimont bore such décor to reveal direction, although much smaller gems were used, and sapphires led south while rubies passed into the north. The topaz and peridot earlier made no sense. Concentrating on Torrac, Greyor knew the battleaxe to be to the south.

He followed the blue stones.

They traversed the hallway for a hundred feet before a pair of large archways appeared, one to either side. They were typical of the arches thus far, with hammers and anvils in bas-relief, and a rail exited from each before heading up the corridor. Greyor walked beside the rail on the left of the columns. Twenty yards farther was an archway on the right, but Torrac remained ahead, and Greyor continued.

Smaller openings soon interrupted the walls, each leading into chambers with no other exits, and after thirty more feet, a single arch provided access to a hallway on the east wall. Still, the rails proceeded, and Clanghorr urged Greyor to do the same. But as he passed the side tunnel, Eraim brought him to a halt.

"Tux..." the elf whispered, but Greyor heard her plainly enough.

"I remember that name," he said.

"The gray elf," Kiryanna added. "He fought in the Battle of the Broken Land, or so I was told."

For some reason, Eraim looked embarrassed that she had spoken aloud. She turned to Kiryanna. "Yes, he did."

"The shortest gray elf I ever laid eyes on," Greyor commented. "Lorylla claims him to be a half-breed. Said it was the only time she heard of such a thing from her race."

Kiryanna's chin lifted. "There's nothing wrong with half-breeds."

"Especially Tux." Greyor snorted a chuckle. "He saved Vayla's life on the battlefield, using arrows from five-hundred yards with deadly precision. He was like a blur, running into battle and running off again to use that bow of his." Greyor furrowed his brow. "But why are we discussing Tux?"

Eraim sighed, staring beyond the archway into the adjoining hallway. "This mark."

Greyor and Kiryanna moved closer to see what had caught Eraim's eye. There was a faded symbol on the wall. It was a vertical white line topped by a horizontal line ending in an arrow pointing toward the corridor where they stood.

Greyor frowned. "A pretty simple mark. Anyone could have made it."

"Yes," Eraim said. "But Tux *always* used this mark, so he would not get lost."

"I hardly see how this matters," stated Kiryanna. "We are not here for Tux. We're —"

"It is old," Eraim pointed out. "But it means he has been here." She turned to Greyor and Kiryanna. "And if he was here, then his marks also lead to a way out."

Kiryanna's expression lightened, but the moment faded and darkness returned. "It matters not until we find the others."

"Of course," Eraim responded quickly. "But we will have a way out *after* we find them. That is, as long as Tux's route still exists."

Greyor nodded. Kiryanna did the same, although slowly. Still, Greyor had no intention of leaving until he located the forge at the very least. That, and he needed to rid the mines of that blasted dragon!

"We should continue," he said.

"Just a moment." Eraim rummaged through her backpack, extracting a hardy sheet of parchment and a piece of charcoal. After strapping her pack in place, her fingers worked frantically, sketching lines onto the paper. Not ten seconds later, and after a sigh from Kiryanna, the elf ceased drawing and looked up. "I am ready."

Greyor thought it odd. He had assumed Eraim committed everything to memory. Perhaps a possible exit was too great a risk to leave to chance.

They moved on. Before long, archways appeared on either side, topped by symbols of mine carts or picks. Another had three wavy lines, and one bore a mushroom. Before the next central column was an old bloodstain, and farther ahead, Eraim's light illuminated larger stains. One looked as if whatever had bled out had been dragged away, the streaks lasting twenty paces before fading. As Greyor and his companions pressed on, the light revealed the skeleton of a lizard resting atop yet another stain.

"Tux must have battled lizards," commented Kiryanna.

"Hmm," Greyor snorted. "I doubt he was alone."

"Oh?" asked Eraim.

"From some of the splatter," he pointed at faded spots of blood on the nearby wall, "the lizards received wounds too large for the elf's arrows or narrow sword. A much wider blade was used. Perhaps a battleaxe. That, or a very large sword."

Eraim pulled in her lips as she glanced at the archways.

"Did he have any friends?" Greyor asked.

"He was with Vecnor when I first met the two of them," Kiryanna said. "They seemed very familiar with each other."

"The swords Vecnor uses would suffice." Greyor lowered his brow in thought. "But he'd have been much too young." He looked at Eraim for any comments.

She shrugged. She was hiding something. But at the moment it mattered little.

"Let's move on." Greyor pointed Clanghorr at the archways to the right. "You two have a peek through those." He turned to the opposite side of the corridor. "I'll check the others."

Greyor found that most of the openings led to rooms bearing rubble or useless gear suggested by the markings above the arches, like mine carts or tools. He was sure some chambers were for storage or equipment, and others were meant for reparations or holding debris removed from newer tunnels until it could be shaped or discarded. The archway with the image of a mushroom opened into a vast garden, much larger than the one in Morimont. A forest of bruskiin grew toward the front left side, the giant fungus ready to be harvested for its wood-like properties, and to the right and beyond were many other forms of toadstools.

Greyor spotted a patch of stone crawlers, and he glanced at the maidens. They were busy with their task, peering through the arch sporting wavy lines. He put his hand into his healing pouch; there were only a few crawlers left. After another glance over his shoulder, he stepped into the room.

The aroma of mushrooms and dirt was almost intoxicating. But as Greyor entered deeper, a moldy odor mixed in—some fungi were obviously past their prime. He reached the stone crawlers and looked around. Glow-shrooms cast a blue light deep inside the chamber, revealing the room's massive depth, and lizards crawled about. Though typical cavern lizards, only a foot in length at most, it was a reminder of the creatures patrolling the mines, and he gripped Clanghorr tighter and scanned the nearby wall.

Nothing.

Farther in to the left, a section of the bruskiin appeared to have been completely burned. Had the dragon been there? No, it would have razed the entire forest.

Greyor moved to inspect the area of ash. Although it seemed old, it remained clear of growth, and half-buried were scattered bones, barely visible. He needed a closer look.

The ash crunched beneath Greyor's boots as he proceeded, and soot replaced all pleasant odors. He reached the nearest bone and noticed it was an arm—the hand was missing. It resisted when he tugged at it, and he yanked it free of the charred soil. It had been attached to another bone. After the ash settled, he brushed aside the area with his gauntlet and discovered more of a skeleton. A dwarf skeleton. Greyor gazed across the field. If every bone represented a corpse, a score of dwarves had met their end in this room. It was a mass grave.

"There you are!" said Kiryanna with a scowl. Eraim was with the marteese. "We found something."

Greyor dropped the bone. "Me too." He walked back to the stone crawlers and kneeled in the dirt. "These will come in handy." He saw no point in discussing the skeletons; they wouldn't help find Baylun any faster. Nor the forge.

"We don't have time for mushrooms," Kiryanna said, her voice growing angrier.

"Stone crawlers!" Eraim rushed to join Greyor and squatted next to him. "He is right. It would be foolish to leave these behind."

Eraim seemed very astute in her mushroom knowledge as she helped extract the toadstools, picking only those of proper age to possess healing qualities. The others might ease pain, but they'd do little else. Greyor then noticed several had been picked already, and not that long ago. Baylun? Lorylla? He hoped the mushrooms served them well.

They harvested more than a score, and Greyor filled his pouch while Eraim took the rest. They then joined the very impatient marteese waiting at the arch with sword ready. Kiryanna obviously understood the importance of the healing fungus, though, and accepted the handful Eraim offered.

"Can we go to the battle scene now?" Kiryanna asked as she secured the crawlers in her pouch.

Greyor frowned. "Battle scene?"

"Oh!" Eraim shook her head, as if disappointed with herself for getting distracted. "Sorry, yes. There are several dead lizards and mine dwellers ahead."

"Fresh corpses," added Kiryanna.

"Mine dwellers?" Greyor's thoughts drifted back to his past adventure through the mines with his cousin Millord. He hoped none of his companions had slain the poor creatures.

They walked hastily along the main corridor until reaching what the maidens had discovered. There were two areas that had hosted battles. The first consisted of dead lizards only, and the second comprised lizards and four mine dwellers. From the injuries, the reptiles' teeth had surely killed the latter. Greyor's shoulders relaxed.

"There are tracks leading away," said Eraim. She stood beyond the bodies, inspecting the floor. "They suggest seven separate people, and four of them wore no boots."

Greyor wandered to where the elf squatted. The survivors couldn't avoid stepping in blood, and distinct footprints were clear. But the trail faded with every step.

"The booted prints are too large to have included Ameilistari," Eraim added, "but I am positive one set belongs to Lorylla, and the other two are from men."

"Baylun," Greyor said. They were on the right path.

"Did one group follow the other?" asked Kiryanna.

"They travel together," Eraim replied. "The consistency of the blood is equal."

"How long ago?" the marteese asked.

Eraim furrowed her brow. "Maybe an hour." She looked at Kiryanna. "It is difficult to know for sure. But I am positive it was close to an hour."

Kiryanna released a frustrated breath.

"They can't have gotten far," Greyor said as guilt set in. Had he not slept after being burned, they'd have caught up to Baylun already. "Let's find them."

CHAPTER 19

THEY'RE EVERYWHERE

Ameilistari sat up with a soft snort. The room was dark and silent. After the lizards abandoned their attempts to gain access, Lornibur quieted, and sleep must have overtaken her. Summoning her magical light, she restricted its illumination to the strength of a candle.

She was on a bench. Nidor shared the seat—they had been resting head-to-head—and he breathed a steady pace while he slept. A splint Tewlon had fashioned adorned her cousin's ankle, and the injured leg rested atop his backpack.

Tewlon sat across the room with eyes closed and his unsheathed sword upon his lap. One of his eyes opened to look at her, and he shut it as he drew a slow breath through his nose and released it out of his mouth. Both eyes then opened, and he stood and sheathed the weapon.

"I trust you're ready?" the elf posed.

Ameilistari nudged Nidor. Her cousin stirred, nearly tumbling from the bench.

"Did we fall asleep?" he asked.

Ameilistari rolled her eyes. "Of course we did, you dolt." She glanced at his ankle. "Think you can walk on that?"

Nidor swung his feet off the bench and bounced his boots on the flagstones. He winced. "It hurts." He looked at Ameilistari. "But it's better. I'm ready."

"It would have been much worse without the healing herb," said Tewlon.

Tewlon had given Nidor a Vermallon dusk, but the elf didn't

seem confident with a procedure. In the end, Nidor put the leaf under his tongue for a minute before swallowing it.

"Another few hours of rest and it would be normal." Tewlon sighed. "Alas, we cannot linger that long. But do not fret; it will continue to improve."

"Don't know what possessed you to leap off the stairs." Ameilistari shook her head. "You're only part elf. You can't do everything Tewlon does."

"One does not need to be an elf to be nimble," Tewlon said.

What a strange comment for an elf to make.

Tewlon crossed the room and squatted to inspect Nidor's ankle. "Yes, you'll soon be fine." He looked up at Nidor. "But you should adjust your stance so you don't lose your balance at the wrong time."

"What?" Nidor lowered his brow. "Stand on one leg?"

Tewlon chuckled. "Draw your sword, and I'll show you."

Nidor stood and unsheathed his blade, and Tewlon proceeded to give a lesson on swordplay. Though they were pressed for time, Ameilistari supposed it was necessary—she wouldn't want anything bad to happen to her cousin. She began to hum.

Over the next hour, Ameilistari battled boredom as she often did, manipulating a small magical sphere between her wiggling fingers to improve her dexterity. Selanna had taught her the exercise, and though she had perfected it already, it was both calming and beneficial. The sphere didn't shed much light; it didn't explode or freeze. It simply existed. While she continued humming, she summoned a second ball for her other hand and worked them both. After a few minutes, she took control with her mind and forced the spheres to move on their own, around her fingers and back again. She then released her mental control and resumed maneuvering them manually.

The room quieted, and Ameilistari lifted her head to observe her warriors. They stared in her direction. The little spheres vanished as fear crept in, and she scanned the wall behind her. No lizards. Her eyes went to the ceiling. Nothing. Ameilistari looked back at her companions to see what had stilled them, and noticed they were staring *at* her, not past her. Nidor chuckled.

"What?" She patted down her hair. Was it that disheveled? Nidor and Tewlon weren't exactly ready to sit for portraits themselves.

"What were you doing?" asked Nidor.

"You have your exercises," she lifted her chin, "and I have mine." Nidor wouldn't make a very good soldier if he teased his commander. If he ever hoped to be her captain, he needed to learn that. But lessons in proper decorum would have to wait until Tewlon wasn't present—elves had their own views on how things were done. "Are you two just about finished?"

"Almost," said Tewlon, and he turned to Nidor. "Once more, all the way through."

Nidor and Tewlon raised their swords, and Tewlon lunged. Nidor spun on his good ankle, using the bad one for balance only, and steered the elf's blade away. He countered, stomping with his right foot and thrusting, and Tewlon danced out of reach. The elf maneuvered around Nidor, and Nidor made quick steps with his wounded ankle while the good one bore most of his weight.

Ameilistari furrowed her brow. She would not have been able to tell an injury hampered him, had she not known already.

Tewlon advanced with a flurry of slashes, and Nidor shifted his weapon from one hand to the other, retreating on his right foot while fending off the attacks—when did he learn to use his left hand so proficiently? With a flourish, he twirled Tewlon's blade aside and switched hands again before moving to the offensive. After a few more slashes, the warriors stopped, and both smiled while Nidor panted.

"Excellent!" Tewlon said.

Nidor grinned, and a genuine appreciation for the elf's expertise reflected in his eyes.

Ameilistari gawked at Tewlon. Were he human, she might consider hiring him to train her soldiers. What he taught Nidor in a short time was amazing.

The elf looked at her. "We can proceed if you're ready," he said.

She cleared her throat and stood. "Yes. We should get moving. Has your master mentioned anything as to where we should head?"

Tewlon scowled, but it seemed more at himself than toward Ameilistari. With a sigh, he stared at nothing for several seconds before frowning. He closed his eyes and shook his head.

"Is something amiss?" Ameilistari asked.

He turned to her. "No. All is… as it was. I believe we're on the correct level. Once we leave this room, we'll turn right." He glanced at Nidor. "And we need to be *very* alert."

"What are you not saying?" Ameilistari posed. The elf was definitely hiding some piece of information.

"Nothing. But we can waste no more time. We must go now."

"All right." Ameilistari looked from Nidor to Tewlon. "You lead the way," she turned to her cousin, "and you protect the rear. Same as before."

Tewlon smirked.

Ameilistari unlocked the door, and the elf listened before opening it to have a look. All was quiet. He crept from the room, and Ameilistari and Nidor followed.

The tunnel stretched nearly a hundred paces to a corridor passing from left to right. To the left, the floor steadily rose, while the opposite direction carried a downward slope. With only the slightest hesitation, Tewlon turned right.

Ameilistari worried the uneven floor would test Nidor's balance, but her cousin kept up without complaint. The corridor traveled twenty yards and leveled off as it turned right, and the following hallway led to an archway. Beyond was a large chamber, dark and quiet.

Willing the intensity of her light to grow, three exits appeared within the immense room, one to either side and another on the far wall. Rails entered from the side tunnels, and piles of debris and upended mine carts were scattered. Above, veins of gold and silver glittered, whirling from one end to the other and entwined at several points, as if performing an eternal dance. Were the mines not so foreboding, the design might have been beautiful.

"I have been wondering," Nidor whispered to Ameilistari as they entered. "Can you make all three of us invisible? Perhaps we can avoid further confrontations."

"I'm not sure." She bit her lip. "A third person would drain my strength much more swiftly."

"It wouldn't work," Tewlon said softly. "The lizards can both hear and smell us."

That was how the creature found her and Nidor in that first encounter! So much for that idea.

Tewlon neared the center of the room, his attention alternating between the side passages. He then halted when five lizards entered through the opposite archway, only one of them using the floor.

"Behind us!" Nidor warned.

Ameilistari looked to see additional reptiles crawling through the entrance she and her companions had used.

"Do we fight?" Nidor asked.

Tewlon seemed torn. There were now a dozen lizards on either side of the room. "No." His voice was calm. "Follow me."

The elf sprinted toward the right archway—Ameilistari was positive he slowed his pace for Nidor's sake. She followed, glancing back twice to make sure her cousin kept up. His limp was more pronounced while he hurried, but he did not fall behind.

They entered a narrow hallway. The ceiling was rounded and only seven feet high—it was the most constricting portion of the mines thus far. Luckily, it wasn't very long, and they stepped into a small chamber with a single exit on the left wall.

"They're pursuing," said Nidor as he hobbled into the room.

Without a word, Tewlon led the way through the exit. The next corridor was similar to the last one, but after ten yards it branched left and continued straight. Behind Nidor, the shadows of lizards danced at the edge of the light.

Tewlon turned left.

The passage remained confining as it curved to the right, and after fifty paces it terminated at a room. The chamber was twice the size of the previous one and possessed five exits: one to the left, another at the far end, and two on the right, one nearby and the other across the room. Six lizards issued from the near archway, each eight feet long, but their scales weren't green or gray. They were red.

Tewlon turned to face the monstrous reptiles. "Cross the room!" he ordered.

There was no time to fret about Tewlon taking charge. Ameilistari obeyed, praying no lizards entered through the archway she approached. She glanced back to make sure Nidor was behind her—she wasn't going alone. Her cousin kept up better than she had anticipated, but beyond him, billowing flames attacked Tewlon, and her eyes widened. Thank the gods the elf rolled aside in time.

Fear drove Ameilistari, and nothing opposed her as she and Nidor passed into the adjoining hallway. Tewlon entered a couple of seconds later.

"Go!" he commanded.

"Did one of them breathe fire?" Ameilistari asked while she resumed running.

"All of them did!" Tewlon's voice carried a tone of anger, not fear.

Who was he angry at? Sure, they were lost in a mine and pursued by enormous lizards, some that could evidently breathe fire, but at the moment there was nothing to do but find another room offering protection. Preferably one with a door the reptiles couldn't burn.

The corridor ended at a descending stairwell, and Ameilistari balked. From what Tewlon had said, they did not want to climb or descend, and they had already performed the latter in the sloping hallway.

"What do we do?" she asked.

"There's no choice!" snapped Tewlon. "Go!"

Unlike the last staircase, this one didn't spiral around a column. It traveled a short distance to a landing jutting to the right, and another set of stairs descended in the opposite direction. This happened two more times, and the steps ended at a large tunnel. It was twenty feet wide, with a massive archway supporting the ceiling thirty feet away. Halfway down the corridor's length was a smaller archway on the left, and Ameilistari hastened toward it.

She hadn't realized how far ahead of Nidor she was, and he limped from the final step as she reached the opening. Tewlon was behind her cousin, and the elf turned to decapitate a pursuing lizard—a green one.

Ameilistari passed beneath the arch and into another large chamber. The opposite end bore the only exit. Looking back, Nidor and Tewlon had joined her, and Tewlon waved for her to proceed.

The air was warmer than in other places of the mines, and Ameilistari's light sparkled off deposits of blue, green, and yellow quartz across the ceiling. As she reached the halfway point, four lizards, two red and two orange, entered through the far archway. Behind her companions, five red lizards pursued.

"Magic!" Ameilistari said to herself, coming to a stop. With all the running, she had forgotten about her stunning spell.

Nidor and Tewlon turned to confront the reptiles to the rear, the elf shouting commands to her cousin she had no time to decipher. She concentrated on the lizards blocking her path—there were eight now. Speaking her incantation, bolts of lightning streaked from her fingertips to envelop the creatures and halt them where they stood.

Ameilistari spun as fire rushed her companions. Tewlon tackled Nidor to avoid the attack, but they had surely felt the heat. She cast her spell again, stunning the red lizards.

Tewlon rose to his feet, his leather armor darkened and anger plain on his face. "I cannot fight like this!" he growled, pulling Nidor to stand.

Was the elf angry with Nidor? Being outnumbered wasn't odds anyone *wished* for, nor was fighting fire-breathing monsters, but her cousin was doing his best. And now, more lizards arrived through the first archway, green ones and orange ones.

Suddenly, Tewlon grew in height and mass. His leather transformed into black steel plates, his sword enlarged, and his ears became rounded as his hair darkened and a goatee formed around his lips. He was massive. He pulled a second enormous sword from his back and hacked into the new arrivals, slaying one with every swing.

Whatever magic was at play, it hadn't come from Ameilistari. She realized she was gawking and returned her attention to the far arch. No more lizards had emerged, and those captured by her spell continued dancing while sparks of lightning raced about their bodies. It would hold a little longer.

She spun back. Giant Tewlon had killed half the attacking creatures, and a few lay dead before Nidor. Four orange reptiles remained out of reach, and their jowls puffed up. They were preparing to spit fire.

Multiple spells rushed through Ameilistari's head. She latched onto one, pulling forces of magic to her as she recited the words and swept her arms from left to right. A force of wind crossed the chamber, veering the fiery breath away as soon as it escaped the reptilian maws. Nidor stumbled while retreating, while giant Tewlon charged, heedless of the fire, and butchered the monsters.

The room quieted for a moment before another dozen lizards entered through the first archway. Tewlon lifted Nidor and turned to Ameilistari.

"Go!" he said, his voice much lower and more commanding than before.

She ran past the stunned creatures and through the archway.

Chapter 20

The Forge

After taking a few minutes to patch up their injuries—the mine dwellers did the same, using mushrooms—Baylun and his companions followed their new guides. The creatures obviously preferred darkness, but they didn't make any motions to suggest Romik extinguish the torch. Instead, they shielded their faces from the light.

The hallway stretched long, finally interrupted by twenty-foot-wide corridors branching left and right while the larger hall continued. A massive amount of rubble climbed the walls around the intersection, and the ceiling was jagged, as if it had collapsed, leaving a rough cavity above the tunnel rising thirty feet. It must have been the cave-in from centuries ago that trapped Mattasun. Perhaps it was the dwarves who had worked with Uustaag that opened it up during their escape.

The dwellers headed left.

Romik attempted to speak with the creatures after the turn, but the one who addressed them earlier scowled and put a finger to its lips. Baylun didn't believe the creature to be angry; it was more like it repeated a gesture it had seen many times.

Before long, smaller archways appeared, and the dwellers passed beneath the second on the right. It was narrower, with a rounded ceiling. After a short distance, the mine dwellers stopped to peer forward and back while one of them fiddled with a spot on the wall. There was nothing marking the area as special other than a small triangle etched near the floor, a detail easily overlooked as part of the scenery. A five-foot-wide section of the wall slid silently open to reveal a hidden passage. How many of these doors had Baylun and his companions missed?

They followed the dwellers into the secret tunnel, and the door closed quietly behind them. The mine dwellers then halted in a small chamber not far away. Contained within were a stone bench and a well, and a hallway exited on the opposite side.

The lead dweller turned to Baylun, putting a hand to its chest and saying, "Poopit Hans."

Was that its name? Why would any parent…? Baylun shook his head. That wasn't important. He put his hand on his chest.

"Baylun."

"Bye'Lin," Poopit said.

Baylun pointed at his brother. "Romik."

"Row'Mick."

He waved toward the gray elf. "Lorylla."

"Lola."

Close enough.

Poopit introduced his companions, naming each in turn. "Bo, Zur, Ka."

Those were simple names, making Poopit's even stranger.

Poopit pointed at the torch ensconced in Romik's hook. "Shut up!"

Did he mean for them to put it out?

The dweller pointed at his eyes. "Blasted eyes!" He spoke with feeling, as if annoyed with his own anatomy. It was as if he repeated something uttered to him before, perhaps in the same manner in which it had been said.

"I think he wishes for you to extinguish the torch," Baylun said to his brother.

"But how will I see?" Romik asked.

Baylun turned to Poopit. "Can't see." He placed his hand over his eyebrows and looked around with his eyes closed.

Poopit nodded in understanding. He reached into a pocket in his lizard-skin and pulled out a mushroom.

"I'm not eating that," said Romik.

Poopit pointed at the torch again. "Blasted eyes!"

Baylun shrugged. "Just drop it in the well. I'll lead you."

Romik scowled as he tossed the torch into the pit, watching it descend until there was a splash and its light winked out. But darkness did not reign. In the torchlight's absence, the fungus glowed blue. It wasn't much, but enough to see Poopit and most of Bo, Zur, and Ka.

Poopit handed the mushroom to Baylun and smiled. "Less go."

The dweller waved for them to follow, and he and his companions moved toward the exit.

Romik seized Baylun's arm. "I don't know where they're taking us, but I doubt it's to find our children."

"Wait!" Baylun halted the dwellers. "Have you seen our friends?"

Poopit frowned.

"Others like us?" Baylun spoke slowly, pointing at himself and his companions.

"Uh-zurs…" Poopit appeared to think. He smiled. "Yes! Uh-zurs. Less go!" He and his companions exited the room.

"I see little choice at the moment," said Baylun. "They helped Greyor before. They might lead us past dangers we're unaware of." His brother was unconvinced. "We will follow for now, but I promise you, we'll get back on the trail as soon as we know they can't help us."

Romik shook his head, but made no further protests. Lorylla was unreadable while holding an arrow loosely to her bowstring.

Baylun handed the mushroom to Romik, and they proceeded.

The tunnel bore straight before opening into a small room. Several mushrooms grew around the edges, shedding the same light as the one Romik carried and bathing the chamber in a soft glow. A door was situated in the far wall, and another was to the right. The lead mine dweller opened the door on the right and passed through. The others followed.

Romik paused, sheathing his sword to pluck a few mushrooms and skewer them onto his hooks. He then nodded to Baylun to continue.

The next tunnel ended at an intersection. A corridor ran to the left, bending away, and to the right, a stairway led deeper into the mines. As they turned left, Romik's sigh of relief mirrored Baylun's feelings—he doubted any of their friends were farther down.

The curving hallway traveled sixty paces and ended. Near the floor to the side of the dead end, a triangle marked the wall. Poopit held a finger to his lips while Bo fiddled with the area above the triangle, and a panel slid silently to the left, revealing what appeared to be the back of an enormous statue. Bo and Ka crept forward with spears ready, making little sound while moving to either side of the sculpture and disappearing from view. Poopit and Zur remained at the secret door, Zur standing in the doorway to keep it from closing.

A chirp sounded from the right. Another answered from the left. Poopit made a chirping noise of his own, and responses came from beyond the statue. Zur then stepped through, followed by Poopit, who beckoned for Baylun and the others to join them. Baylun held the door open while Romik and Lorylla entered first.

The monument was fifteen feet tall and eight feet wide, appearing as an enormous dwarf. As Baylun reached the front, he saw that the statue held a hammer against its chest with both hands, and before it was an anvil five feet high and just as wide. The dwarf did not seem to be a warrior—a smith? Scores of hand-sized claw marks marred its exquisite detail, but the vandalism failed to detract from its splendor—even the scratches across its eyes didn't stop them from following Baylun as he trailed his companions.

"Meldar," whispered Lorylla.

Baylun had never seen the god's likeness before.

Poopit and Zur bowed to the statue while Ka and Bo moved to a set of doors on the far side of the room. One door was ajar, and Ka motioned for everyone to join him while peering through the opening.

Romik gave Baylun a concerned look, likely nervous about

straying farther from their companions. As Lorylla walked toward the doors without hesitation, Baylun felt torn. He gazed at Torrac.

Dwarf-friend… Protect… Honor your oath… Clanghorr approaches…

Had the whispers been there all along? Perhaps they had become so common that his consciousness ignored them. Baylun needed to pay more attention. Torrac wished to proceed, that much was obvious, and apparently Greyor headed their way. But how long before the dwarf arrived? There was no way of knowing.

Baylun turned to Romik. "We must continue for now."

Romik shook his head and sighed, his mounting frustration evident.

Beyond the doors was a small unfurnished chamber with a faded fresco on the opposite wall. Claw marks did their part to aid the ravages of time, making sure that whatever the scene had portrayed remained unknown. A corridor exited to the left, while a narrow hallway with a rounded ceiling bore right.

The mine dwellers took the right tunnel, and an arcing stairwell veered them to the left. It was a gradual climb, rising thirty feet over the course of a hundred steps, and through an ornate archway at the top issued an orange glow. The dwellers shaded their eyes and proceeded. Beyond the arch, a room opened to the left, where the light originated. The mine dwellers hugged the wall on the right as they entered.

Baylun stepped into the chamber, and the temperature rose. Until that moment, he hadn't realized how cool the mines had been. The square chamber stretched twenty feet to the left, where the floor ended with a ledge topped by a wide arch bearing the familiar hammer and anvil in bas-relief. No railing existed. The glow emerged from below, and the mine dwellers appeared hesitant to draw any closer. All except one. Poopit Hans lowered to his hands and knees, still grasping his hammer as he crawled toward the drop-off.

Baylun motioned for Romik to remain, and he followed Poopit's lead. Lorylla joined him, but the elf merely crouched while holding an arrow to her bowstring. Even in her awkward stance, she moved gracefully and without a sound. Baylun couldn't claim the same, and he slowed his pace to dampen the rattling of his armor.

Poopit reached the ledge, and the heat grew as Baylun arrived with Lorylla close behind. Thirty feet down was a massive room. The chamber was oval-shaped, stretching twenty yards to the left and right, and walls darker than other places of Lornibur curved inward as they climbed above the balcony to form a dome. From a trench along the opposing wall radiated the orange glow. Barriers of bronze guided the channel, and within was a familiar sight—how could Baylun ever forget the lava-filled fissures in Helmland? On either side of the duct were foot-wide gaps, each filled with water moving rapidly in the same direction as the molten rock. The system entered through a hole near a large decorated archway at the apex of the rounded wall to the left, and exited through another hole near a matching archway to the right.

Seven forges followed the trench, the middle one larger than the others. It was also the only one bearing a slat of stone suspended a few feet over the trench, anchoring it to the far wall. Smoking gray coals filled the wide hearth of the central furnace, the stone darkened by centuries of scorching, and several levers extended from its side. One lever surely lowered a metallic wheel from the raised slat, a device equipped with blackened scoops to lift magma into channels running about the stone bed of the forge. Another lever appeared to operate a bellows ten times larger than those attached to the smaller forges. Affixed to the flagstones around the station were five anvils, while the others bore one each, and four empty troughs of stone seemed to have been risen from the floor, two to either side. The central forge was the only one not covered in dust.

Rusted tools of the trade were strewn haphazardly, and bundles of old wood—perhaps bruskiin—filled several mine carts scattered about. The area below the balcony bore no furnishings, and the forges shrouded much of it in shadow.

Poopit looked at Baylun. "Aamustall," he whispered, pointing toward the middle forge.

"Aamustall…" Baylun repeated, receiving a nod from the mine dweller. The master forge's name?

Poopit curled his index and middle fingers and held them up to his mouth, as if they were fangs. He hissed at Baylun, and then flapped his arms, as if they were wings, before raising his hands like claws and hissing again.

Aamustall wasn't the name of the forge. A monster?

Baylun examined the oval room again. Other than the lava and rushing water, nothing moved. He nudged Poopit, then put his hand over his eyebrows and closed his eyes before pretending to scan the chamber. Upon opening his eyes, he spread his hands and shrugged to show his confusion. "Aamustall?" he whispered.

Poopit seemed to grasp Baylun's meaning, and he pointed at the central forge.

Baylun still didn't understand.

"Whatever Aamustall is," Lorylla said softly, "it uses that furnace for some purpose. And from the looks of things, it is not for smithing." She obviously spied something Baylun had missed. "The pulsating glow deep within the hearth is unnatural."

Baylun narrowed his eyes until spotting what the gray elf indicated. In the large forge at the edge near the trench, an orange glow throbbed, as if breathing. It wasn't obvious at first, but now Baylun noticed the overall lighting of the chamber pulsed with it. How had he missed that?

Poopit crawled away from the ledge, beckoning Baylun and Lorylla to do the same. Baylun followed Poopit's lead while Lorylla remained crouched, apparently unwilling to remove her hands from her bow and arrow. Once they rejoined the others, they stood, and Poopit led the way to the other end of the room, where he pushed against the wall. It was then that Baylun noticed a stone door. It wasn't secret, for no care was taken to disguise its seams, but the decorative carvings surrounding it made it less conspicuous. The door was probably obvious to dwarves in Lornibur's day… and to mine dwellers today.

The panel swung open with a slight grinding noise—it surprisingly didn't echo into the domed chamber. Beyond, a wide hall ran sixty feet, and in place of the far-left corner was a ledge from the side wall to the back wall. Just as with the first balcony, a decorative arch spanned the opening, and a glow emitted from below, matching the hue of the forge, although dimmer and carrying less heat. Atop the arch was a representation of a dwarf. That, or a stout, bearded man. The figure either rose from a block of stone or stood behind a square wall.

Poopit didn't shield his eyes from the light this time as he crept forward, nor did he crawl. Baylun and Lorylla followed. As they neared, Baylun detected sounds below: scuffling feet, occasional coughs, and hushed voices. He understood nothing that was uttered.

He reached the ledge and saw another large chamber below. It butted against the room of forges and was almost equal in size, and ten feet inside the connecting archway, a massive portcullis blocked further entry. If a winch existed to lift the thick bars, Baylun couldn't see it, but it mattered little since the heavy chain intended to perform that action dangled beside the portcullis, its end appearing to have been melted.

Within the gated area, hundreds of stacked cubes of worked granite formed a twenty-foot-high wall to split the room into two unequal sides. The smaller portion was directly below, hosting dust-covered deposits of ore encased in dirt and stone. Amid the faded glow of the forge, most of the ore was hard to discern, but there were several colors of quartz, and Baylun was sure a large chunk bore gold and another silver.

The larger section of the room comprised three-quarters of the overall space, and Baylun couldn't believe his eyes. Crowded within were mine dwellers. There were no furnishings of any kind, and the creatures milled about like cattle with their heads down. Some appeared to communicate in soft voices, and several toward the far end were sleeping or dead. The cell was dirty, like a neglected barn, and the mingling smell of feces and death turned Baylun's stomach.

Poopit stared with hardened eyes.

"What is this?" Baylun asked in a hushed voice, realizing too late the mine dweller likely understood none of his words.

"Uh-zurs," Poopit said.

"Prisoners," whispered Lorylla, turning to Baylun. "The 'others' of his kind."

Poopit looked from the gray elf to Baylun. He pointed at the captives, then moved his hand to his mouth and began chewing.

Lorylla's eyes widened with horror. "Food!"

Poopit nodded. He evidently recognized that word.

"Food for what?" posed Baylun, glancing at the visible portion of the forge room. It was then he noticed that several bars of the portcullis had been cut, creating a door held in place by a pair of ropes. Not very secure. Yet, the mine dwellers made no attempts to escape. In fact, none of them seemed willing to approach within ten feet of the bars.

While Baylun pondered this, a movement outside the gate caught his attention. It was subtle, just beyond the archway. Squinting, he spotted a figure partially camouflaged by the orange glow behind it; a creature with orange and red skin. It had the look of an insect, although it stood erect and bore only one set of arms and one set of legs. Its head was wide, with bulging, compound eyes similar to a praying mantis, and before its small mouth were jagged mandibles, surely capable of ripping off a limb. The monster was taller than Baylun by a head at least, and its arms were long and thin, segmented as if wrapped in natural armor. One arm ended in a scythe-like blade, while the other bore a hand with four clawed fingers. It was like a statue, facing the prisoners while smoke dribbled from its maw. Was it Aamustall?

Baylun motioned for Lorylla to back away, and she obeyed, her eyes revealing her to have spied what Baylun had seen. He joined her, mimicking her slow movements so as not to draw the creature's attention. Poopit followed, and they returned to Romik and the others at the wall farthest from the balcony.

Romik furrowed his brow. "What is it?"

Baylun shook his head. "Not sure."

"A demon," Lorylla hissed. "A creature not meant for our world."

"And hundreds of mine dwellers held captive," Baylun added, glancing at Poopit. "Our friend here says they're food."

A look of disgust captured Romik's face. He sighed. "I feel for them. I do. But this isn't our problem. We must find our families."

Baylun understood his brother's point. Nidor and Kiryanna were more important than the plight of the mine dwellers. Lorylla's expression showed only anger—whether at Romik's words, the demon, or the overall situation wasn't clear. As Baylun started to respond, the voice of Torrac entered his mind.

Dwarf-friend… Companion of Clanghorr… Hold to your oath…

Baylun closed his mouth. Hold to his oath? But these were mine dwellers, not dwarves. Perhaps Torrac considered them the new citizens of Lornibur, to be protected by the city's ancient weapons. Even so, a demon? Baylun had hoped his days of fighting such evils were behind him. And although Torrac's compulsion to obey was strong, he knew he could resist if he tried. He swore to be a dwarf-friend, after all, not a dweller-friend. As Baylun thought about the past decades of playing the hero in Philen, rescuing and protecting the innocent, a spark kindled deep within, urging him to comply. It was almost like his time in Darum Carumbor, the dark tower that held him captive while he awaited brave souls to rescue him. But on this occasion, he was that brave soul.

Romik stared intently. He didn't understand Baylun's turmoil. If they proceeded, they might die for their efforts, and their families would never learn of their fates. But to turn their backs on those in need…

The dilemma brought pain to Baylun's stomach. He scanned the four mine dwellers. Their expressions, though fearful, revealed determination. Lorylla was unreadable. How badly he wished he had Kiryanna's counsel.

Chapter 21

Nursery

Greyor closed his eyes and concentrated on Torrac. He and his companions had followed the bloody footprints until the tracks faded, and Eraim led them for several yards afterward. But now they faced another intersection, and the elf knew not which way to go. That was when she turned to Greyor.

Taking a deep breath, Greyor slowly released it. *Torrac, where are you?* There was no answer to his thought, but the familiar sensation pulled at him. He frowned at the maidens. "They have ascended. Torrac is higher than our current location." He pointed toward the ceiling and to the right. "That way."

"Baylun must not sense Clanghorr the way you sense Torrac," said Kiryanna. "Otherwise, he wouldn't be moving away from us." Her expression brightened. "Perhaps he pursues Nidor."

A positive thought? That wasn't like the marteese. But she might be correct. Greyor saw through Eraim's mock optimism—the elf's eyes betrayed her lack of support for the theory.

"We take the passage to the right," Kiryanna decided. "And ascend at the first opportunity."

Lacking a better idea, Greyor gave a firm nod and led the way. Eraim quickly added to her sketch as she and Kiryanna followed.

The tunnel bore straight beyond Greyor's sight. After fifty paces, a slight shift in temperature didn't escape his notice. It was warmer. A bit farther, and a door became visible at the corridor's end. It was not bruskiin, but iron, and rust lined its seams.

"Why does it grow hotter with every step?" Kiryanna asked in a hushed voice. "Do we approach the forge?"

An exciting thought, but Greyor doubted it. The entrance would be grandiose, unlike the hallway they followed. He shook his head.

The temperature continued to rise, and as they reached the iron door, it was like sitting by a hearth in a tavern during early summer: not too bad for enjoying a mug of ale, but too warm for one dressed in full battle gear. Greyor removed his gauntlet and felt the door. It was hot. Not enough to burn, but enough to tell him a heat source lay on the other side. He slid his hand along the iron. It was aged and worn, but not from use. The door hadn't been used for a long time. It might not open willingly.

Fangs gnashed at Greyor's face, and he jumped back.

He saw only the rusty door before him.

"What is it?" asked Eraim.

He shook the image from his mind. "Nothing. I guess the fire-spewing lizard has me on edge."

"It was a dragon," Kiryanna corrected him.

Eraim glanced at the marteese and returned her attention to Greyor. "If you saw something, you must share it with us."

Greyor slumped his shoulders. The elf raised an eyebrow, her expression reminiscent of the paladin Merssa, who had organized the war against Trannum. It was a questioning gaze no one but Vecnor had seemed able to deny. Greyor gave in.

"Teeth."

"Teeth?" asked Kiryanna, frowning.

"Fangs," Greyor said. "A nasty set of fangs. Nothing else."

"Could Clanghorr be warning you?" posed Eraim. "Perhaps it has had a horrible experience here."

Greyor recalled seeing a similar vision when he destroyed the unholy symbol of Demoligius. He blamed it on remnants of evil. But what if it had been a warning from Clanghorr, as Eraim suggested? A warning about what, though? Nothing ill came of shattering the talon. In any case, standing outside the door was getting them nowhere. And now Kiryanna tapped her foot as the last trace of patience melted from her face.

"Let's be ready for anything," Greyor said as he reached for the latch.

Eraim stepped back, an arrow held taut against her bowstring. Kiryanna lifted her blade and issued a nod.

Greyor tested the mechanism. It moved, but the iron door didn't budge. Reluctantly, he looped Clanghorr on his waist to free up both hands and tried again. Reddish-orange powder broke loose, coating his gauntlets and left pauldron as he pushed with all his might, but it opened only a crack. A small body then joined him—Kiryanna. Muscles bulged along the exposed arms of the marteese, and she grimaced. The door pivoted slowly, releasing a hot breeze, and opened a few inches before conceding at last. Greyor and Kiryanna spilled into the room.

The marteese landed atop Greyor, but fell to the flagstones as he scrambled to his feet, his hand desperately pulling Clanghorr. Nothing moved within the chamber, save for the steady flow of magma following a trench along the back wall. Bronze plates lined channels to either side of the trench, each carrying swift water, and the glowing stream entered from a wide corridor on the left and exited through a small, finely carved archway next to a tunnel on the opposite side. The sound of rushing water nearly masked the bubbling and crackling of the lava, and the radiating heat brought a twinge of pain to Greyor's back.

"What could this room be for?" asked Eraim, stepping into the chamber with an arrow ready.

Greyor shook his head and relaxed the grip on his battleaxe. "We have nothing like this in Morimont." Perhaps that was the reason Lornibur's forge was special—legends held Meldar's Forge to be filled with lava. "My guess would be that this channel either carries magma to or away from the forge."

"Which way is Baylun?" asked Kiryanna, evidently uninterested in the possibilities the strange room held.

Greyor closed his eyes and pictured Torrac. The invisible force pulled at his gut, beyond the trench and upward. He opened his eyes and pointed. "He's still above us. Straight ahead."

Kiryanna pursed her lips. There was no proceeding in that direction.

"Let us follow the stream," suggested Eraim. "See where it leads us."

Greyor thought it odd the little elf desired to follow the path of molten rock. It was as if she had read his mind. He nodded and headed left.

They hugged the wall away from the lava to minimize the heat. The passage curved to the right, bearing in Torrac's direction, and sweat drenched Greyor as it straightened out and the air grew hotter still. A wide flight of steps then filled the tunnel, rising ten feet, and to its right was a ramp carrying the magma and giving strength to its flow rate. The sound of rupturing gas bubbles increased, becoming clearer over the racing water—the source of molten rock surely lay ahead.

Greyor stopped to drink deeply from his waterskin, and his companions did the same. Kiryanna's red curls lay flat, and sweat beaded on her exposed flesh. How was it Eraim appeared dry? A benefit of being good friends with Selanna? Greyor shook his head and lifted his skin for another gulp, but a noise halted the spout an inch from his lips. Something had moved. Something up the steps.

Eraim slung her bow over her shoulder and pulled Mithkahr. Even in the orange glow, the red tint of the blade was visible. She walked quickly forward without a sound, still hugging the wall as she ascended. Greyor followed with Clanghorr ready, and Kiryanna brought up the rear. Upon nearing the top, Eraim lowered until nearly crawling, and halted once high enough to scan what lay ahead.

With a gasp, she ducked and whispered something in her native language. It wasn't like Eraim to speak Elfish to non-elves—the sight must have truly rattled her. Kiryanna evidently realized Greyor's lack of understanding and repeated the words in Common.

"Demon spider."

Greyor moved higher up, despite Eraim grabbing his arm, and

crawled the final few steps to take a look. Hot air brushed his face as he gazed upon a pool of lava flooding the back third of a rounded room, fed by a stream from a corridor on the left. Partially submerged within the shallow pond were several one-foot-tall eggs, seemingly impervious to the intense heat, but what held his attention was the monster tending to the clutch.

Walking along the ceiling above the pool was what could only be described as a demon spider. The fiend was as big as a horse, and it clung to the stone as if there were no gravity. While the rear segment was large and bulbous, the front end was horrific. In place of the spider's face was that of a woman's. But not exactly a woman. She had two large eyes and six smaller eyes, all black, with the latter arching over the former. Her mouth was too wide for her face, and every time it opened it dripped a blackish liquid from its many fangs. The nightmare's first four legs differed from the spider-like legs to the rear; they terminated in claws, reminiscent of a lobster. Greyor watched with his jaw hanging open while the creature straightened an egg that had fallen askew and crawled to another to issue a couple of gentle taps.

"What vile god is responsible for that abomination?" Kiryanna asked from beside Greyor.

"Exactly as I said," Eraim replied. "A demon spider. It is from Hell."

"Well," Greyor said. "Whatever it is, it doesn't belong here." He stood before either of the maidens could object.

The demon spotted Greyor immediately and scuttled back a few steps, releasing a screech like a pig's squeal. It then spat a glob of black goop across the room. Greyor ducked, and the spittle sailed over his head and landed on the flagstones at the bottom of the stairs, where it sizzled and left behind a charred hole.

"Don't let it spit on you!" cautioned Greyor, charging up the final steps with Clanghorr ready.

A couple of arrows sped past Greyor as Eraim moved to his flank. A ball of saliva intercepted the first, while the second pierced deep into the demon's bulbous rear. The monster scrambled down the side wall and used one of its pincers to splash lava at the elf, and Eraim shrieked as she leaped toward the stairs, narrowly evading the attack.

Greyor halted ten feet from the pool. The spider was out of reach, and he dared not throw his weapon for fear of losing it forever. Kiryanna stopped as well, her eyes scanning the immediate surroundings. The marteese lifted a rock and threw it. The stone bounced off the creature's hide and plopped into the lava, causing no visible harm.

With impressive speed, the demon ran along the ceiling, fixated on Kiryanna. The marteese readied her sword, but in a flash, the spider grabbed her free hand with a pincer and yanked her toward the molten rock. Greyor heaved Clanghorr before the creature could complete its task, slicing through its arm and freeing his companion, and Kiryanna fell backward, avoiding the lava while Clanghorr dug into the wall near the pool's border and became wedged. The demon spider retreated with a screech as yellowish blood issued from the severed appendage.

Eraim loosed two arrows, adding another wound to the spider's posterior and one close to its face. The elf released a third, but the spider intercepted the missile with its spittle, dissolving the projectile into nothingness.

Greyor raced to Clanghorr. The battleaxe was buried deep in the stone above the lava flowing toward the stairs. The heat grew unbearable as he grasped the haft—it was as if he reached into a fire—but the blade released the wall with surprising ease, and he stumbled back. This worked in his favor, as a gob of sludge meant for his head struck his left gauntlet. The acidic goop ate through the steel, and he cast aside the metal glove, sparing it only a glance as it dissolved on the flagstones.

Kiryanna held a defensive stance, and behind her were a couple of smoking holes in the floor. She shouted, switching from Common speech to Elfish while attempting to draw the monster forward, but it seemed content with remaining over the pool.

"Brakkeet!" Greyor cursed. The demon was a coward!

Eraim turned her aim low and released her bowstring. The arrow pierced an egg, and it shattered, splattering thick orange liquid with a yellow center into the lava. It smoked momentarily as it dissolved.

Shrieking louder than before, the demon scuttled along the ceiling as Eraim broke a second egg. The elf rolled away, and black spittle struck the floor where she had stood. She had found the monster's weakness, and it advanced beyond the pond with malice in all eight eyes.

Greyor ran toward Eraim with Clanghorr in his bare hand, shouting to gain the spider's attention. But it was bent on the destroyer of its eggs. He threw his battleaxe before it reached her, and the runes blazed as it sliced into the creature's hindquarters. The fiend dropped to the floor with a screech, turning its sights on him. With no other weapon available, he drew his knife.

"You like these eggs?" Kiryanna shouted, followed by the sound of an eggshell breaking.

Greyor thrust the knife as the giant body reached him, but the blade snapped. A pincer then seized his right wrist, and Kiryanna yelped when another grabbed hold of her. Clanghorr lay twenty feet away, but it might as well have been a hundred as the claw lifted him off the floor. Kiryanna then screamed when the spider's wicked teeth bit into her side.

"Greyor!" hollered Eraim.

The elf held her sword in one hand and Clanghorr in the other. She tossed the battleaxe with impressive accuracy, and the haft spun perfectly to land within Greyor's palm. He brought down the blade, severing the appendage holding him, and as he fell, he drove Clanghorr deep into the demon's front half.

The spider reared as Greyor crashed to the floor, and he saw Eraim thrust Mithkahr into its abdomen. Not wanting to give the monster a chance to retreat, he scrambled to his feet and cut through both of its left rear legs with a single swing. The spider collapsed onto its side. Eraim made several more gashes with her elfish sword, and

Greyor hacked into its body, unrelenting until the screeches and movements ceased—even the few twitches that followed. The spider then turned to dust, and the particles seemed to evaporate before they touched the flagstones.

Eraim rushed past Greyor toward Kiryanna. The marteese crawled away from the lava pool's edge, where she had been dropped. The elf grabbed hold of Kiryanna's right hand and dragged her farther before rolling her onto her back. A blackened wound existed on the left side of her golden armor, where the demon's teeth had torn a hole.

Greyor joined the maidens, scanning the room for any further danger. Nothing else moved. He did notice, however, that the last egg Kiryanna had broken bore a partially formed lizard. Its skin was red or orange—it was hard to tell as it sank into the pool.

Eraim had removed Kiryanna's breastplate, and she rubbed a leaf over the gruesome wound while the marteese released painful gasps. The blackened flesh appeared to be melting.

"Greyor." Eraim handed him a tiny bowl. "Put three stone crawlers in here."

He did as instructed.

"Now mash them with your thumb," the elf said while she placed another leaf. With her free hand, she pulled a small pouch from one of her larger pouches.

Greyor carried out the action with a sigh. They should feed Kiryanna the mushrooms to begin the healing process, not waste precious minutes creating some elaborate remedy.

Eraim handed Greyor the pouch. "Add a pinch of this to the bowl."

He opened the bag. What looked like salt filled half of it. He sprinkled a pinch into the mixture and licked his finger. It was salt.

Eraim removed the leaves from Kiryanna's side while the marteese writhed. The melting of the flesh had ceased, leaving a nasty hole that didn't bleed. Still, it seemed as though the black substance continued to dig deeper, emitting glowing embers as if it were hot coals. Greyor feared to wonder what damage it would have reaped had Eraim not applied the Vermallon dusk.

"Mix it again," Eraim said.

He stirred the ingredients with his finger. "Won't salt hurt?"

Eraim took the bowl from him. "Of course it will." She scooped the mixture with her index finger and spoke to Kiryanna. "Prepare yourself."

"Squeeze my hand," said Greyor, slipping three of his fingers into Kiryanna's fist—his hand was too large.

The marteese tensed as Eraim smeared the stone crawler mush onto the wound, crushing Greyor's fingers. He didn't care. The glowing orange spots then extinguished, and the blackness turned flesh colored; and though Kiryanna had grimaced when the paste first touched the injury, she now relaxed and breathed easier. Greyor stared in amazement.

"Stone crawlers are better applied this way," Eraim explained while she wrapped a bandage around Kiryanna's midsection. "Your process of eating them diminishes their effect by half."

"Hmm," Greyor grunted. Remembering his own pain, he grabbed a couple of crawlers from his pouch and tossed them into his mouth, accompanied by a pinch of Eraim's salt. Delicious!

Eraim rolled her eyes. "Help me move her."

Greyor followed Eraim's lead and gently lifted Kiryanna, Eraim handling the wounded side. They carried her from the lava and to the wall near the stairs. Eraim then produced another Vermallon dusk leaf and placed it under Kiryanna's tongue.

"Keep this in place for a minute, and then swallow it," she instructed.

"Thank you," the marteese said to them both, though Greyor was sure she meant it for Eraim.

CHAPTER 22

RUN!

meilistari ran along the hallway, pursued by Giant Tewlon, who still carried Nidor. She did not believe Nidor to be unconscious, but they could ill afford for him to slow them down. As she stopped at a four-way intersection, Tewlon raced past her and turned right. She followed.

They traversed a few more intersections, Tewlon turning right, then left, and then running straight without hesitation. Just as Ameilistari wondered which would happen first, her legs giving out or her lungs exploding, the tall warrior ducked into a long room and set down Nidor. Her cousin gaped at Giant Tewlon while the elf-human cocked his head to one side. There were no sounds of pursuit, and his shoulders relaxed.

Ameilistari stared at the man. "What in the name of—"

"Hush!" said Tewlon, the authority in his voice giving her no other choice. He wasn't even breathing hard!

He gazed about the room. Like many others, debris piles littered the floor. "I think we've bought ourselves some time." He moved farther into the chamber.

"Hold a moment!" Ameilistari stomped her foot. "Does Eraim know you're… you're… an imposter?"

Nidor moved closer to Ameilistari, his limp seeming to have disappeared. Perhaps the shock of Tewlon's transformation made him forget about any lingering pain.

"I have only heard of one warrior fitting his description," Nidor whispered. "Vecnor!"

The tall man gave a wry smile. "How's your ankle?"

Nidor didn't respond. He looked at Ameilistari. "But he vanished after the War of the North. Grandfather claimed he rode away from camp while the others slept, never to be seen again."

"We can't stay long," said Tewlon, or Vecnor, or whomever the man was. "They'll find us."

Fire-breathing lizards, shapeshifting elves... No wonder Ameilistari's head was spinning. She chewed her lower lip to figure things out. It was magic; that went without saying. But whose magic? She gazed at the tall man. He was imposing to behold. Still, he was too young to be the warrior of legend.

"We'll not take another step until you tell us what is going on." She hoped the slight quiver in her voice went undetected. "Who are you?"

"It must be Vecnor," said Nidor. "Who else could it be?"

The warrior's expression softened. "It's not important who I am or how I got here. You need only realize that it is a good thing I have arrived. I'm here to help."

He was right. But that wasn't good enough.

"Are you Vecnor?" Ameilistari demanded. She knew not why he avoided saying as much.

He stood tall. "I am Vecnor. Rogue Knight. Black Death." He pulled the second massive sword from his back and twirled both of the blades with an impressive flourish. "Weapons Master." He lifted an eyebrow. "Can we go?"

That would do for now. She nodded.

"How's your ankle?" Vecnor asked Nidor.

Nidor rocked back and forth. "It's good. I barely feel any pain."

"Excellent." Vecnor looked about the room. "I saw an exit at the far end when we entered. It heads in the general direction we must go." He began a swift walk toward the other side of the chamber, veering around a pile of broken stone six feet high — it had obviously fallen from the ceiling. "And we still need a way up."

Ameilistari and her cousin followed, a grin splitting Nidor's face.

"Vecnor..." Nidor shook his head, watching the giant warrior.

"He slew Uustaag and—"

"I know the stories," Ameilistari whispered. "But how is he here? And how is it he looks so much younger than our parents? He traveled with our grandparents!"

Nidor gave a snort, as if she were being silly. "He's probably not even human." He kept his tone low. "With everything he has done, how could he be? But he's here, and that gives me hope better than I have felt since joining this affair."

The archway exiting the room became visible. Vecnor continued at a brisk walk, and every so often Ameilistari and Nidor took quickened steps to maintain the pace. As they approached the dark opening, Ameilistari couldn't keep her mind from pondering.

Vecnor… It had to be him. But was he really Tewlon? Or was Tewlon him? And why the charade? According to Ameilistari's studies, Vecnor had been friends with Vikur, her great-grandfather. This couldn't possibly be the same person. Unless Nidor was right. Maybe Vecnor wasn't human. Perhaps he was a spirit of Brondor, the deity he supposedly worshipped.

She pushed aside the queries and concentrated on their situation. Vecnor was with them; the greatest warrior in nearly every story of import. Suddenly, the mines didn't seem as scary as they had moments ago.

They entered a corridor with a rounded ceiling; it wasn't far from the top of Vecnor's head. Farther on, a staircase spiraled upward. As Ameilistari's spirits lifted, Nidor voiced a warning.

"They found us!"

She glanced back to see green, orange, and red lizards scurrying over debris piles and along the walls—some crawled on the ceiling. There were at least thirty of the monsters.

"Up the stairs!" Vecnor said, standing aside for Ameilistari and Nidor to squeeze past.

Unlike the other spiraling stairwells, this one did not circle a solid column. It was more like a hollow tower with steps climbing along the wall, round and round until reaching the next floor. Except that it didn't reach the next floor. The stairs ended after twenty steps, leaving a gap to the level above. And there was no debris to suggest they had collapsed.

"There's no way up!" Nidor called to Vecnor.

Ameilistari released a slow breath. It was not a time to panic. "I have a way," she said, loud enough for Vecnor to hear.

"Then do it!" he shouted as the first lizard arrived, only to be decapitated with a single swing.

Ameilistari turned to her cousin. "Remember in my room, when I lifted Daymyn?"

He frowned, then nodded.

"Good," she said. "Stand still and relax."

She recited the spell she had used to levitate her younger cousin. Pooling energy beneath Nidor, she moved her palms upward, as if lifting an invisible object, and he rose, his eyes suddenly nervous. In friendlier surroundings, she might have giggled to see his response, but she needed to stay focused. This was too important. Tensing every muscle in her body, she pushed harder with her mind, and Nidor ascended faster until hovering beside the upper level.

"Pull yourself into the room!" Ameilistari said through clenched teeth. She hadn't mastered lateral movement yet.

Nidor grabbed the nearby wall and guided himself over the floor.

Ameilistari released the spell, and a sudden fear overcame her. Were there lizards above?

"Is it safe?" she called up.

"Yes!" her cousin answered.

She expelled a relieved breath.

At least a dozen dead reptiles filled the corridor behind her, and Vecnor continued slicing and kicking all within reach. Orange and red lizards were closing.

"Nidor is up!" she said.

"You next," he hollered as he gave ground while continuing to defend the tunnel.

"I'll have to take my light," she said, unsure if he could still see in the dark, now that he appeared human.

"I'll be fine. Just go!"

She repeated the spell and floated until reaching the next floor. Nidor was there with his sword poised, watching the darkness. Nothing moved except for her cousin as he pulled her into the room, and she turned back to the shaft.

"I'm ready for you!"

The large warrior appeared below, an enormous shadow backing up the steps with arms flailing. Fire then filled the stairwell, lighting up his black armor, and he crossed his swords as if the maneuver afforded him protection against the flames. It amazed Ameilistari to see him unscathed.

She again cast her spell, but after raising the warrior a few feet, her body shook — how much did he weigh? Summoning more energy, Ameilistari lifted Vecnor at a steady pace while he continued slashing reptiles attempting to pursue. An orange lizard breathed its fiery breath, and had Ameilistari not needed to maintain her concentration, she might have gasped at the sight of it having cooked five of its green cousins upon the wall.

Vecnor reached the top, and Nidor grabbed the man's backplate to guide him over the floor. Ameilistari panted as she released the magic.

"Now is the time for fire," Vecnor said with urgency.

The red and orange lizards were scaling the walls.

"What if it doesn't hurt them?" Ameilistari asked.

"Not down the shaft." Vecnor guided her and Nidor away from the opening. "At the ceiling above it."

That made better sense.

She concentrated on the fire spell, but lost her focus when the room spun. She coughed.

"Is something the matter?" asked Nidor, grabbing her arm to steady her.

Ameilistari shook her head, but the dizziness didn't abate, and she suddenly craved sleep. She concentrated again, and her head spun faster as she pulled magical forces to her, making it difficult to hold them—it was like putting water in a bucket riddled with holes.

"Now!" Vecnor commanded.

Extending her palm, a small flame appeared. But it fluttered and almost faded—she couldn't focus. She thought of the fire-breathing lizards, narrowing her eyes to stabilize her vision, and put what energy she could into the spell. Did the flame grow? She wasn't sure. But she had no time and willed the fiery ball away—hopefully in the right direction. There was an explosion, and she collapsed.

CHAPTER 23

UNDERSTANDING

Baylun." Romik's eyes were pleading within the blue glow of the mushrooms on his hooks. "We must prioritize our families over these… creatures."

Baylun scanned the floor. There were no answers there, and the pull from Torrac to protect the mine dwellers grew stronger. It was as if he were being torn apart from the inside.

"Bye'Lin," said Poopit. The mine dweller had huddled with its companions and now beckoned for Baylun to follow.

Romik shook his head.

"Let's see what he wishes to show us," Baylun said.

"That's how we ended up *here*," commented his brother. "The 'others' he wished to show us were *his* 'others' and not ours."

Baylun looked at Lorylla, hoping for a suggestion. She gazed back, saying nothing.

"Any thoughts?" he asked. What did he have to lose?

Her brow lowered as if considering. "As I mentioned earlier, I believe Torrac is speaking to you. You must listen if you wish to hear."

A lot of help that was.

Baylun turned to his brother. "We have no idea where to go. And I don't know why, but Torrac wants me to help these people. It's what I must do."

Romik exhaled loudly through his nose. "I pray to Cafior this leads somewhere."

With that, Baylun nodded at Poopit.

"Less go," said the mine dweller, leading the way back.

They passed through the heated room and headed downstairs to the chamber with the unrecognizable fresco. Returning to the statue of Meldar, they used the secret door and followed the curving hallway to the intersection. They had originally come from the corridor on the right, but this time they proceeded straight and down the stairs.

After descending, the tunnel arced to the left for several paces to another intersection passing left and right. The dwellers turned left. The next passage contained ascending stairs, and it abruptly ended. Zur worked a lever on the wall to the side of the dead end while Poopit put a finger to his lips to caution Baylun and his companions.

A door opened into a wide corridor. It traveled a short distance to the right and stopped, while to the left it extended beyond sight with central pillars shaped like giant hammers, each holding a yellow gem. The dwellers headed right, and Zur opened yet another hidden door on the opposite wall.

Baylun gasped while staring at the prison of mine dwellers. The secret door was near the blocks of granite forming the divider wall of the cell, barely within view of the gate at the far side. A massive crowd of dwellers filled the space between. Prisoners acknowledged the opening of the door, and immediately elbowed or tapped those who had not noticed, the gestures passing through the throng like a wildfire.

Four prisoners approached, and as they did so, Poopit, Bo, Ka, and Zur removed packs from their shoulders and handed them over. The captives nodded—and possibly smiled—before accepting the gifts and turning away. From the bags, they pulled chunks of raw meat, and handed the packs to others, who took a piece for themselves before passing them on again. The packages soon disappeared into the crowd, and Zur stepped back to allow the door to close.

Baylun tried to understand. The prisoners had a way out. Yet, they remained in the dismal place under the watch of a horrific jailer, waiting to be eaten. It made no sense.

The mine dwellers passed Baylun and his companions, heading back to the previous secret door.

Romik frowned, his thoughts likely echoing Baylun's. Lorylla was unreadable.

They returned through the hidden panel and to the last intersection, and Poopit continued straight. Forty paces later, they stopped at a bruskiin door appearing to be in better condition than those Baylun had seen thus far. Poopit knocked once, waited, knocked again, waited again, and knocked twice. After a moment, three knocks sounded from the other side, and Poopit added one more knock. The door opened. In the entryway stood a mine dweller dressed in lizard hide, and he stepped aside, his eyes widening upon seeing Baylun's group.

The room was thirty feet square. There were no other exits, and benches lined the walls, each holding at least a dozen mine dwellers while another score stood, all of them wearing skins and wielding rail spears. Weapons rose when Baylun and his companions entered, but Poopit held up a hand, speaking in their unknown language, and he continued talking as the spears lowered. Suspicion remained in the dwellers' eyes, however, and no less than three kept watch on Baylun at any moment, some issuing scowls, some seeming curious, and others showing apprehension.

Baylun sighed as he gazed at Torrac, his frustrations mounting. How could he help a people he couldn't understand?

Torrac's runes took on a soft glow. Suddenly, the mine dwellers spoke the Common tongue perfectly.

"…don't see how these topsiders can aid us," one was saying. "We remember the last time, when they led our best warriors to their deaths!"

"I was one of those warriors!" snapped Poopit. "With Gray'Or and Mill'Or, we accomplished more than any of us have for centuries. We greatly injured Maak Maak, restricting the monster to the royal quarters. And now the beast lies dead by their hands." He pointed at Baylun's group.

Baylun looked at Romik and Lorylla. The two stared blankly at the exchange.

"Excuse me," he said to the dwellers.

The conversation halted as they turned to Baylun with mouths agape.

"Why do you leave your kin in that prison?" he asked. "Waiting to be eaten?"

The room was silent for several seconds. Romik furrowed his brow, watching Baylun.

"It is for… survival," Poopit replied. "To remove them would be to reveal our freedom. We would then be hunted and slain, leaving no one to gather food."

Baylun pondered the dweller's response. They left their people to be devoured by whatever the insect creature was so that they could hunt? He turned to his companions for help.

"What are you doing?" Romik asked, his brow lowering further.

Even Lorylla's expression had changed. She studied Baylun with those white on black eyes.

"Since when do you speak their language?" posed Romik.

Speak their language? What was Romik talking about?

"But they're using Common —" Baylun followed Lorylla's gaze to Torrac.

"It is your weapon," she said. "It translates for you and allows you to communicate."

"But…" Baylun struggled to think clearly. "That makes no sense. I swore my oath to Lornibur, yes. But as a dwarf-friend. Not…" He looked at the mine dwellers and back to his friends.

"Do you not see?" Lorylla asked. "They *are* dwarves." She regarded the group of dwellers observing them. "They have likely been here since the fall of Lornibur, unknown to the outside world."

"What are you two talking about?" demanded Romik. "Torrac is translating? What does that mean? What are these creatures saying?"

Baylun's head reeled with additional questions. Could the mine dwellers really be dwarves? They didn't look like dwarves. They were too skinny, for one thing. But if they had been enslaved for a thousand years, starving and mistreated, they could be.

Romik stared at Baylun, awaiting an answer.

"Apparently," Baylun glanced at the dwellers, "these are hunters. They supply food for their kin, who remain where they are so the hunters can work unnoticed by their captors." He turned to Poopit, who frowned. "Is that correct?"

Poopit shook his head. "I understood nothing of what you said until the last few words. I know not if you are correct, because you used your foreign language."

Baylun sighed. Torrac allowed the dwellers to understand him, but only when he spoke directly to them? That complicated things a little.

"I do not think they comprehend your words when you speak to us," said Lorylla, agreeing with his theory. "Just as we do not understand you when you speak with them."

"How is it you speak our language?" Poopit asked. "Why did you not tell us earlier?"

Baylun dreaded trying to explain. He was just a dumb warrior. Kiryanna would know what to say.

"It is this weapon." He raised the battleaxe, causing some of the mine dwellers to retreat a step. "I mean you no harm," he quickly added. "This is Torrac, and I am bound to it. Bound to Lornibur and its folk. Bound... to protect you." If it were possible, Torrac felt lighter in his hand after his words.

A smile crept across Poopit's face. The other dwellers didn't appear so relieved. Their expressions remained skeptical.

"And we will begin by freeing your people," Baylun said. "Torrac demands it."

Many grunts ensued as the dwellers looked at one another. Apparently, the grunts weren't actual words.

"We cannot do that!" insisted a mine dweller. "They will find us, capture us, and discover our way in and out. Beyond that, they will treat us even worse than they already do."

"What your kin are enduring is not living!" Baylun put more force behind his statement than he intended, and even Poopit flinched.

"You know not what we face!" said a voice from the rear of the group. "The aamustall are only part of the danger."

Apparently, aamustall wasn't a single creature. A race of insects?

"There are also the boola, the kreela, and the kreedorim!" added the same speaker.

Whatever those names were, Torrac didn't translate them to anything Baylun was familiar with.

He looked at Romik. His brother's expression, though touched by confusion and impatience, told Baylun to proceed. He turned to Lorylla and saw the same expressionless countenance he was used to. But in the light of the glowing mushrooms, he caught a slight difference, an upturn at the corner of the gray elf's mouth, and realized it wasn't for the first time. Thinking back, Baylun recalled several subtleties that might have shown her true emotions over the past days. And although she surely understood nothing of what was said, she encouraged him to continue.

Baylun returned his attention to the room's occupants. "Our objective is to make these mines safe for you and your folk. The first task is to locate a place from which to defend your kin. You seem to know a lot of secret tunnels, and we will use them to our advantage. With them, we will usher those held prisoner from their cell while me and my companions and your strongest warriors protect the escape. Once that is complete, we regroup and go on the offensive to defeat your enemies."

Brows furrowed, heads were scratched, and many glances were exchanged. But none of them spoke for or against the idea.

"That is the objective," Baylun reiterated. "Now, I need to know everything so that we can make a plan."

Chapter 24

Evolution

Greyor assisted Eraim in making sure Kiryanna was as comfortable as possible under the circumstances—the spider bite was horrid and the heat of the room uncomfortable. Fortunately, the sleeping marteese was already on the mend after the elf's treatment of Vermallon dusk and stone crawlers. Greyor and Eraim then stepped away, so as not to disturb her.

"Why is it the demon vanished?" Greyor asked, thinking back on the spider's demise.

"They cannot be destroyed unless killed in their own world," replied Eraim. "In the end, we only sent it home."

"Does that mean we cannot die in their world?"

She shrugged. "I doubt it."

Greyor looked at the spot where the body had been. The spider's blood still stained the flagstones. "That's hardly fair."

Eraim released a chuckle. "Tell that to the gods."

Indeed. Given the choice, Greyor would rather have fought a krahluk or a zreekan, the strange gorillas and tentacled creatures that opposed Vaeldor's united army in the Battle of the Broken Land. When they were killed, they stayed dead.

"Did you see the last egg Kiryanna broke?" Greyor changed the subject.

Eraim shook her head.

"It was a lizard."

The elf frowned. "In lava?"

"I think its scales were red or orange."

Eraim twisted her lips to the side. Her eyes then opened wide and she gasped. "Baby dragons!"

Greyor wasn't sure how to respond, or if he was supposed to. He was no expert. With the creatures' thought-to-be extinction, was anyone? "I suppose anything's possible at this point." He eyed the surviving eggs. There were nearly two dozen. "Should we destroy the rest of them?"

Eraim let out a deep sigh. "Life is a treasure. It should never be taken without reason."

"If they're dragons," said Kiryanna from her seated position against the wall behind them, her voice slightly hoarse, "what choice do we have? Do you propose we hatch them and teach them to be nice?" The last part contained obvious sarcasm—the marteese's wound had surely improved further.

Eraim shook her head, her face contorted with conflicting emotions. Her eyes watered, as if she might cry.

Greyor had never known anyone so torn about doing what must be done. He felt sad for Eraim. He glanced at the quiver strapped over her shoulder. Maybe a dozen of the long arrows remained. "You haven't enough arrows to complete the task."

Her attention snapped toward him. "I will not waste another arrow in that lava! If we must destroy them, we shall do it Kiryanna's way and throw rocks."

A good idea.

Greyor and Eraim moved closer to sit near the pool. There were plenty of loose stones, and they began the process. Eraim was much better at the task, hitting three eggs for every one of Greyor's. Who knew throwing rocks could be so hard?

"How are these here?" Eraim asked between throws.

Greyor shrugged. "Left over from the Dragon Wars?"

The elf shook her head. "Impossible." She grimaced as she destroyed another egg. "If any had survived the war, they would not have hidden. They were predators." She turned to Greyor. "And predators do not fear. They hunt."

Greyor scowled as he missed an egg for the fourth time. But when the stone struck one farther out, spilling its liquid into the pool of lava, he nodded, as if it were his original target.

"Has Clanghorr said anything lately?" Eraim asked.

"No. Not since the fangs before we opened the iron door."

Eraim destroyed another egg. Only four remained.

She furrowed her brow. "Do you remember when it became a double-bladed weapon?"

Greyor frowned. What in Meldar's name was she referring to? "What do you mean?" His next throw splashed down, striking nothing but lava.

"Before I left home to join you on this quest," she said, "I looked back through my journals." She broke another egg.

Greyor sank a stone without success. "You keep journals?"

"Many people do." She knocked the number of eggs down to two. "Would it surprise you to learn that Vecnor does—did?" She shook her head as if irritated with the utterance. "Anyway, to prepare myself, I looked back to when I first met Poluran on Korban Bridge, before the Necromancer War, and Clanghorr had only one blade." She dropped the eggs to one after Greyor missed twice. "I do not see it having two blades until years later. Before the War of the North."

"Perhaps you recorded it wrong," said Greyor. "Those were chaotic times."

She eyed him. "I do not make mistakes about such things." She gazed at the lava. "Still, I could not recall Clanghorr with a single blade. So I shared this information with Selanna."

Greyor struck the final egg and turned to Eraim with a grin. "Ha!"

She frowned as if confused.

Greyor's smile receded. He probably shouldn't boast too much about his victory over the elf. She was proud, after all. "What did Selanna say?"

Eraim took a deep breath. "Selanna reminded me that Clanghorr is a divine weapon, so it carries the Will of Meldar. She surmises that once Clanghorr began to awaken, meaning once you had wielded it long enough, its true form emerged. And because it contains divine magic, this alteration not only escaped everyone's notice, but it imparted upon their minds that it was the form Clanghorr had always possessed. Even Selanna cannot remember the axe as having been different. But she does not doubt my journal for a moment."

This was a lot to take in. Did it make sense? Did it matter? It was Clanghorr, and it belonged to Greyor. Rather, they belonged to each other. "What are you saying?"

Eraim sighed. "Mostly, I am passing the time while Kiryanna rests. But also, you must realize the importance of paying attention to everything Clanghorr tells you." She put her tiny hand on his arm. "And it is important for you to realize that you are not alone. We are all here to help you."

Eraim really was a special elf. But when did she get so smart? Greyor was lucky to have her on this venture, even if having Selanna would have been better.

"And do not think for a moment that you won whatever game you were playing in your head." She stood and brushed the dirt from her leather gloves. "It is not the one who breaks the final egg. I hit many more than you did."

What did elves know? It was probably better to let her have the victory. He grunted a chuckle and stood.

"Are you two ready?" asked Kiryanna, standing near the wall where she had been resting while buckling her damaged breastplate—the bandage showed through the hole. Her countenance then softened. "Thank you both for your aid. I am ready to find my husband."

Greyor concentrated on Baylun and Torrac. A direct route to reach the krukari was across the pool of molten rock and through the wall on the right. Since that was not an option, they could either go back and find an alternative path, or continue through the corridor on the left. As he pondered this dilemma, the desire to go left overcame him. It was where he *must* go. Not wanting to explain this to the marteese, he pointed Clanghorr toward the hallway. "This way," he said, and walked into the tunnel, hugging the wall away from the stream of magma.

The maidens followed.

The corridor curved to the right, and shortly after, the lava disappeared through a finely constructed archway two feet high. As it fell behind, the heat receded, but the air remained too warm for an underground passage. The hallway ended at another large archway, and beyond was a rectangular room. To the left was a passageway, and steaming water covered the back third of the chamber.

Maak Maak came to mind, and Greyor approached the pond with a tight grip on Clanghorr. Other than the rising steam, nothing moved. As he neared the water's edge, he spied another clutch of eggs, each the size of Eraim's head and submerged ten feet from the shore.

"Eraim," he said, just above a whisper. "Come see this."

The elf and marteese halted on either side of him, staring at the water.

"What is going on here?" asked Kiryanna. "Lava eggs, and now... steaming-water eggs?"

Eraim swiftly raised her bow toward the ceiling and released an arrow. The dark-shafted missile stopped short of the worked stone, and a fifteen-foot lizard fell to the floor, its scales a light blue color. Though the arrow had buried deep in the reptile's back, the creature wasn't spent, and it moved rapidly to face Greyor and his companions.

Greyor needed only two steps to reach the monster, and he brought down Clanghorr as it released a spout of scalding water from its maw at Eraim. The elf somersaulted aside, evading the attack, and Clanghorr decapitated the lizard as Kiryanna's golden sword pierced its side. The body thrashed twice before becoming still.

They stared at the corpse, no one speaking for several seconds.

"It breathed boiling water, just like Maak Maak," said Greyor.

"But it had only one head," Kiryanna pointed out.

Eraim twisted her lips as she looked from the lizard to the pool.

She then turned to the adjoining corridor exiting the room.

"What are you thinking?" Kiryanna asked the elf.

"Follow me," Eraim said, moving briskly into the tunnel holding her attention.

The hallway traveled a short distance to another iron door. Though rusted, it was used often, judging by the scratches along the floor. Eraim pulled the latch, and the door screeched as it swung, releasing a cloud of steam.

"More eggs," Eraim whispered, peering into the next room.

Greyor followed the elf with Kiryanna close behind. The chamber was the same size as the last, but it possessed no pool. Instead, a lava stream entered and exited through two-foot openings on the right side, and a large metal basin protruded from the wall above the flow. Water boiled within, and higher up, a stone spout carved to resemble a dragon's head spewed a constant stream to keep the basin from running dry. Steam rose from the bowl, coating the entire room with moisture. To the left, at least three dozen eggs rested atop damp straw, smaller than those in the previous chamber. The far end bore another iron door.

"Dwarves did not build these chambers," said Greyor, scanning the uneven walls and gazing at the waterspout. Some of the dragon's details were jagged, as if worked by unsteady hands.

"They are laboratories," Eraim said. "Each one is a step in the evolution of the eggs."

"To what end?" posed Kiryanna.

Eraim turned to Greyor and the marteese. "To return dragons to the world." She shook her head. "Maak Maak must have been an earlier result. Perhaps a failure. It had two heads and did not breathe fire."

"Who would do such a thing?" asked Kiryanna.

Eraim glanced at the eggs. "A priest. A Demoligius priest."

"We found that Demoligius symbol in that bedroom," Kiryanna said.

"Clanghorr has shown me two such persons," Greyor admitted,

shaking his head. "In earlier visions, before we discovered the item, I saw robed humans in Lornibur. They must have been Demoligius priests."

"But dragons were not extinct before Lornibur fell," Eraim stated, almost to herself. "Unless…" She sucked in her lips while working through her thoughts. "Yes. Dragons born for a specific purpose." She looked at Greyor and Kiryanna. "We must go back."

"But…" Greyor gazed across the room. "What about the door? Perhaps we'll learn more if we continue."

Eraim shook her head. "I am positive we shall find more laboratories with more eggs. But the direction we are moving will eventually lead to a hatchery of the lizards we have been fighting since we arrived. The first stage of their evolution. We should go the other way."

"For what purpose?" Kiryanna asked. "To fight the dragon that nearly killed us?" She turned to Greyor. "No offense to you and Clanghorr, but if we are to face a dragon, we need Baylun."

"I do not intend to face the dragon," Eraim said. "But I must see if there is anything more I can determine from the later stages."

Greyor didn't know what to think. Although he desired to rid Lornibur of the reptiles, Eraim's interest in the eggs was a little suspicious. But he had no better ideas. He nodded. "Yes, we'll head back. I sense Baylun to be in that direction, anyway."

Kiryanna frowned. She then lifted her chin before giving a nod.

CHAPTER 25

A Fireside Chat

meilistari plummeted into darkness. Below was a distant light, but no matter how far she fell, she got no closer. She reached out, but there was nothing to grab hold of. She was helpless.

Take my hand.

The voice was familiar, but she couldn't recall where she had heard it. A hand then appeared in the blackness beside her; a disembodied arm ending at the elbow. Ameilistari grasped it, and it pulled her.

The darkness gave way to a forest clearing. Ameilistari stood among towering trees surrounding a small cabin, and logs formed benches around a campfire. There was no sign of the hand that had dragged her from her descent, but a figure sat on the log facing the fire; a female with long blonde hair and pointed ears. An elf.

"Come, sit with me," the elf said.

It was the voice of the arm. Ameilistari knew she should recognize it, but the name of its owner remained out of reach. With a deep breath, she rounded the figure to sit on an adjacent log. The fire was pleasant, warming her to the perfect temperature, and the elf maiden was beautiful with kind emerald eyes. There was something familiar about those eyes.

"Drink this," the elf said, offering a mug that wasn't there before.

Numb, Ameilistari received the cup and drank deeply. The contents were thicker than wine and as sweet as… chocolate? What was chocolate?

A tingling sensation filled her stomach and quickly spread to her extremities. The forest spun, but only for a moment, and as the trees slowed to a stop, Ameilistari remembered the answer to her last question. Her father had purchased chocolate from a merchant out of Fendora and given it to her on her tenth birthday. It was the most remarkable thing she had ever tasted. She briefly wondered if her cousins had ever sampled it—the realm of Philen neighbored Fendora, after all.

Her cousins! Nidor! The mines! She turned to the elf. It was Selanna!

Selanna smiled. "Welcome back."

"Am I… dead?"

The mage chuckled. "Of course not. But you need to pace yourself. You gathered more energy than your mind is ready to handle, and nearly exhausted yourself to… Let us not worry about that right now."

Ameilistari looked around. "Is this your home?"

Selanna nodded once.

"How am I here?" Ameilistari gazed at the flower beds growing alongside the cabin. The blooms of yellow, red, and blue were absolutely stunning. She then gasped as thoughts of her cousin returned. "Nidor!"

"Calm yourself," Selanna said. "It will not do you well to get worked up while your body recovers."

"Recovers?"

"You are still in the mines," Selanna assured her. "Nidor watches over you."

"This is all so confusing," Ameilistari said. She then smiled. "But it is also wonderful." She inhaled deeply and released it. It was the cleanest air she had ever tasted. "Are there no limits to what magic can accomplish?"

"Of course there are limits," Selanna held a level gaze, "as you have hopefully realized. Your mind can only survive the pressure you placed upon it so many times before it shuts down."

"You mean… death?"

Selanna shook her head. "A fate worse than death. You will lose the ability to grasp the energy altogether. It will constantly seem within reach until you attempt to harness it, and it will escape you. And *that* is a life no mage can endure."

A chill crept along Ameilistari's spine at the thought. Never feel the surge of life granted by the flow of magic coursing through her body… She recalled her last spell of fire, and how the energy had been hard to contain. She needed to be more careful.

"I do not require knowledge of *how* I am here," Ameilistari said after a moment, "but *why* am I here? Did you rescue me?"

Selanna lowered her brow in contemplation. "Let us say that I am sparing you from the remainder of your mind's journey through the void."

"The void…" Ameilistari murmured to herself. What would have happened had she reached the light? Would she have awakened as herself? Or as an ordinary girl that used to harness magic, cursed to live out her days in sorrow for her loss? She wasn't sure she wanted to know.

"As to why you are here," said Selanna, "it is because I wish to speak with you." She lifted a long pipe from the log, glanced at it, and set it back down. Had it been there earlier?

Ameilistari looked at her hands. The mug was gone. *This is inside my mind*, she told herself and turned to Selanna. "Are you going to ridicule me for sneaking into the mines?" She dreaded the answer and didn't wait for a response. "But I am ready! Even Rauzel agreed I need more than the stone walls of a laboratory to cast magic at."

Selanna smirked. "I believe her intent was to take you into Marcove for some controlled spell casting."

Ameilistari sighed. "But I'm ready to do the things that stories are made of."

The elf released a small chuckle as she stared at the sunny sky. "I remember feeling the way you do." Her eyes leveled on Ameilistari. "But a mage must resist the urge to show what they are capable of until their mind is properly conditioned. They must learn to allow magic to flow through them; become its vessel and not its warden.

You see, you are like someone new to swimming. You exert more strength than is necessary to accomplish what an experienced swimmer performs with ease." She shook her head. "You are not quite ready for the task you have imposed upon yourself because you think too much. You need to listen, so the magic can speak to you."

Ameilistari's twinge of confusion must have been obvious, for Selanna's smile returned.

"Tell me," said the elf. "How has your adventure fared?"

Ameilistari bowed her head. "Horribly."

Selanna's brow rose, like a mother waiting to hear her child admit the truth.

"We were separated, just as when you and Eraim passed through Lornibur." Ameilistari's shoulders slumped. "And we cannot find the others. It is just myself, Nidor, and… Tewlon." She wasn't sure what to call the warrior anymore. She narrowed her eyes at Selanna. "Who is this friend of Eraim's? He goes by the name Tewlon and pretends he cannot speak. And now he's the largest man I have ever seen, and Nidor insists he must be Vecnor. But Vecnor disappeared after the War of the North. If he is still alive, he is likely retired somewhere to live out his old age. Unless Brondor sent him to help us in our time of need. A warrior angel?"

Selanna laughed. "My dear child."

She hated Selanna calling her that.

The elf's expression became serious. "I am going to share something with you. But you must swear never to reveal this information to anyone. Not a soul." Selanna emphasized the last three words.

Ameilistari nodded. Hopefully, her old mentor was about to teach her some new magic.

"The man you travel with is indeed Vecnor." Selanna paused. "And he is with you at my bidding."

"But he is too young," Ameilistari pointed out.

Selanna raised her brow. "You, of all people, know better than to question the powers of Vou."

How could she forget? Another thought then struck her. "You're his master!"

Selanna smiled. "As much a master as anyone can be to Vecnor."

Ameilistari gazed at the fire to sort through the reality of the situation. She was traveling with the actual Vecnor of legend! And he appeared every bit as capable of doing the things she once thought to be exaggerated.

"But you cannot tell anyone about him," said Selanna.

Ameilistari snapped free of her thoughts. "Can't tell anyone?"

"As I said," the elf explained, "Vecnor is with you at my request. I never intended for his true identity to be revealed, but circumstances being what they were…"

"Does Eraim know?"

Selanna laughed again. "You are such a darling young lady."

Ameilistari didn't get the jest.

"You must also make Nidor understand he cannot speak of Vecnor's presence," Selanna continued. "You need not know the true reason, only that this is what I ask of you."

Ameilistari nodded. But what explanation would her cousin accept?

"You will think of something," said Selanna.

The elf was reading her mind!

"If I may," Ameilistari said, "why *did* you send Vecnor? Did you know about the fire-breathing lizards?"

Selanna's smirk dissolved. She stared, as if choosing her next words carefully. "There is a prophecy. I shall not reveal it to you in full, for there is not enough time. But I will show you some of it."

A fog engulfed the clearing, billowing like a waterfall from the sky. The ground disappeared, and Ameilistari stood atop a cloud within a mountainous cavern. Below was darkness, but it wasn't complete; a light flickered in the center, almost invisible.

Lornibur houses something terrible. Selanna's voice came from every direction. *The dwarves attempted to bury it, but they only aided in its secrecy.*

The flame erupted, filling the vision, but then receded and

darkness returned. Something moved within the shadows, slithering like a snake. But it wasn't a snake—it had arms and legs. A giant lizard?

Hidden beneath the mountains, Selanna's voice continued, *evil was left to its own devices.*

The flames returned, ten times brighter than before, and upon an outcropping of rock amid the devastation was a robed figure with hands raised. The fire fluttered as another figure appeared, one standing unharmed within the blaze. Ameilistari couldn't make out the newcomer, but she was sure its skin was red and its hair was made of fire.

And now, its task is nearly complete.

She raced upward, through soil and stone until reaching the night sky. The scene below was of mountains, and nearby was a walled city. Charndova?

Left unchecked, much of Vaeldor will burn.

Flames surged among the mountains, spreading until they engulfed the city. Ameilistari rose higher to spy plains and forests, and the fire expanded until everything burned.

It was hard to breathe. Smoke rushed into her lungs, and she coughed uncontrollably. Soon, the very cloud supporting her became black smog, and she fell through, rushing toward the fiery landscape.

The vision ended. Ameilistari sat atop the log in the clearing, panting. She looked up. Selanna was on the bench to her left.

"You see," Selanna said, "it is most important that Vecnor helps you and the others find this hidden evil before it completes its task."

"Did Fenreil the Seer show you this?" Ameilistari managed between breaths. Surely the information came from the Council of Wizards.

"The Seer knows of what I speak."

Selanna must be acting in support of the Council. Ameilistari would never have guessed that she worked so closely with the group of human mages out of Tikken City.

"I see," said Ameilistari, the information hanging like a weight on her shoulders. Sneaking into the mines now seemed a horrible idea. She and Nidor were supposed to defeat a few giant lizards and meet mine dwellers, not battle fiery reptiles and a man with flaming hair. Maybe she should have slept late the morning Greyor's company departed.

"It is nearly time for you to wake," Selanna said.

Ameilistari wasn't ready to go back. Not yet. The clearing was peaceful, while the mines were scary. Perhaps she could stay in the world of dreams a few more hours.

"But first, I will share with you one more piece of information," the elf said. "There is a reason I chose to mentor you in the beginning. Have you noticed how much easier it is for you to cast spells of fire and water than some others?"

Ameilistari slowly nodded. But weren't those types of spells easier for all mages?

"The reason is that you are an elementalist."

Ameilistari wrinkled her nose. "A what?"

"An elementalist. It is a rare type of spellcaster. In fact, you are the first known elementalist in my lifetime."

Ameilistari stared at nothing, absorbing the news. But it was confusing. "What is a...?"

"Elementalist." Selanna pronounced the word slowly this time. "You work well with the elements; they come naturally to you. Which is why you need to be careful. Summoning them can be so effortless that you accidentally release too much power, as you did with Maak Maak. You must learn to control it."

An elementalist! And Ameilistari was the only one. She knew there had to be something special about her. She could feel it in her bones.

"Yes," Selanna said, "it is very exciting. But heed my warning."

Ameilistari suppressed her smile. "Of course."

"And now you will leave this place and awaken. Tell no one about this conversation." The elf raised her brow. "And keep my secrets safe. Prove yourself trustworthy, and we shall discuss more in the future."

Another fog billowed into the clearing.

CHAPTER 26

A PLAN

Baylun exited through the double doors of the large chamber where the mine dwellers—or dwarves—were gathered. It wasn't far from where he learned he could communicate with the ancient race. Unfortunately, none of the secret chambers were big enough to house the prisoners, so the dwellers led him and his companions along a wide hallway supported by central pillars to a room appearing to be an ancient temple. Its high ceiling vaulted over cracked benches facing a destroyed altar and a toppled statue. Like other grand rooms, veins of gold, silver, and copper made random patterns toward the apex of the dome, where a diamond was affixed.

While in the temple, Baylun received a better understanding of the obstacles they faced. Several arguments broke out between the dwellers during the briefing, but Poopit appeared to be a figure the others could not deny for long, especially once the dweller set his mind on a course of action. And with Poopit's support, Baylun developed a plan at last.

Romik and Lorylla had remained in the antechamber, having nothing to contribute. Lorylla sat on the floor next to the double doors leading back to the maze of tunnels, likely relying on her ears to keep guard. Romik was on one of the stone benches running along the sides of the room, fiddling with a crack on his wooden arm. He appeared to be testing its strength. His determined expression shifted to concern at Baylun's approach.

Baylun understood his brother's distress. As for himself, he focused on the task before them, trying to keep thoughts of Kiryanna and Nidor from pushing him into hasty—perhaps deadly—decisions.

One thing aiding that focus was news provided by the mine dwellers; information he hoped would put Romik at ease, even if only slightly.

He sat next to his brother. "Ameilistari is alive."

Romik perked up. "Where is she?"

"I don't know exactly." Baylun saw the spark in Romik's eyes wane. "But the mine dwellers have seen her... and Nidor and Tewlon." He glanced at Lorylla, who watched with interest. "The dwellers observe all things foreign within the mines to determine if they're a threat. They trailed our kids. Even tried to capture them."

Romik frowned. "Capture?"

Baylun nodded. "Ameilistari has done well for herself. She has survived more than one lizard attack."

"So where is she now?"

Baylun sighed. "The dwellers are not completely sure at the moment. It seems Tewlon led them into an area heavily populated by lizards, and... some of them apparently spit fire." Before Romik could express any fears, Baylun added, "But they escaped. The mine dwellers couldn't follow afterward, but scouts are making their way around the nest to find them. Once they do, they'll try to guide them here."

Romik sighed. "I suppose that's the best news we can hope for at the moment."

Baylun nodded his agreement.

"It is curious," Lorylla said, remaining on the floor. "You know them to be dwarves, yet you continue to refer to them as mine dwellers."

"They're not like any dwarves I ever saw," muttered Romik.

Baylun had to agree with his brother. Still, he needed to get used to the notion.

"Any news about your wife and the others?" the gray elf asked.

"They are not far away," Baylun replied. "But..."

Lorylla narrowed her eyes while Baylun tried to think of how to explain.

"Just say it, brother," Romik said.

"They are currently in a part of Lornibur even more deadly than where Tewlon took the kids."

"Worse than a nest of ten-foot reptiles spitting fire?" asked Romik.

Baylun lifted his brows. "Apparently so." He glanced from the elf to his brother. "There are eggs being… made."

Romik frowned. "What do you mean, *made*?"

"The jailers have been taking eggs from the lizards, or boola as the mine, er dwarves, call them, and experimenting on them. The eggs have evolved over the course of many, many years. Centuries." Baylun still had a hard time understanding it. "That is how Maak Maak came into existence, as well as the fire-spitting lizards, or kreela. But they didn't stop there. Kreela were developed into kreedorim. The mine, er dwarves, describe the kreedorim as enormous reptiles that breathe fire. They are typically twenty feet in length, but recently, a beast forty feet long was spotted."

"A… dragon?" Lorylla asked. It was the palest Baylun had ever seen her.

"Nonsense." Romik waved off the idea. "Surely the dwellers exaggerate."

"Maybe," said Baylun. "Maybe not. But this kreedorim is between my wife and us. It's the reason the dwarves abandoned watching her."

The temple doors opened, and a dozen Lornibur dwarves exited. Zur led the contingent, nodding at Baylun as they passed through the antechamber doors.

"Where are they going?" asked Romik after the doors shut.

"To gather more spears," Baylun replied. "Once we free the rest of them, they'll need weapons if they're to help in their own defense."

"What about aamustall?" posed Lorylla. "What does that mean?"

Baylun dreaded that question. But he needed to get to it eventually. "Demons, as far as I understand. Several of them."

Romik's face blanched. Lorylla didn't seem surprised.

"They come from the main forge we saw," Baylun added. "They

literally emerge from the coals. The dwellers—dwarves!" He scowled at himself. "The dwarves don't know how they came to live in the forge. Poopit claims the demons have always been there, and they keep the dwarves to torture and eat them. He doesn't know when the secret door at the rear of the prison was discovered either; it was long before his time. But they dare not leave for fear of being slaughtered. So only the strongest sneak out to gather food and water so their people don't starve. Apparently, the aamustall aren't interested in fattening their prisoners. Perhaps they feast on souls."

"I still don't understand allowing your people to suffer such a fate," said Romik.

"We cannot judge what we have not been a part of." Lorylla looked at Romik. "You have never walked their path. Right or wrong, they preserved their existence, and have lived with that decision for centuries."

Romik sighed. "I suppose."

"But now they have changed their minds," Baylun said. "Once we get the prisoners into the temple, they will be armed and given basic training to fight. Poopit has declared it time to take control of their destiny."

"Dragons are bad enough," remarked Romik, "but demons? How are we to fight *them*? As you know, I lost my father to the demon Ragab."

Baylun understood that fact all too well. Romik's father had closed a gate to Hell by leaping through it with a magical key. It was the only way to send the hundreds of demons that had entered Vaeldor back to their accursed world. "Yes." Baylun put his hand on his brother's shoulder. "I know this. But we have Torrac. And Torrac had no problem destroying krahluks in Lormin Dmurr. I believe it will be equally effective against the aamustall. And at my urging, the dwarves are sending a party to assist Greyor and bring him. Then we'll have Clanghorr as well."

"This is more than I was expecting when I joined this mission," Romik admitted with a wry smile. "I wish Selanna were here."

"You and me both," said Baylun.

"So what is the plan?" Lorylla asked.

Baylun cleared his throat. Right. The plan. "The first part is to get the dwarves out of their cell."

Chapter 27

Dilemma

Greyor led Eraim and Kiryanna back to the lava pool and down the stairs to the corridor they had not taken. The hallway was rough, and chunks of stone protruded from various locations about the walls and uneven floor, forcing him to watch his step—no dwarf had had a hand in its construction! After a few paces, the passage began a steady climb.

"Where is this taking us?" asked Kiryanna in a hushed voice.

Greyor shook his head. "This is not part of Lornibur."

Eraim twisted her mouth to the side. She didn't know either. But why would she? This wasn't a forest.

After two hundred feet, a breeze brushed Greyor's cheeks as the passage curved to the left. It rounded what was surely an entire loop before opening into a cavernous chamber so large that Eraim's light reached none of its walls. The floor was jagged, rising and falling at steep angles, and loose stones were everywhere. To the left, crude steps led higher into the shadows. But darkness did not entirely capture the room. An orange glow illuminated a ledge atop the stairs, obviously cast by lava. But Greyor felt no heat. On the contrary, the wind was cool, and twice as strong as it had been within the tunnel.

A horn sounded: a short blast reminiscent of a goose, but ten times as loud. Greyor stilled, his eyes shifting left and right and scanning the darkness overhead. A hiss followed, and a roar echoed across the chamber.

"The dragon?" Kiryanna whispered.

Eraim furrowed her brow, her gaze fixed on the top of the stairs.

Dragon or not, Greyor came to clear the mines of all vermin, and he grasped Clanghorr tightly and marched upward.

"Wait!" Eraim grabbed his arm.

Greyor continued.

There must have been thirty steps. As the ledge came into view, Greyor's suspicions of a lava pool became a reality. The area bore into the wall twenty yards back with the molten rock bubbling toward the rear, and next to it was a rounded tunnel. The passage was oval-shaped, ten feet high and fifteen feet wide, and from it emerged an orange reptilian head twice the size of a horse's. Its maw was eight feet above the floor, and as it entered further, it revealed a long, serpentine neck.

Greyor did not know whether the monster could breathe fire. If it did, how was he to get close enough to swing Clanghorr without being roasted?

"You kill it!" said Kiryanna, dashing onto the ledge and racing to the right.

The lizard's front claws entered, and its neck swung as its eyes followed the marteese. Greyor could not believe her bravery—perhaps stupidity—in risking her life as a distraction. He couldn't let the beast get her.

He leaped over the top step, placing his hand on the rough floor to launch himself in the reptile's direction. Just as he feared, the creature's head reared as it drew a deep breath—it prepared to spit fire! He had no choice, and he threw Clanghorr. The weapon rotated once before picking up speed, making it appear as a circle of silver with a bronze core.

The monster lunged, and fire gushed from its open mouth, rushing between fangs as long as daggers. Kiryanna rolled as the flames nearly engulfed her, evading the attack, and Clanghorr ended the blast as it buried into the creature's neck. Had the flames continued, the marteese would have been burned or worse.

The reptile thrashed, but it didn't collapse. Several broken-horn sounds emitted from its maw, and a long-shafted arrow penetrated its skull, causing it to rear and crash into the wall near the pool. The jerking motion broke Clanghorr loose, and the battleaxe fell.

Greyor charged while the monster attempted to right itself. He lifted Clanghorr to finish the beast, but another arrow sank into its chin, piercing its skull, and it collapsed. The bubbling magma was then the only sound.

Greyor had never seen a lizard so long. But was it a lizard? Its neck was six feet long—much longer than those encountered thus far. It looked like a small, wingless dragon.

Turning to the tunnel, Greyor detected nothing else coming. His companions held their weapons ready, Kiryanna with the golden sword and Eraim with her bow, but the chamber remained quiet. Greyor then noticed the breeze didn't originate from the passage. It came from above.

"Send your light up," he said to Eraim.

She complied, and the bauble soared into the darkness overhead until revealing a hole roughly fifteen feet in diameter. It bore into the jagged ceiling.

"An exit," Greyor mumbled.

Kiryanna studied the corpse. "Only for creatures that fly."

Indeed, there was no other way to reach the tunnel.

"Apparently, neither of you noticed the dragon that chased us earlier had wings," said Eraim, her light returning to hover above her head. "We must not allow them to escape into Vaeldor."

"What do we do?" asked Kiryanna. "The three of us cannot go dragon hunting." She glanced at the corpse. "The one we saw was three times the size of this thing." She turned to Greyor. "What was your plan, anyway? Surely you did not expect us to rid the mines of lizards. There are far too many, even if we weren't separated from our companions."

"Indeed." Greyor sighed. It was time to be honest. "You are correct. It'll be an army of dwarves that exterminates the creatures." He sniffed. "My original intent was to secure the safety of the mine dwellers. Where they came from is a mystery, but they aren't evil. I cannot have my kin slaying the poor things."

"Is that all?" posed Kiryanna, her brow rising.

Greyor stared at the marteese. "I also seek answers about Clanghorr, before King Lrindon of Rornibur attempts to take possession of it."

"King?" Eraim scrunched her tiny nose. "Since when?"

"Recently." Greyor rubbed his nose. "And now he lays claim to Clanghorr. He believes that because Poluran was its original owner, it belongs to Rornibur." He shook his head. "It would be like losing my arm." Gazing about the cavernous chamber, he added, "I don't know what I hoped to find, but Clanghorr had been whispering to me, and I sensed its need to come here."

"Though I do not fully comprehend what you're talking about," Kiryanna said, "I empathize with your situation, believe me. I have worked to strengthen the resolve of half-breeds for most of my life, encouraging them not to allow others to walk all over them." Eying Greyor, she added, "Perhaps that is something you should consider yourself." She gave a firm nod. "And now, it is time we got back to finding our families and friends."

"Of course." Greyor glanced at the tunnel, the dark ceiling, and finally the steps leading downward. The marteese was right; they needed to rescue their companions. Beyond that, the dragons presented a whole new obstacle he wasn't even sure an army of dwarves could overcome. He sighed. Lornibur would have to remain lost.

Eraim's brow furrowed as if she contemplated something. She nodded to herself and faced Greyor and Kiryanna. "Yes, we should return to our search. But before we go, I will have a look down this tunnel." She turned to Kiryanna. "I shall not be long. But we must know what we are leaving behind."

Kiryanna pursed her lips, and she gave a curt nod. "Be quick about it."

"Stay," Eraim said to her floating light, and she bolted into the passage with Mithkahr in hand.

Kiryanna's countenance softened as she released a long exhale, and she turned to Greyor. "I do not know what Baylun would do if others laid claim to Torrac. That weapon is a part of him, just as Clanghorr is a part of you." Her brow lowered while she pondered. "Perhaps I'd counsel him to declare a Dance of Flames."

"A dance?" Greyor chuckled. "I'd like to see a krukari that can dance!"

She appeared offended. "Were you not at Vayla's wedding party? Baylun danced like a prince!"

Greyor thought back, recalling that night. It was a grand affair with the finest human minstrels one could hope for. He remembered the happy bride and her husband, Macurak, capering among friends. The memory of Baylun dancing with Kiryanna then came to the forefront, and Greyor smiled. It was like watching a frog and a swan. He worked hard to contain a laugh.

Kiryanna smirked. "Okay, maybe not a prince." Her expression turned serious. "But the Dance of Flames is not a dance as you are thinking. It is a competition under Silcor, performed in a ring of fire. In Holindale, the Dales use it to solve many disputes. It is done without weapons, and whoever is cast from the ring is declared the loser."

"That sounds like the way barbarians would handle such matters," Greyor said.

"It is *Silcor's* way," Kiryanna corrected him.

"So it is." He chuckled. He knew very little about the Fire God. Some smithies paid respect to Silcor, hoping to receive divine heat for their forges; that was the extent of Greyor's knowledge. "If only dancing were an option."

Eraim returned, her face paler than usual.

"There are many like this creature," she said, glancing at the corpse. "No less than a hundred in a chamber much larger than this one. And half of them have wings."

Greyor's hopes dwindled further. There was only one way to keep such a brood from Vaeldor. He needed to complete the job the dwarves of old had started, and collapse it all.

"Fret not," Eraim said to him. "There may yet be a path forward for you. But first, we must figure out what to do next."

Chapter 28

Liquid Fire

Ameilistari woke to the clash of steel and grunting.

She opened her eyes. She lay on a stone bed, and the ceiling rose high overhead, illuminated by a flickering light. Why did dwarves prefer such tall ceilings?

The mines!

She sat up to see Nidor and Vecnor sparring within a small bedchamber by the light of a torch in a wall sconce. The room contained a single door, and a few stone furnishings crowded one side—obviously moved to make space for the bout. The bed was hard.

She swung her feet over the edge, wondering if the floor might have been more comfortable. Her head was groggy, as if she were overcoming an illness, and she remained seated. The boys didn't seem to notice she had awakened.

"I must be more careful," she told herself, remembering Selanna's words.

"That you must," said Vecnor, lowering his sword and facing her.

Nidor looked at her with concerned eyes. Unlike Vecnor, he panted. "Good," he said. "You're up."

"How long have we been here?" she asked.

"A few hours," Vecnor replied.

"What happened?" She recalled nothing after releasing the fire.

"You blasted that shaft pretty good." Nidor grinned. "Two orange lizards had reached the top, but they went right back down. Nothing's coming up that way ever again."

She offered half a smile. Ameilistari might have been more

impressed with herself were her head not swimming. But that didn't stop her thoughts from churning. She traveled with the real Vecnor, but she couldn't tell anyone. And she needed to convince Nidor to do the same. The mines contained danger far beyond anything she had imagined, and now thousands and thousands of people counted on her and those she entered Lornibur with to protect them from a fiery torment, whether or not they realized it. Although Selanna didn't specifically say not to mention that part, she knew she must keep it to herself. The whole adventure was supposed to have been a chance for her and Nidor to prove themselves. It was supposed to be fun. But she wasn't having any fun.

"Are you okay?" asked Nidor.

"She's fine," said Vecnor. He eyed her, as if aware of her visit with Selanna. "She just needs to take it easy for a bit."

There was no time to take it easy—perhaps she read too much in Vecnor's eyes. She stood and put on her bravest face. "I'm ready."

Vecnor gave a wink. "Then let's be on our way."

They gathered their gear, and Vecnor opened the door. He peered to the sides before heading right into the adjoining corridor, and Ameilistari summoned her light and followed with Nidor close behind.

The tunnel was eight feet wide with a rounded ceiling, and the craftsmanship remained consistent with the rest of Lornibur—Ameilistari wasn't sure why she had expected anything different. They passed two sets of stairs and four intersections, Vecnor ignoring the former and pausing at the latter. At the second intersection, he had closed his eyes and listened before picking a route.

They continued without stopping, and strength returned to Ameilistari with each step. It seemed an hour had transpired when they reached a wide corridor passing from right to left. Like others of its width, pillars lined the center at sixty-foot intervals, but unlike those hallways, most of them lay in ruin, and cracks raced across the ceiling twenty feet overhead, interrupting the usual dance of gold, silver, and copper veins.

"Is it safe to take this passage?" Ameilistari whispered as Vecnor looked both ways.

The warrior glanced upward. "Stay near the wall," he said, and headed left.

Rubble crunched beneath their boots, and they inadvertently kicked stones while hugging the left side. The few columns intact showed cracks and evidence of deterioration, and dirt occasionally sifted from fissures in the ceiling.

"Strange that this tunnel has fallen into ruin while the others appear strong," Nidor mentioned quietly.

"This did not fall into ruin," Vecnor said softly. "It was destroyed."

Farther along, scattered bones decorated the hallway, and scorching intermittently marred the walls.

"The orange and red lizards have been here," Ameilistari said.

"Only if they're eating their own." Vecnor glanced at the bones. "These are lizard remains."

"Large teeth gnawed through this." Nidor's voice was a bit distant.

Ameilistari turned to see him twenty feet behind, kneeling and holding what was surely a spine. She had forgotten that her cousin was a skilled hunter.

Vecnor halted. "How large?"

Nidor rotated the bone, scrutinizing where it had been snapped. He set it aside and studied a couple more before looking up, his eyes troubled. "*Very* big."

Ameilistari grew nervous as Nidor walked to the center of the hallway and stooped to peer at the floor. Vecnor had told them to remain to the side.

"Whatever moved through here was enormous," Nidor said. "There are two sizes of clawed feet, one set larger than the other." He looked at Vecnor. "I'm not as skilled as my father, but I'd say it was a single creature moving on all fours. At least thirty feet long."

Vecnor took a deep breath and blew it out. "Move back to the wall," he said at last, and Nidor obliged. He then considered Ameilistari. "Remember that the opposite of fire is water."

She frowned. Everyone knew that. Before she could respond, the warrior continued along the corridor.

Less than thirty paces farther, a section of the wall appeared to have collapsed. No. Exploded. The rubble that once formed a barrier between the passage and what lay beyond covered the floor. Surely one of the fancy archways had separated the two spaces, but Ameilistari spied no evidence of its prior existence.

"Did Maak Maak do this?" she asked.

Vecnor shook his head. "I'm not sure."

"I don't believe so," said Nidor, crossing the hall to gain a better view. "The Maak Maak tunnels were dug out. Whatever did this used force." He overturned a chunk of debris with his boot. "And several pieces have scorching and pitting, as if weakened by fire. Maak Maak spit scalding water."

Ameilistari's cousin continued to surprise her with his knowledge. His father and grandfather were truly skilled to have taught him so well.

"It's as I feared," said Vecnor, peering into the dark hole. "A dragon."

Surely Vecnor was mistaken. Dragons were things in stories told to children; monsters long extinct. They were mystical creatures that cast magic, visited your dreams, or swept you away to palaces atop clouds; flying reptiles as small as a bee or as large as a castle, and every size in between; legendary beasts that breathed fire, snow, or rainbows. Little boys slew them. Little girls rode them and kept them as pets.

Vecnor stepped over and around rubble to inspect the neighboring room. He stared into the darkness as if it posed no hindrance, his gaze moving from side to side and up and down.

"It must be done," he said to himself. Or perhaps he had spoken to Selanna. He turned back. "If we encounter this dragon, you two are to run the other way." His expression left no room for argument or compromise. "Fight only if your lives depend on it."

Ameilistari glanced at Nidor. Her cousin showed disbelief—whether at Vecnor telling them to run or the thought that a dragon existed, she couldn't tell. Her chest constricted with anxiety, and she swallowed the lump growing in her throat and addressed Vecnor.

"If what you say is true, how do you expect to handle the beast alone?"

He turned back to the darkness ahead. "I've done it before." He pulled his second blade.

Ameilistari's apprehension grew. Vecnor was serious. With a deep breath, she entered the adjoining room, and Nidor followed, both of them lagging twenty feet behind their courageous leader.

The light revealed more of the chamber with every step, and the rubble dwindled until only a smooth floor remained. As the wide room continued beneath its vaulted ceiling, broken stone furnishings were strewn, creating moving shadows and putting Ameilistari's nerves on edge. The original purpose of the fixtures was impossible to discern for most of them, but a few tables and chairs were intact. If it had been a dining hall, it could have easily seated a couple hundred dwarves.

"This will likely connect to another wide hallway." Vecnor interrupted the sound of their footfalls. "The monster will have broken that wall too, as well as several others to gain access to different parts of Lornibur."

"For what purpose?" posed Nidor, his voice half the volume of Vecnor's.

"It could be searching for a more desirable lair," the large man replied. "Or maybe it's hunting, or ridding the surrounding tunnels of pests." He shook his head. "Who really knows?"

A thought occurred to Ameilistari. "What about its breath? How can you survive that?"

"My gear is specially forged to resist fire," he said without looking back.

That was how he remained unharmed after the lizards belched

their flames! But how did one forge gear to resist fire?

"What if it breathes ice or snow?" Ameilistari posed.

Vecnor turned and grinned. "Dragons breathe fire." He proceeded forward. "Everything else is just stories."

She thought about the battle in the throne room. "Maak Maak didn't breathe fire."

Vecnor paused with a frown on his face. "You have a point. Still, with the scorching we've seen, what else could it be?"

He resumed the march.

Rubble again adorned the flagstones, and the far end of the hall came into view. Indeed, the wall was toppled, and beyond stood another thirty-foot-wide corridor, this one running straight ahead. From the splintered wood, Ameilistari guessed there had been a set of double doors that once separated the room from the tunnel. As with the previous hallway, pillars that once supported the ceiling lay in various states of ruin at twenty-yard intervals.

The sound of sliding stones emitted from the darkness ahead. It was distant, yet it caused Ameilistari and her companions to freeze where they stood. Vecnor looked back with a finger to his lips, and motioned for them to stay put. Ameilistari turned to Nidor. Her cousin gave her a half-hearted smile.

As Vecnor approached the edge of the light, Ameilistari wondered if she should move it with him. He was human after all, and humans couldn't see in the dark. But he had had no issues back in the tower after she levitated to the next floor, so… She didn't know what to do, and she dared not ask. As the giant warrior faded into the shadows without a word, she had her answer.

Her anxiety grew. Nidor appeared just as unsettled. She wished desperately to fill the silence, to speak with her cousin, if for no other reason than to dispel the haunting sound of Vecnor's diminishing footfalls. But she could not. Her breathing became shallow—she wanted to run and hide. But Vecnor was alone and might need help. Her heart sank. She and Nidor couldn't possibly defeat a dragon.

A growl halted her thoughts. It was faint, but unnerving all the same. The growl then evolved into a roar, and a light interrupted the darkness ahead — the corridor was long.

"Run!" commanded Vecnor, his diminutive silhouette approaching in haste along the middle of the passage.

The distant illumination was fire, and it filled the tunnel like a billowing orange cloud, but ended short of Vecnor's position.

Nidor carried out the command while Ameilistari remained. Terrified as she was, she had to see the monster for herself. Willing her light forward, it hastened to join Vecnor as another roar sounded, filling her ears as it reverberated along the hallway — it was getting closer. The floor then shook as the beast came into view, and Ameilistari gasped.

The dragon's head was larger than either of Maak Maak's, and mostly covered in red scales — groupings of orange surrounded the ears and angled above its reddish eyes to make it appear angry. Sleek horns spiraled back, curving like waves from the top of its head on either side of bony black protrusions along its neck. The creature's mouth could swallow Ameilistari whole — Vecnor might be another story — and bright orange liquid drooled over hundreds of fangs, smoking as it touched the flagstones. Its front legs entered the light; scaly appendages ending in claws smaller than Maak Maak's, but no less deadly in appearance.

The reptile was nothing like the stories Ameilistari had heard growing up. This creature would not fly her away to a palace in the sky or create rainbows to brighten her day. It had only devastation in its snarl. It gained on Vecnor, but ceased its forward progress and reared, its horns scraping the ceiling. After a deep inhale, it lunged.

Ameilistari's legs wouldn't move. Nidor grabbed her arm, but her eyes remained fixed on the dragon's destructive breath. It wasn't fire, but more of the orange liquid splashing the ceiling, floor, and walls, and everywhere it touched, flames sprouted. Vecnor raised his sword in defense, and the weapon and more than half of his armor ignited. He retreated again, waving his blade as if trying to extinguish it and rapping the fire on his breastplate with his gauntlet. As the erupting flares from the walls, floor, and ceiling united, a billowing cloud surged forward.

Vecnor had claimed his equipment resisted fire, but this was no ordinary fire, and Ameilistari sensed him to be in distress. Her mind raced as the flames threatened to engulf the warrior.

…allow the magic to flow through you… came Selanna's voice.

…water is the opposite of fire… said Vecnor's.

She reached out to the invisible energies of magic, pulling them to her in haste. Nidor must have noticed her actions, for he released her arm, and her lips moved as she voiced her spell. It was an incantation she used to water the gardens atop Ironside Keep during the dry season, but this time, she drew in more power. She channeled it through her arms, and what began as a spray became a gushing burst. The rush nearly knocked Vecnor off balance as it doused his body and kept the surrounding fire at bay.

The dragon halted, as if curious or nervous—its angry eyebrows made it hard to know for sure.

Ameilistari eased the pressure so as not to slow Vecnor's withdrawal, but the flames upon him didn't die. They sputtered and reignited. She used her free hand to gather more energy, and while part of her brain maintained the flow of water, another part formed additional words upon her lips and turned the water to snow. The spell worked, and she released her hold on the magic as the fires died at last.

Vecnor continued on his path, his armor sporting a different hue of black than it had before. The beast became enraged and released an ear-splitting roar at the ceiling.

"Run!" Vecnor shouted, now within twenty feet.

Ameilistari called her light to her and chased after Nidor. Vecnor's heavy steps drew nearer, and heavier footfalls soon followed, growing closer with every thump.

"Through the door!" commanded Vecnor.

An archway was ahead on the right, and wooden remains lay to the side of the opening, badly charred. It must have once been a door, and as there were no other archways visible, it was surely the direction Vecnor meant. Nidor obviously reached the same conclusion as he bolted into the unknown beyond.

Ameilistari joined her cousin, her light revealing another long room with a vaulted ceiling. Rows of stone benches to seat shorter folks faced the opposite end, the only proof of decline consisting of a few cracks. Though similar to a chamber of worship, Ameilistari was confident it wasn't a temple of any sort.

As she followed Nidor into the central aisle between the benches, the far end came into view, where a four-tiered stage met a rounded wall. The lowest and largest stage held four long tables, each set before eight chairs that faced the room. Four shorter tables bearing half as many chairs occupied the next stage, and the next level had four single-person tables. The smallest and highest tier hosted a throne-like seat. The chairs were obviously meant for nobles, as the care taken in their craftsmanship was evident even at a distance, and the higher the stage, the fancier the furniture appeared. The throne reminded Ameilistari of the high-backed chair in the tavern of Ironside Keep, and her light sparkled off what could only be gems adorning it.

"Blast!" Vecnor growled, now behind her.

Ameilistari and Nidor spun. The tall warrior scanned the room, his face burned in several areas and his facial hair singed.

"There are no exits." He shook his head. After another glance along the room's length, he said, "Get to the far end." He turned to the doorway, where Ameilistari expected to see a large reptilian eye peering through. It was not so. "I'll find a way to get you out of here."

"You need our help," Ameilistari insisted. "That wasn't fire it breathed on you."

A rustle outside the room drew their attention. The entrance remained empty, but the dragon was surely there.

Vecnor looked back. "No, it's not ordinary fire. It's worse." After a moment, he added, "Assist as you did before, but only if you must. And do so from farther back. Neither of you can survive what comes from that creature."

Nidor gave a nod, appearing eager to carry out the instructions. As for Ameilistari, she did not need to be close to use her spells. She nodded her assent.

A loud sucking sounded as the dragon pulled air into its lungs. It was getting ready to release its breath.

Nidor grabbed Ameilistari's arm, breaking her from her trance, and she ran with him deeper into the chamber. Behind them, the rush of the dragon's exhale drowned out all other noises. Ameilistari was halfway to the stages when she spun to see the result.

There was nothing but the illumination of fire burning in the entryway. But then an area of the wall glowed, roughly two feet in diameter. And another area. And another. The liquid fire was eating through the stone!

A dozen radiant sections were now visible, and the room shuddered. Something had struck the wall, creating cracks from glowing spot to glowing spot, as if completing a diagram or tracing roads on a map. With the next strike, parts of the wall crumbled, and fissures spread along the ceiling. Flames then illuminated the holes where the lighted areas had been. A second later, the wall crashed down, several of its chunks alight, and the dragon entered with a roar.

Ameilistari's heart raced — Vecnor was missing! She searched the rubble, but he wasn't there.

The dragon eyed her, almost seeming to smile.

From the corner of the room came the giant warrior — perhaps he had had the foresight to move from the beast's path before it breached the wall. He darted below its long neck unseen, but several stones were kicked, and the reptilian head turned downward. It could not react before he thrust his right sword into its chest, however, and as he pulled the blade free, he spun, scoring a gash with the other sword. The dragon lunged like a snake, its teeth clamping shut with enough force to sunder a tree, but Vecnor dashed from the spot and to the other side of the monster before the fangs could strike.

Keep your head, Ameilistari cautioned herself. She reached out, finding the magical energy around her, and repeated her previous spell. But she held it at her fingertips, not wanting to hit Vecnor with the attack she had planned.

The dragon maneuvered away from Vecnor, crumbling the remaining edges of the wall, and sucked in another breath. Vecnor lunged, scoring a wound on its right claw before retreating. The creature then surprised Ameilistari when it turned its head toward her and expelled its orangish fluid. It was clever enough to know it didn't want her interference again, and it allowed Vecnor to add another slash to its neck to accomplish the feat.

Fear nearly broke Ameilistari's concentration, but she remained focused and released the surge of water and snow. The liquid breath streamed around her, unable to penetrate her blast. She pushed harder, allowing energy to enter through her head, shoulders, stomach, and from the stone beneath her boots, and the water and snow became ice. It pierced the dragon's breath and invaded its gaping mouth.

Dizziness threatened, and Ameilistari reluctantly reduced the flow of power. Ice became snow, and snow turned into water. The spell then ended. Hopefully, she had done enough.

The hue of the dragon's scales appeared faded, as if the creature had paled, and it reeled. Vecnor pressed, attacking with savagery Ameilistari never thought possible from a human. His blades swung as fast as an elf releasing arrows from a bowstring, and each strike sliced as deep as a dwarf wielding a battleaxe with both hands. The dragon recovered and wheezed, as if attempting to spew its liquid fire, but harmless trails of steam were all it conjured. The monster then resorted to clawing Vecnor's black armor and knocking him back. Somehow, he kept his feet.

Vecnor made a move to the right, and the reptile countered with its claw. He pulled up short and cleaved three of the toes from its foot, driving his enemy to retreat into the corridor. He pursued, and its monstrous head descended like lightning; and though Vecnor evaded most of the teeth, the blow knocked him to the flagstones.

Ameilistari needed to help. But the strands of magical energy now dangled on the outskirts of the burning benches around her, and when she tried to draw them closer, her head swam. She was spent.

Vecnor proved as agile as any elf and dodged the next strike while rolling to his feet. Before the giant lizard pulled back, he gashed its lower jaw, his blade passing completely through lip, teeth, gums, and bone. The reptile countered with its good claw, and Vecnor used both swords to veer the attack aside. He followed with a spin, and his blades sliced the scales on the dragon's front leg, penetrating deep.

The surrounding heat intensified, and a feeling of dread overcame Ameilistari like a dagger in the heart. She spun.

"Nidor?"

Most of the benches were ablaze—the trail of fire passed all the way to the first tier of tables and chairs. Her cousin was nowhere to be seen.

"Nidor!" she cried, following a path untouched by the orange liquid—her spell had protected it.

Three rows away, Nidor lay between the benches on the left. The dragon's breath had failed to reach his lower body, but most of his torso and head were burning. Without thought, Ameilistari pulled a single strand of energy to her, her will too strong to be denied, and she blasted snow from her extended hand to smother the flames. The spinning of her head nearly overwhelmed her, and she ended the spell.

The fires on Nidor no longer burned, but he was badly charred and unmoving. Turning to Vecnor, Ameilistari witnessed the neck of the dragon slamming to the floor, causing dust to rain from the cracks overhead. Vecnor stood before the beast, covered in smoking orange blood.

"Vecnor!" she cried.

Chapter 29

Step One

Baylun squatted on the balcony overlooking the prison. He could not see the creature that had been guarding the gate earlier; perhaps it roamed the other chamber or had returned to the coals. He looked at Lorylla. She scanned the room below, her slender fingers loosely holding an arrow to her bowstring. It was the first moment Baylun had had to admire her weapon's beauty. The wood was gray, nearly matching the hue of Lorylla's skin, and etching of leaves flowed from top to bottom, as if falling from a tree. Above her left hand that clutched the bow, notches marked the shaft, so fine that they could easily be missed. Surely there weren't enough to represent everyone slain by her arrows. What then? Baylun made a mental note to ask her one day.

He looked towards the rear of the prison cell. From his vantage point, he couldn't see the secret door. But it was there, and Poopit and other dwarves were gathering behind it with Romik. He mouthed a silent prayer to Silcor to see his brother safely through.

"It is nearly time," said Lorylla in a hushed voice. She studied Baylun, as if reading his mind. "It is a noble task you have accepted."

Maybe she didn't read his thoughts exactly.

She turned back to the prison cell. "Do not fear for Romik. He has shown himself a capable warrior. Besides," she eyed Baylun, "of our missions, his is the least dangerous."

Perhaps she *had* read him correctly. And she was right. But even though Baylun and Lorylla bore the riskiest of the tasks, Romik's was not without danger.

Baylun took a calming breath and slowly released it. Pulling a slip of parchment from his pouch, he glanced at it. The soft glow of the forge revealed the crude map he had drawn; his route to the rally point. "You have your map?" he asked the elf.

She patted a pocket on the side of her breeches.

"Be safe," Baylun said, turning to report to his post.

"*Mulaattü espruul,*" she said back to him. "May the wind remain beneath your feet."

A strange saying. A bit of Elfish Baylun had never learned. He gave a nod and crept away.

Baylun crossed the room and passed through the door to the chamber overlooking the forge. As he approached the ledge, he dropped to his hands and knees and crawled until the orange light touched his face. The forge was empty.

He took another slow breath as he tightened his grip on Torrac. At any moment, Poopit would open the secret door. The dwarf would then begin the exodus, having the captives toward the front stay put so the demons hopefully didn't notice their depleting numbers until most of them were safely away. Until the enemy realized their actions, Baylun would remain still and watch.

Minutes passed. He detected nothing from the prison through the archway on the right. His heart rate increased.

"Calm yourself, Baylun," he whispered.

If anything had gone wrong, he'd have heard or seen Lorylla by now. Surely the small folk were filing through the door at that very moment, following Zur and Ka while Romik and Bo waited with fifty dwarves to protect their escape. If demons had somehow entered the prison without Baylun seeing them, Poopit would have whistled to summon Romik and the others into the room.

Patience.

The central forge glowed brighter, and Baylun held his breath. The mantis creature exited the furnace, as if hopping from the coals, and landed on the flagstones of the oval-shaped chamber. Fearing it might spot him, Baylun backed away until only his eyes and the top of his head showed. The hard feet of the demon clicked as it walked toward the archway leading to the cell, its actions showing no alarm, and upon reaching the opening, it stood perfectly still.

Had Poopit Hans not begun removing his people? Dread roiled in Baylun's stomach.

The mantis moved—its mandibles snapped twice. Did that mean something?

Baylun continued observing.

The creature stepped through the archway, and as it disappeared from view, a high-pitched screech echoed. A second later, the demon stumbled back beneath the arch with three arrows protruding from its body. Another arrow struck, exploding upon impact, and the mantis reeled.

The coals flared, and four demons leaped from the forge. The first was tall, with the head of a dog that had been badly burned. Vicious fangs were evident through holes in its cheeks and charred fur covered its body, and it held a wicked spear with three tines as thick as knives. The second fiend stood half the height of the first. It possessed a scorpion tail rising to dangle over its deranged, chicken-like head, and it released an ear-piercing screech reminiscent of a bird of prey. A dark exoskeleton enclosed the rest of its body, and its arms resembled the front appendages of a praying mantis. The final two creatures were human-like from the waist up, except for the horns atop their heads, and one had bright red skin while the other was blood red. Both had muscular torsos and lower bodies of goats. The first twirled a chain with a pair of spiked balls, while the second wielded a sword wreathed in fire.

A roar sounded from the prison. The dwarfish warriors had charged.

None of the demons took notice of Baylun, and he rose to his feet while they headed for the archway—the mantis must have reentered the other chamber. An arrow then exited the prison, piercing the dog monster in the chest and releasing a small explosion—Lorylla had surely leaped onto the wall of granite stones to have hit her target. The attack staggered the demon, and it responded with a lion-like roar.

Baylun raised Torrac. The glowing runes didn't escape his peripheral vision — it was ready. He heaved the weapon, and it picked up speed as it streaked toward its victim, its runes appearing as a circle of white light. The battleaxe arced right, then left, and severed the scorpion tail from the second demon's body. The fiend stomped about in obvious pain, and the goat-legged demons turned to spy Baylun. He reached out his hand, and Torrac returned.

The blood-red demon shouted unintelligible words, and the coals lit up again. From the forge bounded a dozen tiny creatures with pointed tails and two-tined spears. They appeared to be naked humanoids and hopped like rabbits into the prison. More monsters emerged, but Baylun lost track of them as the bright red demon swung its chain in his direction. Although the fiend stood sixty feet away, the links extended to close the gap in a hurry.

Baylun moved his head aside as a spiked ball struck the wall next to him; the other ball narrowly missed his ear. He brought Torrac across in haste, severing the chain before the monster could recall its weapon, and followed the action by throwing his battleaxe. The demon attempted to dodge, but the spinning blades remained on target, following the fiend's every step and cutting it in half. The creature disappeared within a cloud of red smoke.

Baylun caught Torrac as it returned.

"We must go!" yelled Lorylla from behind him.

The dwarves had exited the cell and were on the run.

As Baylun turned to follow the gray elf, an enormous demon materialized from the forge, causing him to balk. It was over ten feet tall, with the head of a bull and red eyes a couple of shades brighter than its crimson skin. Hair of a darker hue dangled from its chin and the sides of its face, and its eyebrows were thick. The monster's torso appeared as a grossly muscled man, and it held a great axe in its human-like right hand while its left arm ended in a pincer. Just as with the humanoid demons, its lower body was goat-like, and its hooves cracked the flagstones where it landed.

"Now!" Lorylla insisted as the bull head turned to face Baylun.

He tore his eyes away and raced to follow the gray elf, who was already descending the stairs.

Everything was going according to plan for the most part. Baylun's primary job was to remove the scorpion tail—Poopit explained the beast's venom to be a fate worse than death, as it drove its victims mad with a thirst for blood. Lorylla's task was adding support from above while the prisoners filed through the door. Next, he and the gray elf were to report to the rendezvous point. Unfortunately, Poopit Hans and the dwarves didn't know how many demons the forge contained. They had only ever seen the mantis, the red-skinned demons, and the scorpion-tailed fiend. Nothing was said about tiny hopping creatures or the dog and bull monsters. Baylun prayed there were no more surprises.

Chapter 30
Now What?

Having decided to see the dragon lair for himself, Greyor followed Eraim and Kiryanna along the tunnel. Eraim moved without a sound, while Kiryanna emitted only the slightest noises. Greyor didn't mind trailing at a distance of ten yards if it meant the dragons would not detect their approach, but every loose rock and protrusion of the unworked floor pressed into the bottom of his bare feet. Worse than leaving his boots behind, he regretted having removed his armor in a vain attempt to make him stealthy. There was a reason dwarves didn't pursue careers in thievery! And if Eraim covered her mouth one more time, a signal he was breathing too loudly, he might explode. For all they knew, dragons could smell them as easily as hear them. They'd wish Greyor had his armor then! How had Eraim tricked him into agreeing to this horrible plan? The elf said it was the only way to see what she had described, but he had his doubts. She was an elf, after all, and he recalled a day when a few cavern lizards had made her nervous.

Eraim turned, glaring at Greyor and placing a hand over her mouth. Blood rushed to his head as he took a deep breath and held it.

The passage grew warmer, and a light revealed a room ahead. Greyor gripped Clanghorr tighter—he'd sooner remove his arm than leave the weapon behind! Eraim and Kiryanna paused at the opening, and Greyor joined them, receiving another glare from Eraim as he released the air from his lungs. He ignored her—embarrassing the elf in front of Kiryanna wouldn't benefit the mission.

The chamber was horrific, roughly four hundred feet in diameter with a glowing chasm occupying two-thirds of its center. An orange light from below gave the entire cavern an ominous glow, revealing the giant lizards Eraim had reported, although the shadows made it appear there were twice as many. Most of the reptiles were longer than the dead lizard down the tunnel.

The creatures moved about a spiraling ledge beginning to the right of the entrance and completing nearly two circles as it rose a hundred yards overhead. The ramp varied from twenty to sixty feet wide, and outcroppings of stone and loose boulders riddled its length. Higher still, winged lizards perched upon shelves like giant birds—Greyor spied no access to their nests. A ceiling infested with stalactites completed the space, adding to its sense of foreboding.

Eraim waved at Greyor and pointed into the pit. He inched forward, his eyes darting between the reptiles and the glowing hole until reaching its edge. The monsters appeared to take no notice of his presence—some were feeding, some slept, and a few were playing or fighting. He peered downward, his face greeted by hot air. A lake of bubbling magma lay two hundred feet below. But that wasn't what Eraim had been drawing his attention to. Crude steps descended to a ledge circling the shaft, and along its circumference were at least a hundred eggs, taller than any seen thus far.

The view made Greyor's head spin, and Eraim grabbed his shoulder to steady him as his weight shifted forward. His gaze went to the monsters. They still seemed unaware or uncaring that anyone watched them.

The small elf pointed back down the tunnel, and Greyor followed as she and Kiryanna headed back. They halted at the dragon corpse, where Greyor immediately put on his boots.

"How is this possible?" Kiryanna asked no one, her eyes staring blankly forward. "Legends hold dragons to be fearless." She looked from Greyor to Eraim. "Why would they hide for all these years, pretending to be extinct?"

"They are not survivors of the Dragon Wars," Eraim said. "They were created. A process needing centuries to complete."

Greyor strapped on his breastplate.

"How do you know this?" demanded the marteese.

Eraim looked down the tunnel, as if watching the giant lizards crawl about their lair. "Like you said, dragons have no fear, and would not have hidden this long." She turned back. "And when you take into consideration other things: the Demoligius symbol, Greyor's visions of evil priests, the laboratories… Demoligius is the Dragon God, and Velgaad was a dwarf king bent on power. It is possible they worked together to achieve their goals. The priests needed a remote place to create their special dragons, and the dwarf desired weapons of terror."

"But dragons already existed back then," Kiryanna pointed out. "Why create new ones?"

Eraim glanced at the corpse. "Like I said earlier, they are being bred for a specific purpose. But I hesitate to guess as to what that purpose is."

Fire burned in Greyor's veins just thinking about Velgaad working with evil. He recalled Balmorak's words, warning Mattasun about the king dealing with a couple of dragon priests in the forge…

The forge!

"We must get to the forge," he said.

Kiryanna glared his way. "You and that forge!"

"No." He released a frustrated breath. "In my vision, Velgaad dealt with the clerics in the forge. That's where they can surely be found."

"Who?" posed the marteese. "The priests? They must be long dead." She turned to Eraim. "So who has carried on the task of creating these nightmares?"

Eraim shrugged. The elf had spoken with the wisdom of Selanna, but was now at a loss for words? After a moment of chewing on her lower lip, she reluctantly spoke. "Demoligius has legions of demons at His call. Perhaps He has employed them in this matter. After the downfall of the dragons, He was greatly weakened and would not wish for this experiment to fail."

Kiryanna turned to Greyor, her expression a combination of exasperation and defeat. "Which way to the forge?"

Greyor sighed. "I cannot say with certainty. I can only follow my knowledge of dwarfish construction, and hope Lornibur is no different."

"Which way?" The marteese enunciated each word.

Greyor thought of the tunnels they had traversed. If the forge used lava, they needed to follow its stream. Tracing a path in his mind to the iron door when they first discovered the magma, he angled his body in the direction the molten rock had been flowing. He pointed across the chamber and toward the wall. "That way."

"And where is Baylun?" Kiryanna asked.

Greyor concentrated on Torrac. "The same."

"Of course he is." She shook her head. "Leave it to my husband to find the most dangerous part of Lornibur." She turned back to Greyor. "Let's find this forge."

"What about the lizards?" He pointed Clanghorr down the tunnel to the dragon lair.

"We shall have to deal with them later," Eraim said. "We must unite with our companions before..." She huffed, as if frustrated. "Lornibur is too dangerous a place for our fractured party."

"Agreed," said Kiryanna.

Greyor nodded. "Let's go then."

Leaving the reptiles behind plagued his mind, but there was nothing he could do. Even if they found their companions, what could be done? Again, Greyor wondered if his efforts to reclaim Lornibur had failed. But that was a question for another day. He needed to focus on one thing at a time, and finding the forge was next.

He led Eraim and Kiryanna back to the room with the rusted iron door, where the magma flowed through the channel along the wall. There, Greyor stared at the small archway guiding the molten rock from the chamber.

"What is it?" asked Kiryanna.

"We need to follow this stream," he replied.

"Well." Eraim gazed at the lava exit. "There's no entering that tiny tunnel, not even for me." Her eyes moved up the wall, along the ceiling, and down to the door that remained open. "I believe I can guide us in the desired direction," she said at last, "through corridors we have passed by already."

Follow an elf to the forge? These were dwarfish tunnels! Greyor could find the way, given half a moment. But… Eraim was yet to fail him. He released a slow breath and nodded. "Lead on."

The small elf walked briskly through the iron doorway and along the corridor, her eyes darting across the walls and ceiling for unwanted company. But it seemed the lizard population had thinned, and they saw none—that, or the creatures were uninterested in showing themselves. She paused upon reaching the first intersection, where six tunnels connected, and appeared confident as she picked the one to the immediate left.

That's the one Greyor would have chosen.

They followed the hallway for over a hundred paces to another intersection, and Eraim continued straight. At the next junction of tunnels, she turned left, and farther on, an archway opened into a grand corridor more befitting the approach to the forge. It was thirty feet wide, with pillars shaped like hammers spaced every twenty yards to support the forty-foot ceiling. Each column to the right bore an emerald, and those to the left held citrines. In Morimont, green stones led east while yellow passed into the west. Was it the same here?

Eraim turned right.

Greyor concurred, but he checked with Clanghorr to be absolutely positive. Torrac lay to the right.

In contrast with most of the recent corridors, this one was unscathed by Maak Maak's claws or any other vandalism. The squaring was perfect, and the decorative borders where the floor and ceiling met the walls were flawless. Though the hammerheads seemed separate pieces from the ceiling, Greyor was confident they were attached, and the handles were slender, yet thick enough to add necessary support—each appeared as a weapon made for a giant.

While they walked, Greyor's heart soared with anticipation, despite the assumed evil ahead. A hundred feet farther, several archways appeared on either side, staggered from left to right and each no less than ten yards from the next. The sound of dripping reached Greyor's ears, but it lasted a few seconds and then halted. Moments later, it happened again from another direction.

Eraim stopped, holding up her hand for Greyor and Kiryanna to do the same. "We're being watched."

Chapter 31

Fire Begets Fire

Ameilistari gaped in horror. Burns plagued nearly all of Nidor from the waist up—he must have been standing behind a bench—and his breathing was shallow and raspy. Never had she believed her little adventure could lead to this.

She stared at Vecnor. The giant warrior ran toward her, his armor covered in soot and a mixture of red and orange blood. Though wounded, he moved as if he bore no pain and kneeled beside her.

Vecnor bled from his nose, and his skin was pink and blistered—he had taken more damage than Ameilistari realized. As he lowered his gauntlet to lift Nidor into a seated position, a steady stream of blood flowed from beneath his armor, where a gouge ran along his vambrace. A glance told her additional gashes adorned the rest of his body as well.

"Nidor!" Vecnor said, dropping the gauntlet from his left hand, which appeared unharmed. He tapped Nidor's burned cheek.

Nidor's right eye opened—the other was swollen shut. Blood filled the cornea and most of his iris, distorting its brown color. He looked blankly forward as his lips quivered, but he spoke no words.

Ameilistari sobbed.

"Don't give in!" Vecnor ordered the young warrior, as if Nidor had a choice.

A long breath escaped, and Nidor's head fell back.

Ameilistari's eyes blurred with tears. Vecnor gently laid her cousin on the floor, and she spied a cinder upon Nidor's chest that had survived her spell of snow. She wanted to attack the glowing speck; to summon a burst of ice to spare him further harm at the hands of the dragon's breath. That blasted dragon!

The cinder grew brighter, and she backed off, afraid the dragon's liquid fire was reigniting. Vecnor rose, pushing her farther away as she wiped her eyes.

It wasn't a cinder. It was Nidor's necklace; a present from his grandfather, Gruelenor. She understood it to be all that remained of the original Nidor, after the fire opal had shattered in Lormin Dmurr to release the paladin's spirit. The shard was a token holding only sentimental value, but there it was, glowing as bright as the sun, and from the jewel sprang a surge of fire in every direction. Ameilistari could not avoid the ring of flames, but it did not burn. It passed over her and to the edges of the hall before dissolving, and her magical light winked out. The room went dark.

Fear stilled Ameilistari's tears as she suddenly felt alone, and she hastily summoned another light. Vecnor was there. He stood gaping at Nidor…

Her cousin rose to his feet, appearing as if the dragon's breath had never touched him. The necklace no longer glowed. It no longer existed. A leather thong hung around his neck, and as he glanced about in confusion, the cord fell to the floor.

Ameilistari's eyes blurred with tears again. Was she dreaming? Did the fire kill her? If this were Heaven, it looked like the room where she had met her demise.

"What's going on?" Nidor asked, inspecting his body in wonder.

"It's the Will of Silcor," Vecnor said, his expression one of amazement.

"Silcor?" Ameilistari posed. "But… how…?"

She moved closer to Nidor to touch his face. His eyes were normal. His skin was normal—no burns, no soot, no blisters. Even his gear appeared as it had before the attack. "Is it really you?" she asked.

Nidor nodded. "I don't know what just happened. I remember being covered in burning liquid… It was the worst pain I have ever known." He gazed at Ameilistari. "Then you yelled my name. And then Vecnor's. And then fire returned, but it did not harm me. I thought it was a strange dream, but when I opened my eyes… I feel fine." He scanned the room. "But it couldn't have been a dream. Look at this place!"

The dragon's fire no longer burned, but the blackened benches provided evidence of the heat the furnishings had endured.

"It would seem that sliver of opal still possessed a part of Paladin Nidor's spirit." Vecnor cupped Nidor's chin to stare into the young man's eyes, as if searching for something. "I believe your family's undying faith in Silcor allowed that spirit to remain." He released Nidor's chin, apparently satisfied. "You have been touched by divine strength. It is a rare gift, and not one to be taken lightly." He turned to Ameilistari. "In fact, my own injuries are mended."

Indeed, the tall man's visible wounds had ceased bleeding, and his gashes had vanished.

Ameilistari closed her eyes and sensed for surrounding fields of magic. They rushed to her, eager to fulfill her command. She released them — she had no need to cast spells at the moment. Her fatigue was gone as well. "Silcor…" she said, staring at nothing. It was the god of her mother and Dale relatives. Her appreciation of Father allowing her to follow in their footsteps grew.

Nidor shook his head. "But why would Nidor, or rather Silcor, care about me? I'm no hero. I'm… nothing, really."

Vecnor smiled. "It is not within our ability to understand the gods." He picked up his discarded gauntlet. "They work in Their own ways, in Their own time. All we can do is accept this most divine gift and return to the mission at hand." He took a deep breath and glanced at the destroyed wall, where the dragon corpse had not moved. "And get back to it we must. Lornibur holds more than just mine dwellers and reptiles."

Selanna was surely speaking to Vecnor, informing him of matters elsewhere. Ameilistari gave a firm nod.

Chapter 32

The Chase

Baylun followed Lorylla through the tunnels; they needed to get into position to execute the next phase of the plan. They relied on their ability to see in the dark as they completed five turns along the two hundred yards of passages—luckily, no lizards emerged to slow their progress. The gray elf kept a quick pace, often slowing for Baylun to keep up. He was grateful, but also cross with himself for being a burden. He quickly realized the elfish phrase, *May Galenfial carry you on winged feet*, was not just a collection of words.

As they made the last turn, Baylun saw a light in the distance. It wasn't torchlight, but a flaming sword wielded by a bipedal fiend, its reddish skin almost glowing. Four demons of similar height followed the creature, and small jumping imps bounded along the corridor to join them. The lead demon struck the wall with the fiery blade, collapsing it—the secret door Baylun and Lorylla aimed for.

Baylun's heart leaped into his throat. How had the enemy found the door? He and Lorylla needed to stop them from entering.

The gray elf surely realized this, and she let out a loud whistle to gain the demons' attention. She then fitted a couple of arrows to her bow, one after the other, and released them in less than two seconds. The arrows flew swiftly, piercing a demon in the head and another in the chest. With each strike, a small explosion resulted. The monsters turned angry eyes on the elf, and three of them charged.

"Return to the forge!" Lorylla said, heading back.

Baylun followed, unsure of her intentions. Perhaps he and the elf could defeat the creatures if only the three gave pursuit, but if they summoned others, it would likely be a different story. His thoughts then went to his brother's safety—Romik had passed through that secret door. The plan was unraveling.

The light footfalls of the enemy made it hard to tell if the distance between Baylun and his foes lessened. As the temperature increased, he was sure they closed the gap. He peeked while taking the first turn to confirm that suspicion.

The pursuers comprised three red-skinned demons, each approximately Baylun's height. One had four arms and wielded two swords in the upper hands while the lower ones held long daggers. It had fangs protruding from its maw, two each from its upper and lower jaws, and from its wide nose issued smoke. The next demon had a wolf-like snout, and fur covered its arms from its elbows to its clawed hands. The third demon had a pair of short horns atop its bald head, and its snarl revealed black pointed teeth. It carried the flaming sword, and attached to its back were bat-like wings.

Baylun concentrated on the way ahead—Lorylla obviously slowed so he wouldn't fall too far behind. They made the next couple of turns, and the distance between him and the gray elf increased as she picked up speed. She then turned, fitting an arrow to her string, and released it. Baylun felt the breeze of the projectile fly past his head, and a moment later he heard an explosion.

Lorylla continued once Baylun neared her location.

The next couple of corridors were short, and as Baylun exited the wide hallway into a narrower one, the stairs to the room overlooking the forge lay ahead. Lorylla leaped over the first five steps before touching down and springing higher up. As Baylun reached the stairwell, he turned and threw Torrac.

The runes lit up, and the spinning axe raced at the four-armed creature twenty feet away. The demon hesitated, and Torrac passed through its torso, spraying the nearby wall with smoking red blood. Baylun focused on his weapon while the halves of the corpse fell to the floor and vanished into puffs of red smoke, and Torrac returned to his hand.

The remaining demons glared, and the one with black teeth spat a gush of fire from its mouth. The flames gave chase, but never reached Baylun as he rounded the bend in the stairwell.

Lorylla awaited Baylun atop the stairs within the orange light saturating the chamber—the glow had intensified since Baylun left. She loosed two arrows in succession, one to either side of him, and a couple of explosions sounded not far away. It seemed the attacks served only to slow the fiends down, but that was all he needed to gain access into the room.

"Go to the door!" said Lorylla as she bolted toward the balcony overlooking the forge.

Baylun understood her intent. Kiryanna often had him stand apart from her when dealing with ranged attackers, so the enemy had to split their attention. And by separating, the black-toothed demon couldn't reach them both with a single breath of fire. He neared the door and spun with Torrac ready.

The demons entered, with black-tooth leading the way. Its eyes moved from Lorylla to Baylun, and it exhaled fire at him again. Whispers filled his head, and although he didn't understand them, he was compelled to raise Torrac like a shield. He obeyed, and the runes lit up, parting the flames as if a barrier existed. Baylun felt the heat, but not a hair on his body was singed.

The demon appeared furious, and it turned its sights on Lorylla when an arrow exploded on its flesh, leaving a third blackened mark. It leaped toward the gray elf, the flaming sword held forward, and its wings spread to close the gap in haste.

The wolf charged Baylun.

Baylun readied to throw his battleaxe, but the demon dropped to all fours and covered the distance in two bounds. The wolf lashed out as fast as lightning, gouging his pauldron with its claw before he could react—a burning sensation surged through the wound. The injury challenged his balance, and his counterattack missed.

Baring its fangs and a forked tongue, the wolf moved in for a bite, and Baylun retreated, falling into a seated position as he stumbled. The jaws chomped at the air above him. He thrust the spike of his haft, puncturing the demon's abdomen, but he couldn't put his full strength into the attack and only caused it to fall back a few paces. It was enough to regain his feet, however, and Baylun clenched his teeth as the pain increased.

Beyond the wolf creature, Lorylla fought the winged demon. Her sword glowed blue, and blood flowed from charred gashes on her left arm and shoulder, as well as her stomach. One of the fiend's arms hung limp, and it bore three bluish wounds packed with ice.

Baylun focused on the enemy before him as the wolf attempted another bite. His axe was heavy in his left hand, and to gain momentum, he spun. It was a risky move that could lead to dire consequences if he missed, but his right arm was useless, and he needed to help Lorylla. As he came around, the runes lit up, and the blade landed true. The fangs were inches from Baylun's face, but came no closer as Torrac sliced through the demon's chest cavity. The creature vanished in a cloud of red mist.

Near the balcony, Lorylla backed against the wall as the black-toothed demon pressed with its flaming sword. Baylun threw his weapon with one hand, and the momentum caused him to flop onto his stomach. The aim was poor, but the spirit of Torrac took control, and the glowing runes intensified as the blade decapitated the fiend. The monster dissolved into a red cloud.

Lorylla dropped to a knee and issued a nod of thanks as Baylun caught his weapon. She then scanned the chamber below and shook her head. A roar sounded, like the nightmarish call of an angry bull—apparently the giant demon had not left the forge.

Turning to Baylun, Lorylla said, "Prepare yourself!"

Chapter 33

Communication

Greyor crept toward the first archway Eraim claimed had emitted a dripping noise, a sound she said was mimicked and not the result of actual water falling from the ceiling. The elf had dimmed her floating light to the strength of a candle, so as not to fully expose Greyor, and sent it forward. As he reached the arch, Kiryanna moved to his side with her golden sword ready. Greyor gave a nod, and Eraim willed the light to grow brighter as they charged into the room.

The chamber appeared to have been a feast hall. Several round stone tables lay in various states of ruin to the sides, while a long table dominated the middle. An archway provided an exit at the far end, and scattered about with arms over their eyes to protect against the burst of illumination were half a dozen mine dwellers. One of them shrieked, and all of them lifted spears made from the rail system.

Greyor grabbed Kiryanna's arm as he halted. "Lower the light!" His command was unnecessary, as Eraim had already returned it to a softer glow.

The mine dwellers relaxed, and Greyor lowered Clanghorr and took a couple of steps forward. He then detected footfalls behind them, and four mine dwellers filled the entrance beyond Eraim. It was a trap.

"Gray'Or Clay'Gor?" a dweller in the room asked, approaching on hesitant feet.

Greyor grinned. It was how the mine dwellers said his name the first time he traversed Lornibur with Selanna and Eraim; when he and Millord rallied a group of them to fight against their long-feared enemy, Maak Maak. The sole surviving mine dweller must have made it back to its people to have taught them that. He put his free hand on his chest. "I am Greyor." He held up his battleaxe, causing several dwellers to flinch. "And this is Clanghorr!"

Mine dweller heads bobbed, and a few seemed to smile from beneath patchy mustaches.

"These are the creatures you spoke about?" asked Kiryanna.

Greyor nodded. "They mean us no harm. They want only to survive the horrors of this place."

Her eyes became hopeful. "Perhaps they know where the others are."

Definitely a possibility. But getting information out of them was another story. Still, Greyor had to try.

"Maybe you should lower Clanghorr," suggested Eraim.

A few dwellers maintained their spears in defensive positions.

Greyor lowered his weapon, and the humanoids did the same. He then addressed the one who had spoken.

"Have you seen our friends?"

The mine dweller furrowed its brow.

Greyor sighed and pointed at the speaker. "You…" he shaded his eyes with his hand, "…see…" he pointed to his chest, "…my…" he motioned at Kiryanna and Eraim, "…friends?"

The mine dweller pointed at the marteese and elf. "Fends!"

Greyor dropped his head and shook it. This was going to take some time. He looked up. "My *other* friends." He pushed down his nose and tried to stick out one of his bottom teeth while frowning. All he received in return were a quizzical expression from the dwellers and a frown from Kiryanna.

"Have you seen Baylun or Nidor?" asked the marteese.

She was apparently lacking in patience for Greyor's interrogation method. But he had communicated with them before, and he could do so again.

"Bye'Lin! Row'Mick! Lola!" The mine dweller grew excited. He pointed toward the hallway and to the right.

Kiryanna looked at Greyor and Eraim. "He knows where Baylun is!"

"Can you take us to him?" Greyor asked, earning another confused look. He put his hands out, palms up to symbolize a question. "Can..." he pointed at the dweller, "...you—"

"This is ridiculous!" Kiryanna stepped in front of Greyor. "Where is Baylun?" She sounded out each word.

"Bye'Lin!" The dweller set aside his spear and raised a hand, as if holding something. He brought down his fist to strike his palm, and repeated the gesture a few more times before positioning both hands before him, like he was looking through a barred window. The dweller then tiptoed a few paces and pushed open... a door? He waved as if beckoning someone to pass through the door, then lifted his hands as if they were claws. The dweller growled while swiping in random directions.

The show captivated Kiryanna. Greyor moved beside Eraim, who watched with a frown and a wrinkled nose.

"Reminds me of a mine dweller named Blar," he whispered.

She glanced his way. "They have names?"

Greyor nodded. "Millord called Blar Puppet Hands. Poor creature accepted the name like it were a medal."

The mine dweller smashed down his nose and tried to stick out a single bottom tooth, mimicking Greyor's impression of Baylun.

Greyor grinned. The dweller had understood.

The humanoid swung its arms left and right, as if wielding a heavy weapon. Probably Torrac. He then pointed at Clanghorr.

"Baylun fights something." Kiryanna turned to Greyor and Eraim. "A dragon?"

"Most likely," said Greyor.

"I am not so sure." Eraim twisted her lips to the side. "He made no gestures to suggest breathing fire." She looked at Greyor and Kiryanna. "I believe it is something else he fights. Something as bad as dragons. Maybe worse."

How did the elf get all of that from the puppet show? Was she watching the same performance? Still, doubting Eraim was as dumb as walking through Lornibur with your eyes closed. Greyor had to accept the possibility.

"What could be worse than a dragon?" posed Kiryanna. "Short of Uustaag?"

"Remember our conversation about the demons?" the elf asked.

More demons… Why couldn't the spider have been the only one? Perhaps the dwarves of old had been justified in trying to bury Lornibur. How had the mine dwellers survived dragons *and* demons?

Kiryanna's shoulder's slumped.

Greyor tightened his grip on Clanghorr—destroyer of Death Lords, krahluks, and zreekans—and confidence surged through his body. His ancestor, Balmorak, had failed to save Lornibur. This was his chance to set it right. "Take us to Bye'Lin," he said to the mine dweller.

"What about Nidor?" the marteese asked, her shifting eyes revealing the turmoil that haunted her. "If Baylun faces… demons or dragons or whatever, what perils threaten Nidor and Ameilistari?"

Were the children even alive? A morbid thought, and Greyor shook it from his mind. He turned back to the mine dweller. "Nidor…" he smashed his nose and put his index finger to his ear to emulate a point.

Kiryanna sighed.

"Tewlon…" Greyor clenched his fists, stuck out his chest, and flexed his muscles—probably pointless with the armor covering his torso. He placed his finger to his ear to show that the warrior also possessed pointed ears. He then mused. How should he portray Ameilistari?

The mine dweller pointed at Greyor, growing excited again. He mimicked the flexing pose and used his fingers to indicate pointed ears.

Greyor's grin returned. Of course the creature understood.

The dweller raised a hand just above his head. Was he showing Tewlon's height? The humanoid shook his head and moved his hand as high as he could reach. He then put his fingers to his ears again, but curled them to represent rounded ears.

What in Meldar's name was the dweller talking about? Greyor wished Puppet Hands were here.

"I believe he says Nidor and Ameilistari are well," said Eraim.

What? Greyor saw nothing to make such an assumption.

"For all we know," she added, "Baylun has found them already." She turned to Kiryanna. "I think we should find your husband."

The marteese continued to visibly struggle. After a long exhale, she asked, "How? These mine dwellers don't understand a word we say."

While Kiryanna spoke, the dwellers in the archway backed off as those in the room exited. The speaker looked at Greyor, motioning toward the arch.

"Less go Bye'Lin."

Good enough.

"Let's go," said Greyor.

Chapter 34

Discord

Ameilistari needed to be more careful. More thoughtful. She figured out how to help Vecnor against the dragon, but completely forgot about her cousin. She had failed as a leader and as a spellcaster. But thanks to Silcor, she had a chance to handle things better. Selanna would never have made the same mistake, Ameilistari was sure. Was Selanna watching? Did the mage witness her blunder? She had to do better.

"We had best get moving," said Vecnor.

"One moment," said Nidor.

He turned away and whispered to no one. Ameilistari wasn't positive of everything her cousin uttered, but she heard enough to realize he spoke a prayer of thanks to Silcor. She closed her eyes and mouthed the words to do the same. Once finished, Nidor nodded his readiness.

Vecnor led them through the demolished wall, where the massive dragon lay dead. It must be fifty feet long! It was amazing Vecnor had survived. Sure, Ameilistari's spell prevented it from spraying him with its diabolical breath, but still… It could have crushed him. He was every bit the hero described in stories.

Smoking blood splattered the flagstones, pitting the floor and marring it forever. Vecnor made a couple of leaping steps to avoid the fluid, and Ameilistari and Nidor followed his lead. As the carcass fell behind, taking with it the odor of charred destruction, Ameilistari ventured to ask Vecnor a question.

"What kind of dragon was that?" She didn't know if there were different types, but she had never heard of one expelling burning liquid.

Vecnor shook his head. "Unlike any dragon I ever encountered. I have no name to put to it."

"How is it you've encountered dragons before?" she asked. "I thought their extinction spanned centuries."

Vecnor sighed, appearing annoyed with himself.

"You needn't worry," Ameilistari assured him. "We are tasked with keeping your help in this matter a secret." She gave her cousin a meaningful stare. "And you can be sure that is exactly what we intend to do. So you can tell us anything."

He stopped before a massive hole in the wall.

"Wow," said Nidor, obviously seeing more in the darkness beyond than did Ameilistari.

She sent forth her light, expanding its glow to reveal buildings as far as the illumination allowed. Why would a giant cave need buildings?

"This is what the dwarves call a quadrant," explained Vecnor. "It could have been for housing, shops, storage… just about anything."

"Is that where the dragon lived?" posed Nidor.

"Perhaps," Vecnor replied. "But it's too vast for us to go poking around in. No telling how many creatures live in those structures."

They resumed their trek, and Ameilistari realized Vecnor never answered her question concerning dragons. She opened her mouth to repeat the query, but he halted again.

"What's this?" He stopped to peer at a small hole in the wall. Below the breach near the floor was a carving of a triangle.

"It's a hole," Ameilistari said. "Now, about the dragons —"

"I think it might be a door." Nidor kneeled for a closer look.

"A secret door," Vecnor corrected her cousin.

"There's a tunnel," Nidor said.

"Step back," ordered Vecnor.

Nidor complied, and the giant warrior struck the area with his boot. Several cracks extended from the hole, reaching up the wall. He gave another kick, and the three-inch stone separating the main hallway from the smaller one crumbled, adding to the ruination of Lornibur.

Ameilistari's light floated into the tunnel. It was narrow with a low ceiling, and Vecnor ducked as he entered.

"Why follow this?" asked Ameilistari, trailing after the large warrior. She did her best not to sound like she disagreed with Vecnor, as she had with Tewlon earlier. She honestly wished to know what the man thought, so she might emulate him more in the future.

"Dwarves have a way of making secret passages," he replied. "But they aren't always for hiding treasures and such. Most serve as shortcuts, or contain rooms for resting."

She wrinkled her nose. "Why hide a room for resting?"

Vecnor shrugged. "I suppose it gives workers a place of solace, so to speak. A chamber where they can recover without interruption."

Rocks plagued the way ahead, having fallen from the ceiling some time ago. Vecnor kicked them as he proceeded.

"Look here!" Nidor grabbed their attention, staring at the wall.

Ameilistari noticed that a part of it was shifted back. It fit in with the decaying tunnel, but the seams were too straight. Vecnor's giant shadow probably hid it from her as she passed by.

"Another door, I think," Nidor said.

Ameilistari guided her cousin aside so Vecnor could see.

"That it is," the large man commented.

He used his gauntlet this time to push the wall, and it collapsed into a small chamber.

"A secret room within a secret tunnel," he mused. "That's unusual."

He entered, and Ameilistari and Nidor followed.

The ceiling of the tiny room was eight feet high, allowing Vecnor to relax. It contained a desk and a chair, and little else. Upon the desk sat a stack of old parchments and an ancient candle—whoever used it last left two inches of unused wick. On one side was a quill next to a bottle of what had surely held ink, its contents now dry.

"A den?" asked Ameilistari.

"Dwarves call it a small room," Vecnor said. "A place where they keep records, make plans, and such. But I have never heard of a secret small room before."

He wandered to one side of the desk, and Ameilistari moved to the other. The surviving sheets of parchment appeared as fragile as the scroll Lorylla had found in the hearth earlier.

Vecnor looked at Ameilistari. "It's written in Dwarfish," he said. "None of those strange runes."

"I understand Dwarfish," she offered.

He nodded. "Just... be careful."

She sighed as she sat on the hard stone chair. She needed to be better than last time, when the scroll disintegrated under her care. Luckily, the parchments were stacked and not rolled, so handling them would be kept to a minimum.

Whispering her spell, she blew steam onto the paper, and the discoloring lessened. She then used her finger and thumb to remove the top sheet, of which very little was legible.

The second page was obviously a continuation of the one before it. Ameilistari understood most of the words, but a few were beyond her knowledge. Still, she followed what was written.

"It's a journal," she said. "It speaks of dragons." Her heart skipped a beat as she continued. "Lots of dragons. And there is mention of priests..." she shook her head. "I cannot make out the letters revealing their deity."

"Demoligius is my guess," said Vecnor.

"The evil God of Fire," Nidor added.

"Also known as the Dragon God," Vecnor pointed out. "They were His greatest creations, and He suffered greatly after the Dragon Wars."

"The dwarves worked with the priests," Ameilistari said. She had kept reading while the other two spoke, dividing her attention between the conversation and the journal. She removed the page to see the next one. "The priests desired to use the heat of Lornibur's forges. The king, Velgaad, told his people they were there to make the forges burn hotter, but that was a ruse." She reached the bottom of the parchment, and it crumbled as she lifted it, reminding her to keep a delicate touch.

The next page rambled on with nothing of interest until two-thirds of the way down. "It says Velgaad made a pact with High Priest Kradur, allowing the human and his following to make dragons that could be controlled and used as weapons. In return, Velgaad would be a king within the new empire the dragons created under… Demoligius." She couldn't read the name, but she recognized it as the same word as before. She slowly removed the page.

After scanning the top of the next sheet, she gasped. "Velgaad intended to betray Kradur!" She looked from Nidor to Vecnor and returned her attention to the parchment. "Velgaad had a suit of dragon armor forged, and planned to wear it when he slaughtered the priests and claimed the dragons for himself."

"That's madness!" said Nidor. "How did he expect to rule such wild creatures without the priests?"

"Velgaad was not known to be a sane individual," Vecnor commented.

"He would don his armor and 'enter the portal'," Ameilistari said as she continued reading.

"Portal?" Vecnor sighed. "Great…"

Ameilistari moved on to the next page. "Velgaad believed that if he entered the portal and killed the Dragon Master, he would assume rulership over the creatures. And he would use them to conquer all of Vaeldor."

"He truly was mad," said Vecnor, as if speaking to himself.

"Obviously, none of that came to pass," Nidor pointed out. "But before their plans fell apart, they must have created the dragon we faced."

"Though we have seen only the one," Vecnor said, "I doubt it was alone. Maak Maak must have been an earlier version of their experiments, and they made it a guardian while they continued with their work."

Ameilistari scanned the bottom of the page. "It says this is being written in case things go awry, so the true story might be known, and it's signed by Lord Ellibrus Brisomer." She faced Vecnor and Nidor. "Ellibrus Lords are like princes in Morimont. When a king retires or passes on, a new one is chosen from among them." Finally, her pointless studies paid off!

Vecnor grinned, apparently pleased with her knowledge. "Velgaad was an Ellibrus Lord before taking the throne," he said, "and Brisomer replaced him as Ellibrus of the same House. That is why the other Houses considered Brisomer's entire following to be tainted after Lornibur fell." He looked from Nidor to Ameilistari before adding, "As history tells it."

It wasn't a history lesson Ameilistari had learned. But she didn't doubt him.

"That means Brisomer was aware of Velgaad's schemes..." Vecnor said to no one.

"Yes." Ameilistari didn't know how else to respond. The dwarf had written the pages, so that conclusion was obvious.

"After the fall, he moved his House to the Serpent's Range, probably out of guilt," the large man added, still not seeming to speak to Ameilistari or Nidor. Did he converse with Selanna? He cleared his throat. "We should move on."

Ameilistari nodded. Nidor appeared confused.

They returned to the tunnel. It bore straight for a long stretch before ending, and from the wall to the left protruded a small lever. Vecnor pulled it down, and the wall at the end opened, allowing a blast of heat to wash over them.

"The forge is near," said Vecnor.

CHAPTER 35

No End in Sight

Baylun moved to Lorylla's side to see the room below. The bull demon occupied the middle, pointing its enormous axe at the balcony where he and the gray elf stood. Advancing in response were a dozen of the small humanoids with short tails.

Baylun's view of the imps was better than before. They ranged from one to two feet in height and possessed large almond eyes of pure black, and dark forked tongues lashed between their pale lips and tiny fangs. They bounded instead of running, and Baylun held no doubt they could leap all the way to the balcony once they drew near enough.

"Let's move," he said.

They headed toward the stairs, but an orange glow filled the stairwell, and they halted. Something approached from that direction as well.

"The other room!" Lorylla said, and she hurried to the door connecting to the chamber overlooking the prison.

Baylun followed, looking back. Three of the small humanoids had reached the balcony, and a demon slightly taller than himself climbed the final steps. The creature had a flaming skull with horns, and its eyes comprised glowing red dots. Tattered, soot-covered chain armor exposed areas of burned flesh and blackened bones, and twinkling orange particles constantly fell from its overheated body. Covering its left forearm was a battered wooden shield, and its gauntleted right hand wielded a sword appearing to have just been removed from the coals of an active forge. Baylun briefly wondered if Lorylla could make her blade burn that hot. A high-pitched shriek escaped the skull's mouth, putting his nerves on edge. The hopping creatures, meanwhile, drew nearer.

Baylun bolted through the open door and shut it behind him. Lorylla stood on the balcony overlooking the cell with her bow ready, though less than a dozen arrows remained in her quiver. From the prison came the clamor of battle.

The door didn't reopen right away—perhaps the smaller demons lacked the strength to move it. Baylun rushed to join the gray elf and peered down to see a score of dwarves within the visible section of the prison. Hadn't they left with the others? They must have, for these dwarves wielded rail spears and fought a dozen of the jumping demons, as well as four taller ones. The bigger fiends appeared as armored men with deep black skin, pointed ears longer than Lorylla's, and yellow fangs and horns. Three brandished swords while the fourth held a barbed whip; its other hand clutched a long, curved dagger. Baylun then noticed his brother.

Although grateful to see Romik alive, a chill ran down Baylun's spine to know the Lord of the Keep was so near to the bull demon. What was he doing down there? That wasn't part of the plan. Of course, Baylun and Lorylla weren't supposed to have returned to the observation rooms either.

He turned back to the door as it opened. Standing there was the skull demon, and the imps bounded in before it—were they giggling?

The two-tined spears didn't pose too much of a threat, so Baylun threw Torrac at the larger foe. The runes lit up as the axe spun toward its target, but the fiend lifted the shield, and somehow the tattered piece of wood deflected the attack. Torrac struck the wall, cutting into the stone before responding to Baylun's mental command to return; and as the weapon sped to his hand, a pair of smaller demons descended onto him, one on his shoulder and the other atop his head.

The skull demon absorbed an exploding arrow with its shield while Baylun attempted to shake the imps loose, but the little beasts clung like spiders. They found openings in his armor and penetrated his skin with their spears. As expected, the pain was bearable, but the injuries grew moist and started to burn. It was at that moment he remembered his father speaking about the tiny creatures. Gruelenor had faced them before, and mentioned that their acidic spittle paralyzed their victims.

"The small ones spit venom!" he warned Lorylla as the wounds became hot.

He slammed his back against the wall, dislodging the pests. The fiends bounded to the floor, and arrows pierced one and then the other, dispatching them in clouds of smoke. The pain in his left shoulder and neck didn't compare to the wolf venom plaguing his right arm, but now his left arm stiffened. He would soon lose the ability to wield his battleaxe.

The skull demon arrived, slashing with its sword and spinning with a shield bash. Baylun parried the blade but was struck by the tattered wood and knocked into the rear wall. He wouldn't have thought the shield could hit so hard. The monster pressed, thrusting the smoldering weapon, and Baylun moved aside—it pierced the wall by at least three inches, leaving a blackened hole.

There was no telling how long Baylun's functioning arm would be of any use, and he dared not allow the wicked sword to touch him. He gathered what strength he possessed and brought Torrac down. The runes lit up, seeming to aid his motion as the demon lifted the shield, and the bronze blade sliced through the wood, splitting it down the middle and cutting through the creature's forearm.

The skull shrieked, bathing Baylun in a hot blast of wind. Its screech was even more unnerving than before.

Normally, Baylun would follow the attack with the spiked handle, and it surprised him to find the weapon nearly weightless, allowing him to do so now. It was a reminder that Torrac had learned his combative style and worked to enhance it; something his brother had explained long ago when gifting the battleaxe to him on his eighteenth birthday. Ribs snapped as the bronze spike impaled the demon's chest, driving the fiend back and giving Baylun a chance to reset his feet.

His enemy showed no pain at the loss of its shield arm, and it didn't bleed from the injury, nor from the puncture to the chest. It lunged, thrusting its sword, and Baylun steered the weapon aside. The skull demon then attempted to sink its fangs into his neck. Baylun danced back. He countered, bringing the axe upward with surprising ease and adding a gash to the monster's torso. The armor split, as did the rotted flesh and bones beneath, and from the wound sprouted writhing black tentacles.

The flames surrounding the demon's head turned blue. It screeched again, this one lasting longer than the others, and its skull shook as its eyes grew white. Baylun held forth Torrac in defense as the creature exploded. Heat washed over his body, but Torrac pushed the blue fire around him, leaving him unscathed.

The demon vanished, and the smaller foes were gone. Lorylla was gone. But the sounds of battle continued.

Baylun rushed to the balcony and spied the gray elf. She had apparently leaped to avoid the blast of the demon's demise and now clung over the edge of the wall of stones—a jump she should have easily made. Baylun noticed lines of blood running down her thigh, where a tiny spear had surely struck. If an imp had spat onto the wound, she was likely working on one leg.

Within the prison were a dozen jumping demons, from what Baylun could see. Were they the original imps? Or reinforcements? It was hard to know for sure when they left no proof of their demise. The armored, black-skinned creatures were gone, and replacing them were four demons about Romik's height and one twice his size. Two had wings and hovered while tossing balls of fire. Of the others, one held a halberd, the taller one a hammer, and the last demon was frog-like and attacked with clawed hands.

Romik battled the frog. He appeared to have a wound on his side, but wielded his sword like a veteran while dweller dwarves fought with desperation. Nearly a score of Lornibur's denizens littered the floor, unmoving, and more rushed in from the area of the secret door.

The entryway from the forge exploded as the bull charged into the room, not bothering to duck beneath the arch.

Chapter 36

To Battle!

The mine dwellers led Greyor and his maiden companions farther along the wide corridor before opening a hidden door in the wall. At the lead dweller's insistence, Eraim extinguished her light—the creature pointed at the hovering bauble and mimicked throwing it to the floor and crushing it beneath his foot, to which Eraim said, "Certainly not!" Luckily, Greyor and his friends could see well enough in the dark. He just hoped no coldblooded creatures roamed the intended path.

They followed a narrow passage for over a hundred feet before opening another secret door and traversing a wide hallway to an intersection. After turning into a normal-sized tunnel, the dwellers slowed to search their surroundings, often pausing to listen. A couple of them walked several paces ahead, mimicking noises like water dripping, beetles chirping, and lizards hissing. The sounds held obvious meanings that Greyor could not comprehend.

At the next intersection, the lead humanoid studied each direction. All was deathly quiet. It made a shushing noise, followed by a couple of chirps and a rising whistle, and the mine dwellers became uneasy.

They headed right at a slower pace, depressing the sound of their movements. This mattered little with Greyor present, and he received several glares of frustration from both the dwellers and Eraim. The corridor then widened, and a pair of double doors lay ahead, one of them open and revealing a dull blue glow.

The lead humanoids moved to either side of the open door and peered inside. One then looked back and let out a low whistle while beckoning the others to approach. The mine dwellers quickened their gait, sliding their bare feet along the flagstones.

Beyond the doors was a large chamber that looked to have hosted a battle. Glow-shrooms grew at the edges — Morimont used the fungus in farming areas only — and dully illuminated stone tables and chairs appeared to have been shoved aside and out of the way. Blood splattered much of the furnishings and collected into pools on the floor, but the only corpses were those of mine dwellers. The far wall held another set of double doors.

Eraim moved among the bodies while the mine dwellers searched the area.

"There is blood on their weapons to suggest an enemy," the elf said. "Not all of it is red, and some is smoking."

"Dragon?" asked Greyor.

Eraim shook her head, her eyes filled with concern. "Demons."

The hope that demons didn't roam Lornibur quickly faded. What had Velgaad done?

A mine dweller made a couple of *yipping* sounds, grabbing everyone's attention. The humanoid studied the wall next to the entry doors. Greyor joined the others in moving closer to find strange writings. The author had dipped their finger in blood and used symbols similar to those etched on Clanghorr and Torrac. The mine dwellers gasped, almost in unison. Did they understand the runes?

The dweller that had spoken in the other room addressed the squadron in his strange language. When he raised his spear and the others did the same, they surely readied for battle. The dweller pointed his rail weapon at the far doors, and they charged, abandoning all thoughts of stealth. Greyor and the maidens followed.

They ran along three different corridors, all of them no less than fifteen feet wide and possessing supporting arches. The mine dwellers didn't hesitate in the slightest at intersections, and their expressions remained urgent. As they approached yet another junction of tunnels, Eraim gasped.

"I hear combat!" she said.

They turned into a wide passage with hammers for central pillars, each one holding an emerald, and screams, shouts, growls, and howls reached Greyor's ears. A roar followed, like an angry bull, silencing Lornibur for a moment. It was reminiscent of the battle cry of a minotaur, but ten times as loud. It came from straight ahead.

A hundred feet farther, archways opened to either side of the hallway, and from the first on the left emitted sounds of fighting. The humanoids slowed to peer into the chamber beyond.

It was an ancient room of worship, judging by the toppled statue, cracked granite altar made to resemble an anvil, and broken benches. Toward the back were scores of mine dwellers combating a dozen strange creatures. The monsters ranged in size from a couple of feet to twice Greyor's height. Some wore armor, some exhibited exoskeletons, and others appeared naked or had patches of fur. Arms varied from human-like to claws or pincers, and while most had two, a few possessed three, four, or six. Half of the fiends had tails, some short and pointed, others snake-like, and many held weapons such as swords, curved daggers, flails, spears, or spiked chains—some of them alight with fire. They were demons, and though outnumbered, they had the upper hand against the mine dwellers. The humanoids used their crude spears to the best of their abilities, somehow showing no fear in the face of their enemies.

The leader of the mine dweller group barked orders, and half of the platoon charged into the room to reinforce their kin. He then resumed racing along the tunnel until reaching an archway where more signs of battle were obvious. The chamber might have been a grand hall at one time with its vaulted ceiling, but there was nothing left of its furnishings to confirm this. Several creatures battled another fifty mine dwellers inside, and three of the demons flew on bat wings, using bows to launch wicked arrows into the melee. More of the squad Greyor traveled with advanced, leaving him and his friends with four dwellers, including the commander.

Farther along, flames moved about and a third battle became evident. Greyor and his depleted group continued, finding hundreds of mine dwellers fighting demons in the tunnel. The humanoids fought valiantly, showing more combative skills than those in the prior two rooms, and the hell-spawn vaporized whenever a killing blow was achieved. Still, dozens of dwellers lay bloodied on the floor. The leader beside Greyor screamed a war cry, and the four dwellers charged with their spears.

Beyond the melee came the sound of shattering stone. Shortly after, the roar of the angry minotaur echoed again, and Greyor saw mine dwellers rushing through a small door ahead, where the noise had surely come from.

"We must get to that door!" said Eraim.

Greyor agreed. Something big existed beyond the door, and Clanghorr would be needed. Not only that, but a feeling overcame him that Torrac lay in the same direction.

He entered the scrum with Eraim to his left and Kiryanna to his right, and a blob of orange and brown with large pupilless eyes quickly opposed him. It stood no higher than himself, and a tendril grew from its mass to swat at him. Greyor swung Clanghorr, severing the tendril, which transformed into a puddle of greenish-yellow fluid on the floor. He brought his weapon up and back down, slicing the creature in half. It disappeared in a cloud of smoke, leaving behind a larger collection of the grotesque blood.

On his right flank, Kiryanna joined a mine dweller against a squat demon with no head. Its sinewy arms and legs ended in talons, and a pair of big eyes were on its chest while its stomach opened to reveal deadly fangs. It raked the marteese with a claw, leaving a scratch on her forearm, and snatched the mine dweller and pulled the poor thing into its mouth, which bit the humanoid in half.

On Greyor's other flank, Eraim skewered a cat demon possessing blood-stained white fur and red eyes. The monster disappeared in a puff of smoke. She quickly sheathed her sword and grabbed her bow, releasing a pair of arrows at a flying demon wielding a handful of fire. The long-shafted missiles penetrated its head and chest, and it vanished.

Greyor dodged left and right as he hastened toward the far door. Mine dwellers fought in groups around him, stabbing demons several times to achieve their victories, but losing two to five of their own in the process. Eraim remained with Greyor, now swinging Mithkahr, and Kiryanna hastened to catch up.

Another demon barred Greyor's path, a monstrosity appearing as a bipedal jackal with tentacle arms. He brought down Clanghorr as one of its appendages wrapped around his waist, severing the limb, but a new tentacle quickly grew in its place. The other arm lashed out, and he cut it loose, only to see it replaced as well. The creature then spat a yellowish liquid onto Greyor's breastplate; the filth smoked as it began eating through the metal.

Greyor had no time to deal with the hellish phlegm, and he pressed. Both tentacles reached for him, and he cleaved one while the other wrapped around his neck. Eraim was then behind the fiend. She thrust Mithkahr into the demon's back, and the point protruded from its stomach. The monster dissolved into smoke. A second later, Kiryanna emptied the water from her flask onto Greyor's armor, dousing the spittle.

Nothing now barred their way, and they ran through the open door. Beyond was a long chamber filled with mine dwellers and more demons—how were there so many? At the far end, before a mangled set of bars and a destroyed archway, stood the tallest of the demons. It was like a demented minotaur, except the bulging muscles of its torso and arms were hairless. The behemoth held an enormous axe in its right hand, while the left arm ended in a pincer.

Between the minotaur and Greyor hopped little demons with almond eyes and short tails, wreaking more havoc than he would have thought possible. Several mine dwellers lay on the floor, seemingly unable to move as they cried out while the creatures poked them with two-tined spears and spat a black substance onto the wounds. Some imps jumped as high as ten feet to land on the shoulders of standing dwellers, where they clung like bugs with their tiny feet.

Protect…

The whisper came from Clanghorr. The battleaxe wished for Greyor to help the mine dwellers. A confusing request, but he wasn't about to question the weapon with which he had recently bonded.

He charged into the smaller demons, and a couple attempted to jump on him. Spinning Clanghorr overhead, he easily sliced the little monsters and turned them into tiny clouds of dissipating mist. He then kicked one from the unmoving body of a mine dweller, intercepted another with Clanghorr's spike as it lunged at him, and crushed a third beneath his boot.

Six imps focused on Greyor, lowering their spears and spreading out in a semicircle. He readied his axe, waiting for the attack. Three of them jumped high while one leaped straight at him, and the final two bounded toward his flanks — savvy little monsters!

The imp in front of him arrived first, and he met it with his spike.

Poof!

He twirled Clanghorr overhead, ending two of the descending demons on the spinning blades while the third landed on his helmet. As well, the flanking pests leaped, and Greyor cut one in half. He spun back, but the other fiend never reached him — it vanished in a puff of smoke. He spied an arrow flying toward him, and before he could react, it pierced the imp clinging to his helmet.

Poof!

Atop the wall, a barrier created by the stacking of massive granite blocks, was Lorylla. She gave Greyor a nod, and his spirits soared. He then noticed Romik fighting in support of the mine dwellers. The Lord of the Keep had taken several wounds, but didn't slow.

The minotaur demon moved farther into the room, and Greyor refocused. The lesser demons scattered from its path, and the mine dwellers coward at the sight of it. Greyor roared as he charged, gaining the demon's attention, and it brought down its giant axe. The blade drove into the stone floor, cutting several inches deep as he rolled to the side. Greyor recovered and spied the minotaur's pincer coming his way, but the appendage stopped short when a spinning circle of bronze struck it.

It was Torrac!

Torrac sliced the demon's forearm, leaving a large gash. Then, to Greyor's amazement, the weapon curved back and flew high into the chamber. He followed its trajectory and spotted Baylun on a balcony beyond the granite wall where Lorylla perched. The krukari had not been visible when Greyor fought closer to the stone blocks, but he saw the warrior plainly now. How had Baylun made Torrac return?

The minotaur snorted flames through its nostrils. From its pincer arm flowed smoking orange blood, and it turned angry eyes on Baylun.

Chapter 37

Rendezvous

Ameilistari followed Vecnor with Nidor close behind. They continued along the corridor, passing a couple of rooms where she spied pools of magma. Her giant leader appeared unconcerned with the chambers, sparing them only glances. It almost seemed he knew his way about Lornibur, except he paused at each of the three intersections they encountered before picking a direction, and after one of his choices led to a dead-end room, they doubled back to make a different selection. She thought of asking him if he needed any assistance, but what help could she offer? One person guessing was enough; adding her speculations would only make decisions take longer. No, she would keep silent and follow. Vecnor had accomplished magnificent feats throughout his lifetime, and she would trust in his experience.

As they reached the end of the present passage, a broad corridor crossed their path. It was similar to other thirty-foot-wide hallways with supporting pillars in the shape of hammers, but there was something grander about it. The hammerheads to the right each held an emerald, while those to the left bore citrines, and veins of silver and gold raced across the ceiling and descended like forks of lightning through the columns. Where the walls met the floor and ceiling, beveled edges exhibited patterns of multi-colored quartz that reflected Ameilistari's light, generating a pleasant show along the tunnel.

Vecnor froze when a strange noise echoed: a distant roar rising in pitch and lasting a couple of seconds. A dragon? Ameilistari tried to read Vecnor's expression. He showed no emotion and headed right, providing her with no information.

A light appeared in the distance. As Ameilistari and her companions drew nearer, the corridor widened to fifty feet and terminated at a pair of tall brass doors, each with a large pull ring. Etchings of giant anvils with hammers decorated their centers, and several indentations formed circles around the engravings, where small objects may have once existed—gems? On either side of the magnificent entryway hung lamps emitting blue flames that illuminated the area. Strangely, they shed normal light. Vecnor didn't seem to notice them as he reached for a pull ring.

The large man easily opened the door. Ameilistari had expected to see veins bulging from his neck for the effort, but it was not so. Beyond stood a wide hall, and additional lamps with blue flames illuminated most of the room. The ceiling rose forty feet, and scattered to the right were workbenches crafted of granite and rising no higher than two feet—the perfect height for dwarves. Destroyed barrels, boxes, and racks that might have once held weapons or armor lay near the furnishings. On the left, broken and crumbled workbenches splayed away from a fifteen-foot-diameter tunnel that bore into the wall. Shattered lamps accompanied the debris, leaving puddles that emitted blue flames upon the flagstones. The tunnel was definitely an addition to Lornibur after the dwarves forsook their home. It was larger than the Maak Maak tunnels, and Ameilistari didn't wish to know what had created it.

Vecnor strode across the room to a large archway topped by an anvil and two hammers in bas-relief. An orange light glowed beyond, and as Ameilistari neared the midpoint of the chamber, she detected the sounds of battle. Her fearless leader must have heard the noises as well, for he picked up his pace to a jog. Thus far he had led the way with only one of his swords in hand, and as he drew the second blade, his jog became a run.

Heat blasted Ameilistari as they entered a large hall. They stood at one end of an oval-shaped room, and other than a high balcony to the right, a toppled wall was the only visible exit on the opposite side, appearing to have been destroyed by something massive. A stream of lava mirrored most of the left edge, entering through a hole and following a channel until exiting before the demolished wall, and spaced along the trench were several dwarf-sized forges. The apparatuses appeared forgotten and unused, except for the largest unit in the middle. Its coals were alight and throbbed to an unheard rhythm.

From the far opening came the sound of combat, swirling about the domed ceiling — roars, screams, and battle cries. Strange giggling sometimes accompanied the noises, like children at play. A colossal roar then brought all commotion to a momentary halt; the same call Ameilistari had heard not long ago. It was bovine-like, as if a giant bull cried out in both anger and pain, and sent chills down her spine. For a moment, she ceased breathing while staring at the broken wall, and she suddenly noticed stout, hairy legs with enormous hooves. It resembled the lower body of a gigantic goat, but the comparison ended at the waistline, where a human-like torso began, crimson in color and grossly muscled. She saw no more when the creature moved away and the clamor resumed.

"What's happening?" asked Nidor. His unsettled expression proved he had seen the monster.

"A battle for Lornibur," said Vecnor. He stood, watching the far exit as if awaiting something. "The mine dwellers fight for their freedom against minions of Hell."

Ameilistari thought it strange that they moved no farther. The Vecnor she had learned about never shied away from combat. He had fought Uustaag in the War of the North! Still, she had no desire to enter the melee in the other room. What could she and Nidor possibly do against the monster she glimpsed?

Nidor gulped. Perhaps he agreed. But then his next words took Ameilistari by surprise.

"I'm ready when you are."

Her heart skipped a beat.

Vecnor gave a firm nod, as a leader acknowledging his

subordinate. "We remain here," he said, allowing her to breathe again.

"But…" Nidor's eyes moved from Vecnor to the broken archway and back.

Her cousin was either brave or crazy. Maybe both. Dragons were bad enough; she didn't wish to know what the dwellers fought in the other room.

"Wait for what?" Nidor finished his thought.

Vecnor turned toward the far end. "Eraim."

A moment later, the small elf dashed through the opening with Mithkahr in hand.

CHAPTER 38

DESPERATION

Baylun could see only the torso and head of the bull demon as it entered deeper into the cell. Lorylla, meanwhile, kneeled atop the barrier of stones and trained her bow on the battle below. Romik had moved closer to the wall and out of Baylun's sight. Hopefully, the gray elf kept his brother safe.

Baylun pulled out his map for a quick look. Running along the corridors to reach the melee was going to take a couple of minutes—if only he had Lorylla's jumping ability. And although the burning of his wounds had somehow eased, his shoulders ached. He prayed Torrac continued assisting him. As he turned to leave, he balked. Greyor had arrived, followed by Eraim! Baylun held his breath, watching for Kiryanna and Nidor. No one else entered that he saw.

Lorylla sent a couple of arrows into the scrum, depleting her quiver's stock. She slung her bow over her shoulder and pulled her sword. Meanwhile, the bull moved forward, and Greyor ran to meet it. As the demon swung the enormous axe, Greyor dodged, leaving the weapon to penetrate the flagstones.

Baylun lifted Torrac, and as the giant fiend reached for the dwarf with its claw, he threw his battleaxe. The runes glowed brightly as the blades spun, and it sliced into the creature's arm. But the limb was thick, and Baylun failed to sever it. The monster roared while Torrac returned.

The demon's eyes turned on Baylun. It lifted its injured arm toward him, and as the claw opened, an invisible force jerked him from the ledge. There was no stopping the evil magic, and he couldn't alter his path; the jagged edges of the pincer became clearer as he neared.

Something struck Baylun, knocking him free of the energy pulling him. It was Lorylla. The gray elf had leaped from the wall and kicked him free of the wicked spell. Unfortunately, she now sped toward the deadly claw.

As Baylun hurtled to the floor, he spied a glowing circle—Clanghorr was flying. The axe sliced the demon's arm, completing the wound Torrac had begun, and the claw fell to the flagstones. Lorylla crashed down, her injuries disallowing her usual graceful landing.

The room was fully in view. At a glance, Baylun saw over a hundred corpses of Lornibur dwarves. Still, those fighting outnumbered the demons, and Romik fought beside them.

Lorylla rose to her feet with blood trickling from her nose and mouth and her left arm held close, her eyes focused on the larger enemy. Greyor stood beyond the bull, but Clanghorr was not with the dwarf. Baylun spotted the battleaxe across the cell. Apparently, Greyor hadn't learned how to make it return. And now the monster charged, intent on trampling the dwarf.

Baylun again cast Torrac, and the spinning blades struck the demon's back. Though a deep cut, it wasn't lethal, but it allowed Greyor to evade the thunderous hooves, and the beast crashed into the wall with its massive horns. Large holes then marred the smooth stone, and cracks traveled from floor to ceiling.

The demon spun, its red eyes tracking Baylun as he caught the handle of Torrac. Greyor rushed to reclaim Clanghorr, and Lorylla limped to Baylun's side, appearing more haggard than after the War of the North concluded. But her expression remained determined. She raised her sword, its blade covered in ice and radiating cold.

"I'll get its attention," she said through clenched teeth. "You bring this thing down!"

Before Baylun voiced an objection, she moved away with surprising speed. But what could she do in her condition? If only he hadn't allowed the demons to infect his arms with their poisons. Then he could mount a proper fight against this creature!

He took a defensive pose, lifting Torrac with some difficulty while the bull lumbered forward, twirling its weapon left and right like a seasoned warrior. The axe was twice the size of Baylun's, and he was in no shape to even attempt knocking it aside. If he threw Torrac and it wasn't a killing blow, its return might not be in time to aid him.

Clanghorr flew again, and the beast halted to deflect the weapon with its axe.

Baylun turned to Greyor. "Will it to come back!" he called. Seeing the dwarf didn't comprehend, he added, "Call Clanghorr with your mind!"

There was sudden understanding in Greyor's expression, and he reached out his hand. His eyes then widened as the spinning axe returned—Baylun remembered fearing he might lose his fingers the first time. But Clanghorr landed firmly in Greyor's grasp, and a grin captured the dwarf's face.

The bull advanced again, faster than before and holding its axe as if to drive Baylun back. Lorylla was then beside it, having jumped from twenty feet away, and she impaled its abdomen with her frosty blade. The demon halted, slamming its hoof and sending her sprawling.

Kiryanna was then behind the bull, and her golden sword struck its thigh twice. Baylun's heart leaped into his throat as fear grabbed hold, and he was powerless when the beast kicked backwards, striking her breastplate and knocking her several feet through the air. He threw Torrac with what strength he possessed, but the demon deflected the weapon as it had done to Clanghorr.

"We must attack from opposite sides!" shouted Greyor. "It can't stop both of us!"

The dwarf was right, and Baylun withdrew deeper into the room while Greyor ran toward the mangled prison door.

Neither Kiryanna nor Lorylla moved, and Baylun's fear grew. He stared at Kiryanna, willing her to get up; to make a hand gesture;

anything.

"Baylun! Watch out!" called Romik.

Baylun's thoughts had distracted him, allowing the demon to swing the giant axe uncontested. But Romik pushed him to safety, and he watched from a prone position as the weapon continued on its path—it was like being back in Lormin Dmurr, fighting against Uustaag. The axe struck the wooden arm raised in defense, and Romik crashed to the floor.

Dread set in. It all started with that blasted letter sent by Greyor. And now Baylun had doomed everyone he traveled with to early graves. He should never have helped the dwarves.

But Romik wasn't dead. His face was scraped and smeared with blood, but he scrambled away as quickly as he could with one arm—his false arm lay in splinters.

The bull roared, spinning in the other direction, and Baylun saw Clanghorr circle toward its master. Upon the monster's back gushed smoking orange fluid from a gash deeper than Torrac had inflicted.

Baylun knew not whether Kiryanna or Lorylla lived. He knew not whether Tewlon had kept Nidor and Ameilistari safe. And regardless of his decisions, this was the situation he found himself in. The demon needed to be stopped.

To Baylun's rear, the dweller dwarves occupied the other fiends, who seemed happy to remain clear of the area where the bull fought. At least he needn't worry about being attacked from behind. He turned back to the giant beast, and though his shoulders argued, he forced them to raise up Torrac.

Chapter 39
The Architect

Ameilistari received only a glance from Eraim as the elf hurried across the oval room to join her and her companions.

"There you are," Eraim said to Vecnor, not a hint of humor in her tone. Nor was there anger. It was relief mixed with urgency.

"I arrived before you," the large man commented.

"I pray we have enough time." Eraim looked at Ameilistari and Nidor as she bit her lower lip.

What were they talking about?

A roar emitted from the far room.

"We must be quick about it." Vecnor glanced over his shoulder at Ameilistari.

"What about these two?" posed Eraim.

Vecnor shook his head.

"You ask her," Eraim said. "I will get to work."

Ameilistari faced Vecnor. Ask her what?

But he didn't speak to Ameilistari. He closed his eyes and remained still. When he opened them again, he stared blankly at the floor, as if listening. But if it wasn't *her* Eraim had meant for Vecnor to ask his questions, then who? Selanna! It must be.

Eraim, meanwhile, stood next to the middle forge; the only one showing use. She turned away from the furnace and took ten careful steps alongside the lava-filled trench before facing the wall.

"Now what?" she asked no one, her voice barely audible above the clamor in the other room.

Ameilistari moved closer as Eraim squatted. The small hero

fiddled with the flagstones and seemed surprised when one of them slid over the magma to create a narrow bridge. She hopped to the other side, apparently unwilling to test the inch-thick stone, and bent down to inspect the wall with her fingers splayed. Two feet above the floor, her right hand stopped, and all but her index finger retreated to her palm. She kept the finger in place while fishing something from her pouch. It was the key Greyor had found; the one hidden in the bedroom… how long ago was that? Ameilistari had no concept of time anymore.

Eraim put the key into the wall next to her finger and turned it three times. Upon completion, she fiddled with the area next to the key, attempting to slide the wall up, down, and sideways. Nothing happened. Sweat drenched her hair and spotted her face as she pushed, and a panel pivoted open slightly, five feet tall and three feet wide. The elf had no choice but to step onto the bridge to open it further. The platform held.

Within a closet beyond the door was a suit of red armor accented with black outlines. It was artfully crafted, with dark scales running along the sides and horizontal rows of brighter scales down the front. The scales continued from the pauldrons to form vambraces and ended in claw-shaped gauntlets. The helmet was even more exquisite. Constructed for a wide head, horns protruded from the top, and an elongated snout with an open mouth and fangs provided a window through which the wearer might see. It was the dragon armor Velgaad had intended to wear when he slew the Dragon Master.

Eraim seemed unconcerned with the fancy armor and hastily searched around it. She then pulled an item from behind the left sabaton and rushed from the bridge to Vecnor. A second after she stepped off the bridge, the flagstone retracted to its original place.

"Here it is," Eraim said.

The elf held a brooch. It appeared to be silver, but Ameilistari realized it to be made of platinum, and it possessed three diamonds. Marring the otherwise perfect piece of jewelry were small runes etched in black. But they weren't the dwarfish runes she expected.

They were arcane. Eraim clutched a magical key.

"We must enter now," Vecnor said to Eraim. He turned to Ameilistari. "And she's coming with us."

Ameilistari grew nervous.

"To Hell?" Eraim's expression revealed shock. "But—"

"She must," insisted Vecnor. "You've never been there. We'll not survive the heat." He looked at Ameilistari. "She can protect us."

Vecnor took the brooch from Eraim and handed it to Nidor.

"Hold this," the large warrior said, "and make sure no harm comes to it. When we return," he pointed at the central forge, where the glow continued to intensify and relax like a slow-beating heart, "cast it into the coals at once."

"Hell?" Ameilistari repeated, her voice struggling to be heard.

Another roar echoed, and the floor shuddered as a crash resounded.

"I am sorry," Eraim said to Ameilistari. "There is no time to explain."

"You will use your powers to keep us from burning up," Vecnor instructed. "Now, focus and cool the air around us."

"Please," added Eraim.

Ameilistari took a deep breath. This was a lot to take in. But the expressions on her companion's faces told her she must act now.

Keep your mind, she thought to herself to steady her nerves. Eraim and Vecnor surely carried out Selanna's wishes, and she needed to do the same. With another deep breath, she pulled magical forces to her, swirling cool air around her and freezing all moisture. Suddenly, it was as if a winter wind had embraced her, yet the room remained calm. She expanded the energy until it encompassed Vecnor and Eraim.

Eraim rubbed her hands along her arms, and her breath became visible. Vecnor nodded in approval and reached out his hand.

Ameilistari grabbed hold, and he pulled her close with strength greater than she imagined, yet he was as gentle as her father hugging her goodnight. A feeling that nothing could bring her harm enveloped her, even with the surrounding evil; even with the knowledge of where Vecnor intended to take her. He wrapped Eraim in his other arm and turned to the furnace. Lifting them both, he jumped.

A gasp nearly escaped Ameilistari as they descended onto the pile of embers. But she maintained her concentration. As Vecnor touched down, his boots did not displace the coals. They passed through as if the forge were an illusion. Ameilistari held her breath, as if she were plunging into a lake.

But it wasn't a lake.

They entered a chamber, moving parallel to the stone floor as if Vecnor had jumped sideways instead of downward. He crashed onto his back, curling Ameilistari closer to his chest to spare her from too much jarring. At first, she thought his attempt was in vain, for the cool air faded, but she realized the energy still swarmed around them. How hot was the room? Vecnor rose quickly and set down Ameilistari and Eraim before pulling his swords. Eraim unsheathed her fancy sword as well.

The coals were a gate, and Ameilistari stood at one end of a strange room. Behind her was a circle of stones set into a wall of dark red bricks and highlighted by illegible runes. The writings held a blue glow, and a shimmering of the same hue filled the circle. At the far end, an archway of black bricks awaited. Three-foot-high windows occupied the middle of the tall walls to either side, stretching the length of the chamber, but they contained no glass and no bars; just an open space exhibiting a world on fire. As Ameilistari gazed upon the dancing flames, she spied faces emitting soundless screams, and the longer she stared, the warmer the room became. It was as if the faces drew closer.

"Ameilistari!" said Eraim. "Concentrate!"

Ameilistari realized the aura of cold had shrunk. She pushed outward with her mind, struggling as the environment resisted her. But she won the battle, and the heat retreated.

"This is Hell?" she whispered, afraid to speak too loudly.

Vecnor nodded, his eyes fixed on the archway.

"Why?" she asked. "What are we here for?"

Eraim faced Ameilistari. "You have spoken with Selanna, so I will get to the point."

Vecnor moved forward, and Eraim urged Ameilistari to match his pace while she continued.

"We knew only that the source of Vaeldor burning originated from Lornibur. We learned recently that it is the development of dragons from cavern lizards that will give rise to the event."

A hiss interrupted, and everyone halted. It came from nowhere. The sound ended after a few seconds, and they resumed their forward trek.

"It is absurd to think Velgaad capable of such work," Eraim said. "It had to be a powerful wizard or the assistance of an evil entity. Once we discovered the symbol of Demoligius, it was obvious. Now, to gain the aid of their vile deity, the priests had to have opened a gate, and when dealing with Demoligius, that gate could only lead to one place." She looked at Ameilistari. "Hell."

"Selanna taught me about gates," Ameilistari said, still whispering even though Eraim spoke only in a hushed voice. "And you obviously found the key. Why not close the gate in the forge?"

"It would have been fortunate if we could have just sealed the door and banished the demons back to their world."

Eraim didn't finish the thought, for they had reached the archway. Vecnor paused to gaze through the opening while Eraim peered around the warrior's right side. Ameilistari maneuvered to see around the left. The room was circular, at least a hundred feet in diameter, and four pits, two to the front and two to the rear, held raging bonfires. Three archways were to either side, their passages leading downward, and each radiated a throbbing red light.

In the center of the chamber, a circular dais filled most of the room, its entire perimeter providing three steps for access. To the left and right atop the platform, the upper bodies of two red dragons jutted from the floor, as if emerging from below, and their necks extended high above to where their jaws interlocked, as if biting one another. They appeared real, but didn't move. Beneath the dragons, a pair of podiums held open tomes, the pedestals shaped as scaled necks leading to dragon heads with wide-open mouths to support the books. Between them sat an altar of red stone, seeming to hover above fire, and upon the slab lay the shriveled body of a mine dweller.

A man dressed in black robes with red trim stood above the corpse, holding the talon of a large bird clutching what appeared to be a black heart. The heart throbbed, and with each beat the man's eyes glowed red while his wrinkled skin tightened and his hair changed from gray to brown. Had he sucked the life-force from the victim on the altar?

Behind the robed man, in the shadows of one of the rising dragons, was a female figure. A pair of short horns extended from her forehead while bat wings twitched behind her, as if deciding whether to take flight. She was scantily clad, and an evil grin crossed her face. Beyond the woman and to the side, an archway sculpted as an enormous dragon head with a wide-open mouth emitted a shimmering blue light.

"Just as Selanna thought," Eraim whispered. "Another gate."

The body on the altar turned to dust, and the black heart ceased beating. The eyes of the man holding the wicked item stopped throbbing, and he focused on the entryway.

"You should not have come here," he said, his voice catching Ameilistari by surprise—it was completely normal, even with his heavy accent. "I am amazed you made it this far. But your luck has run out."

Vecnor moved forward, allowing Ameilistari and Eraim to enter. "Your experiments end now!" His words reverberated about the chamber.

"You know nothing!" the priest hissed, baring his teeth as if he had fangs.

The female stepped from the shadows, offering Vecnor a seductive smirk to match her sensual stride. Her eyes were as black as her hair, her cheeks rosy, and her lips dark red. Although her smile failed to conceal a set of fangs, they did not detract from her beauty. She wore a slip, leaving little to the imagination; the material was nearly transparent.

"My, aren't you a tall one," she said to Vecnor, her voice deep, though not so deep as Lorylla's. "You are a perrrrfect specimen of a man." Her words oozed like honey.

Vecnor took a step forward. "Your flattery is wasted on me, witch!"

The demon stuck out her lower lip, like a disappointed child. "And I was soooo hoping to get to know you better." She sighed, her chest rising and falling. "Tis a shame." She stepped to the priest's flank and playfully ran her long black fingernails through his short hair and down his neck to his shoulder. "Kradur, my love. They think they can make a difference."

Kradur! The priest mentioned in the journal. But he lived centuries ago. How many souls had he stolen?

"The fools are too late," Kradur said, and with the last word his eyes glowed red. "And now they shall pay for their intrusion!"

He raised the talon, and the dark heart began beating. The demoness spread her wings and took to the air, a wicked smile transforming her countenance from alluring to vicious. To make matters worse, howling and chattering came from the downward-slanting tunnels—more creatures approached.

"Keep us protected!" Eraim said to Ameilistari with urgency.

The elf took a couple of hasty steps toward Vecnor and jumped. Vecnor seemed to anticipate the maneuver, and lowered his right arm, giving her a place to land. He then flung her upward, and she propelled herself at the demon.

Ameilistari's mind raced—she couldn't expand her aura to encompass the entire room. But there was no time to think, and she reacted, curling her fingers as if holding a ball and thrusting it at Eraim. Just as she had hoped, a piece of the sphere separated, and the elf smoked only briefly before it enveloped her. As Vecnor advanced, Ameilistari used her other hand to surround him, creating a third bubble. It wasn't a feat she would have believed herself capable of, and it amazed her she maintained all three at once.

Above, the demon flew at Eraim with fangs bared and claws out—her fingernails were more bestial now. Eraim swung Mithkahr as they came together, cutting the monster's arm, while the demon raked Eraim's neck. The fiend shrieked, having obviously received the worst of the injuries, and dark blood gushed from the wound. The demoness then climbed higher while the elf plummeted. Eraim landed with the skill of centuries, rolling to her feet, and winced as she placed a hand over three long scratches below her ear.

Ahead of Ameilistari, Vecnor ascended the steps of the altar. Kradur opened his mouth, his jaw dropping much farther than what should have been possible to reveal wicked fangs, and from it spewed fire.

Ameilistari knew Vecnor's armor provided some protection, but she remembered how the liquid fire had affected him. She couldn't risk it happening again. She pulled additional energy through her body to empower his sphere, and the flames washed around him as he strode over the next two steps to arrive at the stone table.

Vecnor continued his momentum, planting a hand atop the altar and leaping over the fixture. As he did so, the priest ceased the attack and jumped straight up. Shadows gathered behind Kradur to form dark wings, but Vecnor's reach was long, and he caught his enemy by the ankle before the man could escape. He hurled the cleric down and through the podium on the left. The tome crashed to the floor.

Ameilistari checked on Eraim. The elf held an arrow to her bow, unblinking while tracking the flying monster. Less than a dozen arrows remained in the elf's quiver—she needed to make each one count. The creature circled the platform, seeking an opening, and Eraim released the bowstring. The arrow traveled swiftly, but the demoness evaded the projectile.

Ameilistari stared in disbelief. Eraim never missed!

The elf put another arrow to the string, and as she let the fletching go, she quickly pulled back a second arrow and did the same, sending it in a slightly different direction. The demon dodged the first, but couldn't avoid the second. Instead, it caught the missile with a clawed hand and snapped the shaft in two.

Ameilistari searched her mind for a way to help; Eraim had to win the battle before reinforcements arrived from the side tunnels. But there was no way to maintain cooling auras for all of them if Ameilistari shifted to attack spells. The air warmed as the stress of the situation nearly overwhelmed her, and she forced her concentration back to the spheres—Eraim glanced her way, as if having detected the rising heat as well.

The demoness plunged at Eraim. The small elf made a valiant effort to evade the creature's claws, but as the fiend passed over, its tail lashed out, and a barb at the tip sliced the leather across Eraim's back. The elf grimaced and released four arrows in swift succession. Again, the demoness evaded the first missile; the next two were snagged within clawed hands. The woman appeared to have dodged the fourth as well, but as it passed over the demon's shoulder, it pierced the bone of the bat wing, and the appendage folded. The monster crashed into the nearby wall before plummeting to the floor.

Back on the platform, Kradur's eyes still glowed while blood issued from his scalp and cheek—Ameilistari wondered if he was beyond pain. And now, a ring of fire surrounded him. The priest raised the talon clutching the beating heart, and above him, the dragon heads released their clasping bites to gaze at the melee below. At once, they spat flames onto the dais.

Ameilistari transferred part of the cold from her sphere to Vecnor's. The air about her became uncomfortably hot, but around Vecnor, ice crystals hung motionless—the warrior nearly turned blue. The attack washed over him, making him a silhouette in a shower of fire.

Sweat ran down Ameilistari's forehead, stinging her eyes, but she remained focused even as she shifted more of her protective barrier and her skin burned. The pain grew intense, and she wanted to scream out—it was worse than any she had ever endured. The spouts of flame then ended at last. Vecnor seemed unscathed, as did Kradur, and Ameilistari returned the strength to her sphere. Though the burning eased, the agony remained, and a few blisters dotted her arms.

To her right, Eraim squared off with the demoness. And from the six tunnels, creatures wreathed in fire emerged, one from each. The newcomers had subtle differences in appearance, but all were hideous, like deformed cats standing seven feet tall on their hind legs. Their fangs were long and their claws bear-like, and their reptilian tails ended with bony spikes.

"Kill the child!" commanded the demoness, pointing at Ameilistari as Eraim plunged Mithkahr into her abdomen. The fiend smiled as the sword's hilt struck her stomach—smiled? She vanished in a flash of black smoke and was gone.

Ameilistari had learned that demons could be killed in their own world. Why, then, had the demoness vanished?

It was a pondering that would have to wait, for the reinforcements turned their yellow cat-like eyes on Ameilistari. She knew not whether the chilled sphere would protect her from their fiery shrouds, but that mattered little if their claws ripped her to shreds. Defending herself, however, required abandoning her companions' protection.

On the platform, the dragon heads descended with gnashing fangs, and Vecnor used his swords to knock one aside while sidestepping the other. The priest watched, still holding the beating heart high.

There was no choice. Ameilistari had to help before the cat demons finished her. Selanna had faith in her, and she couldn't fail the mage, nor her companions. She focused on the aura surrounding her, shrinking the sphere until it became a ball of ice the size of her fist. The hot air moved in, and she was sure her hair ignited. Swallowing the pain, she thrust the orb forward. She wasn't positive she could accomplish such a spell, but she let the magic flow through her, acting as a conduit, and imagined the ball as a spike. It worked, and the dark heart exploded in a burst of black fluid as the spike pierced it. The dragons froze, returning to an inanimate state, and in their new positions they collapsed. Debris rained around the priest, shattering like stone, and a large piece knocked Vecnor to the platform.

Ameilistari dropped to her knees as she renewed her sphere. She was amazed she still maintained all three protections.

The priest hissed at the loss of his item and tossed the empty, blood-stained talon aside. He then chanted strange words, and a ball of red light appeared over his raised palm. He made a move, as if to cast it at Vecnor while the large warrior rose from the debris.

Vecnor was swift, however, and he thrust one of his giant swords from several feet away, skewering the priest's chest. The sphere winked out as the glow of Kradur's eyes faded.

But the priest didn't fall. He chuckled as blood seeped from his mouth. "You're too late."

Vecnor's second blade came around, severing Kradur's head. The man's knees buckled as the body collapsed.

The cat demons arrived, but there were only five. To Ameilistari's right, Eraim rushed through the smoke of the missing demon's demise—likely upon the edge of Mithkahr. Vecnor scrambled over the altar, but he would never reach Ameilistari in time.

A light appeared to her left; a green glow hovering just above the floor. It was another portal, and through it sprung a warrior dressed in a chain shirt and wielding a sword. He seemed familiar, but Ameilistari couldn't place him, especially with the chaos surrounding her. But he was definitely not a demon. He came down on the back of a cat, driving his sword into the fiend's skull, and followed with a long dagger in his other hand. The man grimaced as the thin blade pierced the demon's torso, his hand surely burned by the fire enveloping the creature, and the cat vanished in a puff of black smoke.

The remaining demons hissed as they descended on Ameilistari with their claws. She had no choice and withdrew the spheres from

Vecnor and Eraim, pulling them to her—the protections would abandon her companions anyway if she were struck down. Time then slowed as she shot her hands outward, forming ice shards with her mind. Not wishing to injure her friends, she envisioned the attack following invisible channels toward the enemy only, and was relieved to see the spell work. The cats released hissing screeches, and the fires surrounding them extinguished. Their hides were then as charred fur.

Eraim destroyed one abomination, and Vecnor arrived, cutting down two others. The stranger finished off the final demon.

Ameilistari teetered on the edge of exhaustion. Magical energy had been rushing through her nonstop since they entered the strange world, and she didn't think she could handle anymore. But as Vecnor's armor smoked and his skin turned another shade of pink, as did Eraim's, there was no other choice.

She pooled nearby strands of magic, forming them into another protective sphere. It wasn't as cold as before, but it was the best Ameilistari could conjure—hopefully, it sufficed. The air warmed further when she stretched the area to include the stranger—he had protected her, and she couldn't leave him to suffer the burning environment.

"Ballrik?" Vecnor asked, his expression one of confusion.

"It *is* you!" Eraim declared.

Ameilistari knew that name, but she wasn't thinking straight. Her mind wished to shut down, and it was all she could do to stay awake.

"There's no time," Ballrik said with urgency. "We must close the gates."

Eraim put an arm around Ameilistari, helping her to remain standing. "Lean on me. Let my strength be your strength."

Ameilistari leaned on the elf, who stood a bit shorter than herself, and her legs stabilized slightly. Eraim led her to the platform, following Vecnor and Ballrik while the two scoured the dais.

Ballrik... That was Ameilistari's grandfather's name. But her grandfather was dead. It must be a man sharing the name, like her cousin was named after the late paladin.

Vecnor rose from the priest's corpse, holding an item Ameilistari couldn't focus on. He tossed it through the dragon sculpture's mouth, and the blue glow vanished.

"Now let us make haste!" said Eraim, turning back.

The newest gate, the one Ballrik had used, was gone. Had it ever truly been there?

"I've got her," said Ballrik.

He swept Ameilistari off her feet, and Vecnor and Eraim ran ahead, leading the way through the arch and across the long chamber with the blue glow at the far end. Ameilistari looked up. Her arm was around Ballrik's neck. He glanced at her, and in that moment a smile was there and gone.

"You'll soon be safe," he said. "Then you can rest."

Eraim jumped through the gate first. Then Vecnor. Ballrik entered last, and Ameilistari's head spun as they returned to the chamber of forges, the room oriented in a way that caused Ballrik to fall hard onto the floor next to the furnace. Eraim was on her feet, as was... Tewlon?

Vecnor was an elf.

Nidor stood holding the brooch with wide eyes.

"Throw it in!" commanded Tewlon, his voice boyish again. "Now!"

Nidor did as instructed, casting the platinum jewelry into the coals, and it vanished. A moment later, hollow screams filled the air as wispy shapes of monstrous creatures rushed past, pulled through the gate and back to where they belonged. As the final smoky demon disappeared, the coals turned black.

Chapter 40

Unfinished Business

Greyor faced the great bull demon. He had placed a nasty gash on its back when it opposed Baylun, and now it had eyes for him. Thankfully, Baylun had figured out how to make their weapons return, and passed that knowledge on to Greyor. It was so simple—how had he not figured it out for himself? And with the monstrous fiend charging, being without it was not an option.

The demon swung its axe in wide arcs, to its front and overhead—the massive blade struck the ceiling several times, raining debris onto the chamber. Dodging the evil weapon was impossible; Greyor wasn't nimble like Lorylla or Eraim. And with the rage in the bull's eyes and the flames shooting from its nostrils, there was no hope that an attack from Torrac would stop the demon's momentum. So Greyor did the only thing he could. He attacked.

Stepping forward, he put all his strength into his swing. But it wasn't meant for the beast. He aimed for the axe headed his way. The weapons collided, and Clanghorr cleaved the giant blade, breaking it into a thousand fragments. The force of the impact ripped Clanghorr from Greyor's hand and sent him sprawling.

He hastily regained his feet. His arms and knees shook as if he had worked in the mines for a week without rest, and his teeth hurt. The demon staggered as well, but quickly recovered.

Clanghorr lay thirty paces away. Greyor summoned the weapon with his mind, and thank Meldar, it responded. In seconds, it was in his grasp, and his body felt better for it.

The demon roared at the ceiling, and Greyor spotted the cause of its distress—Torrac flew from its back. It stomped its hoof, and the room erupted. Narrow fissures extended from the beast, and random areas of the floor rose while others fell. Mine dwellers suffered from the attack, as did the demons the dwellers fought—the bull didn't seem to care who was affected. Atop a jutting piece of floor lay Lorylla, and Greyor gasped. The gray elf had been immortal in his eyes. How could she have fallen?

The demon lunged at Baylun, lowering its head, and the krukari attempted to dance back. But the jagged terrain caused him to stumble. Greyor threw Clanghorr, and the weapon slashed the monster between the shoulders, where three gashes already bled, but it didn't stop the creature's charge. With nowhere to go, Baylun swung Torrac and cut loose one of the bull's horns. But the fiend struck, and the krukari flew twenty feet before bouncing twice.

Greyor again threw Clanghorr, scoring a hit to the demon's massive head. As the battleaxe came back, the monster spun, exhaling fire. It wasn't the billowing flames the dragon had breathed earlier, but a stream moving faster than Clanghorr could return.

There was no defense, and Greyor cringed. But he felt only a trace of heat as the fire dissipated before reaching him, and all at once the demons transformed into misty figures. Though the air remained stale, it was as if a great wind blew through the chamber, sweeping the smoky forms through the toppled wall. Other forms entered through the secret door, and they too passed through the breach.

The mine dwellers froze where they stood, their eyes nervous and untrusting of the occurrence. Silence reigned.

"How are you back so soon?"

The youthful speaker was barely audible from the other chamber. It was Nidor.

"You entered only moments ago," the lad continued.

Though Greyor was more than glad to hear Nidor's voice, there were more immediate concerns, and he scanned the room for his companions. Baylun rose on wobbly legs, blood seeping from several wounds, and maneuvered across the broken floor to a small body in golden armor. It was Kiryanna, and he helped the marteese to her feet—thank Meldar she had survived!

Greyor's eyes then went to Lorylla, afraid to know the elf's fate. She shifted and rolled onto her back, and his heart lifted.

"Baylun!" he called. "Nidor's in the next room."

Baylun stood up straight, as if to see if Greyor spoke the truth. The krukari and marteese then moved toward him in haste, forgetting all of their woes.

Romik assisted Lorylla to stand, and Greyor noticed the Lord of the Keep was without his false arm as he helped her traverse the uneven floor. Greyor knew not whether Ameilistari was with Nidor, and chose not to mention that fact as hope entered the lord's eyes. As Romik neared, Greyor relieved him of his burden.

Lorylla leaned on Greyor's head while Baylun, Kiryanna, and Romik rushed through the collapsed wall. Greyor couldn't help smiling at the gray elf. What would he have done had she perished?

"Alas, my quiver is empty," Lorylla said, showing just a hint of a smirk. "My service to you has reached its end."

Greyor snorted a laugh and dug into his pouch to withdraw a handkerchief. It was a cloth he often carried but never used—no self-respecting dwarf would be caught dead possessing such frilly items! But when you traveled with maidens such as he did, it was worth the risk. He handed her the handkerchief, and as they entered the next room, she wiped the blood from her lips.

Greyor froze at the sight. It was the legendary forge of Lornibur! And standing near the largest furnace were Nidor, Tewlon, and Eraim, the elves appearing to have walked through a fire. But how had Eraim gotten ahead of him? As he pondered that question, he couldn't recall seeing her in the battle against the bull demon. He then noticed Ameilistari in the arms of a stranger, her head lying against the man's shoulder—she also exhibited burns and singed hair. The warrior was an older human, perhaps fifty or sixty years in age, and cradled the lass like a father holds his sleeping child. Greyor had never seen the man before, yet there was something familiar about those eyes and cheekbones.

Romik rushed to his daughter while Baylun and Kiryanna ran to Nidor—where did they find the strength? The krukari and marteese took turns embracing their son, Kiryanna arriving first.

"Stari?" Romik brushed the child's disheveled hair with his fingers.

"She's all right," said the old warrior, his voice strong. "Only a bit of fatigue."

Romik froze while staring at the man, his mouth agape. "Father?" he uttered, just above a whisper. "But… how…?"

Ballrik! Romik's father, lost years ago when he jumped through a portal to close a gate to Hell before the Necromancer War. Rumors claimed he had died. How could he have survived in such a place for so many years?

"I'm not sure I can explain," Ballrik said.

Tears formed in both of their eyes.

Lorylla moved her hand to Greyor's shoulder. He looked up, fighting back a tear threatening to portray him as a sentimental fool.

"Is the dust getting to you?" posed the gray elf, her smirk moving to one side.

Greyor shook his head and jammed a knuckle into the offending eye to disperse the moisture. "Blasted place hasn't been used in centuries. There's dust everywhere."

"Our job is not yet over." Eraim gathered everyone's attention. "Dragons infest Lornibur, and we discovered clutches of eggs that will hatch into more."

"Dragons?" Baylun lowered his brow. "Surely you're mistaken."

Kiryanna grabbed the krukari's arm. "I'm afraid not, my love." She looked from Eraim to Greyor. "There is a giant nest of them." She glanced back at the other chamber, where mine dwellers bearing various injuries stood at the breach. "The demons have been breeding them."

"We saw only one dragon," Nidor said, looking at Eraim. "But Vec—" He glanced at Tewlon. "But it is dead."

"The nest lies above a pit of lava," Greyor announced. "If there were a way to cause an eruption… maybe we can destroy them. But…" he looked at the mine dwellers, "I fear what might happen to these creatures. What if it buries all of Lornibur? Destroys their home?"

"These creatures?" Baylun frowned at Greyor. "You don't know? They're dwarves. And the cell in the previous room *was* their home."

"Dwarves!" Greyor snorted. Perhaps the bull demon had rattled the krukari's brain.

"It is true, my friend," said Lorylla.

Greyor studied the dwellers. Was it possible? Perhaps they did not flee Lornibur with the others centuries ago. Maybe they had been unable to do so. But how could they be dwarves? They were so… thin.

"Why don't they speak Dwarfish?" It was the only question Greyor could think to voice aloud.

He spied a particular mine dweller stepping forward. The dweller spotted him as well and smiled wide while raising a crude hammer overhead.

"Gray'Or!" the creature said with excitement.

Greyor grinned. "Puppet Hands!"

"Puppet Hands?" Baylun murmured. "That makes better sense."

Puppet Hands dropped the hammer and shaded his eyes as he rushed to meet Greyor—neither Eraim's nor Ameilistari's magical lights were present, but the lava was bright. Greyor met Puppet halfway, and they embraced.

Turning back to his companions, Greyor said, "This is one of the courageous mine dwellers that helped us fight Maak Maak." He gazed at the floor, remembering the rest of the story. "The only one of the group who survived." He turned to Puppet Hands. "Good to see you!"

"I have pondered your question." Eraim walked to stand near Greyor's reunion. "About their speech." She narrowed her eyes at Puppet Hands. "Their language *sounds* dwarf-like. That is, when they actually speak. But the words seemed jumbled. Some of them, perhaps, spoken backwards." She turned to Greyor. "They have endured great evil for centuries. I believe that in their quest for survival, they might have altered their speech, so the enemy would not understand them." She glanced at Puppet. "And over time, it became their new language, and the old one faded from memory."

Another moment of Eraim's fleeting wisdom? Could she be correct? As Greyor thought about it, the dwellers' words *did* seem dwarf-like. How had he not noticed? Still… dwarves? Looking at the mine dwellers and their wiry frames, patchy beards, and varying degrees of balding heads, it was hard to imagine. But the prospect was intriguing, if not exciting.

"But we must return our attention to the matter at hand," Eraim said, facing their companions. "These dragons have been bred like attack dogs. The nest must be destroyed before the monsters escape into the world."

Greyor let out a slow exhale. "There are too many. I can think of no other way than the magma." He glanced again at his ancient kin, now over two hundred in number, most of them watching from the shadows of the other room. "But…"

"Dwarfish construction is unmatched by any other race," said Lorylla, the slight shaking of her deep voice revealing the pain she endured. She looked down at Greyor. "Even your ancestors could not bury this place."

The gray elf had a good point. He needed to have faith in his people. He nodded. "Still, that leaves us with the question of how."

"I can do it," said Ameilistari. The young lady now stood, and her skin was paler than Greyor had ever seen it.

"Nonsense." Romik frowned. "I have only just found you. You'll not be put in harm's way again."

"Father!" The mage's voice exuded authority. "I am capable of more than you believe."

"You must trust her, son," Ballrik said to the Lord of the Keep. "Deep down, you know of her strength. You have seen it."

How could Ballrik know any of that to be true? Perhaps he *had* been dead, gazing upon his descendants from the heavens.

Romik appeared torn by the statement and remained silent.

"She speaks the truth," said Nidor. "She saved our lives more than once."

Ameilistari smiled at her cousin, a proud expression capturing her. She took a deep breath and faced her father. "I'll admit I am afraid. But you have trained me for a couple of years now, and if I am to be Lord of Ironside, I must stare down adversity and proceed in a disciplined manner to accomplish the task before me."

Romik failed to conceal a flash of pride. But it was short-lived. "I appreciate your words," he said at last, "as well as all you have accomplished since *sneaking* onto this mission. But even if what you say is possible, how can you be sure you're not consumed by lava? Or any of the rest of us?"

"Your fears are warranted," Eraim confessed. "But you must remember what is at stake. If these monsters escape Lornibur, they will devastate all of Vaeldor. And they will strike the area of their departure first, which includes Ironside Keep."

"Son," said Ballrik, placing a hand on Romik's shoulder. "You have no reason to trust me; you don't even know me. But this is the time when heroes step forward to do what must be done."

Eraim smiled fondly at Ballrik. The elf surely remembered the sacrifice the warrior had made all those years ago in the evil kingdom of Selt. What Ballrik said weren't just words. He truly believed them.

Romik pulled Ameilistari in for a tight embrace. "Remember to leave yourself a way out," he said in a hushed voice that echoed into the dome.

Chapter 41

Pressure

Ameilistari's head was awhirl, and not just from the power she expended while in Hell. She survived that horrid place, her grandfather returned to save her life, and the rest of her companions were alive, although most of them were in a terrible state.

Uncle Baylun and Aunt Kiryanna limped heavily, and their conditions exceeded the worst images Ameilistari could have envisioned in her scariest nightmare. She had believed them to be invincible. Still, Baylun's giant hand swallowed Kiryanna's tiny one while they walked beside Nidor, who held his sword as if ready to protect his legendary parents.

Lorylla was another warrior Ameilistari thought incapable of taking serious harm. The gray elf was intelligent, swift, and able to do amazing things. Yet, blood matted her silver hair—likely her own—and she hobbled as much as Uncle Baylun and Aunt Kiryanna. As well, cuts and scratches marred her beautiful visage.

Outside of Nidor, who bore no injuries thanks to Silcor, only Eraim, Tewlon, and Greyor seemed unhindered. Scrapes adorned the dwarf's visible skin, and dried blood on his armor suggested a few hidden wounds, but one wouldn't know the dwarf endured any pain.

As for Ameilistari's father, the sight of Romik without his wooden arm was a bit shocking. But he was alive, and that's what mattered. She knew he wished to protect her from danger, and it surprised her he agreed to allow her to spearhead the task of destroying the nest. Perhaps he finally saw her as the accomplished mage she was.

Presently, they followed a wide corridor, led by Eraim and Vecnor, the large man posing as an elf. Ameilistari didn't understand

Tewlon's presence—she preferred the giant warrior for the mission ahead. The elves kept an easy gait so as not to push the injured. Had Eraim not taken an hour to patch up wounds with what remained of their healing herbs, things would have been worse. Even so, there hadn't been enough to do the job properly, and the elf decided who got how much. The mine dwellers—rather, ancient dwarves— offered more of the stone crawlers Greyor possessed, which helped immensely.

Ameilistari thanked Silcor that she required minimal care, for she detested mushrooms. What she needed most was rest, but that wasn't possible beyond the hour spent mending wounds and however long it took to reach the nest. Ameilistari still knew not how she would accomplish what she already claimed she could do, and she tried to work it out in her head. When Greyor suggested they needed to erupt the magma, it was as if she heard Selanna's voice telling her she possessed the means, and she spoke before thinking. Hopefully, she developed a plan before it was too late.

Her father walked to her right, and her grandfather to her left. She still could not believe Ballrik was alive, but there was no time to be emotional; best to leave that for after the mission. She had expected Father and Grandfather to carry on a conversation, since they had never actually met, but they said nothing, walking in silence with their eyes forward. Perhaps they focused on what lay ahead, or maybe they just didn't know what to say.

In truth, it seemed no one knew what to say to Grandfather. Father introduced Baylun to the man, and Ameilistari's uncle called Ballrik "sir" at least twice, while Kiryanna held an expression of doubt or curiosity. Ameilistari noticed her grandfather speaking with Tewlon every once in a while, and true to character, the muscular elf didn't respond verbally. But Tewlon's facial expressions, though subtle, were evident to anyone caring to pay attention. Some unknown connection existed between the two, and it frustrated Ameilistari that she would likely never know what it was. This belief was fueled further by the fact that her grandfather had said nothing about Vecnor's disappearance upon exiting through the gate. But Ballrik had been trapped in Hell for decades, so what connection could there possibly be? Also, how had he survived the extreme heat? And how did he open a gate to arrive when he did? Ameilistari might have thought Selanna to be behind it, but the looks of shock on the faces of Eraim and Vecnor were genuine when her grandfather arrived.

Most of the conversations during the walk were between Greyor and Eraim at the head of the group. Besides Tewlon, Puppet Hands also walked with the two — Ameilistari swore she heard Uncle Baylun call the mine dweller Poopit. It was almost comical watching Greyor communicate with the leader of the mine people before they departed for the dragons' lair; they used their hands to make gestures while speaking either slowly or loudly or both. Somehow, they eventually understood each other. Greyor explained to Puppet where they were headed, and what they intended to do. Puppet seemed to be aware of the area, but was adamantly against the plan.

The time necessary to convince Puppet might have been much longer had Baylun not revealed the ability to speak with the Lornibur dwarves. Ameilistari's uncle explained it was Torrac that granted his comprehension, and Greyor appeared upset that Clanghorr didn't do the same. In the end, from what Ameilistari gathered, Puppet organized his people to help once they completed the task, and he now guided them to their destination.

They traversed secret tunnels, narrow passages, and wide corridors by the light of glowing blue mushrooms supplied by Puppet Hands. With every step, the heat steadily increased. The temperature climbed higher as they passed through a rusted iron door and into a room with a stream of lava. Magma entered from a corridor on the left and exited through a finely carved archway a couple of feet high. Ameilistari was uncomfortable within the chamber, as the silver eye herbs hadn't finished repairing the damage from Hell. But as Puppet led the way to a tunnel on the right, her grandfather shielded her from the radiating heat while she hugged the wall, providing some comfort.

The hallway was wide, and its craftsmanship paled compared to the rest of Lornibur—an obvious addition by the priests. And although the temperature remained warm, Ameilistari's pain faded as the lava stream fell behind. A bit farther, a gentle breeze greeted them—a refreshing change. The passage seemed to spiral upward, and the company slowed to conserve their strength.

At last, they reached a cavernous room. Eraim had produced her light while they approached, much to Puppet's dismay, but the mine dweller shaded his eyes and marched dutifully forward. The bauble illuminated most of the chamber, revealing boulders and loose stones upon an irregular floor, and crude steps scaled the wall to the left. An orange glow highlighted the end of the climb, suggesting lava, but the constant wind provided cool relief. Ameilistari suspected the rushing air came from the ceiling.

Eraim turned to face the company. "At the top of the stairs is the passageway leading to the nest," she said, without fear of being overheard. "There are a lot of dragons, so we need to be prepared." She looked at Ameilistari. "Are you ready?"

The walk had taken some time, but Ameilistari still had no idea what might cause an eruption. Selanna called her an elementalist, meaning she held some kind of control over the elements. Was lava an element? She needed more information. "How does magma work, exactly?" she asked Eraim, her voice coming out dry and cracked.

Eraim's lips parted as if to answer, but Greyor interrupted.

"It's molten rock," said the dwarf, "filled with gas that creates bubbles. If the pressure gets too great, it erupts. This makes it a dangerous tool, but apparently the dwarves of Lornibur knew how to use it safely."

Eraim closed her mouth. A second later, she nodded.

Ameilistari shut her eyes and concentrated. Threads of magic surrounded her. *Let the magic flow through you,* she reminded herself. She reached out and sensed the lava in question. There was a lot. She pushed farther and detected a river nearby, an underground current below them and to the right—she never realized she could perceive such things! The ice-cold water hurried on its way to become a river the people of Vaeldor were familiar with. Did it flow into Sardina? Or Marcove? That didn't matter. It was an element she could use. She opened her eyes and nodded to Eraim.

Eraim turned to Greyor, and the dwarf addressed the company.

"Eraim, Baylun, and myself will accompany Ameilistari into the nest."

Romik's mouth opened to voice his protest, as he did the first time the dwarf made the announcement, and Greyor raised a hand for silence.

"Your daughter is in the best of hands," he said. "I will die before I allow harm to come to her. And as Trannum and Uustaag discovered, defeating me is no easy task."

Greyor was a true hero, and his words halted Romik's objection. A realization then struck Ameilistari of the danger she had accepted. She was so focused on the magma that the hundreds of dragons hadn't registered. It was suddenly hard to breathe.

"Ballrik and Tewlon will await us atop these steps," Greyor pointed Clanghorr at the rough stairs, "ready to reinforce us or protect our retreat." He eyed the others. "The rest of you will remain here to do the same. And if I understand our friend here," he glanced at Puppet, "the Lornibur survivors are clearing our path of all dangers. They shall then lead us to the tunnel to Ironside Keep."

It appeared as though several shoulders became lighter with the last part. Ameilistari was ready to go home as well. She should never have sneaked onto this adventure.

Greyor nodded at Puppet, and the dweller shuffled his feet as he sped back down the corridor.

"Let's go," Greyor said to the company, and he headed up the steps.

Ameilistari's heart pounded as she ascended, walking between Ballrik and Baylun while Greyor, Eraim, and Tewlon led the way. The climb took forever, yet when they neared the top, it was as if no time had elapsed at all. To compose herself, Ameilistari focused on the river. Her heart rate sped up, as if matching the water's flow, and every nerve in her body came to life.

Beyond the stairs, a wide tunnel penetrated the cavern wall, narrowing as it delved forty feet deep and became an oval-shaped passage. To the right, a pool of magma bubbled, and before it lay the corpse of a dragon, its neck nearly severed. A pair of Eraim's arrows protruded from its skull, and charred stone suggested the reptile had breathed fire. The dragon paled in size to the beast Vecnor had slain, but it sent a shiver down Ameilistari's spine nonetheless.

Eraim carefully removed the arrow from the corpse's forehead, wiped it clean, and added it to her quiver. She attempted to remove the second one buried in the monster's chin, but the shaft snapped. With the additional arrow, the elf had six available.

Greyor headed into the rounded tunnel, and Eraim followed. As Ameilistari did the same, she felt the giant, reassuring hand of Uncle Baylun on her shoulder. She glanced up, and he winked, summoning one of his smiles that typically put strangers on edge, afraid he had grown angry. But it was endearing to Ameilistari, and it calmed her slightly.

The tunnel grew warmer as they proceeded. Eraim walked several paces ahead of Greyor with an arrow to her bowstring, the elf as silent as a mouse while the gap between them increased. Her ball of light then winked out as it hovered to her, and she placed it into her pouch, leaving an orange glow as the only illumination to guide them.

The passage grew hotter still as it curved toward the light, and Eraim vanished against the wall in the distance. When Ameilistari next saw her, the elf stood peering into another massive cavern. Greyor paused, holding up his gauntleted hand until Eraim beckoned them forward, and they continued.

The cavity was larger than Ameilistari could have imagined. It was rounded, the far end distorted by a haze emerging from a glowing pit taking up most of the space, and the floor comprised a wide ledge ascending to the right as it circled the chamber twice, ending high above. Shadows moved upon the ramp at various heights, revealing hundreds of dragons, and along the spiraling rise protruded a score of rock shelves where most of the creatures congregated. Higher still, additional ledges beneath jagged stalactites held even bigger dragons—reptiles with wings. Some of the monsters took notice of Ameilistari and her companions but seemed unconcerned. Eraim surmised it resulted from having had caretakers since their births. Hopefully, that provided time to do what needed to be done.

Greyor gave Ameilistari a gentle nudge, and she walked to the edge of the drop-off. A rush of hot air stung her skin as she gazed into the depths of the chasm at a lake of magma below. To her left, crude steps descended to a ledge encircling the pit, where hundreds of large eggs basked in the heat. As she stared, an egg cracked, and a dark claw pushed through.

She took a deep breath, grateful for the power she had recovered during the long walk—hopefully it was enough. She had kept her connection with the river, as using existing elements was less taxing than summoning it from nothing, and reached out to harness the cold air rushing about the neighboring chamber. Employing a single strand of magical energy, she called upon the water, and it responded, finding every tunnel, hole, and crack to obey her command. While it approached, she routed the swirling breeze through the tunnel behind her.

The wind arrived first, and the impact nearly pushed Ameilistari into the pit. But a firm hand grabbed her collar and steadied her— probably Uncle Baylun, as Greyor was too short. It gave her confidence that he was near. The cold air circled the hole in accordance with her wishes.

More of the dragons took notice of her presence.

Ameilistari sent the wind into the pit, but the only response was more eggs cracking open. Water then entered the chamber, like a five-foot-wide river suspended overhead. She directed it into the magma, and a dark spot formed where it struck.

A dragon roared somewhere above, and several roars and squawks answered.

Ameilistari's idea wasn't working. Although the water disturbed the lava, it didn't appear to mount any pressure. She wanted to give up—it was beyond her ability. Selanna should be here!

No. There was no time for childish self-pity. If Ameilistari failed, the people she loved would perish. She calmed her mind.

Pressure… She needed to build pressure, like putting a lid over a pot of boiling water. Though she had never performed such an action, she had watched cooks do it in the keep's kitchen when Father insisted she know every room within the stronghold and how it functioned. She remembered when the water boiled over, wreaking havoc with the fire below it. The cooks didn't appreciate her giggling.

Ameilistari cooled the wind further and used it to form ice. She then covered the area above the magma, but the heat immediately turned it to steam. She needed more power.

Pulling additional threads of magic through her body, she fueled the rate at which the water froze, building a lid forty feet above the molten rock. As it melted, she cooled the steam and added layers of ice on top. She continued the process, slowly sliding the lid lower and lower. Despite the freezing gusts tossing about her hair and robes, sweat beaded on her forehead while she fought the extreme heat, and soon she had a solid mass over ten feet thick.

The screeching of dragons pierced the wind in her ears.

Chapter 42

Extermination

Baylun eyed the giant reptiles stirring along the rising ledge. Though Eraim claimed the dragons were surely accustomed to people entering their nest, they evidently realized something was amiss. The monsters appeared restless when the wind first entered the chamber, and after the arrival of floating water, restlessness became agitation.

The last time Baylun glanced into the pit, Ameilistari was forming ice over the magma. Ice? Baylun would wager all of his gold on the lava if anyone were willing to take that bet. But he needed to have faith in his niece. She continued with her task, and the ice completely obscured the bubbling lake—the glow diminished enough that Eraim released her bauble of light.

"Right side!" said Eraim above the wind and rushing water.

A dragon took flight from a high shelf, its wings spread wide. But it narrowed its wings and fell into a dive, aiming at Baylun and his companions.

Greyor hurled his weapon, and Baylun did the same. Though the gap was substantial, Baylun knew his axe was capable of closing the distance after the first time he threw it in Helmland, when a skeletal dragon flew off with Romik. The battleaxes picked up speed, becoming rings of light as they reached their target. Clanghorr struck one of the creature's wings while Torrac tore through the other. The reptile screeched as it plummeted a hundred feet onto a ledge, stirring the dragons perched there. The body bounced from the jutting stone and fell again, landing on the rising path where it ceased to move.

Baylun reached out to catch his returning weapon, and Greyor did the same.

"Left! Left!" said Eraim.

Another dragon took to the air while a pair of giant lizards without wings rambled down the sloping ledge. Knowing the latter wouldn't arrive too soon, Baylun set his sights on the flying beast and threw Torrac. Clanghorr followed in the axe's wake. Torrac struck the dragon's neck, and Clanghorr finished the job, cutting the head loose. The corpse descended into the pit, landing atop the thick ice, and the surface cracked. But the fissure quickly sealed as additional water froze on contact.

The battleaxes truly worked well together! Baylun hadn't even aimed; he simply threw the weapon, and it struck the reptile's neck. He wondered if it was the same with Clanghorr.

Four wingless dragons now lumbered down the slope while two more launched from the high perches.

"Guard the ledge!" ordered Eraim as she loosed one, two, and three arrows at the flying enemies.

The charging dragons moved at a swifter pace than Baylun originally thought. From the lead creature's mouth spewed flames, but it was too far away to reach him and his companions.

"Now!" said Greyor.

The axes flew, and Clanghorr took a direct path while Torrac veered over the pit before circling back. The dragon released its fiery breath onto Clanghorr with no effect, and the weapon cut into the monster's jaw. Shortly after, Torrac sliced the side of the dragon's head. The combined wounds felled the beast, and the axes returned.

The other three dragons drew to within sixty feet, and a flying reptile plummeted into the pit, joining the corpse that was now half-buried in ice. The floor then quaked.

"Grab the girl!" hollered Greyor.

"Not yet!" Ameilistari said, halting Baylun as he reached for her.

The ground rumbled harder, spreading into the walls, and the dragons shifted their attention as stalactites descended, piercing several of the beasts or crashing onto the floor. A dozen cone-shaped formations drove into the ice that somehow still plugged the pit. One stalactite approached Ameilistari while she focused, and Baylun threw Torrac, shattering it to pieces. He then stood over his niece to protect her from the ensuing shower of stones.

Ameilistari snapped out of her trance, turning to the tunnel. "Run!"

Baylun moved last, following the others as the hovering river ceased its flow and washed the corridor. Though he had taken several injuries during the battle with the bull demon, the healing Eraim administered had improved his condition, and his limp was gone. Still, he needed to pace himself to trail Greyor—the dwarf's short legs only carried the warrior so fast. Now he knew how Lorylla had felt when she slowed for him earlier.

Roars resounded behind them, and there was a sudden blast of heat. Baylun grabbed Greyor and leaped forward. The dwarf grunted under his weight as they hit the unforgiving floor, and fire raced over them. It reminded Baylun of the battle against Maak Maak, except this time he was not badly scorched... and it wasn't Ameilistari's fault.

He and Greyor scrambled to their feet once the fire subsided, and moved swiftly from the tunnel. Tewlon and Ballrik stood on either side while Baylun sprinted past Greyor, and he didn't slow until reaching the top of the stairs.

Eraim and Ameilistari had avoided the fiery attack altogether, and they rushed down the steps. Below, Nidor stood with Kiryanna and Romik, all of them holding their swords ready. Lorylla watched the exit.

Baylun turned back to see a dragon head emerge from the passage. It was red with a yellow underbelly, and its cat-like green eyes were set wide on its triangular head beneath a jutting brow. It filled the chamber with a roar.

Baylun and Greyor raised their weapons, but the dragon released another stream of fire, and they half-jumped-half-tumbled down the first several steps—why hadn't they used their axes to deflect the flames? The attack didn't last long, and Baylun raced up to see Ballrik and Tewlon assaulting the monster. Ballrik fought with a sword in one hand and a dagger in the other, scoring a shallow wound with the longer blade while the knife failed to penetrate the beast's scales. Tewlon drove a single thrust into the dragon's neck, burying the sword to the hilt.

The dragon turned on the elf. Tewlon had nowhere to go with the lava close behind, so Baylun heaved his battleaxe. Torrac arrived before the monster made good an attack, cleaving the creature's left eye and surely blinding it. As the weapon returned, an orange glow within the tunnel grew bright, and the ground trembled.

"Get out of here!" said Greyor.

Tewlon left his sword buried in the reptile, and the dragon slammed its head into the ceiling as it reeled in pain. Ballrik and the elf then retreated, and Baylun ran down the steps ahead of them.

"Ameilistari!" called Nidor. "Collapse the dragon tunnel!"

Eraim and the young mage had joined Lorylla, and Ameilistari turned. Baylun noticed the color she had regained while traveling to the nest was gone—it reminded him of the time Teliya had suffered a horrific illness after consuming bad berries. Eraim said something to Ameilistari, and his niece shook her head before gently pushing away the elf's supporting arm. She made gestures as Baylun and the others touched down from the final step, throwing her hands forward.

Baylun glanced to see a ball of flaming lava rise from the area of the magma pool. The thrashing dragon was nearly all the way through the passage, and three more heads emerged from the entrance. The ball flew as fast as Torrac, striking the tapered ceiling, and an explosion resulted.

Everyone rushed from the room, Baylun exiting last. He looked back again to see the tunnel atop the stairs had completely collapsed, burying the lead dragon, which no longer moved. There were no signs of the other three. As the floor vibrated, he detected another explosion. No. An eruption. Ameilistari had done it!

Fear entered Baylun's heart at the thought of lava bursting through the pile of rocks. Would the debris hold back the flow?

He fled from the chamber, ushering everyone ahead. Ballrik carried Ameilistari, and Eraim led the way by the light of Mithkahr's blade along the arcing corridor — she must have put away her bauble. Nidor ran beside the elf, Baylun's son amazingly unharmed during his adventure with Ameilistari and Tewlon, and Lorylla and Kiryanna were next. Romik remained alongside his father and daughter, trailed by Tewlon and Greyor. Baylun quickly caught up.

The hallway shuddered as they reached its end, and a distant explosion echoed behind them, followed by a constant roar. The company scurried through the iron door as a rush of hot air struck them, chased by an intense orange glow filling the tunnel they had just traversed.

Greyor slowed to force the door shut, and Baylun gave aid. The two of them made easy work of the task, and they exited before pulling it the rest of the way.

Farther up the hallway, a pair of Lornibur dwarves held glowing mushrooms and waved for the company to hurry. Baylun and Greyor caught up with Tewlon, and the three of them looked back to see the iron door shining in the distance. It appeared to be melting.

The mine dwarves opened a secret panel to an ascending staircase. Eraim led the way, and they ran single file up the thirty-foot climb. Upon reaching the top, another pair of dwarves opened a door into one of the grand corridors of Lornibur, and after the company passed through, the four dwellers followed.

The shaking eased, and they stopped to catch their breaths. It seemed everyone was too exhausted to continue, but when the floor rumbled again, they found strength enough to jog.

They traversed several more tunnels and chambers that might have been beautiful in their day. But as usual, broken furnishings, destroyed pillars, and marred walls did nothing to support such beliefs. The patterns of gold, silver, and copper along the ceilings, however, escaped most of the vandalism. Every hundred feet, more

Lornibur dwarves stood like sentinels within the corridors and rooms, and they remained at their posts as the group passed.

Another explosion sounded. And another. But they were different. More like cave-ins than fiery blasts. The company then entered a chamber where a dozen Lornibur dwarves gathered, including Puppet Hands, and Eraim came to a halt. Puppet nodded at the elf, and she returned the gesture before facing the company.

"We can rest now," she said.

Though Baylun was more than happy to catch his breath, he feared they needed more distance from the lava. Puppet Hands explained earlier that his folk had prepared areas of Lornibur to collapse—it was part of an original scheme to escape their captors—and they should be protected from the eruption. Baylun prayed to Silcor the dwarf was correct.

"Won't the lava exit the mountain altogether?" posed Romik, his eyes suddenly filled with dread. "Will it hit Ironside Keep?"

Greyor's shoulders slumped. The dwarf evidently hadn't thought about that possibility.

Eraim supplied an answer.

"We are far enough from your keep," the elf said. "Do not fret. Ironside is safe."

Romik didn't appear satisfied. Baylun wished he could offer comfort to his brother, but what could he say?

Ballrik set Ameilistari down to sit against the wall, and he nodded at his son, as if expressing his faith in the elf's words.

That seemed to help, if only slightly.

"I wonder how much more of Lornibur is now lost," mumbled Greyor. He looked up at Lorylla, who frowned. "I suppose that isn't what's important."

The gray elf shook her head and placed a friendly hand on the dwarf's shoulder.

Baylun took the opportunity to join his wife and son. He overheard Nidor speaking to Kiryanna as he approached.

"You should have seen her," Nidor was saying. "Ameilistari is amazing!"

"That she is." Kiryanna smiled, appearing beautiful even with the dirt and blood smeared on her face. Baylun also noticed a hole in the side of her armor, exposing a pinkened bandage. She looked at him and released a deep sigh. "Still think you could have completed this mission without me?"

"We're not out yet," Baylun said, regretting the words after he uttered them. Being pessimistic helped nothing.

She furrowed her brow. "I meant to ask earlier, how long have Torrac and Clanghorr been returning after you two throw them?"

Baylun lifted his weapon. How could he explain his new responsibility to Lornibur? The oath he took without consulting her? Now wasn't the time. "Torrac continues to amaze me," he replied. He looked at Nidor. His eldest. The voice claimed his firstborn would succeed him once his service was done. Perhaps he should have spoken to Nidor before obligating them both. Then again, he wouldn't have survived without his oath. "You finally have stories of your own," he said.

"I'm not so sure." Nidor frowned. "It was mostly Ameilistari and Ve—uh, Tewlon."

"I charged you with Ameilistari's life," said Kiryanna, "and she is doing just fine. I'd say you did your job perfectly. You'll make a great Honor Guard."

Nidor looked across the room to where his cousin sat, and Baylun did the same. She gazed back and smiled while Romik and Ballrik held a conversation above her. Baylun's attention then drifted to Ballrik. He still could not believe Romik's father was alive. Part of him rejoiced for his older brother, but another part, a jealous part, wondered if it would change their relationship. But why would it?

"Is everyone ready?" asked Greyor, gaining the eyes and ears of the room. "According to Puppet Hands, we're about to pass from the living quarters and back into the mines, and the explosions seem to have stirred the lizards. There's likely no avoiding them."

Of course not. Why couldn't it just be over?

"Stay with your cousin," Kiryanna told Nidor.

The young warrior nodded and walked across the room to join Ameilistari as Romik pulled her to her feet.

"And you keep watch on your son," Baylun said to his wife.

She let out a small chuckle. "Yes, sir!" she responded with sarcasm, adding a wink.

Chapter 43

A Path Home

Greyor glanced around the chamber while everyone prepared to depart. Meldar willing, they would soon exit Lornibur. It was both disheartening and a relief. The history of the place still held him in awe, but he needed to get topside so that plans could be made.

Puppet Hands led them from the room, and they climbed a staircase spiraling around a solid pillar adorned by veins of silver and collections of red jasper. The stairwell passed through the ceiling and into a wide corridor with a rail running along its center and exiting through decorative arches to either side.

Progress was swift after that, as Puppet and half a dozen Lornibur dwarves shuffled their feet, choosing what was likely the most efficient route. Giant lizards appeared here and there and were easily dealt with, but there were never more than a few. Maak Maak tunnels then marred the mines, and Puppet revealed a keen ability for spotting unsafe areas of the floor. There were more traps than Greyor thought.

A skirmish occurred in a vast chamber containing several exits possessing rails that joined a broken circle in the middle. Piles of stone and debris lay scattered, as did round tunnels crafted by Maak Maak, two in the walls and one each in the ceiling and floor. A couple dozen lizards advanced from multiple directions and approached from every angle.

Nidor showed off his skills, switching his sword between his hands when it suited him. He skewered and slashed his foes, slaying no fewer than three. Kiryanna was beside her son, and easily complemented his style, as if she had fought with him for years—it was amazing how her abilities adapted to those around her. She dispatched only a couple of the monsters while watching Nidor's flank.

Ballrik and Romik kept Ameilistari between them, unwilling to leave the enemy a path to the young mage. She remained pale, and made no attempts to assist with magic, but her eyes tracked the melee, as if she might change her mind at any moment.

Tewlon, Eraim, and Lorylla stood close to each other. Tewlon did most of the work while Lorylla rested her wounded body—she voluntarily received less healing from Eraim before approaching the nest, and suffered more than anyone. Eraim held her last arrow to her bowstring, watching the battle unfold while Tewlon slew half a dozen reptiles. Greyor was impressed with Tewlon's skills, but he wondered where the elf had procured another sword, since he left his behind in the dragon's neck.

The Lornibur dwarves fought better than expected. Greyor had seen them in combat in the past and never considered them too much of a threat; it had been their numbers that made them strong. But Puppet's group must have been the best of them, for they exhibited the skills of many years.

Greyor and Baylun worked together, throwing their battleaxes to aid their companions and slaying half of the lizards—Greyor loved fighting beside the krukari! Once the battle ended, Eraim took a moment to treat minor injuries received.

The rest of the trip lasted a few hours. Greyor recognized the room where they first discovered Ameilistari and Nidor, when the two nearly fell through the floor. The others obviously realized how close they were to freedom, and their expressions became energetic as they picked up the pace—no one seemed interested in retrieving their ropes from the hole in the corner.

Upon reaching the breach to the secret tunnel of Ironside Keep, the Lornibur dwarves lifted their fists, as was their way of saying goodbye. Puppet Hands was the last to depart, and the temptation to try to convince the warrior to leave the mines dangled on the tip of Greyor's tongue. He had tried it before, years ago during the Necromancer War after the battle with Marfesna, the ice demon, but Puppet refused. This time would likely be no different, so Greyor raised his fist. Puppet Hands surprised him with an embrace. But the hug was short, to Greyor's relief—any longer and the others might think him soft.

"We will meet again very soon," Greyor said to Puppet, using his hands to communicate the words. He had explained it before, and Puppet understood immediately.

"Can we leave now?" posed Romik, releasing a small chuckle.

Greyor sniffed back the mucus threatening to escape his nose and wiped the touch of moisture from his eye. "Let's go."

The air in the secret tunnel was just as stale as Lornibur's, maybe more so. Nobody seemed to mind. They filled the corridors with conversation while they journeyed over a day and a half, but Greyor didn't listen to most of their words. Their spirits were up, and it appeared life was returning to normal. After facing demons and thought-to-be-extinct dragons, that was a good thing.

One particular conversation, Greyor couldn't help overhearing, since Lorylla walked beside him. It was between the gray elf and Nidor. The lad had maneuvered to walk near Lorylla and asked her a few questions.

"Do gray elves live only in Orlenfel? Or do you travel around Vaeldor? Do you ever make it to Dakreal Forest?"

"You showed great skill in that last battle." Lorylla left the questions unanswered.

Nidor blushed. "Tewlon taught me a few things. He really is knowledgeable."

Lorylla considered the muscular elf, who tilted his head, as if hearing the statement. "Indeed."

Nidor didn't seem willing to explain further.

"Your father is very unique," Lorylla said after a moment.

"Uncle Magneer—that is, Duke Magneer—depends on Father

to keep the realm safe." Pride shone in Nidor's eyes while he gazed at Baylun walking next to Kiryanna. "He trains me when he can."

"I speak not only of his combative skills," Lorylla said. "He is a genuine hero, and a good soul." She glanced at the lad. "And he has likely trained you more than you realize, and not just in combat."

Greyor thought about the gray elf's words, realizing he didn't really know Baylun beyond their weapons. Yet, he sensed Lorylla to be correct. He needed to spend more time with the krukari when the opportunity presented itself. His thoughts then shifted to the battleaxes, and he wondered...

Closing his eyes, Greyor reached out with his mind, feeling for Torrac. He detected the weapon just ahead of him. He then attempted to speak to Baylun without words.

Baylun. Scratch your head if you can hear me.

He opened his eyes. Baylun continued walking, making no movement to comply.

That didn't work.

Greyor focused.

Torrac. I need you.

Baylun looked back at Greyor. The krukari smirked and nodded. He had surely received the message. That was a start.

Greyor gazed at Ameilistari. Unbeknownst to anyone, the little sneak had joined the mission. But could they have succeeded without her? She walked between her father and grandfather, who spoke to one another nonstop and laughed often. Greyor didn't know who had fashioned the Lord of the Keep's wooden arm, but he planned to contract the best craftsman to make one even stronger once he returned to Morimont.

Morimont... Would the representatives of Rornibur be there when Greyor arrived? It didn't matter. He had news for the dwarves of all mountain realms. Big news. News that King Kolermane would not turn a deaf ear to. As the Morimont kings before him, Kolermane held on to the old ways, and with the knowledge that Lornibur had been discovered... It was just the thing the aging monarch needed to retire happy: leading his subjects back to the beginning. Back to the true home of Clanghorr and Torrac.

Greyor gazed again at Baylun. He and the krukari would have a serious conversation once they reached the keep.

Chapter 44

Ironside Keep

The company reached Ironside Keep at last, breathing fresh air for the first time in what felt like months. But it had only been a week. Captain Marlajin immediately informed Romik of a volcanic eruption in the south. Just as Eraim promised, it never threatened the keep, but it shook the foundations and put everyone on edge.

The next report was not well received. Marlajin informed Romik that his most loyal subject, Morsum, had decided to live with family in the north, and departed two days prior. The news saddened Romik and Ameilistari. Romik didn't understand why the old gatekeeper left while he battled in the mines—a face-to-face departure would have been preferred. In truth, he would have offered rooms for Morsum's entire family to stay in the keep. The aging soldier said goodbye to no one, opting to drop a note instead. The last person to see Morsum, according to the guards, was Rauzel, Ameilistari's mentor. Apparently, Romik's daughter had missed a lesson with the marteese, who passed the hour having tea with Morsum in the gatekeeper's chamber. When asked about Morsum's actions afterward, she replied, "He looked so tired. Claimed he wanted nothing more than to spend his remaining years with his family. Who am I to stop him?"

While the captain discussed Ironside matters with Romik, Daymyn and Teliya ran to reunite with their parents and older brother, and didn't leave their sides for the better part of three days. They had enjoyed meeting King Cavalor of Marcove immensely during the Lornibur mission, but the only thing that kept them from spiraling into fear and sorrow was the arrival of Naiandillis, Lorylla's eldest daughter. The gray elf had been exploring Mentrial Forest when she learned of her mother's visit to the keep. She then made the trip to surprise Lorylla, and discovered her mother had joined a mysterious quest and had not been heard from since. Naiandillis resolved to stay until Lorylla returned, and she spent most of her time entertaining the children that shared in her worries.

Arriving on the same day as the company's return to the keep was Selanna. The elfish mage claimed she had expected Eraim in Vermallon a few days ago, and had made the journey to be sure her lifelong friend was safe. No one was happier to see Selanna than Ameilistari.

Though fatigue plagued the adventurers, and they desperately wished to rest, a feast was prepared that first night to celebrate their return. Tavern tables were rearranged and the keep's guests were invited to attend, and Romik allowed Vikur's chair to be moved temporarily so musicians could perform. It was odd that traveling minstrels were passing through at the time; they couldn't even recall where they were going. Eraim visited each member of the Lornibur company hours before the event to reapply herbs where necessary, since Selanna happened to bring an abundance of Vermallon dusk.

❊ ❊ ❊

Romik still could not believe his father had returned. The man had been lost to Hell for so long... How could anyone survive such a predicament? Ballrik must truly be a great warrior!

They spent hours talking, and Romik found it strange that his father didn't pose more questions about his missing arm or his life in the keep—the man's interests seemed focused around Romik's earlier years. Explaining that his mother, Lorin—Ballrik's thought-to-be widow—had remarried, and to a krukari, wasn't as difficult as Romik anticipated. Just as his stepfather explained decades ago, Ballrik and Gruelenor had been great friends, and Romik's father appeared genuinely happy the two discovered love. It was then easier for

Romik to explain that Baylun was his brother, and his father accepted that information as easily as the rest, commenting on what skilled warriors they both were.

Ballrik spoke highly of Ameilistari and encouraged Romik to help her attain her goals, instead of molding her into the image he created in his mind. Romik presented protests about loyalty and responsibility, to which Ballrik said, "You cannot predict what the future holds. I was never Lord of the Keep, but the stronghold endured, and the rightful master is firmly in place."

Romik appreciated the end of that statement. A part of him had wondered whether his father harbored any desire to assume control.

When asked about his time in Hell and how he had escaped, Ballrik's response was cryptic.

"Some things are better left in the past," he said, "and some things are best forgotten. I choose to look only to the future, and the time I have left. And unless you object, I would love to spend that time here, in any capacity you see fit."

Romik was more than happy to hear those words, and readily accepted. When his father suggested a bedchamber he had "admired as a youth" to house him, Romik frowned.

"That was Morsum's quarters," he said. "We have much larger rooms."

"That room is perfect," Ballrik insisted.

❄ ❄ ❄

Nidor spoke quietly with his father about his near-death experience once they arrived at Ironside Keep. Baylun's face paled more than he had ever seen upon describing the liquid fire washing over him and the excruciating pain accompanying it. When he mentioned the healing flame that pulled him from death's door, his father smiled.

"It's a feeling unlike any other," Baylun said, putting a powerful hand on Nidor's back. "Silcor blesses our family, and the man we named you after is our guardian angel." His expression became serious. "But do not count on such a miracle in the future."

"Believe me," Nidor chuckled, "I never wish to experience that kind of pain again." He looked at his father. "I will not waste this second chance Silcor and Nidor have given me."

Baylun gave him a crushing hug.

Nidor was elated to be reunited with his siblings—he thought he'd never see them again at one point. But shock overcame him when he saw them in the company of a gray elf maiden. Naiandillis was her name, and she was obviously related to Lorylla, but younger. As it turned out, she was Lorylla's daughter.

Naiandillis stood nearly a head taller than Nidor. She wore a fine white blouse that shone against her grayish skin and black breeches that hugged her well-defined legs. Just like her mother, her eyes were enchanting—he'd never tire of white irises upon black eyes. A braided cord held her silver hair in a ponytail hanging halfway down her back, with a tuft of hair out of place that dangled over her forehead. He saw her only briefly before she greeted Lorylla with an embrace.

That night, Naiandillis wiggled her way to sit next to Nidor during the feast, when the dining was nearly complete.

"Mother says you fought valiantly in the mines," she said, her voice low, but not so much as Lorylla's. Perhaps it would deepen further with time.

"I almost died," Nidor responded, wishing he hadn't.

She smirked. "And honest, too." She gazed about the table at the many people talking, laughing, and toasting as music began to play. "She also tells me our race fascinates you."

Nidor stopped breathing. Why did Lorylla say that?

"I am fascinated with your race as well," Naiandillis said, as if reading his thoughts. "Tell me, do you hunt?"

The tension in the air eased, and Nidor relaxed a bit—he had been hunting for years. "Of course." He hoped he had spoken with confidence. "My father and grandfather taught me to track, trap, and use a bow." After a moment, he hastily added, "Although I'm sure I'm not as good with a bow as you."

She raised a silver eyebrow. "You assume I use the bow because I am an elf?"

He hadn't expected that response. He was no better than those making assumptions about him and his family.

She laughed.

Did gray elves laugh out loud?

"Of course I use a bow," she said. "I have been staying in Mentrial Forest for the past year. Perhaps we can hunt sometime."

Nidor's world crashed down around him, and he sighed. "I expect we'll be returning to Philen soon. That's where we're from."

"Pity." She gazed at the open space in the middle of the tavern, where people started to sway to the music. "Do you dance?"

Nidor watched his mother drag Daymyn to the dance floor. She had done the same thing to him many times in the past. If only he had paid more attention to how she moved instead of dreading the occasions.

"Come." Naiandillis held out her hand. "We will dance."

Her slender fingers wrapped around Nidor's hand, and she pulled him from his seat. Her grip was firm. As she led him around the table, he wondered if she could jump like her mother or make a sword glow with heat. He also wondered if she possessed any talents that Lorylla did not. If only there were time to find out.

They danced, and Naiandillis smiled often—probably at Nidor's awkwardness. Still, the smile relaxed him, and he gave up caring. As they continued, he noticed Sybin watching him while dancing with one of the keep's young soldiers. He felt nothing for the captain's daughter. Ameilistari was correct; Sybin wasn't the girl for him. Even if he never saw Naiandillis again, he realized there existed someone who *was* right for him. He told his father he wouldn't waste the second chance Silcor and Paladin Nidor had given him, and he meant it. He returned his attention to his dance partner.

❋ ❋ ❋

After feeding his belly three platters of food, Greyor sought Baylun and dragged the krukari to a secluded corner of the tavern. There, they had a drink while music, dancing, and laughter filled the room.

"We have much to discuss," Greyor said.

Baylun watched the dancers, where Kiryanna twirled Daymyn. "Torrac speaks to me more often now." He looked at Greyor. "Not in words, but it speaks to me. I feel Clanghorr as well, and I sensed you summoning me back in the tunnel."

Greyor bobbed his head. "Did Torrac require an oath?"

"One hundred years."

Greyor grinned. "Our weapons are linked. And now we are as well."

"That's kind of what I figured." Baylun stared at his mug.

Greyor snorted a chuckle. "A dwarf and a krukari. No one will believe it!"

Baylun's eyes returned to his wife. "If I'm to serve Lornibur, I suppose I'll need to move closer. Perhaps Romik can house us here in the keep." He shook his head. "I just hope Kiryanna takes it well."

Greyor glanced at the marteese. It amazed him to see her go from vicious warrior to loving mother. "You have the greatest wife one could ever hope for." He eyed Baylun. "Explain it to her. She'll understand."

Baylun held a wry smile. "I pray you're right."

They proceeded to share everything they had experienced in Lornibur. Greyor grew more excited with every bit of new information, although the death of Mattasun at Uustaag's hand was disheartening. How could dwarves side with such a monster? Then again, those same dwarves supported Velgaad.

"What's next?" Baylun posed after their tales were complete.

Greyor drew a deep breath. "There are the lizards that need to be controlled or exterminated. And I doubt every dragon was slain, so we'll have to do some hunting. But I'm sure Morimont's best warriors will assist us."

Not a trace of fear entered Baylun's eyes with anything Greyor said. He was going to enjoy working with the krukari.

"Other than that," he continued, "Lornibur needs to be mapped out, tidied up, and made ready before my kin call it home. Your services aren't necessary for that part." He eyed Baylun. "But before all that, you must come to Morimont with me."

Baylun frowned. "Will your folk allow that?"

Greyor snorted. "When they hear what I have to say and see what the two of us can do, they'll have no choice."

"I'm not sure what time I have left." Baylun sat back. "My kind aren't known to live long lives."

The krukari looked at Nidor. The young warrior danced with Lorylla's daughter. Greyor wondered if she was the same daughter wanting to make a life beyond Orlenfel Forest—a trait unheard of among gray elves. He could think of no dwarves desiring a home outside the mountains.

"I suppose I'll have to speak to Nidor about his inheritance," Baylun mumbled.

"Do not plan your funeral just yet," said a female voice.

It was Selanna. The mage's blonde hair flowed freely past her shoulders, and her emerald eyes sparkled in the candlelight. How had she approached unnoticed by two veterans?

She sat next to Greyor. "I can sense the change in you already," she said to Baylun. "Your blood has been altered. You made your oath to serve for a hundred years, and Torrac will hold you to that."

Baylun wrinkled his forehead. "I don't understand. What do you mean, 'altered'?"

Selanna smiled. "As you know, the flow of magic offers longevity to wizards. And now, a similar magic flows through you. For the next century, you will notice practically no change to your physical presence. It is almost as if your aging has been postponed, at least until you have honored your commitment to Torrac and Lornibur."

Baylun eyed the table while considering the elf's words. The corner of his mouth twitched as tears formed. He grimaced—maybe it was a smile—and stared at Selanna, as if wanting to give her a hug or a kiss. Perhaps both.

Selanna chuckled as she stood. "A good evening to you both." And she walked away.

Though surprising, the mage's information came as a tremendous relief. Nidor was a fine young warrior, to be sure, but Greyor looked forward to having Baylun at his side when times called for it.

"Well, Bye'Lin." Greyor grinned. "Looks like you're stuck working with me for a long time."

❈ ❈ ❈

Once the feast ended, Baylun joined Kiryanna in the children's room to bid them goodnight. Baylun wasn't sure if it was the right moment, but he decided to share his news.

"I have something to discuss with all of you," he said, "and I pray it isn't met with ill feelings."

Kiryanna sighed audibly. "We're moving, aren't we?"

How did she know? Baylun found no words.

The kids gaped as if they had yet to formulate any replies.

"I thought it strange," Kiryanna said, "but Selanna kept speaking with Eraim within earshot. She talked about Torrac, some oath, and your responsibilities to Lornibur."

Her tone was difficult to interpret. Baylun worried she would not join him.

"You oaf!" She put her hands on her hips. "Of course we will move! It is just another of life's grand adventures."

He truly had the greatest wife!

"I have already discussed it with Romik," she added with a sly grin, "and he cannot wait. There isn't enough room in the central tower, so he has issued orders to convert rooms for us in the Great Hall."

"We're going to live here?" asked Nidor, his incredulous expression hard to read. His eyes darted to the door. "I have to do something!"

Before Baylun or Kiryanna could object, Nidor raced from the chamber.

Baylun turned to his other children. "What do you two think?"

Daymyn frowned. "I'm not sure. What about Grandfather, Grandmother, and Uncle Magneer?"

"We will visit them often," Kiryanna replied.

"What about my friends?" posed Teliya.

How many friends could the little girl have?

"We will visit them too," Kiryanna said, elbowing Baylun—how did she always know what he was thinking?

"Okay." Daymyn nodded. "We'll give it a try."

Baylun chuckled. He had the greatest family.

After kissing Daymyn and Teliya goodnight, Baylun and Kiryanna went to their room. Baylun stood before the closed door after entering until his wife looked back.

"What is it, my love?" she asked, her expression moving to concern.

"Did Selanna mention my oath has obligated me to a hundred years of service?" he inquired with a straight face. "I'm afraid Torrac will not let me age a day until that duty is fulfilled."

Her resulting smile reminded Baylun of the day they married; the times she discovered she was pregnant; and the moments their children were safely delivered into the world.

Life was good.

❋ ❋ ❋

Ameilistari didn't enjoy the feast as much as she might have liked. There was plenty of excitement with having survived against impossible odds and the emergence of her grandfather, not to mention Selanna's attendance at the keep. But she still had not recovered from the power she expended. She was content to watch the festivities while nibbling from a plate of food.

Several young soldiers asked her to dance, but she politely

declined. Of the invitations, she regretted dismissing only one: Ellik; a boy her father considered too old for her. He was seventeen. Of all would-be-suitors in the keep, he was the most polite, the most sincere. But her father had nothing to worry about. Ellik was the only trainee more absorbed with his duties than with wooing girls.

Watching Father dance with Naydrel after the music began bugged Ameilistari. But why? The barmaid never did anything cross to her and seemed to have genuine feelings for her father. Better yet, the woman didn't seem to mind prancing about with a clumsy, one-armed man. And he was smiling. His smile made Ameilistari smile. Perhaps she needed to take a step back from the situation. Father had been without companionship for most of her life. And he was a grown man. This new way of thinking made her feel more like a woman and less like a child. She was proud of herself.

Although Aunt Kiryanna dancing with Daymyn made Ameilistari giggle, seeing Nidor with Naiandillis was priceless. Her goofy cousin looked hilarious while trying to keep up with the gray elf. But Ameilistari kept her laughter in check. Even though she was sure Nidor committed more stupid mistakes than she did within Lornibur, he had earned a festive night without her making fun.

Equally entertaining was Sybin. The captain's daughter plopped down beside her with a look of outrage.

"Who is this strange elf?" Sybin posed, with more than a trace of jealousy.

"Lorylla's daughter, I believe."

Apparently, it wasn't the response Sybin had wanted. After a huff, she said, "How long are these *people* going to be here? What if the keep were suddenly under attack?"

Ameilistari grinned. "Relax. That's why we have your father."

Captain Marlajin was indeed absent from the party, as it was his duty to man the towers during such times, in case Sybin's words rang true. But Ameilistari didn't think for a second that Sybin worried about a surprise invasion. The girl was simply an intolerant, self-absorbed, condescending person. But Sybin was also her friend.

"Cheer up," she said. "A few weeks ago, I saw Father speaking with a soldier from Kalmaar who offered his services. A handsome young man. I'm positive I can convince Father to give him a position."

"Oh?" Sybin's focus shifted to Ameilistari. "When will he arrive?"

So much for Sybin's heartache.

Toward the end of the night, Father sat next to Ameilistari.

"Have I told you how wonderful you are?" he asked.

She wasn't sure how to respond. Maybe it was the beer talking.

"I just need one promise from you," he said.

"What?"

"Keep me informed of your intentions," he stated plainly. "Although I won't always agree with your decisions, I will support you in the best way I know how. Life is too precious to let pass you by. Just… If you decide not to run Ironside, you must tell me. And I promise not to try and change your mind."

She smiled and hugged her father. "You will be the very second to know."

He frowned.

"Well," she gave a wry smile, "I have to inform myself first."

He patted her hand and headed toward the bar, where Naydrel was cleaning mugs.

After exchanging many goodnights, Ameilistari retired for the evening. Her mouth fell agape to find Selanna, Eraim, and Tewlon in her room. Eraim sat on the bed, Tewlon leaned against the wall near the window, as if keeping watch on the night, and Selanna sat at Ameilistari's vanity.

"I sense you have questions," Selanna said as Ameilistari shut the door.

"So *many* questions…" Ameilistari sighed. "Where do I start?" She glanced around the room, and Tewlon gave her a wink. "Could…" She looked from Tewlon to Selanna. "Could Vecnor join us?"

Selanna raised her brow. "You dislike Tewlon?"

"He's fine," she answered as quickly as possible, so as not to insult anyone. "But—"

"As you wish," said Selanna, and Tewlon transformed into the giant warrior.

Ameilistari rushed to give him a hug.

"I prefer this form as well," he admitted, giving her a gentle squeeze. Somehow, his deep voice made the world seem safer.

"Both forms are pleasing," commented Eraim with a smirk.

Vecnor winked at the elf.

Perhaps the rumors about the huge man and the little elf were true. Ameilistari couldn't imagine it. She turned to Selanna.

"The minstrels," she said. "Are they your doing?"

Selanna stifled a laugh. "That is your question?"

Ameilistari smirked. Of course Selanna had brought them. But that was unimportant. "What about Grandfather?" she asked. "How is he here?"

"From what I have been told," Selanna replied, "he arrived through a gate."

"Yes, but…" Ameilistari frowned. "But how did he open a gate? Why was it green while the other two were blue? And how did he know where we were?"

"The gods work in mysterious ways," Selanna said.

A disappointing answer. Ameilistari decided not to press the matter, nor the fact that Grandfather and Tewlon seemed to be acquainted with one another.

"What about the demons we faced?" she asked. "You said that when a demon is slain in Hell, it stays dead. The ones we defeated disappeared in clouds of smoke, as if being sent home."

"What do you know about Demoligius?" the mage inquired.

"Evil deity of fire," she replied, trying to think. "Silcor's nemesis."

"Ruler of demons," added Eraim, receiving a disapproving glance from Selanna.

"Yes, Eraim." Selanna turned back to Ameilistari. "It was not Hell that you entered, but a corner of Demoligius's world. The priests opened the portal to conduct their experiments, and the second gate you saw was a door to another part of Vaeldor."

The answer produced additional questions. Like how did Selanna know all of this? Where in Vaeldor had the other gate led? And if they weren't in Hell, how had her grandfather found them? But it was obvious Selanna would not provide those answers. Ameilistari had no choice but to respect that decision and keep her wonderings to herself. Perhaps one day she would figure them out.

"What about our time in… the evil world?" she posed. "Nidor claimed we had just entered after we returned. But we were there for an entire battle."

"Time does not work the same between worlds," Vecnor explained. "In Hell, the hours move much slower than in Vaeldor." He acknowledged Selanna's impatient stare, and said, "What? I knew the answer to that one."

"Is it possible that we defeated all the dragons?" Ameilistari asked Selanna to change the subject.

"Do *you* believe it possible?" posed the mage.

Ameilistari turned to Eraim with a wry smile. The small elf offered no help this time.

Why ask questions if you had to answer them yourself?

"I doubt it," Ameilistari mumbled. "Did the Seer say if anything has changed? Did we save Vaeldor?"

Selanna glanced at Eraim, who held a raised brow. Ameilistari wondered if they were teasing her; playing a game.

"It is not always easy to see the future clearly," Selanna said at last, apparently sensing Ameilistari's mounting frustration. "It would be arrogant to say the eruption consumed every dragon. And it is wise to keep your eyes open. Although I no longer see fire engulfing Vaeldor, I sense distant, smaller flames. I do not believe they spell devastation for Vaeldor, as they once had, but there is danger yet ahead."

Selanna stood, and Eraim dropped from the bed and walked to stand by Vecnor.

"We must go," Selanna said, "but I'll leave you with this. You have many decisions to make in the near future, and please know that you have time to make them. Enjoy life to its fullest! But danger is constantly around the corner, so be wary of the signs."

"Please," Ameilistari grabbed Selanna's hands. "Before you go, you must tell me. Can one be a mage and still find the time to be Lord of the Keep?"

"Or *Lady* of the Keep?" asked Eraim with a smirk.

"As I said," Selanna lowered Ameilistari's hands and gently let go, "you have time to make the many decisions before you. And only you can say what you're capable of, be it lordship, wife, mother, or whatever else comes your way." She smiled to one side and moved toward the door. "Continue with your studies, and mind your teacher."

"Rauzel..." Ameilistari sighed. "Can you please tell her to be more like you? More fun?"

Selanna chuckled. "I will speak with her."

Vecnor again became Tewlon, and the three visitors exited.

Ameilistari sat on her bed. The world was the same as she had left it, yet it was different. She was an elementalist, and the full weight of that knowledge was upon her. She closed her eyes and concentrated. A wind blew outside her window, and an underground river cut through the mountains miles below. Within the keep, twenty-two hearths held fires. Though they lacked sentience, they leaned toward her, as if eager to answer her call.

She opened her eyes. It was all so new and amazing. She wondered what adventures lay ahead, and if they would be as dire as her exploration into the mines. Hopefully not.

Ameilistari inhaled to blow out the candle, then paused. She ordered it to extinguish with her mind, and it obeyed. Climbing beneath the covers, she turned her thoughts to the present. She survived her first adventure; her grandfather had come home; and Nidor and his family were moving in permanently. If she chose to be Lady of the Keep, perhaps her cousin would consent to being Captain of the Guard. Sybin wouldn't take it well, but First Lieutenant wasn't a bad position.

So many thoughts, so many decisions. Ameilistari wondered if she would get any sleep. But if Selanna spoke the truth, she had plenty of time to sort it all out.

This Concludes

LORNIBUR

But the journeys continue…

Look for more adventures in Vaeldor in the future.

Acknowledgements

Praises continue to go to my wife and son, Justiina and Ronnie. The constant support, feedback, and map creations make my stories possible. And as always, Mary J. Nichols plays a key role through the editing process. Thanks to all my readers; your comments keep me working on the next adventure!

About the Author

Ronald G. Bellar was born in Ohio and raised in Michigan, one of the middle children in a family of ten. He has degrees in electrical engineering and automated manufacturing, but his love for numbers led him to a life in tax accounting. His passion for medieval fantasy began at age 11, when he was introduced to Dungeons & Dragons, and it was cemented after reading The Lord of the Rings by J.R.R. Tolkien. He began writing when he was 15, but did not take it seriously until encouraged to do so later in life. A huge sports fan, he has returned to coaching football and has now logged 33 years. He currently lives in Michigan with his wife and son.

Ronald G. Bellar has also written the Fate of Vaeldor Trilogy, including Alas! The One that Evil Brings, Might and Strength of Evil Bone, and Eyes Open in Shadowy Hall, followed by The House of Elgarroth, my "peek behind the curtain" story. And the adventures in Vaeldor will continue…

Look for additional novels in the future.

Glossary of Names

Aamustall (AHM-oo-stahl): Name given to the mine dwellers' enemy.

Ameilistari (uh-MEEL-uh-STAR-ee): Daughter of Romik. Young mage.

Arkor (AR-kor): Younger brother of Vikur. Granduncle to Romik. Had only one arm. Raised Romik to govern Ironside Keep.

Arrikan (AIR-ik-in): Mountain ranger. Late mother of Duke Magneer. Good friend to Greyor. Traveled with him through Lornibur during the Necromancer War. Died of old age.

Azoumee (uh-ZOO-may): Of Dale descent, born in Marcove. Late wife of Romik. Mother of Ameilistari.

Ballrik (BAHL-rik): Son of Vikur and nephew to Arkor. Father of Romik. Saved the realm of Nira from a demonic invasion by jumping through a gate to close it. Returned as aged soldier, Morsum.

Balmorak (bahl-MOR-ik): Last King's Champion of Lornibur before its downfall. Wielder of Clanghorr.

Barrelda (buh-RELL-duh): Female Pavish barbarian married to Desser, son of Duke Magneer.

Basallor (BASS-uh-lor): Ellibrus Lord of Greyor's House in Morimont.

Baylun (BAY-luhn): Krukari son of Gruelenor and Lorin. Half-brother to Romik. Cousin to Desser and Daymyn and nephew to Duke Magneer. Wielder of Torrac. Commander of Duke's Honor Guard. Married to Kiryanna.

Benasti (beh-NAS-tee): Forest in northern Kalmaar. Largely inhabited by evil tribes of hobgoblins, krukari, and ogres.

Blar (BLAR): Mine Dweller that accompanied Greyor and Millord while they hunted Maak Maak during the Necromancer War.

Bleer (BLEER): Lieutenant in Ironside Keep. Expert crossbowman.

Blorin (BLOR-in): Dwarf king of Rornibur in the Stone Eagle Mountains.

Bomahni (bo-MAHN-ee): Tribe of Pavish barbarians. Helped defeat the forces of Uustaag in the War of the North. Home of Desser and Barrelda.

Boola (BOO-lah): Name given to giant lizards by the mine dwellers.

Bormungdaher (BOR-muhng-DAR): Ancient dwarf king of Varlimor. Commissioned the construction of Palidur Bridge and aided in the construction of Palidur. Only Ellibrus Lord of the four Houses of Lornibur to remain in Varlimor Mountains after the city's downfall.

Brakkeet (brah-KEET): Expletive in the Dwarfish language.

Brisomer (BRISS-oh-mur): Replaced Velgaad as Ellibrus Lord after Velgaad ascended to king.

Brondor (BRAHN-dor): Deity of battle.

Broxen Lord (BROKS-in): Lowest of the lords in the dwarfish hierarchy, consisting of four Houses. Each House has eight Broxen Lords who hope to ascend to become Harkan Lords.

Brunux (BRUHN-uhks): Companion of Balmorak. Opposed King Velgaad.

Bruskiin (BRUSS-keen): Giant mushrooms possessing wood-like properties. Used by dwarves to create "wooden" doors and furniture.

Bye'Lin (BYE LIN): How mine dwellers pronounce Baylun's name.

Cafior (CAF-ee-or): Deity of the land.

Cavalor (CAV-uh-lor): King of Marcove and father of Vayla. Adopted son of Merssa and Borse. Fought in both the Necromancer War and the War of the North.

Charndova (sharn-DOH-vuh): City in Sardina on the western edge of the pass through the Varlimor Mountains.

Clanghorr (KLANG-or): Ancient dwarfish battleaxe. Wielded by Greyor. Special weapon with strange powers.

Clarna (KLAR-nuh): Name listed among the heirs of Torrac before

Gruelenor and Baylun.

Clay'Gor (KLAY GOR): How mine dwellers pronounce Clanghorr.

Coranthiar (kor-ANN-thee-er): Mountains across northeastern Vaeldor.

Crynora (kry-NOR-uh): Former name of West Palidur before Duke Rholmar changed it.

Dakreal (DAY-kree-uhl): Forest in Philen. Home to Dakreal elves.

Dale (DAYL): Barbarian denizen of Holindale. The dark-skins.

Darum Carumbor (DAIR-uhm cuh-RUM-bor): Ancient watchtower of Helmland during the reign of Uustaag. Baylun had been stranded in the tower with his cousin, Daymyn, during the beginning of the War of the North.

Daymyn (DAY-min): Son of Baylun and Kiryanna. Middle child. Also name of Baylun's late cousin, who died during the War of the North. Desire for power led him to betray his family in Darum Carumbor, and Baylun felt responsible.

Demoligius (dem-uh-LIDG-ee-us): Evil deity of fire and reptiles. The Dragon God.

Denvale (DEN-vayl): City in Marcove on the eastern edge of the pass through the Varlimor Mountains.

Desser (DES-sir): Mountain ranger who married a Pavish barbarian, Barrelda. Son of Duke Magneer and Kalette. Cousin of Romik and Baylun.

Dornux (DOR-nuhks): Father of Balmorak. Previous King's Champion.

Dowar (DOW-er): Companion of Balmorak. Opposed King Velgaad and aided Balmorak's self-banishment.

Dragon Wars: Battle between dragons and all of Vaeldor. Led to the extinction of the giant reptiles, greatly weakening the evil deity, Demoligius.

Elgarroth (EL-guh-roth): Former elfish seer and mentor to Selanna.

Ellibrus Lord (EL-uh-brus): Highest of the lords in the dwarfish hierarchy, consisting of four Houses. Each House has one Ellibrus Lord, who is in line to become the next king.

Eraim (ee-RAYM): Salenti elf. Master of many talents and friend to Selanna. Wielder of Mithkahr.

Fendora (fen-DOR-uh): Kingdom in southwestern Vaeldor.

Fenreil (FEN-ree-uhl): The Seer in the Council of Wizards of Tikken City.

Frayorna (fray-OR-nuh): Deity of the forest. Mother of Nature.

Galenfial (guh-LEN-fee-uhl): Deity of the elves.

Gray'Or (GRAY OR): How mine dwellers pronounce Greyor.

Gray Elf: Elf from Orlenfel Forest. Tallest of the elfish clans. Most known for their grayish skin, white irises on black eyes, and natural magical abilities.

Grellmor (GREL-mor): Ancestor of Vikur and Arkor. First Lord of Ironside Keep on the pass through the Varlimor Mountains.

Greyor (GRAY-or): Dwarf from Morimont in the Varlimor Mountains. Wields the legendary battleaxe, Clanghorr.

Gruelenor (GREW-len-or): Aged krukari. Married to Lorin. Father of Baylun and step-father to Romik. Fought in both the Necromancer War and the War of the North. Retired.

Gruzim (groo- ZEEM): Death Lord destroyed by Vecnor during the Necromancer War. Father of Gruelenor. Grandfather of Baylun.

Hardor (HAR-dor): Companion of Balmorak. Opposed King Velgaad.

Harkan Lord (HARK-in): Mid-level lord in the dwarfish hierarchy consisting of four Houses. Each House has four Harkan Lords, who hope to ascend to become the next Ellibrus Lord.

Helmland (HELM-land): Wasteland north of the Stone Eagle Mountains where the War of the North was fought.

Holindale (HOE-lin-dayl): Barbarian territory south of Tenvale. Home to the dark-skins.

Ironside (EYE-ern-side): Keep governing the pass through the Varlimor Mountains. Surname to Romik. Home to Lord Romik and his daughter Ameilistari.

Kalmaar (KAL-mar): Kingdom in eastern Vaeldor. Known for its dedication to the worship of Brondor.

Kiryanna (keer-YAHN-uh): Female marteese warrior. Wife of Baylun.

Kolermane (KOHL-er-mayn): King of the Morimont dwarves in the Varlimor Mountains.

Kradur (KRAY-der): High priest of Demoligius, responsible for experiments in Lornibur.

Krahluk (KRAH-luhk): Gorilla-like monster from the world of Thard'Dun. Hairless with jet-black skin.

Kreedorim (kree-DOR-uhm): Name given to fire-breathing lizards by the mine dwellers.

Kreela (KREE-luh): Name given to enormous fire-breathing lizards by the mine dwellers.

Krukari (kroo-KAR-ee): One possessing both human and hobgoblin blood. Outcasts.

Lola (LOH-luh): How mine dwellers pronounce Lorylla.

Lormin Dmurr (LOR-min duh-MER): Ancient citadel of Uustaag the Dark, Ancient Enemy of the North, in Helmland.

Lornibur (LOR-ni-ber): Ancient home to the dwarves. Original birthplace of the dwarfish race.

Lorylla (LOR-i-luh): Gray elf of Orlenfel. Daughter of Xorlunder. Good friend to Greyor.

Lrindon (LER-in-dahn): New king of Rornibur, dwarfish city in the Stone Eagle Mountains.

Maak Maak (MAHK MAHK): Giant, two-headed lizard that lives in Lornibur. Defeated by Selanna, Eraim, and Greyor during the Necromancer War.

Magneer (MAG-neer): Mountain ranger. Duke of West Palidur in Philen. Father of Desser and uncle to Baylun and Romik.

Marcove (MAR-kohv): Kingdom south of Kalmaar.

Marfesna (mar-FEZ-nuh): Ice demon defeated in the Varlimor Mountains by Greyor, Selanna, and Eraim during the Necromancer War.

Marlajin (MAR-luh-shjin): Captain of Ironside Keep. Father of

Sybin.

Marteese (mar-TEES): One possessing both human and elf blood.

Mattasun (MAT-uh-sun): Last wielder of Torrac before Baylun.

Meldar (MEL-dar): Deity of the dwarves.

Mentrial (MEN-tree-ahl): Forest in Marcove.

Merssa (MER-suh): Late Cafior paladin. Hero of Palidur. Short in stature, but possessing enough courage and faith to make her seem giant. Led the allies during the Necromancer War. Grandmother of Vayla.

Mill'Or (MIL OR): How mine dwellers pronounced Millord's name.

Millord (MIL-ord): Stone Eagle dwarf from Rornibur. Late cousin to Greyor. Died fighting Maak Maak in Lornibur during the Necromancer War.

Mithkahr (MITH-kar): Ancient elfish blade possessed by Eraim.

Moclen (MAHK-lin): Kingdom west of King Arman Lake.

Morimont (MOR-i-mahnt): Largest city of dwarves in the Varlimor Mountains. Greyor's home.

Morsum (MOR-sim): Elderly gatekeeper of Ironside Keep. Body inhabited by Ballrik, granted to him by Elgarroth.

Mulaattii Espruul (moo-LAH-tee es-PROO-uhl): Gray elf phrase meaning may the wind remain beneath your feet.

Naiandillis (nay-ANN-dil-iss): eldest daughter of Lorylla.

Naydrel (nay-DREL): Barmaid in Ironside Keep.

Necromancer War: The war against Trannum fought almost two decades prior.

New Palidur (PAL-lid-er): Name given to Palidur after the city was rebuilt after the Necromancer War.

Nidor (NYE-dor): Son of Baylun and Kiryanna. Oldest child. Also name of the late paladin of Silcor, a dark-skinned barbarian from Holindale who greatly assisted in the success of the Necromancer War and the War of the North. A good soul.

Nomedd (NOH-med): Southern territory inhabited by Trannum during the Necromancer War.

Orlenfel (OR-len-fell): Forest in northeastern Kalmaar. Home to the gray elves.

Philen (FYE-len): Kingdom in southwestern Vaeldor. Home to Baylun's family and Duke Magneer.

Poluran (POH-ler-uhn): Late Stone Eagle dwarf from Rornibur. Former owner of Clanghorr. Cousin to Greyor. Died before the Necromancer War while trying to take back Ironside Keep from the enemy.

Poopit Hans (POO-pit HANZ): Lead warrior of the mine dwellers.

Qes Perishanta (KEZ per-eesh-AHN-tah): Gray elf phrase meaning my quiver is yours.

Radaam (ruh-DAHM): Death Lord seen during the Necromancer War and the War of the North.

Rauzel (raw-ZEL): Female marteese mage. Mentor of Ameilistari lessons after Selanna stepped aside from the same position.

Rholmar (ROHL-mar): Paladin of Arronaus. Moved to Crynora from Palidur to become Duke and renamed the city West Palidur.

Rivercross: Large city in Virch near the Korban Bridge.

Romik (ROH-mik): Lord of Ironside Keep. Father of Ameilistari. Son of Ballrik and Lorin. Older brother of Baylun. Cousin of Desser. Lost his arm during the War of the North.

Rornibur (ROR-ni-ber): City of dwarves in the Stone Eagle Mountains.

Row'Mick (ROW MIK): How mine dwellers pronounce Romik.

Salenti (suh-LEN-tee): Forest west of Moclen. Home to Salenti elves, the shortest of the elfish clans. Original home of Eraim and Selanna.

Sardina (sar-DEE-nuh): Kingdom east of King Arman Lake. Houses New Palidur.

Selanna (suh-LAHN-nuh): Elfish seer originally of Salenti Forest. Lives in Vermallon Forest with Eraim and Vecnor. Was mentor of Romik's daughter, Ameilistari, until she sensed tension between her and the Lord of the Keep.

Selt (SELT): Kingdom north of Nira. Theocracy dedicated to the worship of Demoligius.

Seltan (SEL-tuhn): Citizen of Selt.

Sendorum (sen-DOR-uhm): Kingdom north of Sardina.

Silcor (SIL-kor): Deity of fire.

Stromburn (STRAHM-burn): Broxen Lord of the House of Basallor in Morimont. The House Greyor belongs to.

Sybin (SIB-in): Daughter of Marlajin in Ironside Keep.

Stari (STAR-ee): Nickname given to Ameilistari by her father, Romik.

Tedonis (teh-DAHN-is): Former compound before the Necromancer War. Evolved into a city and was named after the original surname of the late paladin Merssa.

Teliya (tuh-LIE-uh): Daughter of Baylun and Kiryanna. Youngest child.

Tenvale (TEN-vayl): Kingdom of Wizards known for its strange laws.

Tewlon (TOO-lahn): Abnormally muscular elf warrior. Name used by Vecnor when in his elfish disguise.

Thard'Dun (thar-DOON): Evil deity. The Dark One.

Tikken City (TEE-kin): Free city located in Moclen.

Torrac (TOR-ak): Bronze axe wielded by Baylun. A birthday present from his brother, Romik. Special weapon with strange powers.

Trannum (TRAN-nuhm): Ancient necromancer. Destroyed at the conclusion of the Necromancer War and returned as the Shadow to free Uustaag. Defeated for good at the conclusion of the War of the North.

Trelibrum (TREL-ib-ruhm): The age at which a gray elf journeys to discover their path in life.

Tux (TUKS): Nickname of Eslimil Tuxendora. Legendary elf of mixed blood between Salenti and Orlenfel clans. Possessed special powers and the ability to craft lethal arrows. Notorious for leaving the word TUX in places where he roamed. Companion to Elgarroth and Vecnor. Vanished after the conclusion of the War of the North.

Urnumil (ERN-uh-mil): Strange blue fuel emitting a blue flame when burned but shedding normal lighting. Oil never depletes.

Uustaag (OO-stahg): Warlord of Helmland. Ancient Enemy of the North. The Enemy.

Vaeldor (VAY-uhl-dor): The continent of all known kingdoms.

Varlimor (VAR-lim-or): Mountains separating Kalmaar from Sardina. Home to Ironside Keep and Morimont.

Vayla (VAY-luh): Grand Paladin of Cafior. Granddaughter of Merssa.

Vecnor (VEK-ner): Companion of Eraim and Selanna. The Ageless Warrior, also known as Black Rogue and Black Death. Former companion of Elgarroth and Tux.

Velgaad (VEL-gahd): Last king of Lornibur. Evil dealings led to the city's destruction. Reappeared as a Death Lord during the Necromancer War and was destroyed by Greyor.

Vermallon (VER-muh-lahn): Forest separating Harbnum from Nira. Largest forest of Vaeldor and home to Vermallon elves.

Vikur (VIE-koor): Father to Ballrik. Grandfather to Romik. Killed by Radaam in Ironside Keep before the Necromancer War, and reappeared as a dunarchin during the war.

Virch (VERCH): Kingdom north of King Arman Lake.

Vou (VOO): Deity of magic. Provider of magical energy.

West Palidur (PAL-i-der): City renamed by Rholmar when he was Duke of Philen. Home of Baylun and his family.

Wezlok (WEZ-lahk): Lorian elf wizard from Maple Lore Forest.

Xorlunder (ZOR-luhn-der): Gray elf of Orlenfel. Late father of Lorylla. Killed during the Necromancer War.

Zreekan (ZREE-kuhn): Potato-shaped beings from Thard'Dun's world with one eye. Floats above the ground and has four tentacles. No arms or legs. Capable of terrible magic.